Dagger *of* Bone

Legends of the Clanblades: Book 1

BY R.K. THORNE

IRON ANTLER
BOOKS

Edited by Elizabeth Nover, www.razorsharpediting.com
Cover design by Damonza, damonza.com
Interior Design by R.K. Thorne
Map by Terrance Mayes
Version 1.1

To all the members of my D&D group, you are an endless inspiration. Thank you for all the fun. And all the desserts, beer, gorgeous miniatures, taco bars, inspiring crafts, moving stories, tense negotiations, and raucous laughter.

Never thought I'd end up a tank.

The Wilds
The Great Desert
Silver
Bone
The Salt City
Glass
Lands of Mushin

An approximation of the lands surrounding the Empire of the Six Clans, shortly after the Unification period, prior to the Second Break

Artist Unknown

Contents

DAGGER *of* BONE

Chapter 1

Imprinting

"You'll never be a swordmage."

The words would have stung more if this had been the first time he'd heard them. But Nyalin had heard them before, too many times. He hadn't believed it might actually be true, though. "Isn't my fate for the council to decide?"

"They won't override me. The dark dragon barely sniffed her nose at you." His foster father Elix slowed to a stop at the base of the stairs near the door. Dust motes floated in an early morning sunbeam shining through the window, the only motion in the dim sitting room.

It was true. The Obsidian Dragon had had no time for him, no hint that she saw him as any different than the rocks themselves. Her approval wasn't required for young mages be taught, but with a mother as powerful as Nyalin's had been, the expectations for him had been up in the clouds.

And now, well. Those expectations had gone up in smoke.

"My mother would have hated you for this." His fists were balled, but he hid them at his sides. There was no winning here. Nyalin was trapped.

"You don't know what she would have wanted."

"That's because she's dead."

"You'd do well to start remembering that. Go get a job. There's paying work for scribes."

"You shouldn't have given up. On me or on her."

Elix opened the door, warm light and murmurs from the street pouring in. His dark silhouette paused, a hulking bear suspended in time like an insect in amber. "Take your grievances up with the dragon."

Nyalin held up a finger and opened his mouth, because the Obsidian Council was in fact currently meeting, even if Elix wouldn't believe they could make any decision other than what he wanted. Before he could even make a sound, though, Elix had gone. The door slammed shut in his face.

His shoulders slumped. As if he could talk to a dragon. He shouldn't have let the old bear bait him like that. It was in the council's hands now.

Fine. It was all fine. He had somewhere to be anyway.

Down the hallway, back to the servant's stairs, then out into the street. His feet carried him without thought, his mind lost elsewhere.

Each week, he woke before dawn for this trek. He always reached the graveyard before the sun rose above the city walls. He liked the early hour because it usually guaranteed solitude.

Today, though, his luck had run out. In more ways than one.

Arriving at the graveyard, he discovered a single set of footprints marring the white pebble footpath between him and his mother's grave. He glared down at the dents in the sea of smooth stones.

He started forward, his worn boots crunching fresh prints into the milk-white pebbles. He scanned the graves for the interloper but spotted no one. Heard no one. If he'd had magic, he might have sensed no one, but that was precisely his problem.

Why did he keep doing this—showing up to visit a woman he'd never known? Maybe it was a misplaced search for answers. Or a longing for scraps of truth about a past forever lost. Some weeks, he came out of duty. Others, out of habit.

Today, though, he'd come to apologize. He'd failed.

The only thing worse than being in the royal graveyard was being here with an audience. He ran his hand through thick brown hair. It flopped right back down into his left eye, and he sighed.

The air felt charged. This place made his skin itch, like the souls of the dead were dragging nails across his skin and tugging at his very core. He scratched at his thigh, the black linen of his crossover rough against his fingers. No silk for him, not like his so-called family.

His whole future was being decided by that family and the Obsidian Council in the meeting across town. He hadn't been invited, and there was little he could do to argue his case any more than he already had. Only one thing was left to do: to say he was sorry. To apologize.

He'd never known his mother, but he owed her this much.

The Feast of Souls was coming in a few weeks. In preparation, paper lanterns had been hung over the dead; crimson, teal, gold, and emerald globes swayed and knocked in the brisk wind. The decorations had so little regard for the mourners that they bumped cheerfully in the sunlight, soft taps filling the air with a strange, percussive rhythm. Summer was only just waning, but the wind was already sending a chill through him.

He studied the prints in the gravel path again as he neared her grave. The footprints were small, like a woman's, and recent. He reached the final turn toward the grave, and the footprints turned with him. Damn. The monks who tended this burial ground smoothed the pebbles each morning and again and again throughout the day, so someone had been here. And not long ago at all.

With his luck, it'd be a pilgrim. No, a family of pilgrims. With ten children. By the Twins, he'd hoped to be alone today.

He gritted his teeth, then swallowed and tried to calm himself, the way he did when he needed a steady hand to write. It wasn't their fault the pilgrims were so annoying.

He listened. A fresh gust of wind sent the lanterns tapping again and him shivering. No hymns, no snaps of prayer sticks, and no crunches of feet on pebbles. Birds sang, and the wind teased the holy chimes hung in the cardinal corners of the cemetery, bronze characters in the holy language standing for peace, harmony, and, of course, the afterlives.

No one.

He continued on.

His mother's gravestone stood alone. He blew out a breath. Thank Seluvae.

The white marble was inundated with gifts, the hope and suffering of many expressed in azalea branches, roses, chrysanthemums, and white flowers he didn't know the names for. Most of the blooms were too fine to have been purchased. The poor who flocked here had likely stolen their tributes from the gardens that surrounded the emperor's palace. Nyalin could understand. He had little gold or even copper to his name, and only his continued residence in his foster father's house gave him any resources at all.

And who knew if he'd even have that come evening?

What solace did pilgrims find here? His mother had only been a person, albeit a rare and powerful one. Not a goddess. Not someone to pray to.

Clearly the pilgrims disagreed.

Tracking down the basket the monks used, Nyalin filled it

with the oldest, most wilted flowers. Slowly, tenderly, he uncovered her name. He slid his fingers along the smooth indentations, tracing the elegant holy characters carved into the marble. He left the best blooms. It would be full again soon enough.

When the flowers were cleared and he'd dusted off the stone, he knelt in the soft square of sand set aside for prayer.

What had he hoped to say? Should he ask that the Obsidian Council make the right decision? They wouldn't. This was all doomed to failure. Should he pray that Elix would change his mind? As if his foster father ever had before.

He was trapped, and there was nothing his mother could do to help him, powerful or not, alive or not, whether he prayed to her or not. And the secret of who his real father had been, if the man was even still alive, had gone to the grave with her. If he could have asked her for one thing, it would be his father's name. But those were idle wishes.

"Sorry," he murmured into the music of the chimes, the lantern tapping, the quiet birdsong, the morning air. "I failed you. I couldn't do it. I couldn't convince them to keep trying."

What else was there to say?

She had been the greatest talent of her time, the hero who'd saved so many, who'd shot fear into the hearts of the evil Mushin. Her victories had led to the unification of the clans, to unprecedented peace, to even the construction of this city around him. Unification had turned a rickety trading post near two salt mines into the one place in the empire where the six clans strove to coexist. Mostly. No one had expected peace or an end to the war, and she'd found it. Fought for it. Forced it on them, even. And she'd given it all up in the blood of birth, for what?

For him?

For nothing, then. Her torch had burned bright, and he'd

dropped it.

He hated disappointing Grel; his dutiful foster brother believed in Nyalin almost blindly. But even more, he hated to disappoint *her*. There was no one else to disappoint.

"They would've listened to you," he whispered. "By the dark dragon, I wish there was some other way."

He shook his head, staring unseeing at the sand as the wind knocked the lanterns about. His hand closed into a fist.

"I'll just have to find something. A way to make your sacrifice worth it."

How exactly he'd do that, he had no idea. He had nothing but time to figure it out.

A quiet sob floated toward him on the breeze. He winced. There—the other mourner. Not alone after all.

He should go. The longer he stayed, the more mourners would appear.

He rose and brushed the dust off his knees. If he left by the thin strip of grass and not by the pebbled pathway, maybe he could avoid calling attention to exactly who had been whispering like a madman to the dead. Even though Elix and Grel's awful younger brother Raelt thought he was dirt, many people in the city did not feel the same. Much to his chagrin.

Nyalin bowed to his mother, then stepped carefully to the grass that cut a line between rows of milky headstones. A low hedge at the end of the path marked the north exit of the cemetery, the holy symbols for harmony tinkling away above an arbor.

He hurried the last few steps—and almost tripped over the source of the sobbing.

A young woman sat curled on the grass just beside the hedge. One arm hugged her knees to her chest, the other covered her eyes. With her head bent down, only a violent blond tangle of corded ropes and braids and locks was visible. The shining mass of her hair shook with the quaking of her shoulders.

She wore a crossover the color of bone—finely embroidered at the edges with soft ochre thread—and leggings of the same shade. Bone Clan, then? Someone of some wealth and standing, though, even amid the poorest clan. He couldn't see her ear stud beneath her hair to be sure. No charms or blades hung at her belt, not that he would have expected any on a woman. Her crossover hung loosely and too short and revealed nothing of the shape of her body. It contrasted sharply with the tanned skin of her hands, tough and strong hands that gripped her elbows like a dragon clutching its prey.

Given the shaking of her shoulders, she was still crying, but she made no further sound. Had she missed his quiet approach in the grass? Apparently.

She didn't want to be noticed either, did she? He should slink away now, and they'd both get what they wanted. He knew as well as anyone—dead was dead. He could try to offer words of comfort, but what was the point? There was no comfort but time. If that.

But wouldn't it be cruel to simply walk away? As if her display didn't matter, as if it didn't hurt to see her hurt, as if the suffering of another was as insignificant as a blade of grass swaying in the wind?

That was the way Elix treated people. Irrelevant. As if suffering was only significant based on who felt it. Or Raelt, who would delight in an opportunity to revel in someone's misery, especially that of a woman with social standing lower than his own.

He wasn't like them. He aimed to be as different from them as possible. And her silent sobs were not insignificant to him. His chest panged again as another wave shook her shoulders.

He glanced around, looking for something, anything to offer. He jammed his hands into the pockets of his crossover and discovered a clean handkerchief. Before he could second-guess this rare moment of boldness, he crouched down and tapped her elbow with a finger, offering the soft black cloth.

Her head snapped up, eyes catching on his offering and widening. Ah, the dark color of the handkerchief told her much before she even took him in. She glanced up, fire sparking in her features and tingeing the sadness. Hmm, or was that despair? All familiar feelings.

"Are you all right?" he asked softly. Stupid. It was obvious she wasn't.

Her eyes stopped him short. Like everything else about her, they were a golden brown. They stared out at him like deep wells, intelligence alight amid a maelstrom of emotion. Her delicate, pale lips were parted on the edge of a word. Tears had slipped down each cheek, leaving a faint trail.

In a fit of certain madness, he reached forward and brushed the most recent teardrop aside with his thumb.

She froze. Her skin was warm and smooth under his. The pad of his thumb tingled at first and then stung sharply, a spark of energy knifing up the nerves of his arm.

She jerked back, scrambling to her feet. Had she felt it too? She backed away a few steps and must have worried she had snot coming out of her nose—which would have been completely normal considering the circumstances—as she snatched the cloth from his hand and covered her face.

He straightened too and took his own steps back to give her space. "Pardon the interruption. You looked—"

"I've—" she cut him off, but then stopped just as quickly. "I thought I was alone."

"So did I."

Her eyes flicked down at the handkerchief, then widened as she realized she could not simply hand it back to him. Damn. Her eyes darted around, as if she suspected a trap.

"I've got to go," she blurted, and she sprinted past him, around the hedge, and out of the cemetery, taking the handkerchief with her. The scent of cedar brushed past him, as if chasing after her. Strange, there was no reason for such a scent here.

He sighed. That had gone well. He had such a way with people.

Shoulders slumped, he trudged out of the cemetery and back toward the Obsidian complex to await his fate.

~

Lara sniffled and jammed the Obsidian's enchanted black handkerchief into her pocket as she strode over dew-covered cobblestones. The last thing she needed was to be seen with it. An item from another clan so sopping with magic would raise lots of questions she didn't have the answers to. Stranger still, it didn't seem to carry any particular spell—just energy. It was just like an Obsidian to throw around magic like they threw around gold. And what had been that strange spark that had hit her when his finger brushed her cheek? Every clan practiced the same spells, and she'd never learned anything like that one. And what could be the purpose of shocking a crying girl anyway? Probably just a stray charge, built up by accident, nothing more.

She sighed and squared her shoulders. Time to put the tears—and the handkerchief—behind her.

Smoothing her hair back, she marched herself through the gardens and up the path toward her father's workshop. She had made a lot of good memories in the little building that squatted behind the Bone Clan's mansion, in a corner of the estate near the far back wall. Their estate was odd in that the place was only walled on three sides, something she had never quite understood. It left the grounds more secured than no walls at all—and looking slightly more important than the residences around them. But it still invited the average clan member in, without a fancy gate or some such snobbery to stop them.

Hopefully that was the original intent. It was either that, or they'd run out of money.

Was that Obsidian boy going home, even now, to his family's ornate iron gate, nodding to some butler? Most Obsidian-District estates were walled and held only single families, and rich Obsidians dwelt in houses larger than any in the Bone District, her own included. Meanwhile, building Da's estate had required the pooled resources of the entire clan—and that probably hadn't been the wisest use of funds, considering all their other needs.

But no one was asking her.

Then again, her home served a dozen purposes. It housed classrooms, meeting rooms, diplomats. What did a single Obsidian family do with all that space? Employ a legion of servants?

Yes, certainly. Her clever-eyed, black-clothed benefactor was probably strolling merrily along a line of servants even now. All were gorgeous women clothed in black—probably scantily. They'd shower him with figs and wine and nuts and treasures. What else did one employ a legion of servants to do? Perhaps please him in other ways?

She frowned. Her jealous fantasies weren't usually this... suggestive. She put a hand over her stomach as it gurgled. Hmm. Figs and nuts sounded delicious just now. These bizarre thoughts were clearly just the product of extreme hunger, nothing more.

After all, all the poor man had done was give her a handkerchief. And be wealthy. And have those... wonderful eyes of his. Bright and piercing, intelligent and concerned. They were engraved on her eyelids they'd hit her so powerfully. Like something inside her had shivered and sprung to life.

Like he'd actually seen her, when no one else did.

How dare he try to be kind. He didn't deserve her bitter imaginings. She sighed, smoothed down her hair again, and quickened her pace.

A bell tinkled as she opened the door—the bell was as much for his guards as her Da. Two men lounged in armchairs provided for this purpose in opposite corners, thankfully both awake. It was still early.

The rest of the place was lined with pegs full of tools, the center crowded with tables filled with projects in wood, some in bone or ivory. Was that a chair under construction? Or maybe it was a birdhouse.

Da did not need to earn a living as a carpenter, and that was a lucky thing, no matter how much he loved working with wood.

The smell in his workshop had always made something stir, something warm and happy and yet a little anxious too. Warmth and sawdust hit her in a wave, a small stove in the corner stoked and heating the place. Barely. Da should at least put those guards to work keeping the fire going. But that wasn't the sort of thing he remembered to do.

Her room would have been much cozier. She hadn't ventured out of it for weeks, though—or more likely months—and it was time for that to end.

Today was six months since her brother's death. The day she had decided that since the rest of the world was forcing her to move on, she would start to comply.

Or at least play along.

She'd pulled on a heavier crossover and marched to the first place she could think of that wasn't her bed—the cemetery.

So moving on hadn't gotten off to such a great start, but she'd had some prayers to pray. Forgiveness and permission to ask for.

Because today she was playing along, but only playing. She had plans of her own.

"Good morning, Da," she said as he turned.

"Lara! So good to see you out here."

"Well, you know, six months, I thought I ought to start pretending that life moves on."

He sighed and set down the wax crayon and metal triangle he'd been using to plan his next cut. Did his hand shake with the movement, or was it her imagination? "Yes. It does. And it doesn't."

She nodded. "I wanted to remind you. You need a companion to take to the emperor's banquet." She had long ago taken on these duties of her late mother's, but they'd fallen by the wayside in her grief. She'd shirked them long enough.

He squinted, scratched one bushy eyebrow. "Which ball?"

"The one for the Feast of Souls. It's not even two weeks away."

He waved her off, picked up his triangle. "There's plenty of time."

"Not for your companion to make a gown fit for an emperor, if she doesn't already have one." Or to alter one. Buying fancy gowns for every feast was a thing other, richer clans did.

"Eh." He waved at her again and picked up the black stick of wax wound with thread.

"What about the new Winor woman?"

"The one who's barely got all the yak fur off her skirts? While Pavan does enjoy meeting his people fresh from the steppe, I'm expecting this might not be the best occasion for that. No, my love." His bushy eyebrows frowned at her. He took a sip of the tea that sat nearby on the bench, then narrowed in on marking the wood. "Can't I take you?"

"No. I ought to attend on my own." They probably expected her to cave and bring Andius. That wasn't happening.

"I'll deal with it, my little mother hen."

"Come now. I'm just trying to help."

"This isn't about the ball, is it?"

She dodged the question. "There's always Rior Delacrew. She's lovely."

"She's a decade younger than me."

"So? It's just a ball. Although..."

"Don't start."

"...you never know!" She brightened, leaning on the workbench conspiratorially. "You might find a suitable longer-term interest among many of these ladies—"

He dropped the tools and pivoted to face her. She thought he might shout, but instead he laid a hand on each shoulder, gentle as usual. When she met his sorrowful gaze, all her forced mirth dried up. His fingers squeezed once before he spoke. "My darling dragonfly. Our situation is what it is. Your mother is gone, and now your brother too." He stopped, swallowed, overcome for a moment.

"Myandrin. You can say his name, Da. It won't hurt anything."

"We are stuck where we are stuck." His sad eyes stared at her. He still hadn't said it. "There's nothing to help it." His voice was rough, and she understood. Her throat was tight too.

"We could change it. We could try." She straightened a little. "We *should* try."

"We can't control who we've lost. Nor the consequences. We must simply do the best with what we have left." He patted her shoulder and turned back to his work.

They weren't talking about balls or companions anymore, of course. But she persisted in pretending anyway.

"What about Menin's sister Qela?"

"What about her?"

"She's young and fair, and, and—" Lara groped at the air. There had to be *some* other good quality about her.

"*No*, Lara."

"She's not so bad." She crumpled back against the dusty workbench. What were the guards making of all this?

Da raised an eyebrow, took another sip of tea, and said nothing.

"Okay, maybe she's that bad. But she seems to like you. And she's young! Won't you at least consider it? For me?"

"Lara, I can't—"

"It matters, Da. Any of those women would gladly go to balls with you. Permanently. As a wife. Carrying you a nice new heir—" She jiggled her hands over her belly.

He let out an exasperated sigh. "Women are not just jars for babies, Lara."

Her eyes flashed, suddenly angry. "You think I don't know that?"

"Those women all deserve love, companionship. And that is something I cannot give them or even offer. Or force."

"What about *my* chance at love?" She stabbed a finger at her chest, restraining herself to a mere snap instead of a shout.

"People like us do not get to choose whom we love, Lara." His voice was gentle, but the words stung. She had never really disagreed, but when Myandrin had been alive, she would likely have avoided it. Or sidestepped the matter until she was too old—or independent—to be desirable. It wasn't something she'd grown up expecting to deal with. She was probably already too independent, but there was no choice now.

It was stupid. Some stupid part of her persisted. Probably the part of her that was smart enough to know that it wasn't fair.

"I know this is about Andius," he said into her silence. His voice was soft enough the guards were unlikely to hear, although they couldn't have missed her words. Andius was popular with many of the clan guards. He was popular with everyone, because the parts of the day he didn't spend bragging, he spent kissing asses. "I'm sorry, my child. I wish there was something I could do."

"It's not about *him*." That was not entirely true. She didn't want to marry anyone, but especially not him. "It's about me. About my life. My happiness."

"I live for your happiness, my little fig pie. You know I wouldn't have it this way if I could. It was supposed to be—"

She cut him off. "That doesn't matter now. He's dead."

Da winced. "Even if I remarried, the possibility that I might at some point conceive a child that *might* be a son? That is not going to change their minds. Especially not so soon after Myandrin's death, with no one carrying the clanblade. I've given it up, and I won't retake it. And the dragon won't have me anyway."

"Surely the dragon can be reasoned with."

He laughed softly. "If you'd spoken much with dragons, you'd understand. Darling, all a marriage would do is deny those women any hope of happiness."

And make them richer than they could dream of being. But her father had already thought about it. She could see it in his eyes.

"Something has to change their minds. It *has* to." The words fell from her numbly because she needed them to be true, not because she believed them.

"It's not our choice, Lara. These laws are generations old."

"You are the clan leader. Change the laws."

"Attempting that would only make things worse for you."

She didn't meet his eyes, not wanting to admit he was right on any angle. She was being obstinate, but it couldn't be helped. Reality was hard to stomach at this point.

He continued. "We would be certain to fail at any change. I don't have the support. Andius is popular with the council. They won't make any change he is against, because they'll have to deal with him much longer than they'll have to deal with me. They were already through with me. It was Mya's turn."

Her turn to wince at that. "But you could try—"

"If I went to serious lengths, it would be obvious that it's personal. That it's not about what is proper as law, but about a petty attempt to keep Andius from the seat of power."

She bit her lip. It'd be obvious because it was the truth. Keeping Andius from the throne was exactly what she wanted. No, to be more specific, she wanted to keep him from her bed. Unfortunately, now that her brother was dead, taking one necessarily required him to take the other.

"He'd retaliate against you. And you know it."

She smirked to herself. "I thought Andius could do no wrong. Everyone's darling. He'd never hurt a fly, unless it was hurting one of his precious people." Bastard put up a good facade.

"I've taught him for fifteen years. You think I don't see through it? I can't put you in that position—"

"I'm already *in* that position."

"This would be worse."

"Can't you at least consider remarrying?"

He straightened his crossover. "I won't. It wouldn't do what you think it would, Lara. Even if I immediately had another child, they'd be only a baby. It'd be more than a decade before they were grown and able to take the mantle and blade. I would have to retake the clanblade, and I can't. The child would be irrelevant. There is no stopping Andius now."

She blew out a breath. He was right, and she hated him for it. "Save it, Da. I'm going for a walk." She spun on a heel and headed for the door.

"Wait. Does this mean you'll be in class later? And go to the ball with me? Lara!"

He called after her, but she didn't answer, and she didn't stop. Something had to be done. She refused to believe that there was no way out of this situation, out of enslavement to this gilded snake of a man.

This morning, she'd shed tears on Myandrin's stone, asked his permission and his forgiveness.

Now she would try the one other idea she had. The most desperate one, the one she'd hoped to avoid.

She couldn't blame Da for not wanting to remarry or to quarrel with Andius. He was right in all his arguments. But something had to be done.

He'd left her no other choice.

Dozens streamed past the broad window before Nyalin. The sun beat down on an ocean of robes and crossovers in black. He brushed a strand of hair out of his eyes, feeling claustrophobic just looking at them all, and searched for Grel approaching amid the faceless mass. Their cat Smoke was curled beside him on the window seat, purring as he absently returned to petting her. His knee wouldn't quit bouncing from nerves, but she didn't seem to mind.

"No Grel yet," he murmured.

The people were packed like rolls in a breadbasket, shoving past each other in the din, shoulders brushing. He'd returned from the graveyard through back alleys to avoid entering this fray. Thank the Twins for the back servants' gate.

Some could take this road, and the crowd gave them a wide berth. Necromancers, for example. One strolled by now with plenty of room to stretch. His ropes of hair were tied back from his ruddy face, and he wore a necklace of mouse and rabbit skulls—hopefully that's what they were—punctuated by bright blue beads. Peacock feathers hung down the back of the man's head, and three black vials hung from his belt, surely filled with blood.

The only other people who could cut a path through the crowd—besides the clan leaders and the emperor in full regal procession—were the bladed women. The reasons for *that* were more complicated than fear, but there were so few bladed women, it hardly mattered. Too many people were uncomfortable with women wielding both magic and a sword.

Inside the Obsidian Clan's manor, the air was still and oppressive with the scents of incense and woodsmoke that never seemed to lift from the lower floor of his foster parents' estate. Servants creaked upon the wood floors of the rooms above him, but these lower rooms were frozen and silent, like air trapped in a jar waiting to be released. Quiet birdsong rose from the back garden. His stomach growled as the scent of some baked blackberry creation wafted from the rear kitchens and caught on his tongue. He longed to quit this place, whether for the warmer kitchens with Dalas or the solitude of his work in the library.

But it didn't make sense to continue copying another tome if tonight he ended up not living here anymore. He ran his hand through Smoke's black fur and waited. Her purring thrummed against his hand. "Just a little longer, surely," he reassured her. Even though he *knew* what they'd decide, he had to hear it from Grel's mouth first. And then he'd have to figure out what the decision truly meant.

The hungry growl in his stomach tightened into a knot of anxious dread.

At his words, Smoke stirred, unfurled herself, and stretched, arching her back with a lazy yawn. "You've got the idea, Smokes," he muttered, hopping to his feet. "Yes, that's it. Expend some of that nervous energy."

He paced the mahogany floors, eschewing the carpets for a circuit from the wide front window, to the marble hearth, to the armchairs and the bear rug, and back past the weapons stands. The lonely bows and daggers called out for some attention.

The third time around his circuit, the tiny chime on the great iron front door tinkled. Nyalin stopped and spun.

It wasn't Grel. His younger brother Raelt met his eyes with a sneer. Smoke fled the room, an annoyed growl in the back of her throat.

"I beat him back, didn't I?" said Raelt, grinning.

"What did they say?" He tried to keep his tone flat, emotionless, although nothing would keep his sadistic "brother" from savoring the moment. At least if the council had finally doomed Nyalin, he could get away from this fool.

Raelt swaggered forward and leaned against the arch that separated the grand entry hall from the sitting room. Nyalin looked pointedly at the decorative ceremonial daggers that had conveniently ended up beside him.

Raelt snorted. "Have you been waiting here the *entire* time we've been gone?"

Nyalin said nothing.

"A whole meeting about you, you'd think they would have invited you." Raelt's self-satisfied grin only widened.

Nyalin narrowed his eyes and waited. He wouldn't take the bait.

Thankfully, the chime rang again. Oh, thank Seluvae—Grel.

"They said a rat's anus has more magic than you," Raelt blurted before Grel could barge in and ruin his moment. Raelt dashed halfway up the stairs, putting a nice buffer between him and Grel. "And they'd rather teach the rat!"

Nyalin just shook his head. Raelt had probably been hoping to cultivate something more stinging to say than that, but Grel had forced his hand.

Grel stopped in the doorway, pushing his too-long black locks out of his eyes, and glared at Raelt. "What, did you run the whole way? Just to rub it in?"

"I'm just fitter than you," Raelt called down, now out of Nyalin's sight.

"Balls off," Grel snapped at him. "You live to rub salt in wounds. Get out of here."

"Hey, this is my house too. You can't kick me out. Unlike him." He raised his voice. "Your days are numbered, Nyalin, you'll see."

"Oh, what a loss," Nyalin drawled. "How will I stand being without your excellent company."

"Not everything is about *you*, Raelt," Grel growled, stepping in and opening the door wider. "Now beat it before I beat you out of here." Grel started forward, suggesting the threat was anything but idle.

"Fine. I'll leave you two to your crying party." Raelt's feet thundered the rest of the way up the stairs and down the hall.

Grel closed the door behind him and met Nyalin's eyes. His expression twisted something in Nyalin's chest.

"I'm so sorry," he said softly.

"Want me to send some tea?" Raelt called down. "You ladies need any refreshments for your commiserating?"

"Eat toad testicles!" Grel yelled after him. "C'mon, Nyalin. Let's get out of here and away from him."

Nyalin shrugged and followed his brother back out the door to hear the details of how it had all gone down. He'd endure the crowd to get away from Raelt. They shouldered through the throng for a while in silence.

"Toads don't have testicles," Nyalin said as they found their spot in the river of people and began moving toward the east Obsidian market square.

"Yeah, but he's not smart enough to know that." Grel smiled, his arms clasped behind his back, but didn't meet Nyalin's eyes.

Nyalin snickered, but then sighed. "So they said no, huh?"

Grel hung his head. "Indeed."

"So that's it then?"

"I suppose."

They walked in silence for a moment.

"That can't be it," Nyalin groaned.

"I know." Grel clenched his jaw.

"What are we going to do?"

"Let's get some ale. I think I need to get drunk."

"I don't think that'll fix anything. And it's barely lunchtime."

"All the more reason why." They walked the rest of the way in silence, and only when they were settled with two mugs of sweet black brew did Grel speak again. "I argued vehemently, of course."

Nyalin leaned back in his chair, balancing on two legs. "You didn't need to do that. They have their own issues with you. Enough you didn't need to take up my cause."

"Let them." His brother waved a hand at the air. "They're stuck with me, whether they like it or not. I'm not going to turn my eyes when they pull this bullshit later. They might as well get used to it."

That was Grel—always pissing on politics for the sake of principle. "You will need to cooperate with their whims sometimes. Someday. Or the lot of you will never get anything done."

"Well, I don't need to start trying to impress them or build cooperation over *this*. It's not right, and you know it. I would rather fight them on this than abide by it—I have to be able to sleep at night."

"I understand. If you were clan leader already, this would all be a lot easier."

"Yes, but unfortunately the sword smith turned me down for a sword again. And of course, my father is still alive, the old coot."

"You don't mean that," he said quickly, his chair stumbling forward. "And—I didn't mean it like that either." Much as the decision was idiotic and ensured Nyalin would never join the Order of the Raven, let alone become a swordmage, he didn't wish death on someone just to get some education. Even if that someone was Elix.

"Of course I don't. I want him to live to a ripe old age. But I'd also love it if he didn't do stupid shit like forbidding the teaching of the son of the greatest mage who has ever lived."

His face flushed hot. Thankfully the restaurant was empty, so he didn't need to endure curious stares. He didn't *feel* like the son of a great mage. He felt like an orphan who'd grown up mooching off his rich benefactors and turned out not to have any magic anyway. He was an investment that had not panned out, at best. At worst, an embarrassment. And truth be told, a small part of him was relieved. He had never wanted to be a pawn in Elix's game. But he wasn't going to tell Grel that, especially when his brother had no choice but to play.

He tried to shrug it off. "It's not his fault I've got no talent."

"That's horse shit, and you know it." Grel stabbed a finger at him. "Even he won't say for sure."

"Didn't stop the council from saying as much."

"Too bad the Order of the Raven won't accept anything but a straight answer."

"They're picky like that." He hid behind a gulp of his beer. His oldest brother—the only member of his foster family who'd always loved him and treated him like family—had always been surer of Nyalin's abilities than he was himself. He tried not to argue with someone who believed in him, but it wasn't easy to do when this particular subject came up.

"There has to be something you can do," Grel grumbled.

Nyalin shrugged. "Do you think they accept sons of great mages at brewing school? At least I could drink my woes away more cheaply."

"Maybe you can find a sexy bladed woman to teach you in secret." Grel's eyes twinkled over a sip from his mug.

"Sounds dangerous. What about baked goods? Dalas could teach me." The house baker had always treated him with more care and kindness than anyone but Grel, and the scent of blackberries still hung in his mind.

Grel snorted. "You're not giving up that easily."

"Oh, come on, Grel. What choice do I have?"

"Do you *want* to give up?" His brother leaned back and folded his arms across his chest, eying Nyalin.

He sighed. "No. I can't bear that my mother sacrificed everything for it to end like this. I just don't see what else I can do. Teaching myself hasn't worked. None of them can find my magic. What if they're right? What if I *am* a dud?" They were, of course. They had to be. "I need to give up on all this and just find something else." Something meaningful, even if it wasn't magic.

"First of all, you're not a dud. Second of all, even if you were, with your lineage, they should still spend ten more years checking, just to be sure. Especially since they're *not* sure."

"I wish I had your confidence in me." He downed another, possibly overzealous gulp of beer.

"Why are you giving up?"

"I'm not, it's just... I think they *are* sure. It just hurts their bragging rights to admit it. They don't want people to know that I'm not what everyone hoped. If they don't say anything for sure, then the potential for another great mage is still there. News of my failure can't spread."

Grel's face fell. "That's... plausible. You've thought a lot about this."

"Yes."

"But with this—it could spread now. The council always was a bit overzealous. Perhaps my father hoped to keep them to a nonanswer as well but failed." Grel sighed. "You always were the more politically perceptive one."

Nyalin shrugged. "Hasn't done me much good, though, has it?"

"Listen. I have an idea. But I'm only telling you if you are not actually beaten and hoping to give up."

"I'm not giving up, damn you." He set the tankard down with a thud. "What is it? I'll try anything."

"You sure you don't want to spend your days baking

fruit pies?"

"Dalas has kept me sane, but my mother didn't die birthing me so I could make a better fruit pie."

"That's more like it."

"Tell me your idea, damn it."

Grel grinned. "Go to one of the other clans."

Nyalin stared at him. "Excuse me? I must have misheard you. Either that, or you just went insane."

"Get a second opinion. My father and the council will not be easily convinced. But if it's appearances they care about, use it against them. Except instead of telling people you're a dud, you're going to tell them the Obsidians are too foolish to truly search for your magic. You'll ask for their help, and you'll get it. Maybe they'll succeed where Elix and I failed. And if changing the council's mind is possible at this point, your best bet would be another clan leader's opinion."

He raised his eyebrows. "Elix would kill me."

"Exactly. If your theory is right, maybe embarrassing him is just the ticket. But he won't kill you. I won't let him."

"Do you really think they'd talk to me?"

Grel nodded gravely. "Any of them would. Even without magic, it'd be a slight to Elix that any of them would benefit from. You're the politician—am I wrong?"

Nyalin winced. "What a label."

"C'mon."

"You're not wrong. And that doesn't bother you to suggest it?"

"Not at all. He brought it on himself." His brother folded his arms across his chest. "My only question is which clan."

The girl from that morning flashed through his mind. Razor-sharp wit in those fiery, hurting eyes, and a wealth of beauty besides... Who was the leader of the Bone Clan?

"What about Cerivil?" he blurted.

His brother clapped his hands and leaned forward. "I like it. I mean, you'd be starting at the bottom."

"But Cerivil is the one most likely to help," he said, rubbing his chin and turning the idea over in his mind. Cerivil had always kept track of Nyalin, writing and visiting now and then. Cerivil and Nyalin's mother had been friends, and some had speculated possibly more than friends. That was only wild speculation; he'd searched high and low for clues as to who his father was, but nothing he'd found had pointed to the Bone Clan. All clues he'd found indicated the man was likely an Obsidian and somehow connected to the Order of the Raven.

Hence where he needed to go next. Where he'd planned to go if Elix would just pronounce him a swordmage and fit for teaching—or not. He didn't particularly care if he joined the monastery or not, but he wanted answers. And how else was he going to make a living?

If Cerivil *had* been his father, what reason would he have for hiding it? He could have just said so, and the prestige he would have gained would have been beyond worth it. No, it was more likely that his father, whoever he was, either didn't know or had something to hide.

"Yes, I agree. And he has the most to gain. And besides, everyone knows Cerivil is talented beyond his birth. He's also widely respected for his honesty," Grel mused.

Nyalin nodded and then stated the obvious. "But he's... not particularly high in social standing."

"That will work in your favor if he's more willing to help. And it's a very humble choice. No one can accuse you of self-importance there. Of course, some of the stupider council members will ignore him based on his clan alone, but... Father won't. He respects Cerivil. If Cerivil proves your magic exists and Father refuses to listen to even *him*... well, then, that would be beyond rational."

He hesitated. Elix had never seemed particularly rational to him, but he didn't point that out to his brother now. "So... you think I should talk to him?"

Grel smiled and shrugged. "Well, what have you got to lose? The worst he can say is no."

He laughed. "Not like I haven't heard *that* before. Okay—I'll go tomorrow."

"Nyalin." Grel's fingers drummed along the side of the tankard.

"What?"

"I know you too well." His brother eyed him.

"What?"

"Go today. Go right now, or it'll be weeks before you work up the nerve."

Nyalin glared at him and then took another gulp of beer. Grel was right, he was already shying away from the idea. Asking Cerivil, the leader of the weakest clan under the emperor, to consider butting heads with someone like Elix... it was no small request.

If it were just about him, he wouldn't bother. Dalas could certainly teach him how to bake. And to enjoy it, even.

But it wasn't just about him. Someone other than Grel had maybe loved him once, even if only while he'd been in her belly. It was about her.

And about getting answers. Cerivil might be the only person who could give him that.

"All right, fine. I'll split the difference with you. Tomorrow first thing."

Grel narrowed his eyes and took a sip. "I'll be making

sure of it."

Lara's hand hovered over the black velvet interior of the dagger case. Last chance to turn back. She still had time to think the better of this plan of hers.

She breathed deep the cold air that whistled through the armory. Outside, pale curtains flapped in the darkening evening breeze, the foyer empty as the guards rotated through their rounds. It would remain empty for about two minutes more.

She had that much time to decide.

In spite of being called the Bone Dagger, the small knife was not predominantly made of bone. The blade was the length of her hand, perhaps a bit longer, with a thin fuller down its center. The hilt was the ancient part—and the magical part—its lovely bone carved from the Bone Dragon's own scales. The scale piece curved into a natural guard, or something close to one, but as handles went, it was not particularly practical. The design didn't make much sense. Some bitter sword smith had probably deliberately undermined the balance, angry there was a magic more powerful than his own. The handle looked as likely to injure her hand as protect it in a fight.

She wasn't supposed to know about these sorts of things. But Da had always doted on her, given her far more leeway than council members and fancy ladies said he should, especially after her mother had died. And now with the loss of her brother...

Well, it didn't matter. With the way things were, Andius would put an end to all that.

There is no stopping Andius now.

Actually, Da wasn't quite right about that one. She had

this one idea to stop him. It was extreme. Desperate, even. Possibly a betrayal of her clan, her father, and all she held dear.

But doing nothing was worse—a betrayal of herself, one she wasn't sure she'd survive.

She drew out the golden scarf she'd tucked inside her crossover and laid it over the dagger's handle. She'd explored her options, racked her brain. This was all that was left.

The clan leader always carried the clanblade, but Myandrin's death had thrown things awry. Da had already passed the blade down to Myandrin, leaving them in this awkward limbo where no one carried the clanblade. Other, wealthier clans made new blades from fresh scales for each new heir, but this one dagger had always been the royal blade. And there were no Bone sword smiths anymore anyway. The last had died decades ago. They could beseech one in another clan, but that would require trusting them a great deal. There was no sister clan they trusted that much; there had never seemed a need to find one.

And so now the blade awaited a new heir to be chosen. The new clan leader would take up the mantle before the hard of winter came, if not much, much sooner.

If there was no blade for him to take, however...

Then maybe he wouldn't be able to become clan leader in the first place.

She glanced over her shoulder. The guards were still on their rotation. She had another minute, perhaps two. She raised her hand again over the hilt and the scarf she'd covered it with.

Did she really want to do this?

No one would suspect. She'd take it and ride out and bury it in the desert. Or at the bottom of a well. The theft would cause chaos, maybe hurt the clan. They'd be the only clan without a sacred clanblade. But they were already the lowest of the low. The Bone Dragon had already withdrawn most of its power two generations ago, for no reason she knew. What did it matter? They'd survive, as they always did. Maybe they'd be the better for it. Maybe new traditions would grow. Less stupid ones. Less cruel.

And if not? Maybe they'd kill her. Or send her into exile. She'd still end up ahead—and no possession of Andius's.

Never that. No matter what, he wasn't getting this dagger. Or her.

She lowered a hand and carefully gripped the hilt, keeping the cloth between her skin and the scale of bone. With her other hand, she shook open the sack she'd tied at her belt, the kind women used to carry flowers and market goods to and from home. Men couldn't be asked to carry apples home to feed the family, of course. That was women's work.

A fitting container for a dagger they insisted she could not have. She held the dagger over the bag and lowered it slowly. The cloth was slipping at this angle, but she needed it to prevent imprinting. No one was quite sure how the process of imprinting worked, and she wasn't taking any chances. But dropping the dagger any faster might slice through the bottom and give her no way to smuggle it out, not to mention the noise it would make hitting the floor.

Just as the blade was halfway into the bag, footsteps shuffled out in the foyer. She jumped, ice shooting through her veins. Her startle caused the scarf to slip farther, the knife twisting in her grip. Rough bone brushed her sweaty fingers, cold to the touch. She gasped.

Well. Hello, daughter.

The blade dropped the last few inches, hitting the bottom with nothing but a soft swish, as if it were no sharper than her neglected hairbrush.

A sudden rush of wind hit her, the leathery flap of wings filling her ears. No—it wasn't really hitting her. It was hitting her mind. Stars in a brilliant night's sky flew past at an incredible speed. An upsurge, a spin, her stomach leaping into her throat—

And then it was gone.

"What was—" she started. But she clapped a hand over her mouth. Damn—where was the owner of those footsteps? The hall was silent now. And what the hell had just happened?

The imprinting? No—no, it couldn't be. It required pomp and circumstance. Ritual, ceremony, calling upon the dragon to accept the new clan leader. It couldn't be done so quickly. It couldn't.

She mouthed silent curses as she closed the dagger case, hot tears pricking the corners of her eyes. If it was done, there *really* was no going back. If there ever had been. She would have to hope that her gut was mistaken, that imprinting took more than a brush of a fingertip across bone.

She tightened the drawstrings on her bag and hurried out. She had moments before the guards ended their rotation. She left the armory looking just as it had before. Her room was only a floor and a few dozen paces away.

All too easily, it was done.

She shut the door of her room and leaned her back against the simple wood. Her bag and the dagger inside pressed against her knee, demanding further action, to finish the job. Her eyes caught on the black handkerchief where she'd dropped it beside her bed. It still vibrated hot with magic, its scent teasing her. His was something bright and fruity. Maybe lemon? Or no, blackberries? Something of the forest—not something any Bone Clan child knew much about. It was kind of nice.

Strange that the scent was so faint given the amount of

power the handkerchief still held. She should tap it and use it for something more practical. Perhaps that was the intent, stored energy he was sharing with her? A pick-me-up for a low moment? Had he suspected she was a mage too? That would be even more strange, as she'd worn no visible charms or blades or other signs of being a swordmage. She hadn't noticed such tools on him either, but she hadn't been looking carefully.

The memory of his fingers brushing her cheek flashed in her mind. She covered the spot with her hand, savoring the memory, then shook it off. It'd be foolish to get worked up over a small bit of compassion, even with its rarity in this world.

A shame she'd probably never see him again. Or if she did pass him in the street years down the road, chances were she wouldn't recognize him as the one who'd seen into her soul and lit a strange spark that even now was quietly smoldering, craving his touch on her cheek again.

What a ridiculous thing to be thinking about, after what she'd just done. She wouldn't pass him in the street because she'd be dead.

My, she was being rash today. She sighed. Oh, well. It was a rash world.

She had work to do. The kind that required hiding one of the six most recognizable blades in the empire. She knelt beside her bed, drew out her chest of silk undergarments, and set to concealing the blade linked so inextricably with her fate.

"You should have been Elix's wife."

The fire crackled in the hearth. Unira wished it would crackle louder. Loud enough to drown out her father and his reminders of her failings. She'd been pretending to be too engrossed in the demonology book on her lap to hear him for about an hour, but it wasn't shutting him up.

"You should drink less." She didn't look up from the pages, flipped to the next one. A drawing of an exceptionally handsome demon stared back at her from the paper. Her eyebrow twitched. "You are too far into your cups, Father."

"Not at all! I am not far enough." Edyef slammed down his tankard with a grumble. He was full of the roast boar from his dinner, and full of beer too. And nonsense.

She took a much more graceful sip, hoping to keep him from noticing the way her attention had honed in on the page. Her own wine was sweet and tart on her tongue, like a ripe peach. Cold, chilled by ice she'd ordered dragged down from the mountain. Her children—nearly adults now, but always her children—lounged on the plush white bear rug by the fire with their own wine. They ignored their grandfather's grumbling and their mother's reading equally. Typical late evening activities.

"I thought you said I should have been Pavan's wife," she said as she set down her glass. "Make up your mind, Father. We can only be bitter in so many ways."

"Bah. Pavan should never have been chosen. It should have been Elix."

"And I know, I know, we should never have agreed to ally with the other clans in the first place." Every time he was drunk, it was the same. She ran a finger down the page, across the black coat of the man-demon inked in loving detail. He was more man than most of them were. At least in his outward appearance.

"Obsidians have always been superior."

"Father, respectfully... I did not marry Elix, nor Pavan. Bringing up this matter over and over is pointless. I married Giran." She had thought it a fine lot in life too, especially at first, but her father had had years to breed disappointment.

"Indeed." He took another drink, red wine dribbling into his beard. "At least he had the decency to die."

She narrowed her eyes at him. "Did he now." She didn't believe for a second that her husband had simply died. Her father had had something to do with it, obviously; but she had no interest in finding out. No truth would bring Giran back, and they had meant little to each other. He'd inflicted two pregnancies on her and many other discomforts, but the wealth and children he'd left her with seemed a fair trade for all that. She hadn't wished him dead. But she didn't wish him back alive either.

Her eyes flicked to her children lounging by the fire. Neither showed a reaction. They'd heard his ramblings before. Idak's face sometimes held a flicker of annoyance that she prayed did not mean he held some inklings of avenging his father's premature death. But he loved his grandfather as much as he'd loved his father, perhaps more; she shouldn't worry. Jylan's face sometimes danced with a hint of amusement, a pulling at the corner of her mouth. *That* worried Unira even more, and she couldn't come up with any reasoning why it shouldn't.

"Yes," she murmured to appease her father. "Our only blessing." That and Giran's vast silk fortune—and a dozen farms to keep on growing their coffers. She shook her head, doubting he'd hear the sarcasm.

"You've had such freedom in his absence." He chose a chocolate from a gilded plate on the table at his elbow and popped it in his mouth.

Again she watched Idak out of the corner of her eye. In truth, he was old enough to bear the mantle of the household, and he had been for several years. Only by his permission had she kept it. Permission her father had advised him to give, and

Idak couldn't deny the old many anything, he idolized Edyef so. And her father was right about the freedom it'd given her, compared to many women of her station in the Obsidian Clan.

The old man leaned forward conspiratorially—at least the few inches he was able. "How do our plans progress?"

Your plans, she wanted to say. Your plans. Not mine. "Not now, Father."

"Yes, now."

"No." She focused her attention on the book. The demon's eyes shone silver on the page. Some special ink, silver inlay, or something less mundane? It didn't matter. He was more than handsome, she decided. He was fine as an aged brandy, aristocratic and smoky too. This was it. This was the one. She ran a finger below his name but didn't speak it yet, even in her mind.

Her father's voice cut in. "Humor an old man. I can't but shift around in this stupid lounge and long for the restoration of my family's honor."

Inwardly, she rolled her eyes. What did he know of honor? Little, for all he talked about it. Outwardly, she sighed and shut the book. Her demon would have to wait. "Well, Father. Our plans progress very well."

"Is Idak in line for the blade yet?"

"No, but the sword smiths have been thoroughly bought and paid for. They won't be making Elix's son a blade anytime soon."

"But he remains in line to rule?"

"Yes. It is only a matter of time, though. As the seasons pass, the council will begin to question his ascension. And we will be there and ready."

"We must do more to harm that soppy-hearted, sentimental fool. But fine for now. What about the other? Linali's son?"

She schooled her face, as she always did, swallowing the distaste that welled up at any mention of the woman. Her old rival. Her hate was a weakness, and her father had an inkling that it existed, but not its depth. She worked hard to keep it tucked away so he didn't know how deep it ran.

If he knew, he might make her kill Linali. End the obsession. And then what would Unira do for a pet? Get a hobby?

Or perhaps getting her own pet demon would satisfy instead.

"Elix has done our bidding. He won't allow teaching of the boy. He was furious, but he had no choice. Vanae and her treachery finally came in handy for something."

He waved off mention of Elix's wife. "Excellent. They mustn't have Linali's son to fall back on. Idak must be there—ready and waiting."

She nodded as if this were sage advice, as if she hadn't heard this ten times before. Or ten thousand. But he was not one to be hurried, fortunately or unfortunately. Bound to his couch, all he could do was repeat himself.

Of course, the plan was not bad, even if it was not hers.

If it did its job. If it tore apart the empire. Then she would be satisfied. His plan or hers. Idak on the imperial throne, leading the Obsidians against the other clans as they should have done long ago. Sure, putting the clans back at war with each other might destroy them all, rot them from the inside out.

She didn't particularly care. In fact, she liked that outcome better but wasn't sure she could quite affect total destruction all alone. That was where the demon came in. Either way, the empire would fall. And burn.

And she would dance in the ashes. She wouldn't rest until that magical tree of gems was a smoking skeleton stretching up out of the ruins like a claw toward the sky. And Pavan would regret the day he'd made an enemy of her.

She bowed her head again to her father in the silence.

"You've done well, child."

Although she was well into her fourth decade, his praise still gave her a little flush of stupid pride. "Thank you, Father."

"But we mustn't rest on our laurels."

"Of course. The other clans progress. Glass was easily destabilized. They've played right into our hands. And we have a willing puppet in the Bone Clan. I have leverage on him, but I doubt I'll need it. We are close to getting him the blade and the seat of power. Soon it will all be set, all roadblocks eliminated. It's but a formality now, a matter of approvals and ceremonies."

"Excellent. Which clan is next?"

"Lapis. Work has already begun."

He smiled, nodded. "You see? You are so capable. They really should have married you. And your magic might even surpass theirs. Astonishing—for a woman. You've always been so unique, so special, darling."

"Perhaps. But they didn't marry me, Father." And her abilities did surpass them, and only an idiot would be surprised by that. She knew many idiots, however.

He grinned. "Well, perhaps it will work out even better in the end, when Idak will reign over them all."

She bowed her head and let a smile creep onto her face. Or when the empire was brought to its knees, the clans turned against each other, and it all crashed into utter chaos. Either would suit her, really.

But chaos sounded like such a refreshing change.

She was grinning now, although he couldn't see it. "Yes, Father. So let it be."

Chapter 2

Den of Bones

It was hard to act normal afterward, but Lara did her best. The rest of that night had been easier. She'd lain in bed and wondered what in all Dala's dreams she had done. She'd retired early and slept in late, but the new morning was well underway. And she'd promised herself that her days of mourning were over.

Well, truth be told, she'd likely never stop missing her brother. But she needed to get up, get out, and pretend that life continued on. Because unfortunately, it did. Still, acting "normal" after her theft was made more difficult by the fact that nothing had been normal since Myandrin's passing.

Normal should have been going to lessons. But she'd only been there sporadically in the last few months anyway. In part, grief had kept her away, a willing prisoner in her room and her bed. Missing him, alternately raging at fate and praying it was all a terrible dream. If it was, she'd never woken up.

Then again, what was the point?

She leaned against the low wall of the balcony and gazed out at the horizon. Even in the midday sun, the wind whipping by her was cold. From here in their highest tower, she had a good view of the waterfalls to the west and the cliffs they crashed down on, but not the vast plain of dry basin between here and there. She'd often come here and gaze into the distance, so this at least was normal. All her life she had longed to go there—out to that waterfall, to the mountains and the horizon beyond. To explore the wilds beyond the mapped edges of Bone Clan lands. She'd worked hard as a swordmage because she'd have needed magic for the dangerous journey.

Now, though. She wasn't going anywhere.

She shook off the anger. She was trying to do something about her problems. The clanblade lay under her bed and not Andius's. It was a start.

Picking up her satchel in her room on the way, she wandered downstairs and out into the gardens in front of the mansion. Drawing here had once been a favorite pastime. It'd be good for her to try it again.

She hauled a sketchpad from her bag. Sitting cross-legged on a bench, she half-heartedly sketched a nearby flame tree. But the red blooms defied her attempts to capture them. She was so out of practice. And why hadn't she brought anything but black wax to draw with?

Or perhaps it was just her nerves. How could she concentrate on drawing when she was supposed to be pretending she hadn't done something horrible?

She chucked the sketchpad back into the bag. Time to try something else.

The cool breeze gave her a slight chill, so perhaps a walk was in order. The sun shone down on the dusted paths between evergreens and high, majestic trees. Fountains burbled away as she strolled past them, magic powering their idle flow and birds fluttering in their basins.

The walk wasn't cutting it. Maybe if she left her room

more often, she'd realize she needed to wear a cloak. She gazed up at a favorite boji tree as she strolled past—would a climb do the trick?

She dropped her satchel at the base of the tree and soon was pulling herself high into its limbs. The bark was rough and refreshing against her fingers, and her blood heated with the exercise.

Reaching the top, she surveyed the land around her. The dusty plains of the basin, the distant waterfalls, the jagged canyons and rugged mountains—all were more beautiful up here. And the Bone manor seemed perfectly peaceful. No alarms sounded, that much was certain.

Someone could discover the clanblade was missing in five minutes... or in five weeks. Who would go looking for it, until Andius was confirmed in the Feasts of Contest? And that was weeks away. She couldn't spend every waking moment on edge or she'd go insane. Deep breaths. Even if they discovered it missing, they wouldn't likely suspect her above others. She needed to relax.

She eyed a lower limb that had made a fine bench in the past. No sooner thought of than done. She was soon lounging along one thick limb. The day was peaceful, quiet, and it was easy to forget all her troubles and just be. The wind whispered across her skin and flapped her crossover.

Soft footsteps padded toward her on the dirt path.

She frowned, opened her eyes. Students shouldn't be coming and going—class had started and was far from over. The guards didn't do patrols through here. Probably a servant or something. She shut her eyes again and willed herself to relax.

The steps grew louder.

She sat up, then rose to stand on the branch and

squinted. A form was just coming into view around a large, long-needled evergreen.

A form dressed in black.

By Dala's light! She squeezed the limb harder and leaned forward. It *was* him—her young man from the graveyard. He was going to walk right under her. What kind of strange coincidence was this?

His hands were in his pockets, and those cunning eyes of his were turned down, staring at the ground. Occasionally his lips moved. Rehearsing something? His skin was darker than hers, a tawny olive not from the sun, and his hair flopped to one side and seemed just about to poke him in the eye at any second, not that he paid it any mind. The black crossover was simple and unadorned, ending midthigh as many of them did these days, with pants beneath. Likely what he'd been wearing yesterday, but now she had time to examine him freely.

But—what the hell was he doing *here*?

He was about to pass under her branch, which swayed only slightly in the wind. She dug her free hand into her pocket. A leather thong for her hair, the black wax crayon, the handkerchief that she'd taken without really examining why, as it still needed to be laundered.

She pulled it out. She had always planned to return it anyway. Hadn't she? She certainly wasn't doting on it. In fact—just to be sure—she'd return it right now.

As he strode about a foot past her branch, she lobbed the handkerchief at him. For a soft piece of fabric, it flew surprisingly well.

It hit him square in the back of the neck.

She held closer to the trunk and tried not to snicker as he flinched and grabbed at the thing, spinning. He looked around, saw the handkerchief, bent to pick it up, and frowned.

Some slight sway of the branch must have tipped him off, or maybe a snicker *did* escape, for finally he looked up and saw her. "Hey!"

She schooled her features to be stern. "Why are you following me?"

"Excuse me?"

"Two times in two days. Seems a little suspicious, don't you think?"

"Weird coincidence."

"I don't believe in coincidences."

He glanced from her, to the handkerchief, back to her. Baffled. "Does this still have snot on it?"

Her cheeks flushed. "Maybe."

Back to the handkerchief, back to her. Those clever eyes narrowed. "Why are you in a tree?"

"Why aren't you in a tree?" she shot back. Okay, not her brightest comeback ever.

His mouth hung open for a second. Then he shook his head and walked away.

"Hey!" she called after him. "I answered your question. Answer mine!"

He kept walking.

On impulse, she hopped into the air and landed in a crouch near his feet. She lashed out a sweeping kick, hoping to knock him off balance. It was only fair, the way he kept knocking her off balance in her head. Instead, he jumped.

She rounded on him, flowing straight into a high punch.

He'd already spun and caught it.

Okay. Maybe that was a little impressive. His reflexes were good. More than good—honed. Well, they ought to be. He was an Obsidian, and he could afford the best tutors. His skin was warmer than hers, and his eyes glittered, more amused than alarmed.

"No, you didn't answer my question. And yes, I most certainly did answer yours," he said.

"Wait, what?" She'd forgotten what either of them had said at this point.

He gently released his hold on her fist. She straightened and gave him the slight bow a martial superior deserved. She always tried to grant respect where it was due, even if as a noble she didn't strictly have to. He returned the gesture.

"I'm not following you. So no, I don't think it's suspicious," he said, tone mild. "You, however, haven't explained your presence in the treetops. Do you always attack ordinary people who come to visit your clan leader, calmly and respectfully? I didn't think Bone Clan guards wore such fine livery."

Did he really not know who she was? It wasn't like she didn't appear in public at Da's side. She straightened a little and smoothed one hand over her hair. She was only of average height, and he was perhaps an inch taller. "I only attack Obsidians who follow me around. Most don't wander into our den of bones accidentally."

Laughter in his eyes, he shook his head and turned away.

"Hey! Wait. Tell me what you're doing here!" She followed on his heels.

"I'm here to see your clan leader."

She scoffed. "You can't just walk in to see him. It doesn't work like that."

He spared her a glance, then said flatly, "I was going to knock."

Stopping, she propped her hands on her hips and scowled.

"Politely knock?" He didn't stop.

She was shaking her head. "No, no, no, you can't just—stop walking!"

He turned away from her on the path—but it was the right direction. Toward the atrium where Da received visitors, where he'd be right now. How did this Obsidian know where to go?

She hustled after him, not saying anything. It would be nice to see the guards turn him away.

He headed up the main mansion steps. The doors were propped open due to the heat, the main foyer empty and cavernous and refreshingly cool with its stone floors and walls. He crossed the great room and stopped just short of the two guards on either side of the arch leading to the atrium.

"What do you want, Obsidian?" grunted the guard.

Not much decorum, that one. She frowned at him, and he suddenly perked up, noticing her behind the young man.

Their visitor missed it, however, as his dark form was bowing deeply. "I seek an audience with Clan Leader Cerivil."

"Who requests it?"

"Nyalin moLinali."

Still catching up with him, she tripped on the carpet at the words. MoLinali? Mo*Linali*?

"Right away!" The guard leapt to his feet and dashed into the atrium and toward the great dais in the center.

She reached his side. "Wait. You're the son of—?"

He pursed his lips and crossed his arms. "Oh, so that would have changed things?"

"No," she said, defiant. Her cheeks flamed red.

"Right. Sure. Okay."

She opened her mouth but couldn't seem to force out a stubborn lie. It probably *would* have changed things. What did that mean?

"Don't deny it."

She hated him all the more for calling her on it. "Fine.

Maybe I would have been a tad more polite."

"Maybe you should—"

He stopped as the guard reappeared, impressively fast. "The clan leader will see you now."

He gave her a triumphant grin that made something weird twist in her insides. Those eyes were even more intense when they were amused. "Maybe you should be polite to people no matter who their mothers are."

She snorted. "That's a rich thing for an Obsidian to say."

"Nyalin moLinali." The guard cleared his throat, and the young man—Nyalin—started forward. "Right this way. And, uh, you should know she's like that with everyone."

She cackled as his grin faded a little at the guard's words. Perhaps she should be chastising the man, but the comment was gratifying. "He's right, you know. I'm equally rude to everyone. Venerable mothers or no."

"Well, I suppose that's allowable then. And here I thought I was special." He faked disappointment well. His long, puppy-eyed look made her heart twist in her chest a second time. What *was* it about him?

Cheeks heating further, she cursed her skin. What the hell was she blushing over? "Well, I... I'm not always rude while standing in a tree. Perhaps that makes you feel better?"

"Doesn't."

"It really should."

"Do you need my insults to be special? I should think sons of great mages are special enough."

"I..." He blinked. "I'm not..."

The guard laughed. "Only the daughters of clan leaders get to be rude while standing in trees, I guess. Us lowly guards have to content ourselves with doorways."

His eyebrows rose, and she hoped he'd trip in surprise,

falter, something. But he just kept walking, cool as ever. She squished her lips together and resolved to get under his skin. She'd find a way somehow.

Wait—no. He was Obsidian Clan, she was Bone. She'd likely not see him again after today.

Well, then, she had best make use of what time she had to ruffle his feathers. Although it meant she'd likely end up in class, she rushed after him to hear what he had to say to her father.

The girl—Cerivil's daughter?—kept at his heels, which of course only poured acid on Nyalin's already jangled nerves. Hopefully she wouldn't throw another punch or insult at him while he was trying to get his point out without stuttering. As if a respected clan leader and one of his mother's oldest friends wasn't intimidating enough, he had to brave this girl and her wild mane of hair and eyes like sparks ready to start a brush fire.

Small trees and shrubs hugged the manor on all sides of the inner garden atrium. A dusky wooden platform rose at the center from a lush sea of green leaves, dark needles, and red and purple blossoms. Cerivil congregated with a small group of students, all within a few years of his eighteen summers. Each person knelt or sat cross-legged, concentrating on bowls of sand before them. Cerivil sat before them on a little stool, whittling at a stick with a small knife.

Nyalin took the short set of six stairs before his companion could beat him to it, reaching Cerivil just before her.

Not one to be outdone, she called out from behind him. "Da!" She cleared her throat. "You have a guest."

Cerivil's bushy eyebrows rose at the exuberant edge to

her voice, but then a grin broke across his face as his eyes landed on him. "Nyalin. What a nice surprise." His voice was gentle, warm as he sheathed his knife. Cerivil's short brown linen crossover and robe were much the same as the last time Nyalin had seen him, but the clan leader's back was a bit more stooped, his belly a bit more round, his face a bit more wrinkled. A neat brown beard was new and accompanied by a smattering of gray.

In addition to Cerivil's attention, all the other students were eying Nyalin too. Eyes that seemed to bore into his head. He pretended not to notice.

"Lara, glad you're feeling better," Cerivil added. He held out the stick he'd been whittling; he'd transformed it into a simple rugged flower.

Her face lit up with a smile as she took it. "Thanks, Da."

"Joining us?"

"Sure." She tucked the twig behind her ear, circled around the students, and headed toward the back. She hadn't been headed to class as far as he could tell. She was only here because she'd been tailing him. Some sort of slacker then? She didn't seem the type. A mystery, that's what she was.

And he was staring.

Cerivil's hand clapped down on his shoulder a moment later, making him jump. Nyalin remembered himself and bowed low, which was quickly cut short by a crushing hug and several hearty back slaps. "Strength to you, Clan Leader Cerivil," he grunted under the onslaught, using the proper formal Obsidian greeting, although he hated to further remind their onlookers that he wore black and all the arrogant nonsense that went with it. "It's good to see you too."

"And luck to you, Nyalin!"

"Is this a bad time? I should come back—"

"Not at all. If I have to watch these fine students stare at sand any longer, I'm going to fall asleep. Could I trouble you to join me over a cup of tea while they work? I can only find so many ladies to accept my woodcraft handiwork."

He grinned. "If you're sure I'm not interrupting."

Cerivil shook his head. "Not at all. Come along."

He eyed the group as he followed Cerivil, if only to force some of them to stare at their work instead of him. One student sitting toward the front, though, met his gaze rather than dodging it. The young man had to be about his age, with black hair and a strong jaw. Nyalin stared back. There was no way he was going to drop his gaze in the contest of stares that ensued, but he wanted to shake his head. He got enough of these looks from Raelt. Nyalin was no one to fight with or posture around. Why did so many men not see that?

A clatter and shout beside his challenger drew both their gazes before one of them could win. A bowl of sand rocked sideways and dumped its contents onto the student's shoe.

Nyalin was careful not to look back. Instead, he simply followed Cerivil to a sheltered area on the far end of the platform, where trees and a canvas shade pulled taut to filter out the sun slanting down into the atrium. Lara had settled down with the other students in front of a bowl of her own, hands floating palms down over the substance. Something was taking shape there, but he couldn't quite make it out yet.

Water bubbled vigorously nearby, loudly enough that low voices would be lost in the background. Artful. The Bone Clan leader could say what he wished while still keeping an eye on his students. Cerivil gestured for Nyalin to sit down near the low table, and he complied, curling his legs under him.

"How is your family?" he asked, trying to keep up with the polite manners he so rarely got to practice. If only he could have just written a letter, stayed in his library, and avoided people altogether. Elix truly hated him.

The crease in Cerivil's brow alerted him right away that something had happened. And of course. He should have realized—why else would Cerivil's daughter be crying in a graveyard? Someone must be dead. "Well, you met my daughter, Lara," he said slowly.

Nyalin nodded. "Briefly, yes."

"Did she tell you her brother has, uh, gone on?"

The polite term for death—her brother had journeyed on to the next world. No one knew how many worlds there were, or even if any of the others truly existed, but the nuns of the shrines taught that there were many pairs. Each world had its mirrored afterworld, and the pairs were linked in an endless sequence of greater refinement and evolution. Souls journeyed through the sequence. Or so the faithful believed.

"I'm so sorry to hear that, Clan Leader," Nyalin said.

"Call me Cerivil. Your mother did, so should you."

"My condolences on your loss. No, she didn't tell me." Although perhaps he should have asked. If he hadn't been so busy being flippant or breezing past her when she asked him questions, maybe he would have found that out before.

Cerivil raised his eyebrows. "That's interesting. She usually doesn't let anyone forget it." He shook his head and ran a hand over tired features, looking thoughtful. Then he reached beside him, opened a cabinet, and removed a tray with a teapot and cups, already steaming.

Nyalin blinked, then smiled. "That was quick."

"What good is magic if you don't use it, boy?" Cerivil said, his eyes laughing. "This tea set is well enchanted and has earned its keep. Spiced or green?"

"Green, please."

"I like to keep my tea steaming, especially for welcome visitors. Much worse things to use magic for."

"It's funny you should say that," Nyalin said slowly, urging himself on, "because that's sort of why I came to talk to you." He frowned at the unease in his voice.

Cerivil arched a bushy eyebrow. "You came to talk about tea?" He handed a cup to Nyalin.

"Heh, no." His short laugh was high and thin as he swirled the green liquid and searched for words. He took a sip to stall for time; the tea was smooth and hot and a little bitter on his tongue. Perfect. "About magic."

"What about it?"

How could he put this? It was going to be painful no matter what. He might as well just get it over with. "Elix says that I have no magic." And he thought the tea was bitter.

Cerivil's eyebrows rose and froze in place. "Surely you're not serious."

"Oh, I'm very serious. He won't put it in exactly those words, though. He says that he has searched for a long time and that it'd be a waste of resources to teach me."

"He—he forbade your teaching?"

He nodded. "Grel appealed to the council. Defied his father for me."

"He's a better man than they deserve."

"One of the best, I think. But the council formally ruled this morning. The Obsidian Council has 'declined to enroll me in that path.' "

"Does the *emperor* know of this?" Cerivil said.

He took a sip of tea as he shrugged. "If the emperor cared, he wouldn't have sent me to live with Elix in the first place."

Cerivil scowled. "That's not so, Nyalin. Doesn't he come to see you often?"

"He comes to see Elix often. I'm usually there."

"He speaks often of you. And it wasn't like that," Cerivil continued. "When the emperor placed you with Elix... Elix wasn't always like this, you must understand. Vanae, yes, but not Elix. Must be her influence." Cerivil seemed caught between alarm and disgust. "That diamond-eating daughter of a serpent. And Elix is the diamond. And a power-hoarding fool."

"Power? I haven't got any power to take from him."

Cerivil patted one fist against his palm. "Your name is power. He wants you in his pocket, but not able to climb out. This is irresponsible of him, after all the trust Emperor Pavan has put in him. It's lower than I thought he would sink, to be honest. Really, Nyalin, Emperor Pavan could *not* have known how Elix would turn out, you shouldn't blame him. *I* would never have guessed. When we were younger, when your mother was alive, Elix was... a much different man."

Nyalin looked away. Everything had been different when his mother was alive. Mostly better, it seemed, except for the war. His mother had helped the emperor bring about a surprising and lasting peace—at least with their external foes. The clans still fought among themselves a little, but for now they were united against others. Nyalin waved off the subject. "It doesn't matter now. He is who he is. I came hoping for—I'd like to—Well, I'd wondered if you could give me a second opinion."

"A second opinion?"

"Do you think he's right, Cerivil? That I have no magic at all?"

"No."

"I'm not so sure."

"No, you *must*. What he's saying is impossible. How could it happen? Linali—"

"Elix says it must be my father's blood."

Cerivil snorted, his lip curling. "That jealous, horse-arsed bastard."

Nyalin blinked at the intensity in the older man's voice and refrained from pointing out that it was Nyalin who was the bastard.

"You know, everyone supposed Pavan put you with him because *he* was your father. I should have pointed that out long ago. I thought it somewhat obvious."

He stilled. Did people really think that?

"Oh, very few accused him to his face. But most of us suspected it. Many also suspected me, but I can assure you that's not the case. Not that I would have denied your mother, but she never offered. And I was just starting to fall for the love of my life then."

He wasn't entirely sure he wanted to know this. "Well, I have a feeling it wasn't Elix either at this point. He's been far from fatherly."

"Hmm," Cerivil grumbled, as if he were trying to solve some puzzle. The puzzle of Nyalin's parentage perhaps? The clan leader seemed to notice his impatient stare. "Ah. It doesn't matter. Even if your unknown father had no magic at all, it still wouldn't make sense that you lack magic. Magic is dominant in offspring, nearly always passed down. We have many mages with only one parent with the talent."

He leaned forward now, set his cup down. "Cerivil, if I knew *for sure* that I had magic, if I could prove it... then Elix would *have* to teach me. Right?" And the Raven monastery would have to let him in. Not that that would motivate Cerivil much.

The clan leader's face sobered. After a long moment, he nodded. "I see. While I can't guarantee any action on his part, it can't hurt to look. I'm sure it would also give you peace of mind to know for sure."

Nyalin nodded, stomach churning.

Cerivil set his jaw. "Lara!" he called back to the students.

By the way her head snapped up sharply, she'd been paying a little too much attention to their conversation. She strode over, grinning at the invitation. "Yes, Da?"

"I need your assistance for a moment, dear, for a quick procedure with our friend Nyalin here."

Procedure? Now? With *her*? "Surely it can wait—" he started, his eyes on Lara.

"No need. They'll be working with sand for weeks!" Cerivil said. "Besides, she's been missing a few classes due to our mutual sorrow over our loss. Another won't hurt."

Lara ducked her head as she knelt next to Nyalin, not meeting anyone's eye.

"I was sorry to hear of your loss," he rushed to say. "I hadn't heard."

She shook herself, as if visibly throwing off the emotion—and his condolences. "I figured."

Cerivil gave her a soft smile, then looked at Nyalin. "What she means to say is, thank you for the condolences."

He swallowed. His palms were starting to sweat. This wasn't exactly how he'd imagined this going.

"Okay, Nyalin, just lean back here." Cerivil indicated an open area to the side of the low tea table. "That's it. Rest your head. Some people lose consciousness temporarily. Are you ready?"

"Lose consciousness? Elix never tried anything like *that*." he said, hoping his voice didn't falter noticeably as he settled further on his back between Cerivil and Lara.

This was stupid, wasn't it? By the Twins, he was a fool.

No, he should bite his tongue. The twin goddesses worshipped within the Empire wouldn't appreciate being invoked for this pointless, pathetic attempt. If Raelt or Elix were here, they'd be laughing him out of the room—er, courtyard. He didn't have magic. Now he would find that out in front of a bonus audience. Nothing good could come of this. And what had made him think that the Bone Clan could find his magic when the *Obsidian*, the greatest of clans, could not? When the dark dragon herself couldn't find it?

"Every clan has different techniques for identifying talent, Nyalin, even if we all wield the same magic." Cerivil raised his bushy eyebrows. "Ready?"

He swallowed again, squirmed one last time, and nodded.

Cerivil took one of his hands, Lara the other. Her tanned skin was rough against his, his hand cradling between hers, their fingertips brushing.

Balls, he was staring again. He forced his eyes to the ceiling.

A strange flicker twinged in the back of his skull, like a spark of lightning or the snap of a tree branch. His fingers between hers twitched, curled for a moment. Something deep in his head stirred.

He risked one more glance at Lara, who was now frowning. A strange feeling washed through him. Exuberance. Pure and vibrant energy. *Life.*

"Is this... part of the procedure?" he muttered, mostly at her.

She met his gaze, and her lips parted, but she said nothing.

Cerivil laid his hand on Nyalin's forehead. "Let us begin."

Hmm, apparently not.

"Close your eyes," murmured Cerivil.

He squeezed them shut.

Nothing changed for what seemed like an eternity, aside from the vague stirring. Occasionally his hand between Lara's hands tickled, twitched. Itched. He longed to pull it away from her, to escape the sensation, but at the same time, he liked the feel of her.

Cerivil's hand lifted from his forehead.

"Hmm, I don't understand it."

His stomach knotted yet again. Damn. Would Elix lash out if word got back to him that they'd second-guessed his pronouncement?

"That's nonsense. Let me try," Lara snapped. One of her hands left his and clapped down on his forehead.

The world lit up in an explosion of color against his eyelids, falling like torrents of rain out of the sky, blue and green, purple and yellow, obliterating his view of the shelter above him, the sun, reality. All of it slid from view in a riotous fountain of color and light.

He gripped her hand, hard, before he could stop himself.

"Do you feel that?" Lara whispered.

"No. What? I don't feel anything," Cerivil said anxiously.

"It's there, Da—oh, it's there, all right. How can you *not* feel it?"

"*I* feel it," Nyalin murmured.

The image shifted from slicing streams of color to a sudden purple and red mist that loomed in all directions.

"There too," she muttered, like a doctor inspecting a wound. Or wounds. He watched as the image shifted to a hazy golden fog, then a bluish swirl, like he was underwater.

Then she let go. His forehead was cold. Her fingers left his.

The mundane world returned.

"Really? Nothing?" Lara was saying to her father. Then she scowled. "Damn. Well, it was clearly there. Reasonably strong with but a cursory inspection. You really couldn't feel it?"

Cerivil frowned. "Well, when *you* were looking, I almost could. As though just out of my reach. Like a sneeze that never comes. Was it subtle?"

Nyalin started to sit up and then groaned as a sudden streak of pain cracked through his skull. "Subtle as a dragon in a hen house," he muttered. He collapsed back down.

"Sorry," said Lara with a giggle. Nyalin managed a glare and a curled lip in her direction, but she ignored him, cheerily focused on her father. "Not subtle. Not exactly a dragon-sized amount of magic, not that I would know how much that is. But more than a hen." Her tone was proud and a touch defiant.

Cerivil's frown deepened. Nyalin covered his eyes with a forearm, the light making his head ache.

"What? What is it?" she asked.

"Well, Nyalin came to me because the Obsidians have refused to teach him."

She snorted. Then laughed. Then stopped. "You're not serious."

She might be the most unladylike woman he'd ever met. He kind of liked it.

"I'm afraid I am," said Cerivil.

"That's absurd."

Well, that felt good to hear, even if it was the only thing that would come from this damn trip. In spite of her tendency to attack him unprovoked, if he hadn't liked her before, he did now.

"None of them can find it. Clan Leader Elix, the Obsidian teachers, none of them."

The air around him felt still, as if Cerivil and Lara had both realized something he hadn't.

"That's... that's ridiculous. He is clearly very gifted. Could they be lying? Did they try the dragon?"

He nodded under his arm and stifled a groan. "The dark one too. She didn't say no, but she didn't say yes either. Just... waved me aside."

All these people, the sacred dragon of his clan, even his brother and best friend—none of them could find any scent of magic on him, and this girl could? What sense did that make? Who would even believe it? He wanted to groan again, but he stopped himself. "Well, at least we know, right?"

"*I* can't say for sure, Nyalin, it was Lara that felt it. So I'm not sure how well it serves your goal."

He pried his arm away and one eyelid open to peer at Cerivil. "My goal? You mean getting them to change their minds."

Cerivil hesitated, glancing nervously at Lara. "I fear... they won't listen to her."

Lara's jaw tightened. She was silent for a moment, glaring at the ground. "Why do I *even* bother..." she muttered after a moment.

"I'm sorry, Lara. Do you disagree?"

She shook her head. Her nostrils flared as she blew out a breath. Then she glanced at him, finally meeting his one open eye. "I can try talking to them if you need me to. But if your dragon's word goes against mine too?" She shrugged. "I'll try my damnedest, though. It's the truth. They should accept it."

"It's also not just anyone we're trying to convince here. It's Elix," Cerivil said gravely. "He's grown... foolish with his years."

"It's the whole damn Obsidian Council," Nyalin groaned. "What was I thinking? There's no way to fight them. I'm out of luck."

"Even if they're *wrong*?" said Lara. When he opened his other eye, she was glaring from him to Cerivil and back again.

"There has to be a way."

Cerivil sighed. "I don't know if anyone but the emperor himself could change their minds at this point." They all sat in silence, thinking. "It just doesn't make sense."

"Well, then that's what you've got to do." To his shock, Lara punctuated the words with a poke of her finger to his forearm. He gaped at her, pain from the glaring light momentarily forgotten.

"What?" was all he managed.

"Talk to the emperor. Have him *make* them teach you," she said, closing her fingers into a fist.

Cerivil's eyebrows shot up. "That's not how it works."

"Where there's a will, there's a way," Lara insisted.

"Not always," the clan leader shot back, and they glared at each other for a moment. He had a feeling it was an old argument. "But, maybe..."

He looked from Lara's crazed expression to Cerivil's thoughtful one and back. "Maybe what? He won't talk to *me*."

Lara snorted again, as though she thought he was being sarcastic. "Yeah, right."

He stared at her, even more baffled now.

"She might be onto something. Go and speak to the emperor of this. I assure you he will care, and he will speak with you and know what to do."

"I don't know..."

"Trust me, Nyalin. I've known Pavan for years. He would want to hear from you on this."

"If you think there's a chance." Nyalin nodded. He struggled to sit up one more time, and Cerivil and Lara grabbed his hands and shoulders and helped him to his feet.

He swayed, took one step, and almost fell over.

Lara caught him by the elbow, her fingers brushing his

again, and he could have sworn heat flooded from her into him. He steadied.

"I, uh... I'll head over there right now," he mumbled. Grel was right, putting it off would only make it harder.

He took another step forward, more confident this time. Then one knee buckled.

Cerivil caught him this time. "You seem in no shape for that. Lara, get that guard. Nyalin needs somewhere to rest."

~

Cerivil gazed down at the young man while the guard finished laying him onto the down mattress. Nyalin was already asleep. A maid fussed with the room, straightening the bronze coverlet and stoking the small fire.

This boy and his magic—or lack thereof. Something strange was going on. It was hard to be angry with Elix when Cerivil had seen just what his Obsidian peer had seen: nothing. But Nyalin's exhaustion couldn't be faked and only bolstered Lara's claims.

No, they weren't claims. Lara had no reason to lie. It had to be the truth. Lara's observations.

Even after Nyalin was settled, Cerivil dallied, watching. Thinking. The maid tried to appear occupied, but he was starting to believe that she wouldn't leave until he did. Still, a question poked at him.

Was he *really* doing all he could to help Lara's situation? She'd pushed him before but never as hard as this morning, and her accusations niggled at his brain. Was she right? Was there something more he ought to be doing? Him marrying some poor woman was never going to work.

But maybe... Maybe something else would.

He had tried so hard to give her the whole world to

explore. It was a world that didn't want her to explore it, but he didn't care, and he'd taught her not to care too, not to let that stop her. She'd taken the lessons to heart. Nothing seemed to stop her, not even her own father. Or so it had seemed when Myandrin was alive.

That. That had stopped her.

Even as a young father, Cerivil had known what the world wanted of young women. He'd known the choices he ought to have made.

But as she'd grown, it'd been hard to confine his vibrant tornado of a child to any of that. How could he care about silly, stupid expectations, when those big brown eyes blinked up at him, full of hope and wonder and miracles? And determination. Oceans of determination. All the while innocent to the trap she grew inside.

It might have been kinder to shut her down then, rather than letting her grow used to hope. What was the point, if it was only to be shattered in the end? But he wasn't kind or cruel enough to prune her like a bush into the proper shape. He'd had no choice but to let her be who she was. And perhaps now she would pay the price for his cowardice, his inability to mold her into what she ought to have become.

That was his only regret—that she would pay this price rather than him. Paying the price was inevitable.

But looking down at Linali's son now, he wondered.

He couldn't give Lara the choice she wanted, but perhaps he could give her another.

He looked up at the maid, who jumped at his sudden attention.

"Get me my messenger. And my daughter. And two horses ready. I go to see the emperor."

She nodded with a bow and left.

Cerivil took a deep breath. He wasn't willing to take on Andius and his own council members, apparently. But Elix and the whole Obsidian Clan? No problem. He shook his head.

He hoped he wouldn't regret this.

~

Zama.

In the dim quiet of the cave, Unira said his name—first only in her mind. She knelt at the water's edge, the rock cold and hard against her knees and palms, cutting through the silk of her robe. She waited a moment, reviewing the spell, hoping she'd gotten everything right.

A droplet of water kissed the tip of a stalactite, swelling like a pregnant belly before succumbing to its fated journey to the pool below. The *plop* of it into the water was quiet but piercing. The ripples touched every part of the pool.

Now she dared to say it aloud: "Zama."

His name echoed, both ominous and mocking, as if she might simply be talking to herself. The flames of her small white candles flickered, circling the pool and reflected in its service. She'd tossed the requested ingredients into the water: velvet, silk, satin, brocade, and buttons. All odd offerings. She'd been lucky to find all she needed in her workshop. A relief to avoid journeying into town. The depths of the water stirred, and she leaned forward. Yes. Any minute now.

Zama.

The black depths of the hidden pool took on a silvered sheen. The water shook now, twitching this way and that. She'd lined the path from the pool toward her with thick blue candles, appropriate necromancy for a demon of the watery deep. She'd burned fargrass in the air. She'd seeded the water, stabbed her dagger into the earth. The offerings were all fine quality and had disappeared beneath the water's horizon.

Everything should be just right.

"Zama."

She rose, ignoring her creaky knees, her shaking form. She pushed aside fear and excitement and cold. There would be no going back from this.

She would unleash him. Who would win after that was another matter entirely.

"Zama!"

She flung her arms up to the ceiling. Energy jolted through the candles, the seeds under the water. All of it lit the air with the power of death, static charging every inch of the cave, sparks jumping between stalactite and stalagmite, her own arms and those fangs of the cave above her. Each jolt sent pain down her nerves, her arms, her throat, straight to her core.

But she held on. She gritted her teeth and lowered her arms.

And there he was. Tall, dark, handsome. Surprisingly well dressed.

He spoke into her mind, a thrill zigzagging through her. *Why do you call me, necromancer? Why do you seek the watery abyss?*

"I live in an empire of stone," she growled. "I want you to help me destroy it. Wash it away until nothing is left but a few grains of sand. I want to see it burn."

Hmm. Wouldn't you rather a fire demon then? He yawned.

"No." She hesitated, unsure of how much power to give to him. "I-I liked you the best."

His eyes brightened and eyebrows perked. *Is that so?*

"It is. I think we can cause quite a bit of chaos together. Isn't it water that eats away at stone best?"

A smile tugged up the corner of his mouth. *Well then. Say my name again and draw me forth, intriguing woman.*

She shouted it to the sky. "Zama, come forth!"

Immediately a deluge drenched her, water drowning her for a moment. She gasped and sputtered. Coughing, she squinted in the now complete darkness. The candles had all been extinguished.

Two points of silver glowed in the dark, staring at her.

Unira, said the demon.

She clutched a hand to her soaking chest. He knew her name. She hadn't intended to give him anything like that; how had he figured it out? He could use the name to enslave her—or for many other unpleasant things.

But for some reason, he didn't. "I want you to see that I had the power. I could have done it. But I chose not to." He grinned. "For summoning me and bringing me to this new world, I yield to you."

"Zama," she whispered, biting out the word. Taking control.

The candles flared to life, bright and warm.

And there he was, fully in the flesh now and every bit the illustration from her tome. And so much more. He might have been the handsomest man she'd ever seen.

He took a knee at the pool's edge. "Great necromancer... and lovely woman, I am at your service. Shall we destroy this world together?"

She grinned, hardly willing to believe it had worked. But it had.

"Let's."

Chapter 3

Honor the Dead

One shoddy storefront after another drifted by, and as she rode, Lara slumped on her horse and gazed at them with unseeing eyes, her thoughts elsewhere. The road she and her father had chosen took them along the border between the Bone and Glass Districts, but in truth, both sides of the street were plenty impoverished.

The sad scene was nothing new, however. Her brain toyed with the puzzle that was Nyalin moLinali instead.

The horses, with all their fine livery, plodded on, equally ignoring everything around them. Why did his dilemma eat at her so? Maybe it was just an interesting novelty—or perhaps she just couldn't stand that his elders were wrong. How could anyone be so obstinate?

Her mare stumbled a bit on an uneven cobblestone, jostling her out of an empty stare. She caught sight of a dirt smudge on the hem of her crossover and pulled and belted it tighter, hoping to hide the mark. Her dark brown cloak couldn't hide that her clothing had seen the dirt of a graveyard and the limbs of a tree. She probably should have changed. But what did it matter?

Anyone worth their salt would believe her, whether or not she had a dirt smudge on her shirt.

She cleared her throat. "I don't understand this, Da. Why would they lie about this? About his magic?"

"Hmm?" Cerivil perked up at her abrupt question. "Maybe they honestly didn't see it." Da shrugged and stroked the horse's gray mane.

"Even if that's true, why would they give up? He's young. You'd think they'd have the resources. The time."

"I believe he and his foster father are not exactly on good terms."

"Wait." She straightened on the horse. "Foster father?"

"Oh, yes. When his mother died, Pavan sent Nyalin to live with Elix, but no one knows who his real father is. I get the sense that... he's not treated well there. We all thought his father was Elix, but I'm gathering that wasn't the case."

She frowned down at her pommel. Hmm. Perhaps his servant harem was smaller than she'd thought. "Why would I be able to see his magic and not you?"

"I have no idea, my little cherry."

"Has that ever happened before?"

"No. Not that I can remember."

They reached the emperor's palace gate and dismounted. It wasn't far from home, and they could have walked, but the horses added a certain pomp and circumstance, even for the odd occasion. When you were the lowliest clan, easy pomp and circumstance were not something to pass up.

They were received quickly, and a woman dressed in lovely azure robes led them through a tiled, fountained courtyard and into the great meeting hall. A dome of gold, crystal, and lapis stretched high overhead. And inside, underneath it all, was the tree.

The Tree of the Empire. The ginkgo leaves reached out toward the jewel-encrusted ceiling like trumpets. Light streamed in from the east through tall windows. The tree was at least three stories tall and about the same in width, and it vibrated with life. With magic.

Dangling along the branches and amid those fan-shaped leaves were the crystals.

She had no idea what magic the emperor had worked to create such a thing as this tree. He claimed it hadn't been he who'd created it, but the clan dragons working as a team, just as they had when the clanblades had been originally forged so long ago. Some claimed the dragons had wanted a return to war. Others claimed they'd always pushed for peace. She wasn't sure what to believe. But when the six clans had finally united under the emperor, this tree had been planted, and once fully grown, it didn't cast off seeds or nuts or fruit. It bore gems.

Though, bone and obsidian and glass weren't *technically* gems.

Each member of each clan, when they reached the end of their first decade, would come here to see the emperor and, as part of their journey to become full members of the clan, receive their gems. Her own emerald hung in her left ear now. The bone charm was at home in a chest of other important goods; ideally, it'd be carved some day with her most special, most expert spell. But she would have to reach her third decade to decide that.

If she did, and if Andius let her, all of which was not certain at this point.

Surrounding the glorious tree, six pillars held up the dome, each bearing a statue of its clan's dragon. The miniature Bone Dragon sat regally on a bed of moss, an olive branch in his grip.

The statue seemed to eye her as they approached the emperor's dais. As if to murmur, *I know what you did.* She'd thought the dragon wouldn't approve, but she didn't get that sense now. It was more factual, an intensity of awareness. As if its gaze saw her now, more than it had before. The emeralds and bones in the tree seemed to tinkle in her direction, but it must be the wind.

It's only a statue, she thought. Stop with the guilty nonsense.

But as she trained her eyes on the floor, the memory of leathery wings and wind drifted back at her.

They paused at the dais. The last of a flock of people meeting with the emperor were leaving, and a few advisers were being shooed away.

Emperor Pavan nodded in their direction. "Cerivil, Lara, good to see you," he said. "I wish you great honor."

Pavan had long, wavy dark brown hair, eyes like the azure of the woman's dress, and an easy smile. For someone who held such power, he always seemed at ease, even in the striking red crossover. It was no wonder he'd united them all, even if many said Linali had played the crucial role. A blade hung from his hip, and not just any blade. The rough-hewn, savage-looking weapon was named Shadow Wing for its Obsidian dragon scale near the crossguard. During forging, the scale had fractured into a shape startlingly reminiscent of a dragon wing. At least three dozen charms glittered as they swayed from the handle—jade, lapis, several colors of glass, bone, and wood... so many. And each representing a spell mastered. She could never keep herself from staring, trying to make out the extent of his vast repertoire or admiring the mighty profile cut by Shadow Wing. She couldn't even be bothered by the fact that a former Obsidian was supposed to represent all clans; it was all too impressive. Da wore about a third on the thin chain around his neck, although he only carried a selection of those he knew, the ones he used most often. His spells, too, had once hung from the Dagger of Bone, until he'd passed it to Myandrin.

"Luck to you, my friend," said Da. Each clan had its preferred virtue it wished to others in most greetings. As a Bone, what could you have to give but luck? Not much. Da bowed, and she bowed with him, slightly lower.

The room was finally empty a moment later, and the emperor bowed his head. He clapped once to signify that he had sealed the room with a spell of silence, then threw his arms out wide with a grin. "What brings the lovely Bone Clan here to see me today? Some tea?"

"Of course," said Cerivil, smiling. "The tea and your fine company."

"And surely nothing else." He grinned.

His smile was contagious, and there was a fresh spring in her step as she followed the emperor. He led the two of them behind an ivy-covered trellis that backed the throne on the dais. A low table sat with cups and an iron pot of piping-hot tea already waiting. They each sat on a pillow, and to her relief, Pavan immediately poured the tea. Thank the goddesses there'd be no awkward wait to see who would do the pouring. Maybe he still thought of her as a child and she shouldn't be so happy about it. Maybe he thought of her as an equal. Maybe Andius would turn into a fish and swim out to sea!

She sighed as she accepted the warm cup and took a sip. The spiced black liquid sent a wave of rejuvenating heat from her stomach out. It did make her feel a little better.

Tea distributed, Pavan leaned back, brushed off his

shoulder—though it seemed perfectly clean—and clasped his hands behind his neck.

She knew what would come next. Nostalgia.

"Look at you, Pavan," Da said, as if on cue. "Look at you. I would never have wasted a breath on you if I'd known that the poor apprentice thing was just a clever disguise."

"A disguise! You know it was hardly that. I wish I could go back to those days." The emperor was smiling, but his eyes were tired.

"Those were simpler days," Da agreed, his own eyes twinkling. "And more complex too. The war? The unification?" He paused. "Linali?"

A small smile crept onto the emperor's face, and Lara realized Da wasn't just remembering the *past* fondly. "You name another reason I wish I could go back."

Da nodded. "We have all lost much since those days, in spite of what we've gained." He sighed, and Lara felt a stab in her chest at the words, but he continued. "But what of the future, instead of the past? When are you going to look for a woman in your life?"

The emperor laughed and rolled his eyes. "When all of you stop hassling me about it."

"So never?"

"Not today, that's certain."

"Ah, well. I do have another matter I'd hoped to discuss."

"That's good. Hadn't thought my lack of a wife was particularly urgent."

Lara frowned. Da had sent word that this was urgent? Was one young man's magic urgent enough to warrant all this? Certainly as Linali's son it merited some special attention, but... She thought of all the advisors and courtiers being shuffled from the room. That woman must have been something amazing. It was her memory that had cleared those people from the room, more than anything else.

Da smiled. "Yes. I received a most interesting visit this morning. From Linali's son, Nyalin."

Lara's lip twitched. Oh, no, no, no. She would need to keep a neutral facade for this discussion. A seemingly impartial assessment, nothing more.

Wait—she *was* impartial, wasn't she?

"Yes, and...?"

"What do you know of his magic? And his... relationship with Elix?"

Pavan's face grew grave. "I know a little. None of it good."

"I guessed as much. Apparently, they have declared him devoid of magic and denied him teaching."

The emperor sighed. "I see."

"He came to me today to ask for a second opinion."

The emperor's eyes were trained on his tea, but he arched one eyebrow. "And did you give it to him?"

"I did. And it leaves me in a bit of an... awkward situation."

She sat up a little straighter. If she needed to argue on his behalf, she would, and she'd argue hard. It was only the right thing to do.

"You see, I was unable to detect any magic about him—but Lara could."

Emperor Pavan looked up sharply, almost glaring at her father before his features smoothed. "Wait—what?"

"I could almost sense it while she checked. Something *very* strange is going on."

Pavan turned to look at her now, and she swallowed under the intensity of his gaze. It wasn't just a casual perusal. His eyes bored into her as if he hoped to see for himself what had let her detect his magic when no one else had. His casual mirth was long gone. She could tell him about the handkerchief too... But no. Nyalin catching her crying in the graveyard wasn't really something she wanted to explain.

"They must be lying," she said, shrugging. "The abilities are definitely there."

Da shushed her.

"What? If we want them to change their minds, they'll have to admit that they're—" He shushed her again, more sharply this time, and she blinked at him in surprise. "What?"

Pavan looked from Da to her and back. "How could that work? Why would she see it and not anyone else?"

"I really don't know. I was wondering if you knew," Da answered. "I wanted to know if you had any ideas. You see, I was assuming that his abilities might just need awakening. That can be tricky sometimes. But... that can't be the case if Lara can feel them. But what could hide his powers from me and all the others?"

The emperor looked hard at Lara, his eyes searching her as he picked up the cup. "Well, Lara does have a certain charm."

She frowned at him. "I most certainly do not." While other girls her age had grown into beautiful women, she looked more like Myandrin—straight and bony in all the wrong ways. And when other girls charmed men with sweet words, she could never resist the chance to cut into them. Never—it was just too easy. And she certainly hadn't displayed much charm in either the gardens or the graveyard.

The men both smiled, looked at each other. She frowned harder at them.

"But that's not why I'm here."

Emperor Pavan raised his eyebrows again. "And that is...?"

Da took a deep breath, straightened a little, as if preparing for something big. She frowned. How hard was it to say, *Tell those stupid Obsidians to do the right thing and teach the boy?* Idiots.

"Move Nyalin to my clan," Cerivil said. "Let me teach him, if they won't."

Lara's mouth fell open.

Emperor Pavan, however, only stilled for a moment before setting his cup on the table. "You'd do that?"

"Why not? We would be honored to host Linali's son." Da glanced at her, bidding her to chime in, but she just stared.

"What if they are right? What if he has no—"

"They're *not* right," Lara blurted.

By Dala. Interrupting an emperor even. So much charm she had.

But Pavan only smiled at her. They were lucky in their ruler. "I see. Do you expect ire from Elix?"

"Why should I? They have already had their chance. Rejected him. If they are correct, why should they care if we waste our time?"

"They shouldn't," Pavan agreed. "But if they were wise, we wouldn't be in this situation."

"Perhaps." Da fidgeted for a moment. "All right, honestly, I am concerned with how it might affect relations with them. But what else can I do? Linali's son deserves a chance."

Such passion. If only she could have met the woman, lived in an age with a simple enemy, when a powerful woman could make a difference and inspire those around her. It must have been nice.

"And your clan deserves to win the prize if you can uncover that which the great Obsidians could not? It could greatly change the balance of power."

Da's lips pursed. "It's not about that. But yes."

Pavan glanced at Lara. "What is it about then?"

"It's about honoring Linali."

"Only that?"

Cerivil, too, glanced at her now, and hesitated. He opened his mouth but didn't speak.

"It's about the truth," she said. "If he has magic, it should be honored. Honed. It's a blessing to the empire, and we must cultivate it at every chance we can. I could not stand aside and ignore it, having seen it for myself."

Pavan nodded, but he wasn't taking his eyes off Da. Finally, the emperor turned slowly to look at her. "And what do you think of this young man, as a person? Are you willing to have him in your clan?"

She blinked. "It sounds easier than convincing the Obsidians to change their ways. He should be taught. It's only fair."

"And if he is taught," the emperor said slowly, "and he does have magic, and he does well? Excels? What will you think then?"

She shifted from side to side. Did he mean...?

"If you unlock this magic of his, and he wins your Contests, will you regret demanding honor and truth and fairness with me today?" Pavan smiled a little behind a sip.

She started to laugh—if only she could be so lucky—but fell still as a stone. He was serious. Her heart suddenly wanted to pound out of her chest. Of course. How had she missed it? Da hadn't come here to convince the Obsidians to change their ways—he'd come here to make a play for power.

And perhaps, in a long shot, to give her this one choice. The thing she'd asked him for.

If she wished, she could decry Nyalin as an arrogant fool who'd never truly be a member of the clan. She could demand they argue with the Obsidians first. She could simply quit insisting his magic was real.

Or... she could not. Either way, she'd make a choice. It wasn't much, but it was better than nothing.

She brushed her fingers across her cheek for a moment.

"No," she murmured. "I don't think I will regret it."

"Are you sure?" he said.

"How can I be? I hardly know him," she replied. "But... it's about what's best for the clan. Please. Let us teach him. I will do my best to honor the dead."

Pavan raised his eyebrows again. "Interesting turn of phrase."

She didn't see how. "Linali, I mean." And perhaps her brother, who had hoped Andius would never see the inside of the council room, let alone hold the clanblade.

Of course, *she* was doing her best to see that he wouldn't either way.

"Move him to the Bone Clan," Da chimed in. "We will teach him."

Emperor Pavan smiled at them both, warm amusement in his eyes, then clapped his hands. She blinked. In the moment her eyes had been closed, the emperor as she knew him had vanished and now in his place was a green-feathered hummingbird. She watched as he flitted high—or she tried to. He was a blur, the only evidence of his passing the leaves rustling in their part of the tree, where crystals of bone and emerald grew.

Another branch twitched, a hum, and then he was back before her and fully human again. He held out two chips—a bone charm and an emerald stud.

"All right. It is done." He dropped the jewels into her surprised hands. "Accept Nyalin moLinali into your clan. Let me deal with Elix. And luck to you, Lara." He patted her twice on the shoulder. "I hope you don't need it."

A hand shaking his arm jolted him awake. Nyalin rubbed his eyes and blinked groggily as two figures came into focus.

Lara and Cerivil were leaning over him. Lara's mass of hair and braids tumbled over her shoulder, coming close to hitting him in the face. The heat was still oppressive around them, but a gentle breeze blew across him from some unseen window. Walls painted forest green were lit by midday sun—or was it a bit later than that? Closer to dinner? For that matter, how had he gotten here? Had he just passed out on the floor? The other Bone Clan members would sure fear and respect him now.

More important than all that, though, was that they were smiling.

"Nyalin. I hope you'll forgive us but..." Lara started.

"But what?" Groaning, he struggled upright, making them back away. He wasn't sick or tired enough to deserve their hovering.

"We went to talk to Pavan." Cerivil clasped and unclasped his hands in a movement that was dangerously close to wringing. "To the emperor. On your behalf. Without you."

Nyalin fell back on the bed in relief. "Oh, thank the Twins. What did he say?"

"We didn't ask him to make the Obies reconsider, though." Lara was smiling, but there was a warning note in her voice.

"Lara," Cerivil chided. But Nyalin wasn't going to complain about the derogatory nickname. Not like there weren't jokes being made about the *Bone* Clan.

"What did you ask him, then?" Nyalin asked, sitting up again.

“If we could teach you instead.” Cerivil smiled and puffed up his chest, arms crossing.

Nyalin raised an eyebrow and glanced from one to the other. “You look happy. That’s good, right?”

“Yes. Yes, it is.” Lara nodded, placing a hand on his forearm. He pretended not to notice the strange, sharp stab or the heat of her fingers. “I suppose we should have asked your permission first.”

Cerivil made a shushing noise, but Nyalin only laughed. “It’s fine. Not like I had much choice or blood in that clan anyway.”

Lara’s father blew out a breath in relief and bowed just a little. “That’s good to hear. If you’re willing to join our clan, the emperor is all for it. We’d like to extend you a formal invitation.”

If Cerivil’s grin was proud, Lara’s was dazzling.

“Sure,” he said before they could change their minds. “I’m in.”

She raised her eyebrows. “Just like that? Don’t need to think it over?”

“Nope. Maybe I should go get some of my things, I guess? Won’t take long, I don’t have much. But then I can start right away.” He frowned. Where was he going to live? Maybe Grel would loan him some coin.

“Here.” Lara held up a hand, fingers poised to drop something.

He raised his hand, and she dropped the gems of his new clan into his palm.

He stared. They looked strangely naked. You never saw gem chips unless they were on chains, in charms, in someone’s ear. These were just... sitting there.

Waiting. For him.

“Well, go on,” she urged.

"Oh, don't hurry the boy, Lara," said Cerivil. "It's a big change."

Shaking his head, he hurried to set aside the bone chip and remove the obsidian stud from his ear, replacing it with the emerald one. The skin around the piercing only complained a little. He stared at the pale charm and the dark stud on the bronze coverlet beside him a moment longer.

Opposites, like the Twins, the dual goddesses worshiped throughout the empire. One dark, one light—one his past, one his future.

Cerivil placed a hand on his shoulder and chuckled. "Don't look so stunned, Nyalin. Go on, now. Get your things. You should perhaps tell Elix and your siblings the news too. Although the emperor said to leave Elix to him, so you don't have to."

"I'll avoid that if I can." He glanced at Lara at the mention of siblings. The idea of being associated closely with Raelt was dreadful but protesting the term "siblings" would also slight Grel at the same time, so he remained silent.

Cerivil continued. "When you return, you can stay here for now. This room will do. My students are always provided with housing, here or elsewhere. And a small stipend."

"That's generous." Nyalin tried to downplay his surprise, but Obsidian students got no such things.

"We have to. Otherwise they are penniless," Lara put in. "Most of us can't afford not to work, so they wouldn't come if we didn't provide the basics."

"Well, then I should fit right in." By the funny look Lara gave him, she didn't seem to believe him on that matter, but Elix had always been very clear Nyalin had to work for his place since he hadn't been born to it. He hadn't copied all those books for the man out of boredom.

He gradually eased to his feet. No swaying or knee buckling this time. He relaxed. "Okay, I'll be right back."

Cerivil left, humming to himself. Nyalin glanced at Lara, who still sat amused at the foot of the bed.

"Whose idea was this?" he asked her, less because he wanted to know and more to delay the inevitable altercation.

"Hmm? Oh, my father's." She flipped some of her mane over her shoulder. "He didn't even tell me, just dropped it in the middle of discussion right in front of the emperor. And I'd just been gearing up to bad-mouth your family too."

"They're *not* my family." It came out this time before he could think the better of it, so he amended it. "Well, Grel is. And Sutamae maybe. But not the rest."

She cocked her head, studying him. "Understood."

"Sorry. Do you want to, uh, come with me?" He blinked. Why the heck had he just said that? Was he out of his mind?

"Really?"

"Yeah. Uh." He groped for a logical reason. So I don't have to face those fools alone? "You can tell Elix how wrong he is if we see him. There aren't many who get the chance to do that." Ugh, as if *that* would go well. But he couldn't back out now.

She stood. "You know what? That sounds like fun. Let's do it."

His eyes widened. "Have you met Elix?"

"Oh, yes. Yes, I have."

And with that, she was marching ahead of him, out the door, to seal his fate. He grabbed the obsidian stud off the bed, slipped it into his pocket, and hurried after her.

~

Nyalin surveyed his room. His thoughts raced. Smoke

snaked between his legs, purring. "Excited for me?" he murmured to her as he pulled out his pack. Hmm. What did he actually need?

"I'll miss you, girl," he said, ruffling the hair between her ears. He couldn't claim the cat as his, nor ask any more from Lara's family than he was already, but leaving Smoke behind hurt. And worried him. He and Grel took care of the cat much of the time, with some assistance from Dalas and Uli the maid. Much to Elix's continued annoyance. Hopefully Grel would care for Smoke on his own.

He didn't need his clothes—as a member of the Bone Clan, he would be issued new clothes. Browner ones. He had many books, mostly gifts from Grel, and his mother's old pack of things, which was mostly empty. He started heaping books into his own pack first.

"Nice cat. So this is your room, huh?" Lara bent to pet Smoke once before propping her hands on her hips and continuing to survey the place. "This looks more like a... closet."

He winced. "Probably was. Elix has never been one to spoil me. Thought you'd gathered that."

"I did, but I didn't." She was handing him books from the pile now, helping him go faster. Chipping in. Obsidians rarely did such things. He had a sudden feeling he was going to like this new clan, even if he got a lot of harassment from them at first. It'd take years to truly become one of them, most likely. Not like Raelt and his cronies didn't harass him now, so for him, it'd just be more of the same. He refocused on her instead of the worries ahead. She was eying the spines and reading the titles as she handed them to him. "You like books?"

"What tipped you off?" He stuck the last one in his pack, then headed to the closet and took out his mother's old pack and his writing set. It wasn't really his, but what did it matter at this point? Elix could give him a few feathers, knives, and bottles of ink, since he wasn't going to give him an education or a livelihood. "I spent most of the time in the library."

"Reading?"

"Copying."

She raised her eyebrows. "Copying? As in scribing other books?"

"Exactly."

"Well at least you've got one marketable skill, if none of this pans out." She held open his mother's bag for him while he shoved in a few utilitarian items—sandals for the summer, wool socks, his tiny pouch of coins.

"Actually, my plan was always to join one of the orders as a scribe. And maybe someday, if they'll let me, write my own."

"Really? Which one?"

"The Order of the Raven."

"Ooh, shadowy." She wiggled her fingers. "You seem well educated. They won't take you?"

"Unfortunately, it's one of the few that sometimes requires magic. It's competitive to be selected. In my case, they said I'd definitely need magic. So if this doesn't work..." He shrugged. He was acting casual about it, but other monasteries, especially ones that accepted non-mage scribes, didn't house clues to his mother's life and history. If this last-ditch effort didn't work out—and it likely wouldn't—that trail of answers would be cut off forever.

He reached under the bed for the next set of books.

Her eyes widened. "There's more?"

He shrugged. "I haven't got much else."

Soon both packs were filled, and there were still a few books left. Could he part with some of them? They were nearly all gifts from Grel, the only gifts he'd ever received, and they were all cherished. He had only copied three himself. No, he couldn't part with them. But perhaps temporarily? Maybe he could find Grel and leave them with his brother to bring later?

"Give me them. I'll carry them," she said, as if reading his thoughts.

"You're a noble," he said. "Not a pack mule."

"I hate that term. Like I'm some foreign deity of the Mushin. Besides—what does it matter? You're a noble too."

"I most definitely am not."

She grabbed the books from him, her fingertips brushing his wrist as she took them. The touch sent a weird itch shooting up to his elbow. Okay, that was definitely not normal. And he was definitely not bringing it up to her *or* her father. He could hear it now. Uh, yes, every time your daughter touches me I get the strangest sensation... Maybe he could find a book to shed some light on the mystery.

The book battle lost, he shouldered his pack and his mother's pack and stepped toward the door.

It opened before he could reach it. Raelt. Smoke let out a little snarl and hid under the bed.

"Well, well, what do we have here?" Raelt's eyebrows flew up, resting on Lara. "Nice to see you again, Lara."

She was scowling at him.

"You two have met before." Nyalin looked back and forth between them.

Raelt ignored him and kept his eyes trained on Lara. "The one who shows up looking homeless and the one who soon *will* be homeless—a perfect pair. He could teach you a thing or two about laundering clothes, you know. Even the lowliest Obsidian knows that."

Raelt's awkward barbs had long lost their sting, but Lara scowled harder, her cheeks reddening.

"Like you've ever washed anything you own," Nyalin shot back.

"Can the Bone Clan afford soap? Or is it water that's the problem? Who would consider that land of yours anything but a filthy desert, I have no idea."

"Get out of the way." He stepped forward.

Raelt smirked. "Why should I? You're just angry I caught the two of you in here together. Some kind of illicit tryst, I imagine?"

"You know the word tryst? When did you learn to read?"

"But really, Nyalin, did you have to stoop so low? We have *Obsidian* whores—"

Nyalin shoved him into the doorframe. "Not another word."

But of course, he was only encouraging Raelt, who shot him a satisfied grin. "The emperor will want to know. And Father, of course. I—"

Abruptly, Lara ducked and darted past Raelt. She was just past him and almost free when he swiveled and lunged after her.

She was quicker than he was, even with the books. Her kick crunched into the side of his knee, and he yelped, crumpling to one side.

Nyalin didn't wait to see the theatrics that would soon follow. He leapt over his longtime tormentor before the fool could recover and rushed after her. The two of them shuffled as fast as they could down the hall, just short of a run.

His foster brother bellowed his rage behind them.

"That'll draw a crowd," he muttered. "Better hurry."

"Sorry." Her cheeks were fully flushed now.

"Nothing to be sorry for. He deserved worse than that."

"I don't... I just don't like him."

"Join the club." He laughed, but then sobered when he remembered Raelt's exact words. "Look—ignore the idiot."

"Is that what you do?"

"When I can. I've had years to hone the skill. I must say, as much as I hate to inflict him on you, that was a beautiful sight to see. I knew I brought you along for a reason."

"Excuse me?"

"The knee. Wish I'd done it myself." And it was all the more impressive she'd managed it with an armful of books.

"Do you think they'll be repercussions?"

"Oh, no. That's nothing a healing spell can't fix, although it'll be mighty painful in the meantime. Did you hear that crunch?" He grinned.

She fought a smile too. "I hear it's not kind to triumph at the pain of others."

"Ah, but it sort of feels good, doesn't it?"

She chuckled, not meeting his eyes as they approached a turn.

"C'mon." They went left down a corridor, hopefully escaping Raelt and his nonsense. "You do look wild, by the way." He smiled. Like horses on the plains, strong and untamed.

Her head dipped again, though, the smile vanishing.

"I meant—it's a good thing," he rushed to add.

She frowned at him. "*He* didn't mean it that way."

"Ignore the idiot, remember? And in *my* defense, you did attack me from a tree branch."

"Strictly speaking, I dropped out of the tree and *then* attacked you. And I'll do it again if you're not nice. Or drop your books in the fountain."

"You wouldn't."

She raised an eyebrow, an evil smile on her lips. "Try me. You don't know me very well."

They knocked on Grel's door. A long minute passed, but no one answered. He bent closer and listened; there was no rustling or crackling of the fire. Empty.

He shrugged. They tried Sutamae's next, but her room was empty as well.

"Just need to check the library and the kitchen, and then we're free."

She nodded and followed him.

"Are those too heavy?"

"I'm tough."

"I notice you didn't answer the question. Want to switch, carry a pack, and I'll take the books?"

"Uh... sure."

They were down to the first floor, halfway to the kitchens, when a voice from the sitting room halted him in his tracks.

"Just where do you think you're going?" Smooth as a velvet slipper, that voice belonged to the one person worse than Elix—Vanae. His foster mother turned. Her arms were folded across her chest, one arched finger tapping her bicep. She had olive skin, like Nyalin's own, and poker-straight black hair that he suspected she deliberately arranged to draw attention to certain womanly assets. Her robe was black as night, nothing slightly faded for her, and she wore it as dramatically as Sutamae did her own. Vanae's beauty didn't go below the surface, though. Few people's did.

"I'm leaving."

She frowned, looking actually surprised for once. Her eyes searched his face, then flicked briefly to Lara. Then she smiled, suddenly coy. "I see through your little game. Pretending to leave our home will not change Elix's mind, you know. He knows you have nowhere to go, and he doesn't respond to threats."

"This isn't a threat, Vanae." He inched toward the stairs. Lara hung back, hovering behind his shoulder and half out of sight.

Vanae's eyes widened and flicked to Lara. "But surely you must be joking. Who would take a mage with no magic like—" She pretended to realize it just then. "Only someone truly desperate."

Behind him, he could have sworn Lara growled, a deep hum in her throat. He said nothing. That was always the better strategy. Nothing was worth egging his tormentors on.

Vanae polished her nails against her dress, then flattened her hand to study them. But by the way she watched him from the corner of her eye, she was more alarmed than she was letting on. "Your father will not permit it, you know."

Not my father. I don't have a father. "Well, the emperor will," he said instead.

Vanae opened her mouth, but Lara spoke first, stepping forward so that she stood with her shoulder touching the back of his now. "The emperor already did."

His foster mother's eyes flared, angry and hot, but before she could say anything, the front door opened.

Elix stopped just inside the door, surveying the odd scene. His foster father had the stature of a black bear, and a beard to match. His ice-blue eyes, a mirror of Sutamae's, glared out from beneath a black hood that had shaded him from the sun. Those icicle eyes went to Nyalin, to the packs, to Lara, and finally to Vanae.

And then, to Nyalin's surprise, he smiled as he knocked back the hood. "Well, well. What have we here?"

Vanae pursed her lips. "Nyalin says he's leaving. And somehow Cerivil's daughter wandered in from the street. What are you *doing* here, girl?"

Lara glowered at her. Vanae glowered back.

Elix simply regarded them all for a moment.

"Well? Stop him," Vanae ordered, as if his response should have been obvious. "You can't let him leave."

Elix was smiling a little less now, but still smiling. "Why should I care what he does?"

She looked ready to explode. "For once, Grel is right. You're putting jealous nonsense above what the clan needs."

"Tell that to the council, dear wife." He grinned at her and started for the stairs. "Farewell, Nyalin," was all he said as he started up. "Strength on your journey."

Nyalin blinked. Really? Could it really be that easy? He glanced at Lara with wide eyes, and she returned his stare with a shrug.

While Vanae started after Elix, shouting, he ducked down the flight of stairs toward the kitchens and motioned for Lara to follow. Lara glanced back once, as if not wanting to walk away from a fight, then adjusted the pack on her shoulder as she followed.

"I didn't even get to tell him off," she whispered.

He chuckled quietly. "We can go back."

"No. Just trying to make you laugh."

The comment left him smiling as wide as Elix—whatever Elix's smile meant.

The library might have to be skipped. Fortunately, the kitchens were empty save for Dalas, who was just sliding bread into the ovens with a long-handled wooden slide. He turned, dusting off his hands, then jumped when he saw them. "Well, hello. Strength to you both. Did you bring home a visitor, Nyalin?"

"Not exactly a visitor..." He hesitated.

"I have some oatmeal scones with fig jam if you'd like. Or some tea?" He held up a steaming pot with a grin.

"That's very kind," Lara said politely. "But I don't think

we'll be staying." She looked to Nyalin in confirmation, and her brow furrowed at whatever she saw in his face.

So did Dalas's. "Something wrong, lad?" He crossed quickly and laid a gentle hand on Nyalin's shoulder. "You know it's always easier to just spit something out when you have things to get off your chest."

Dalas was right of course. He was always offering such little bits of advice. But what could he say? Dalas had lost his wife and a chance at a family a long time ago. He was the closest thing Nyalin had to a parental figure around here. This was the man who'd read him bedtime stories by the hearth fire, who remembered his birthday with both a toy and a fluffy treat when he was young. Well, and books when he was older. He would rather not abandon Dalas like some common servant who meant nothing more. But what choice did he have? Not like he'd ever have a grand house that employed a baker as well as a cook. He might not even be allowed back in this house after today—at least not until Grel came into power.

When Nyalin said nothing immediately, Lara added, "Perhaps we could take some to go. They sound delightful."

"Of course!" Clapping his hands, which sent flour puffing into the air, Dalas grabbed a linen towel and began heaping it with goodies. "When will you be back?"

He wasn't going to get a better entry than that, but still he swallowed. "That's... that's just it. I won't be."

Dalas faltered, but his face didn't look especially surprised, and Nyalin said so. The baker shrugged. "Well, you are carrying two heaping packs. But where are you going? Do you have a roof over your head? Did that rat bastard upstairs kick you out?"

"Oh, no, no," Nyalin said quickly.

"We invited him to join us in the Bone Clan," Lara offered. Her intervention was a relief; perhaps he hadn't been so crazy to ask her along. Her presence at his shoulder helped him remember he was not crazy, they really were doing this. He wouldn't walk over to the Bone District only to find out there was some misunderstanding and it'd all been a mistake. Or a joke. It was as real as Lara was.

"But are they going to teach you?" Dalas had the linen towel heaped high now and steaming. "Because if not, you should tell them to shove it up their arses. Pardon me, and present company and lovely women excluded." He winked.

Lara only snorted with laughter.

Nyalin shifted his weight. "Teaching me is the plan. Thank the goddesses."

"Excellent! Excellent, excellent. I'm so happy for you." Dalas was beaming as he glanced up the ceiling, then rolled his eyes. "You deserve this. Wish others had as much common sense."

"Yeah, but they don't. And so here we are." He was ready to be done talking about this, in case Elix or Vanae took a fancy to come down and further harass him before he was gone. Or worse, Raelt. No need for them to overhear this discussion. "Is there something with blackberries in there? I caught the smell earlier."

Lara slanted him a funny look. He cocked his head at her. Too mundane a question? Were they in a hurry and he hadn't realized?

"Blackberries? Oh, no, they went out of season weeks ago." Dalas brushed off some unseen dust from his shoulder, then piled in a few more treats. He was surprisingly clean given the amount of flour everywhere.

"Huh. I could have sworn..."

"You wouldn't be the first hungry man to imagine things." The baker grinned, tied the corners of the towel together, and strode over. Then he hugged Nyalin, in spite of the books in his arms, and clapped him on the shoulder, leaving a puff of flour behind.

"Thank you for always supporting me here," Nyalin said in a tumble. "It made an awful situation so much better. Between you and Grel and Smoke..."

Dalas grinned. "There's not much baked goods won't cure."

"You know it wasn't just that."

"Ah, but it didn't hurt, did it?" Dalas's smile was broad, his eyes crinkled with laughter. The man seemed truly happy for him, but Nyalin couldn't help but feel a little pang in his chest. Wasn't Dalas going to miss him? At least a little? He pushed the hurt aside.

"If you see Grel, tell him the news? And keep an eye on Smoke for me?"

"Of course. Cat always comes down here most afternoons anyway. Send word where you are staying, and I'll send some more goodies. I have a delightful lemon pie I'm perfecting."

Nyalin raised an eyebrow.

"From my home. You think I don't bake at home?"

"You don't need to do that." And how did he afford lemons? Elix didn't pay that well.

"It's no bother. And I'll come and visit. If I get a few moments off."

Lara cleared her throat. "He'll be staying at my father's estate. There'll be more than enough food—and baked goods—to go around, so you need not worry."

"Your father's—ah." The baker put two and two together with a lift of his eyebrows. "Still." He held up the warm pack of goodies and smiled wider now.

"I can carry that." Lara, having a hand free, took the parcel. "You are too kind."

"It is your new clansman who has been too kind to this humble baker," Dalas said, speaking only to her. Nyalin felt his cheeks burn. "Honor and truth to you both."

Dalas gave them both a slight bow, and they bowed in return. Odd salutation—but of course, Nyalin would prefer honor and truth and fairness over strength any day. Lara was frowning too as they left out the back door, Nyalin blushing all the way.

Chapter 4

Wear the Mantle

"Here you go—you can grab some food here after we drop off your things." Lara indicated the archway to the kitchens with a jut of her chin. Late-afternoon sunlight shone in from the atrium. "That is, if you don't just live off all these pastries for the next month."

He started to say there were nowhere near a month's worth but stopped. Maybe among less fortunate folk it would be. Either that or he'd sound like a hog. He kept his mouth shut as he followed her up the stairs to what would be his new room.

The Bone Clan's main estate was very different from Elix's Obsidian manor. The home Nyalin had grown up in had been just that—a mansion, yes, but designed for a single family.

This building, however, was a meeting place for the entire clan. There was no fancy dining parlor for entertaining heads of clans and states, at least not as far as Nyalin could see. Instead, long trestle tables sat outside the kitchens in a wide-open meeting hall, and every table was laden with people eating, talking, reading, studying, eating some more... There had been nothing like that at home.

The stairs they trudged up with all his books were wide and made of warm wood, with a strip of green carpet running up the center and tall, broad windows facing out on the garden. Sunlight slanted through luxurious panes, warming the cool stairwell. He was far from the only guest staying there; at least a dozen people were going back and forth, some servants, some swordmages armed with blades, some wealthier, official-looking folk. The hallways were as wide and sunny as the stairs, with the same carpet stretching down until the halls turned out of sight.

"And here we are." Lara opened the door to his room with her baked-good-laden hand, then bumped the door open with her hip.

"I'm glad you remembered which room it was." He immediately slid the loose books in his hands onto the room's small desk and stretched out his aching fingers.

Lara set the packs gently on the bed. "Lived here all my life. It'd be strange if I didn't."

"Well, glad you walked me to it then."

She smiled, propped her hands on her hips, and looked around. An awkward silence stretched out for a moment. He leaned back against the desk.

She cleared her throat. "Well. I'll check with my father about what happens next. He'll probably have you attend class in the morning. We all do."

"Oh?" Nyalin had no idea how many swordmages among the Obsidians were studying, but Grel's classes had seemed to be one-on-one. One more reason why Grel had hated them. But then he was the clan leader's son; perhaps his arrangement was different.

"Yeah." Her voice trailed off, sounding embarrassed.

"I'll be there," he said quickly. "In the atrium?"

"Yes. At the morning gong, the seventh hour. But I'll ask Da and send word." She glanced around again, then fidgeted. "Do you need anything?"

He shrugged, glancing down at himself. "Maybe something that isn't black."

A nervous giggle escaped her. "Right. Anything else?"

"Nah, I'm pretty self-sufficient. Had to be."

"Ah," she said, nodding. "Well, uh, good."

He frowned, uncertain why this had suddenly gotten so awkward until it dawned on him that they were alone together in this small room—and that she didn't want to leave.

But there was no reason to stay.

She ran an index finger down the black leather spine of a book jutting out of his pack. He watched the movement, transfixed. "So did you scribe all these?"

"Not all of them. Most were gifts from my brother Grel." She nodded as if she knew him. There was none of the flinching from before. "Do you read?"

"Not as much as I should. I've always been too antsy to sit still for very long."

He could understand antsy. Even if he was sitting still to read, half the time his leg was jittering. "Are you more of a hang-out-in-trees kind of person?" He smiled and drew the book she'd caressed from the pack—*The Epic of Henera.* He withdrew a few more and dropped them on the bed, but he kept *Epic* in his hands, tracing his thumb along the spine where hers had been.

"My brother was the one who loved books." She ran her finger over the next book nearest her now, a red leather tome with a faintly embossed title, this one on the Mushin philosophy of the last age. "He used to read to me in the gardens while I saw how high I could climb."

"Sounds nice."

"It was."

"When you were children?"

Laughter perked at her lips. "Is seventeen still a child?"

"I think not?"

"Then no. Do you feel like an adult? You must be at least seventeen."

"Eighteen summers, just past."

"Of course, I should have known that."

"No, you shouldn't have. Why should you?"

"Because. Everyone knows the war timeline. And you're..."

"I'm nobody."

She rolled her eyes. "You're *far* from nobody. You're the child of the Ch—" She stopped abruptly. "Oh. I see. Without..."

He pursed his lips and hugged the book closer. "*Without magic*, I'm nobody. Maybe with it too, who's to say?"

She faltered, glancing around the room, searching for a way out of what she seemed to think was an insult. He didn't care. It was just the truth. He'd rather her be used to it.

"I do miss him reading to me." The words seemed to tumble out of her. "Just the sound of his voice. The content mattered less. I always used to say, 'If I can find a husband to read me epic poetry like you do, I'll always sleep well.' " She grinned, then faltered. "Of course, none of that matters now."

His eyes widened at the book in his hands. He tried to shift the volume behind his back as unobtrusively as possible.

She narrowed her eyes at him. Well. That had *utterly* backfired. "What do you have there?"

"Oh, nothing. Just shifting my arms. Those packs sure were heavy, weren't they?" His lie didn't even convince himself.

She frowned harder, reached around him for it. He

jumped back in surprise. This girl was... well, not a normal girl.

"Let me see." She stepped after him, grinning, and reached again from the other side.

He tried to back away but bumped into the desk. A laugh burst out of him at the silliness of her pursuit. He almost held the book as high as he could over her head, but no, she was too nice for that. Instead, he waved it from his other side, away from her, though not by much.

Grinning, she lunged around him, her shoulder brushing his chest. He could so easily close his arms and hug her close... The appeal of that realization made him falter.

She snatched the book from his hands—and let out a bark of laughter. She shook her head, brown eyes gleaming. "Well, I guess you have good taste."

He snorted. "Feeling sleepy yet?"

"You'll have to start reading." She held out the book, then glanced at the sun out the window. "And it's too early for that."

"You didn't like any of it? It's dry, but there are some beautiful passages." He had them marked in the corners.

She gave him a long look he couldn't read. He was suddenly aware that she hadn't moved away and was standing barely a foot from him. That cedar smell was nowhere to be found this time, though.

"I... may have been too far at the top of the tree to really make out half the words," she muttered.

He laughed softly, covering his mouth with his fist. "Well, maybe I'll refresh your memory."

Intensity flared in her eyes, and he realized his mistake. It must remind her of her loss. Or was it a mistake? Was her expression pure pain or gratitude? Possibly a little of both.

He fidgeted under the strength of her gaze. To dodge

it, he flipped the book open, creating a barrier in the slight distance between them, paging through until he found a marked passage. "Oh, this one is relevant for today.

'The lily blooms for the wise man who
Knows no sleep nor sunset nor winter for his studies
The twisted mind spins in the wind until it discovers truth
Be not ashamed of former darkness.' "

He looked back up. Her eyes shone, wet around the rims. Tears. He swallowed.

Shit. He could tell himself he understood. That dead was dead and gone was gone. But he'd never had a mother to lose, really. He *didn't* understand. Being abandoned, left alone in this world—it wasn't the same as having someone ripped from him. When she said nothing, he hung his head, pretending to look back down at the book. He stared at the ink, the letters, groping for something else to say.

She cleared her throat and sniffed. He didn't look up right away. "Well. You're right. That is fitting."

He looked up now. "Are you all right?"

"Of course." She visibly shook off the emotion, forced a smile.

"Did it remind you of him?" he asked softly.

"Yes. And no. He loved truth and knowledge too. That's not sad. What's sad is that such love is so rare in this world."

He shut the book softly, keeping it from slamming like a tomb. "I won't disagree with that. I'd like to untwist an Obsidian mind or two."

She grinned now, the gleam returning to her eyes. "Never mind them. Forget them. We'll untwist *your* mind, and your magic, and then see what they're saying."

He smiled crookedly back. "I hope you're right."

"In the morning. You'll see." She nodded, more as a goodbye than an acknowledgment. Suddenly he sensed just how long she'd lingered. "I suppose I should go."

She patted his packs full of books and strode toward the door, the setting sunlight catching a twinkle on a bit of gold ribbon entwined in one of her braids.

"Lara?"

She stopped with one hand on the doorframe, turning.

"Thanks. For everything."

Her cheeks flushed. "See if you're still thanking me in a week for dragging you into the lowest of the low clans. Magic or no."

He snorted. She clearly thought his life as an Obsidian had been better than it was. "I'm not worried about that."

"I know. But I hope *you're* right." Grinning, she gave him a little wave and left.

Nyalin settled in for what he hoped would be a peaceful first night in the Bone Clan house.

His evenings weren't peaceful often; evenings tended to be either riddled with annoyance and danger if Raelt was around, or full of long talks and parlor games if Grel was available. Truth be told, it was more of the latter than the former. But not tonight. Although he did need to catch up with Grel as soon as possible. If he didn't get a chance soon, he'd have to send a note.

Although Raelt would be sure to update his brother with the news.

New clothes in a proper pale brown were delivered to his room. He changed into them immediately and was glad to see that they actually fit.

The kitchens were bustling with students, laborers, men carrying books, and women carrying baskets. But more students than any of these, which made sense. This house was half home, half school—and maybe a few other things besides. Eyes up and down the crowded trestle tables watched him—some surreptitious, some blatant.

Yeah... maybe he could take something back to his room. The last thing he needed was a pilgrim who wanted a blessing—or worse, to know why his crossover had changed. It was hard to believe that so many recognized him, but he couldn't think of any other explanation for the stares. He was hardly the only olive-skinned, dark-haired member of the Bone Clan.

His new clan.

That didn't seem real yet, but swimming in this sea of Bones was helping. He picked up some deep-fried mutton bits wrapped in pastry being doled out by the bagful from the kitchens.

He retreated to his room and found that Lara had sent a note. Cerivil wanted him to sit in on the morning class, even if he wasn't to participate. Then they'd congregate after lunch and try to get down to the mystery of Nyalin's magic. Or... the mystery that was its absence.

Mutton bites devoured, he found a small shell of a pastry he was surprised had survived the journey from Elix's house. He sat alone by the window, watching the sun setting over the rooftops of the Bone District and munching on the hard-shelled, sweet cheese- and chocolate-filled dessert. He missed Dalas for what he suspected wouldn't be the last time. And Smoke too. Truly, this time of night, Nyalin would probably be hiding from Raelt in some corner of the kitchen, with just this same dessert and Smoke curled up against his leg. He'd trade stories with his baker friend while the man worked. He'd see Dalas again, though. It wasn't like he'd sailed across the sea.

What would his mother think of all this? This moment, this gigantic change. In a way, he had started it all with the visit to her grave.

"Perhaps things aren't so bad," he said aloud, pretending she could hear him. "I'm still sorry. But maybe I won't have to be quite as sorry someday. One of your old friends is taking a chance."

After that he lay on the bed and dug through a history of the empire for more details on his new clan and its hinterlands. He didn't remember much about the Bone Clan and their exploits on the steppes, to be honest, and it turned out that was probably for a reason. It was quite boring—lots of shepherds herding animals that didn't want to be herded and farmers farming land that didn't particularly want to be farmed. There was a bit of squabbling with their two neighboring clans—Glass and Lapis—before they ultimately joined the other clans in the wars against their mutual enemy, the Mushin.

When he'd finished that, he stacked his book collection on the desk and one nearby shelf. He didn't want to presume he'd be staying here long, but he also couldn't use the books if he couldn't see them.

A black leather-bound volume had been a gift from Grel only a few weeks ago, and he paused before putting it on the shelf. *Unusual Magical Phenomena*. A wise choice from his brother, as usual. He hadn't yet had a chance to read this one. Maybe it could explain the strange shock like a sharp, hot jolt he got when Lara touched him. Or his entire magical existence.

He locked the door as best he could, and then just for

good measure, he dragged a heavy chest that held the room's linen stores in front of the door. He'd had too many close calls, freak accidents, and bizarre occurrences while he was sleeping, and while he attributed them mostly to Raelt, an extra obstacle at the door couldn't hurt.

Then he curled up with the book in bed, reading until the candle burned low. The first few chapters were amusing, but nothing he recognized. Nothing that had ever happened to him. Perhaps the Bone library would hold something that could give him some answers. Elix's library had been grand—and Nyalin had bolstered it further by scribing many, many volumes for it—but if this house supported a school, maybe the library here would be even better.

He slept surprisingly well for a strange bed in a strange house with no purring Smoke curled at his feet.

~

She had to put it back.

In her bedroom, Lara lay in the dark and twirled the idea around in her head, like a crystal sphere that reflected the light this way and that as she moved it. The night had grown cold, but the furs and blankets heaped on top of her were more than enough to keep her toasty. The sweat on her brow wasn't from the excessive bedclothes, however.

She had to put it back.

The presence of the blade beneath the bed tugged at her. She'd been so sure she had everything figured out. And then out of the blue—or the black, maybe—this boy had shown up. With his books and his poetry and his too smart eyes—and enough magic to unseat Andius. Perhaps no one knew yet, perhaps no one would admit it, but *she* knew. She had seen it herself.

Eventually everyone else would too. He'd crush Andius at the Feasts of Contest, and he'd win the title of heir, and they'd go to give him the Dagger of Bone.

And it wouldn't be there.

What had she been thinking? What had felt like rebellion at the time looked more like suicide on a long delay. There was no way out of this alive—or happy. What in all the dragons under heaven was she going to do?

She'd screwed herself worse than anyone else had, except maybe Myandrin in dying, and that wasn't his fault.

Yes. Maybe she could sneak it back in. Putting it back was the only way. She'd right her mistake before anyone knew it had been committed. It would be like it had never even happened.

She threw off the furs and sat up. Swinging her feet, she searched for her slippers. She didn't know the guard rotations as well at night, or even exactly how far into the night they were, but how strict could they be? How frequent?

What kind of fool would try to steal the clanblade, especially from within the house? They'd be relying on the perimeter guards to keep anyone truly dangerous away. She wouldn't be surprised to find them asleep.

Her clan wasn't great at the guarding of things. But they usually had so little to guard anyway.

She pulled a robe around her to stave off the chill and then knelt beside the bed.

She sorted through the silk garments, neatly setting some aside and shifting others. The bag waited at the bottom. She grabbed it by the gathered drawstring at the top and stood.

A dark, quiet laugh echoed in her skull.

Her blood ran cold. No. No—it couldn't be too late—it couldn't have—

The laughter echoed again, rasping and deep. Her mind

was a cavern in which the sound echoed infinitely.

She held the bag up at eye level and glared at it. How could it mock her pain, her naive hope that she could better her situation without inadvertently making everything much, much worse?

"Don't laugh," she whispered.

Face me. The words were barely a whisper on the wind, a tease so soft she wasn't sure she hadn't imagined them.

"No. I'm—I'm putting you back. I should never have—"

She staggered as her vision was obliterated by—by something else. By darkness.

A huge eye opened in her mind.

The black of the pupil gaped, as large as she was, deep like a vast chasm she could tumble into and never reach the bottom. An iris of slate purple ringed the darkness. And at the farthest edge, a ridge of bone.

Hello, daughter.

Hello, she replied as calmly as she could.

Luck to you, honored clanswoman.

Luck to you as well. Even as bitter anger pumped in her veins, she knew enough to be polite to the Bone Dragon. Or was this the clanblade?

We are one and the same. My soul is linked with the blade.

She nodded and swallowed hard. Somewhere she could feel her body still staring at the eye-level bag that hid the dagger; the image was transposed in her mind over the great eye. She was experiencing them both simultaneously. It was dizzying. Terrifying.

But most of all, it meant she was too late.

Do not be afraid.

I am *afraid. I've made such a mistake.*

Be afraid of them, but not of me. I am your friend.

She blinked. *Friend? That's hard to believe.* How did one be a good friend to a dragon?

Perhaps aunt is a better term? Godmother?

You're... female.

Yes. And a friendly female. I saw your birth, you know. I know your father's love for you. You have nothing to fear from me.

I wasn't supposed to take the blade, she confessed. *I stole it.*

You seized it. The great dark voice almost held a tinge of... was that pride?

Her brow furrowed. *Is there a difference?*

There is.

This is all a terrible mistake. I've just realized, I've got to put it back.

I am afraid it is too late for that. There came dark laughter again.

Don't laugh at me, she grunted at the dragon.

I apologize, Clan Leader.

And don't call me that.

Why not? It is what you are.

I can't be.

I say you can. Now draw me from the bag and face *me.*

She yanked the neck of the bag open and drew out the blade. The room was nearly pitch-black save for a touch of moonlight, but somehow the blade managed to catch what it could and gleam viciously. The bone was cold and oddly reassuring in her hand.

Good, the dragon purred. *It suits you so. Look how it fits your hand.*

It did fit. It looked made for a small hand, like hers. But she shook her head. *Only men are allowed to wield this blade.*

Only I *determine who is allowed to wield it.* The dragon's voice rose to such a great thunder in her mind, Lara staggered again. *I may have offered part of my soul to protect my people, but I am no slave.*

I'm sorry. It's just... I thought... I didn't take the blade for the right reasons. It was selfish. I don't deserve this. I don't deserve you. Before the eye in her mind, and in her real body, she fell to one knee, holding up the blade horizontal across her palms.

The eye only blinked at her, cold and unfeeling. *Wear your mantle, girl. There is no throwing it off. Certainly not with noble proclamations.*

She dropped her head, lowered her arms, and rose. *Yes, great dragon.*

Call me Yeska. It is short for Yeskatoth.

Her eyes widened. *Of course. Yeska.*

Now that we've gotten that out of the way, down to more important matters. You must tell the others you've claimed me.

She gasped. *But they'll kill me.*

This did seem to give the dragon pause, as Yeska didn't immediately brush off her claim. *That may be true*, she consented, annoyed. *But if they do, I will withdraw my power from them—*

Didn't you already do that, in my grandfather's time?

The great eye scowled. *I will withdraw it even further.*

She pursed her lips. *You're bluffing. Can you even do that?*

Of course I can. Notice I am not withdrawing it from you. Yet. You can learn from their mistakes.

To her surprise, she found herself clutching the blade to her chest. She stared down at its beautiful, softly curving edge and sighed. What a mistake. Perhaps she and Nyalin could have bested Andius and been truly happy. There wasn't a good chance of that, but now she would never know.

Put me back if you're going to mope, said Yeska. *And take me up again when you are ready to fight.*

A smile tugged at her lips at that sentiment, in spite of herself. *I must admit, I do like your attitude.*

We will be friends.

I could see us being friends.

I know. I am usually right.

I'm usually all up for fighting, but you know, it is *the middle of the night.*

The best time to take an enemy by surprise.

Now it was Lara who laughed. *True. But are they enemies?*

It is debatable. Some of them are. If you would wear me during daylight—

I would get to fight all right. To the death.

No.

She shook her head. *Midnight is the time for moping. Perhaps tomorrow, Yeska?*

Sleep well, Clan Leader.

Wincing, Lara murmured her thanks. The great eye faded from her consciousness, not entirely but enough that she could concentrate on returning the dagger to its makeshift home under her bed.

She tossed off the robe, crawled back under the sheet, and pressed her fingers over her eyes to force back any tears. Tears wouldn't change anything. Tears wouldn't undo the imprinting or any of the choices she'd made. They wouldn't bring back Myandrin, and they wouldn't keep Da clan leader forever. Apparently, she'd already usurped that role.

They were all going to be so, so angry at her when they found out what she'd done. And though she had thrown caution to the wind once before, she didn't want to die.

Unless... unless they couldn't find it.

Yes. That was it. She doubted Yeska would approve, but no objection sounded in her mind at the idea. If returning the thing wasn't an option, she'd follow her other plan. She'd take a horse and ride out into the desert and bury the dagger in the deepest hole she could dig.

The damage would still be done, but no one would be able to link it back to her. And then there might be some other future without death or exile as the only options. Maybe even one with poetry in it. And naps.

She went over her plan again, and again, and didn't really notice the quiet, dark laughter that growled through the corners of her mind as she drifted off to sleep.

Nyalin woke with a jolt. He wasn't in his "closet," which was an improvement, but he did have the bed to himself. Smoke's morning stretches and yawns were painfully absent. The small, warm bundle was not in its usual spot tucked behind his knee or near his shoulder. But he twisted to a seat at the side of the bed, stretched, and felt amazingly refreshed, if very alone.

When things settled down, maybe he could bring Smoke here with him. She'd like this room. Or he could get another cat. None of this was forever.

He washed his face in the washbowl, the last hints of his dark mood carried away with the water. He began his first morning as a member of the Bone Clan and dressed like it. The sand-colored linen crossover was crisp and comfortable, if shorter than he was used to. The Bone crossovers were shorter than most clans—with the whispered joke that perhaps they couldn't afford more fabric—but he immediately liked the way it moved, the way it felt. It'd be far better in a fight. Hopefully he wouldn't need to test that out.

There was a heavy sleeved cloak too, and he pulled the

chocolate-colored garment on against the morning's chill. And now breakfast.

While he could have sustained himself on Dalas's stash, maybe he ought to try to make it last a month, as Lara had suggested. Setting the carefully tied pastry bundle on the shelf by the books, he took the stairs back down to the kitchens.

The place was even more packed than the night before. A river of people ran in and out from the kitchens, rushing away with something in hand. A few ate at the trestle tables, but most bustled out, heading to work or class or he knew not what.

He drifted and stopped off to the side, observing it all. He wasn't even sure where to start.

The kitchen itself was separated from the main hall by reddish stone archways a few feet higher than a person. Shelves filled the arches, and cooks and bakers slid food onto them almost as quickly as people scooped it up. The actual entrance to the kitchen was on the far side, around a short corner, but no one really needed to go there if they weren't going to cook or wash or stoke the fires. All the food was readily at hand.

And so *much* of it. What would this all cost? This was the poorest clan, but he could never recall Elix spending so much on something like food for average clan members.

Maybe they weren't average clan members, but all working for the clan leader. If that were the case, for all he knew, the food could be half their pay. Or all of it.

Cutting his way through this chaos and out with something to eat was not going to be easy.

His eyes caught on a baker with a bushy gray beard and brown cap at the far end of the food shelves. The man was blowing and waving his hands over a loaf of bread that was rapidly collapsing. Nyalin shifted closer to him.

The baker glanced up. His eyes were crinkled with laughter, a surprising bright blue. “Looks like another failure. What do you think?”

Nyalin shrugged. “Is it edible?”

Half the man’s mouth crooked up in a smile. “Certainly.”

“Then certainly no more than half a failure. If that.”

The baker grinned, then held it out to him. “Care for half a failure for breakfast?”

“If you’ve got anything to go with it.”

“I recommend the boiled eggs, if you want to grab something and get away from the madness.”

“Is it always this crazy?”

The baker shrugged. “I’ve only just started. But no one seems particularly fazed.” He glanced at his colleagues, then back at Nyalin, tilting his head.

“I’m new here too. Do you know the way to the library?” Nyalin asked. There was about an hour before class started, so he had some time to start on his research. Aside from his room, there was nowhere else he could imagine going anyway.

“Oh, that’s easy. You passed it just after the stairs—but it’s to the right, not the left you took to come here.”

“Thanks. I’ll take some eggs and fallen bread then.”

The baker grinned, tipped his cap, and held out a basket. “Come back tomorrow. Maybe I’ll do better on the next one.”

“Goddesses bless things in numbers of two, don’t they?”

“Yes. We shall hope I don’t need four. Or twenty.”

“Good luck then. Thanks.” Waving and accepting the basket, Nyalin followed the baker’s directions toward the library. Sure enough, it wasn’t far. He pushed open the heavy wooden door.

Huh. It was mostly empty, despite its central location.

Only one young man sat inside reading. His wild blond hair stuck out in a variety of directions, like Lara's, although his only fell to his ears. His wave to Nyalin was surprisingly friendly, but he returned to his book, thank the goddesses. Nyalin was happy to leave the man to his reading and just look around.

He poked his way through the sections and found the collection surprising and diverse. There were *many* books he didn't recognize, and while there were more than a few he'd like to indulge in, he stuck to the tomes discussing magic.

After gathering five promising ones, which was more than he'd dared hope he'd find, he stopped. He'd been planning to abscond with them and get some reading in after class. But he didn't actually know if he was allowed to remove the books from the library. He set them aside on a window seat near the young man and nodded to him. His new clansman responded with a smile.

Well, maybe there were two or three people he could actually be friends with in this clan. He pushed through the doors again. Now that he was outside of Elix's myopic control—and out of his comfort zone—who knew what could happen? This could be good for him in more ways than just magic.

From the stairwell windows, he checked the angle of the sunlight that shone down into the atrium. Nearing seven, although he hadn't yet heard the quieter gong that would sound on the hour. Students were already gathering on the platform.

Ready or not, it was time.

~

"Do you want me to frighten her, perhaps?"

The door had barely opened before Zama began to speak, sweeping into her studio like a tornado trapped in a dark glass bottle. He'd certainly made himself right at home.

He wore a handsome black coat of brocaded silk with a high collar. The garment flowed over his dark tunic almost to his knees. He'd rejected the crossovers she'd offered, as they were not the fashion where he came from, but he had no problem with wearing black. The color seemed to calm the servants after his sudden appearance. Or frighten them into silence about it. He paused near the fireplace, spinning and propping an elbow on the mantel, the image of a dashing young gentleman.

Except for the unnatural glitter of silver in his eyes, of course. And the centuries captured in his slight crow's feet.

Unira shrugged. "I'm not sure Vanae is worth it."

"But I want to be of service to you." His voice was tinged with mockery. Her silver-eyed demon polished his nails on his chest and faked a yawn in a vicious imitation of the woman. Then he grinned at Unira. "She's failed how many times with Linali's son?"

The way he captured the likeness of a woman he hadn't even met before was a little disturbing, but the way he actually *listened* when she talked more than made up for it.

His dark voice had an unnatural roughness and roll, like thunder through dark skies, and it never ceased to send a little thrill through her. Of fear or delight, she wasn't sure. Perhaps they were the same for her, where he was concerned.

What he said was true, of course. As far as investments went, Vanae had been a terrible one.

"Surely there should be some recompense," he purred.

"I love it when you use those fancy devilish words on me." She picked up a rag nearby and wiped her hands, hoping he'd come closer. "More, please."

"Later. She sent us a message. But it hasn't arrived yet."

"How could you know about it then?"

"I have my ways. I thought you might like to catch her early and unawares rather than prepared and waiting. Especially if I'm to frighten her."

"Of course. Well." She paused. "Do you want to frighten her?"

"I do."

"I can frighten her just fine on my own, you know."

"I have no doubt."

Did he actually need her permission to do something, or did he just like to get it? So far, she hadn't been inclined to deny him anything. "I suppose frightening her is only fair recompense for failure."

"Repeated failure, wasn't it?" he pointed out, one clawed finger jabbing in the air. He grinned and clicked his teeth together, fangs bared.

"You're a quick learner." Smiling to herself, she set down the rag and the clay model and stood.

One corner of the studio held a mirror and an armchair. She'd originally installed them for using herself as a model in the mirror, and for taking breaks in the chair. But it was also very handy for reaching out, both figuratively and literally.

She lit the black candle beside the mirror and directed the view to Vanae.

Zama leaned in behind her, his face set in its grimmest expression, like one of Seluvae's stone guardians perched on her shoulder. Truly formidable. His silver eyes seemed larger, yellower, more like a cat's, and his fangs gleamed.

Vanae's face shimmered into focus, and the woman gasped. "Lady Unira! And— By Seluvae, who is *that*?"

The words burst out of Vanae. The woman could get so sloppy when she was caught off guard. Or really anytime. It was all Unira could do not to yawn. She ignored the rude outburst.

Vanae fidgeted in the glass. "I— Have you heard the news? Got the message I sent?"

"I received no message," Unira said coolly.

Vanae laughed, high and nervous. "I, uh, it's on its way. I swear it."

"I'm sure it is. But why don't you tell me what you have to say yourself?"

"I—uh—" She paused, apparently gathering her wits, because she continued a little more evenly after that. "Nyalin. Linali's son. He's moved beyond my reach now."

"How so?"

"He's left the clan. Become a *Bone*, of all things." She spat the word.

Unira rolled her eyes. So many Obsidians were so obsessed with status, but none more than Vanae. Unira herself could hardly fault the boy. Who wouldn't want to do everything they could to wield magic?

Too bad nothing he did would help him.

"I believe you may have run out of usefulness," Zama murmured, reaching slowly toward the mirror. At the last second, he glanced at Unira. She nodded her assent.

Vanae reeled back, sputtering, so he had to lunge forward, his arm plunging into the mirror up to his elbow. Unira fought the urge to laugh.

Zama ruled three afterworlds, yet he was so eager to help her with her problems. Sweet of him, really. Or perhaps he just loved frightening people. Still, he had more than just his helpfulness to recommend him—his clever silver eyes, his sexy fangs that bit demon magic hot and burning into her veins, and that glittering, evil smile. Hopefully all those traits would hang around for quite a while.

At least long enough for them to destroy an empire together. Yes. Together, they would set the world against itself watch it all crumble down.

Part of this plan included keeping Nyalin from a sword, and indeed from magic altogether. She knew what he was, even if the young man didn't himself. Bladed, the boy would be an even greater risk.

So far, Vanae *had* succeeded in forcing Elix to keep the boy from being taught.

It would have been easiest to just have him killed. But Vanae had tried so many times. The fool was unbelievably, uncannily lucky. She had failed at it so often it was almost comical. But it really didn't matter. It might have been vindicating to see Linali's progeny meet his end, but in truth, Unira knew better than anyone that he'd just end up in the next world, and then the next.

While she'd been lost in her thoughts, Zama had spent his time growling and Vanae groveling. Finally Zama relented, shoving her back and withdrawing his hand from the portal.

Unira drew a slow breath. "Fine. You may live. For now. But you will speak to the sword smith again. The right son must get the clanblade."

"Of course. Of course, honored clanswoman."

The amount of pleasure she got from hearing Vanae grovel was probably a bit unseemly. But taking the haughty woman down a degree after all the days she'd spent looking down that long, thin nose... It was impossible not to revel in it. Vanae had beaten her when it came to Elix, but Unira would win the war.

Of course, the "right" son was not going to get the clanblade. The one who deserved it, Grel, would continue to be denied; she had made sure of it from several different angles.

Vanae of course believed that Unira was referring to her other son Raelt as the heir to their clan. What a laugh. The boy might do as a slave or servant to Zama, if the demon even wanted slaves. But neither of Vanae's sons would get the clanblade.

It would go to Idak. Let them think what they wanted in the meantime, though.

Unira dismissed Vanae with a wave of her hand and a sigh.

Zama propped his hip on the armchair and folded his arms. "Think anything will come of this boy and his ambitions?"

She shrugged. "Of Linali's spawn?"

"Yes. Of the half spirit."

"Oh, he's barely a quarter spirit."

"Any amount of spirit is enough." His mirth was fading fast.

"I doubt it. But we'll keep watch, won't we."

"Yes. Yes, we will."

"We could always try killing him again, I suppose." She shrugged. Just because Vanae had been incompetent at the task didn't make it impossible. Although it sure seemed to be.

He reached out and ran a smooth palm across her cheek, his hand hot and a little rough, like stone baked by the sun. "Let's kill him. We've hardly killed anyone so far."

"My father advises caution. I doubt he'd approve of half the things I've done in the name of his goals." She sighed.

"And has caution gotten him where he wanted?" He grinned, silver eyes shimmering and shifting.

She smiled. "Not at all."

"You have a new advisor now. And this one misses the heady fragrance of blood."

She hadn't expected her demon servant to be so... alluring. "All right. Why not? For you, Zama. If nothing else. I'd hate for you to grow bored." She strolled back to her worktable and held up her creation in clay.

He squinted at it, then shook his head.

She crushed it back to an unformed lump, smiling wider.

"Well, shall I open the next portal for you?" He pretended to trudge wearily back to the chair. "A demon's work is never done."

"Yes please. That Bone Clan fellow this time. Hopefully he's seized the charms as ordered and hidden them well."

"Such an easy way to weaken a clan's mages. You'd think they'd keep them under lock and key."

"Some people are more trusting than you, Zama." Her wink alluded to her sarcasm.

"Some people are stupid."

She chuckled. "Not everyone can be as wise as my demon."

Chapter 5
Wishful Thinking

The punch came out of nowhere.

Nyalin had found a spot as far back as he could and sat cross-legged, surveying the atrium once again. A far superior place to have class than a stuffy, dusty classroom, if it was a little cool. Voices hummed among the students and the building around them, and it was easy to feel like this was the very center of the clan. He'd barely turned back to face the front when the air moved, shifting to his right and behind him.

He jerked his head back just in time.

A fist crossed in front of his eyes where his temple had been. But years of surprise abuse from Raelt had trained him well. On instinct, he caught the forearm and pulled, then connected his other palm to the man's shoulder and pushed out and down. Hard.

His assailant tumbled forward, his balance thrown off, and sprawled on his back, staring up at the sky.

Nyalin still held his attacker's arm in a lock. "Can I help you?"

The boy—for he looked maybe fifteen or sixteen—jerked his arm away and glanced up at someone else.

Standing beside them was the heavily muscled young man who'd directed the guards in the kitchens. Up close, he was maybe twenty summers or more. Like the rest of the students, he had no blade, but he did have two or three charms hanging on his belt at his hip. He had a handsome face with a wide brow, full lips, and expressive brown eyes. His thick, black hair fell long around his shoulders, and his dusky skin was only a little darker than Nyalin's.

"Who do you think you are?" The man's words weren't haughty but measured and controlled. Quietly offended. *Almost* polite.

Nyalin blinked. "Excuse me?"

"Who. Do you. Think you are."

Nyalin narrowed his eyes. There was danger laced in the man's civil tone. Nyalin had lived long enough with danger to recognize it.

"Nyalin moLinali," he said simply. "*Pleasure* to meet you both. And you are?"

The man's laugh was light and easy. He glanced at the others. "I'm sure the pleasure is all yours."

"That's Andius," grunted his attacker, who'd shaken his arm free and gotten up as far as one knee. He was glowering and holding his elbow.

Nyalin looked blandly from the kid to the lordly fellow and back. Was that supposed to mean something to him?

When Andius spoke again, his voice was casual even as the words were dipped in venom. "Do you think your mother matters to us here?"

Nyalin shrugged. "It doesn't matter to me if she matters to you."

Andius cocked his head, no doubt surprised at the lack of response. "You were born an Obsidian. You can't just change that by donning a new robe."

"I *wasn't* born an Obsidian, actually," Nyalin shot back.

"Once an Obsidian, always an Obsidian."

"No. I wasn't born anything." Okay, maybe that one had gotten under his skin. He forced a deep breath. Calm. Be calm. Release the clenched jaw. The edge in his voice was what Andius wanted. Nyalin wouldn't give him an excuse to justify his bullying if he could help it. He would keep his words as calm and neutral as the surface of a morning lake.

Andius's face darkened further. "You mock the greatness of our clan. Our clan must grow stronger, more independent of other clans, not accept their rejects. You disrespect us with your presence."

"I don't see how." Nyalin caught Andius's dark gaze now and held it. "I only seek to join your ranks."

"Don't play dumb. You can never truly be one of us." His full lips pressed into a thin line.

"The emperor disagrees." Lara's voice cut across the atrium from the archway entrance.

Nyalin started to smile, but then Andius smiled at her too. It was a smile that sent a chill through Nyalin's bones.

"This Obsidian has been rejected by his clan," said Andius. "That's what I hear."

"Rumors travel that fast?" Lara folded her arms across her chest.

"Because he doesn't have any magic."

Lara's chin jutted up as a dozen sets of eyes flicked to her, even those students who had pretended not to be watching. "He does have magic. I've seen it."

"So you claim."

Her eyes and her nostrils flared. "Are you calling me a liar?"

He snorted. "You certainly have no ulterior motives. Are

you calling your father a liar? The entire Obsidian Clan?"

Lara opened her mouth but faltered. She *had* done that, and she'd do it again, but did she want to so loudly, so soon?

Andius smirked at her. "Is our clan now to accept all the runts and defectives?"

Lara glowered at him. "Well, *you're* already here, so what difference does it make?"

Nyalin cut in, bowing in his seat. "I'm only here to observe. What harm is there in that?"

Andius's amused expression brightened even further, threat cloaked in a playful veneer. "Now who is the liar?"

"Certainly not me, I assure you." Keeping his eyes trained on the ground, Nyalin bowed further to underscore the words—and maintain the moral high ground. He'd sense any blow coming, just as he had the first one. He waited a long moment, then straightened slowly.

"The Bone Clan does not need—" Andius started.

Just at that moment, Cerivil cleared his throat from the archway. He stopped beside Lara, picking up on the tension even if he'd heard none of the words. "What's going on here?"

"We were welcoming our newest clan member," Andius said smoothly, bowing to Cerivil.

"Good." From the edge to the word and his glance at the young man still cradling his elbow, Cerivil didn't believe Andius for a second. "The emperor himself has seen fit to allow him into our clan. We must honor Nyalin as we would any other clan member. And we must respect the honor the emperor grants us in entrusting us with Linali's only son."

Nyalin bowed again even lower, hiding his wince. He didn't think invoking his mother had much effect on people who'd never met her. "I thank you for accepting me, Clan Leader."

His words were muffled into the floor, which he felt was a

nice touch. The bow and the words were nothing he wouldn't have done with Elix, nothing he hadn't done many times. And it couldn't hurt to start working on *not* looking like an arrogant Obsidian. Still, a wave of surprise swept through them all at the gesture. They glanced at each other, whispered. He held the bow an extra second longer. Had he done something wrong? Did they bow some other way? Or perhaps his willingness to bow frightened them because it meant he must have nothing to offer.

Well, he *didn't* have anything to offer, so let them be afraid.

Class commenced after that. Andius and his crony moved to the front and left him alone, and Nyalin listened as Cerivil spoke.

It was a somewhat advanced lesson on variations in the light charm, one of the more common charms swordmages carved. At times, the clan leader backfilled more simple concepts. That and the questions from some students told Nyalin the class's abilities were very mixed. As soon as his training had started to look doubtful, he had read as much as he could in the Obsidian library. Elix had no shortage of magical tomes, so in the end, he had learned a lot—from books. Nothing Cerivil covered was unfamiliar to him. From a theory perspective, he knew a great deal about magic.

He just couldn't actually *do* any.

The group settled into exercises of what had been taught: beaming light into a small, wooden box on its side. The box gave them a darkness to fill. Each student sat cross-legged with a practice blade across their knees or waist, a light charm dangling from its hilt.

As far as he'd read, casting any spell through a charm worked like a prism, only in reverse. Normal prisms took in ordinary light and produced a rainbow of colors. But where magic was concerned, the charm acted as a focus, a funnel, gathering up strands of energy from the blade and the ambient world and focusing them down, down, tighter, spinning the energy into a single, specialized beam: the spell.

Some great theorists he'd read claimed that it was perfectly possible to cast without the charms, but most mages couldn't manage it—or simply didn't train to.

In this case, the blade's energy should—if everything went right—be spun into a glorious flash of light. Holding up a hand, a nearby student waited for a tense moment before an orb formed at his palm and shot forward, filling the box with a splash of light. Meanwhile, older students yawned and practiced different colors and intensities. Younger students faltered. Some didn't do more than wave an empty palm at the box—Nyalin included.

Andius's lights blared bright over and over again, enough to make students around him wince or shield their eyes.

Who could have guessed he'd do such a thing.

Interesting that Cerivil was their primary—possibly only?—teacher. Nyalin alternated between observing them and meditating. After about an hour, Lara took a break and came to sit beside him.

"Sorry about that welcome you got," she said, her soft voice bordering on a whisper. In the back of the class, he sat closer to the burbling water pavilion. She didn't intend for others to hear her words. "I should have warned you about him."

He shrugged. "There hasn't been much time."

"And who wants to spend more time talking about *him* than we have to?"

Nyalin smirked at that. "Who is he?"

She sighed. "Since my brother died, Andius is my father's likely heir. And my future husband."

Nyalin winced, his stomach dropping. His dislike of the man had suddenly doubled. Tripled, perhaps. "So he's won your Contests?" The book he'd read last night said that the Bone Clan kept the tradition of the Feasts of Contest each year. Obsidian hadn't regularly held that feast in recent memory, but several of the other clans continued this particular old tradition. This feast in particular was meant to determine a line of succession and nonhereditary heirs by pitting the clan's best and brightest against each other.

"He was always second to my brother, eight years in a row. But now..." Her eyes were grim. "This year, he'll win. It's a formality, I suppose, but we're just waiting for the feasts to come around. And for him to win it. There's no reason he wouldn't win." Then she shrugged.

Nyalin's mouth jerked open, and he started to say something but choked a little on the words. He'd wanted to say... what had he wanted to say? That maybe *he* could be that reason?

That was extremely wishful thinking. Even if he was able to unearth his magic in this new clan, Andius was at least a decade ahead of him in study. If he wanted to beat Andius, he was already starting off at a major disadvantage.

And he *didn't* want to beat Andius. Did he? He'd seen how miserable being the heir to a clan leader could be. Grel's days were chock-full of political maneuvering, boring talks about nothing over tea, and the occasional actual decision about the clan. And those decisions were so rare because being the clan leader was like being a sparrow in the midst of a dust storm—pulled every which way, and beaten up by it, with only luck to help find a landing place.

Still, as she fidgeted with the hem of her crossover—a more yellowy gold today, edges embroidered with small trees in a deep brown—something swelled in his chest, something confusing.

He cleared his throat. “There haven’t been Contests in the Obsidian Clan any time I can remember.”

“Because they have enough heirs? Or because they don’t care for the tradition?”

“I’m not sure. I should ask Grel. But I’ve never seen a Contest. What’s it like?”

She smiled, gazing around the group. “Exciting. Celebratory. Energizing. They pound drums, and people cheer. Action and activity all around.”

He’d meant more what competitions were involved and what level of skill they required... But perhaps he could learn that from the same book he’d been reading last night, or another in the Bone library. Or he could ask at another time. A time when she was less likely to realize he was thinking about his own participation.

It wouldn’t do for her to ponder that. His magic was far from assured. And he didn’t want to be a clan leader anyway. He had enjoyed the life of a scribe, and intended to resume it, if the Order of the Raven would just let him in.

So why was he making a note to look up the competition list again?

“Sounds like a good show,” he muttered.

She snorted. “Well, it’s more lively than poetry. No offense.”

He grinned. “You just haven’t read the right poetry.”

Her eyes snagged on his gaze and stopped. “Really? Is that a promise to find me the more lively verses?”

“How could I ignore such a gap in your education?”

“I look forward to hearing them. Entertainment or a nap—either way I come out ahead.”

“I’ll meet you after lunch, in the main lobby under the dome,” Cerivil said as class wrapped.

“I’ll be there.” Nyalin brushed dust from his knees as he rose. Imaginary dust, actually. His pants were perfectly clean. Must be an old habit from wearing black. Either brown was more practical or the class platform was especially clean.

“Off to lunch, everyone. See you tomorrow!” Waving, Cerivil left them and headed into the estate.

Andius’s gaze was heavy on him, so Nyalin dragged his feet getting ready to leave. Ideally he’d wait long enough to be among the last to leave, but not alone, to lower the risk of an ambush. But all the others had more equipment set up from their lessons. He had barely a few books to pick up and imaginary dust to brush. Soon he ran out of ways to procrastinate.

He pointed himself toward the eating hall and ambled in that direction as if he didn’t have a care in the world.

A small group of students coalesced behind him before he’d even made it out of the atrium.

He turned the corner and headed toward the library instead, hoping to throw them off. His companions quickened their pace. He tensed, hustling faster while trying to avoid looking outright hurried.

But no blow or vicious words ever came.

Power hit him, slamming him into the wall. Agony shot through his cheekbone, his skull, his shoulder, and he slumped face-first against the plaster wall, struggling to keep upright.

Magic. Pure and hot.

The magical energy was invisible but all too real. It was not an easy spell either, if Nyalin understood correctly. These were likely skilled mages, and if so, he was in trouble. The pain of that first slam was hardly the worst of it. Beyond the shock to his body, his mind had tortures of its own, sensations slicing across it like a hot knife across skin. His mental boundaries were flayed, screaming.

Of all the things Raelt had done, he'd never done *this*. That his brother had never used magic had never struck him as odd before, but it did now. Raelt was as much a mage as any of these young men. Why... Fresh pain reminded him there was no time to ponder it.

Nyalin squeezed his eyes shut, but the pain only increased. The hallway took on a grayish-green cast, everything slowing as he fell toward the ground.

His temple hit the wood floor and bounced. But his grunt and groan were swallowed in a massive rush of wind. Even with the pain, even as he pressed a hand to the side of his head to feel for blood, he blinked and looked around.

Everything around him had changed.

The details of the hallway and his attackers shifted, twitched, then shifted again—left and then right, sliding into and over themselves, going out of focus until they were gone.

Trees and waist-high, waving grass took their place. Then they, too, shifted, sharpened, slid, blurred.

Nausea hit him like a sucker punch to the gut. Or maybe he had also been punched. It was hard to say. He fell onto his back, clutching at his stomach.

Above him, where the ceiling should have been, was a vast, green sky.

What in the world?

The green sky vibrated and shook, flickering with some hint of the real world every few seconds. He could just about make out a student or two leaning over him, talking, looking down, backing away. Fear in their eyes.

The combination was staggering, and to top it off, the scents of lemon and pine and olives clogged the air around him. He wanted to gag.

No, he wanted to throw up. He was *going* to throw up.

He heaved himself up onto all fours and promptly did so. More pain splintered him near his ribs, but it felt distant, blurred.

The green world hardened. The flickering ceased. That eased the nausea but fanned new flames of panic as he fell back onto his heels, staring at the world around him and wiping his mouth on his sleeve.

He sat there panting for a long moment, recovering, catching his breath.

Below him there was only grass—long and soft like the softest woven wool. His fingers stroked it, memorizing the combination of gentle and smooth and fragile. He'd never seen so much grass, and what he had seen was tough and stringy by comparison. The desert couldn't support this; only the Lapis and Glass Clans owned land like this, and the Mushin in their faraway lands.

Conveniently, there was also no vomit. It looked like he hadn't thrown up at all. What in all the goddesses' dreams was this?

Another vague bolt of pain hit him, a blow to his ribs. He couldn't see any assailant who could have kicked him. The actual world, the world of the students, was gone. He finally was steady enough to look around him.

In this world, wind stirred elegant tree branches and delicate stems of the grass. Water tinkled somewhere near, but he couldn't spot a source. A butterfly landed on a nearby green leaf and then flitted away, as though it had just noticed him.

Heavenly.

Nyalin stilled. A man stood beside one of the trees, peering out from behind a gnarled trunk. The wild-haired blond man who'd smiled at him in the library.

What the hell had been in that bread? Was he hallucinating now? If he ever saw that baker again, they were going to have words. This new clan was off to a great start, truly.

Nyalin stood, took a step forward, but had to stop when the world flickered.

The young man's clothing was greenish—just like everything else—and worn, but it looked as though it had once been fine. His hair was almost white here, and his skin shone in the dimness. The wind whipped at his hair and his rags, transforming him into a shining apparition in the green light.

Nyalin swallowed. "Who are—"

In a rush of speed, the green sucked away into nothing, the scents evaporating. The man, the trees, the grass—all vanished. The dark wood panels of the real world's hallway abruptly took its place.

And Nyalin's entire body exploded in fresh agony and pain. He'd been standing, but now he collapsed again to the ground.

All the pain and injuries inflicted while he'd been hallucinating came crashing down at once. He gritted his teeth and stayed completely still, until it passed. An old habit he'd learned long ago, to discourage Raelt.

"Nyalin! Nyalin!"

"Lara?" No, it was a male voice. He forced open his eyes.

Above him was one of the students from class, one of the younger ones, maybe thirteen. The boy's face was creased with concern. He had gray eyes, dusky skin and dark hair like Andius. "Nyalin, are you okay?" Friendly arms helped him sit up.

Nyalin wobbled but managed to stay sitting. He glanced

beside him—sure enough, he had thrown up. His head ached dully, but after the initial burst, much of the pain faded. He'd expected lingering agony. "Dark dragon," he muttered. "I don't know." Then he winced, hearing himself.

The young man only grinned.

"I guess I'll need to swear on something else, eh?"

"I say 'great dragon.' It's not that different. 'Bone Dragon' doesn't have the same ring to it, but 'by Dala's light!' is a classic." His grin broadened, and he gave a crisp, short bow. "I don't believe we've been introduced. I'm Faytou."

"Nice to meet you." With Faytou's help, Nyalin got to his feet. "Where did they go?"

"Ran off." Faytou flicked his fingers dismissively down the hall, then rolled his eyes. "My brother and his cronies like to show off their Energy Slam, but it's their only spell on that level. They're cowards deep down. And idiots."

"Wait—your brother?"

"Andius."

"And you're here helping me?"

Faytou shrugged. "We can't choose our families."

"You're telling me." Nyalin couldn't help but grin at that. Maybe Faytou could tell him what he had missed. What if Andius had threatened something specific that he wanted Nyalin to do? That was how bullies like him worked. How could Nyalin explain he hadn't been able to see them or hear anything they said? Confessing to hallucinations seemed like a bad idea for your first day in a new clan. "I, uh, missed what they said. Did you catch it?"

Faytou waved a hand in the direction they'd gone. "Same old usual epithets and threatening. Rarr-rarr watch your back, rarr-rarr that girl is mine, rarr-rarr."

"Why would they run off when I was lying on the floor,

throwing up?"

Faytou sobered and grabbed his arm. "They ran because you *did* it."

"Did what?"

"What Linali used to do."

Nyalin frowned at him. "Excuse me?"

"Sure, you started off tossing your guts, but you stood up. You started to change."

His frown deepened. "Change how?"

"White light behind your eyes. Like they talk about in the stories. It was like you couldn't feel them attacking. You were invulnerable."

"I couldn't feel it. But I feel it now. Not invulnerable, I assure you."

Faytou did not look convinced. "I thought you might just walk away. I'd have loved to see their faces if you had. What happened? How'd you do it? That must be some spell. You *have* to teach me."

Nyalin blinked. "Uh... I don't know if I can do that."

"Aw, c'mon!"

"No, I mean, I don't know what I did. Or how. Let alone how to teach it."

"Well, you better figure it out." Faytou clapped him on the shoulder. " 'Cause that's not normal spell book stuff. That's brilliance right there. Innovation. And it'll keep Andius away from you too, if you can master it."

Nyalin winced. "I guess some research is in order."

"Hey, I'm first on the list when you get that down to a charm. Or a whole sphere of them! Okay?"

He couldn't help but return the boy's eager smile, especially with his blatant confidence in Nyalin's abilities. While it was unfounded, it was refreshing. "Sure."

"Hey, are you hungry?"

"Will your brother like you hanging out with me?"

Faytou made a rude gesture in his brother's apparent direction, and Nyalin couldn't help but laugh. "He doesn't like anything I do so it really doesn't matter. C'mon. There's a great roaster not far away in the Glass District. Let's run over there and get a drumstick or two, where none of them will bother us."

Nyalin took a step. "Wait—what time is it?"

"That really took a lot out of you, huh? Not sure, but it can't be ten minutes since we left class."

"I need to be back to meet with Clan Leader Cerivil soon."

"Oh, it shouldn't take twenty minutes. We can eat and walk and make rude gestures in Andius's general direction together."

Nyalin hesitated a moment longer, then shrugged. As if to encourage him, his stomach grumbled. What did he have to lose? No man was too rich to not need friends, and he was far from rich. "Okay. Lead the way."

Chapter 6

Deluge

"Let's see." Cerivil cleared his throat as he drew a small wooden chest off a high shelf. "First we'll need some of these..." He set the chest on the long wooden table, its gorgeous grain buffed and shined. "Oh, and this too." He bustled away toward the shelves.

Nyalin should have been excited. They were here—ready to try to solve this mystery once and for all.

He didn't *feel* excited, though. He felt... unsettled. The chicken legs had been delicious, and Faytou had been thoughtful and funny company. They'd made it back on time, too. But the memory of the green world lingered. Pecked at him.

Asked a question and begged an answer.

He sat at a table centered in a complex of Cerivil's rooms. The hard wooden seat was starting to get uncomfortable, and they'd barely gotten started. The complex was delightfully breezy, as evidenced by Lara's locks whipping in the feisty air beside him. She waited with him, picking at her fingernails. What reason did *she* have to be nervous? A large beige rug covered the floor with a dark brown vine-and-leaf pattern. One wall was covered with shelves holding numerous chests, bottles, bowls, containers, and—unsurprisingly—practice swords.

One such sword Cerivil had selected and set before him, and Nyalin eyed it with a mixture of hope and trepidation. He hadn't had much access to magical blades in his life, at least not ones people were supposed to practice with. There had been a few stored on the walls of Elix's house, but they weren't for casual handling, and Nyalin had mostly known better than to test Elix on the matter. Of course, he'd always hoped his better behavior would earn him some teaching, some real access to his magic, not just the loaned magic of a practice blade.

That had worked out well.

"All right." Cerivil set down a stack of books with another small bin balanced on top of them. Lara jumped up and lunged to keep them from spilling everywhere. "Here we are!" Cerivil rubbed his hands together. "Just give me a moment or two to set up. Go on and hold that blade, young man. Might as well get used to it."

Nyalin took the hilt in one hand, the scabbard in the other, and studied them both. The white enameled scabbard was magnificent, the sword light but enticing in his hands. It felt like a bright sword, a fast sword, something he could slash through a stalk of wheat, and it'd take a breath before the severed half fell. He longed to take it for a few rounds with a practice dummy.

He didn't feel any different, holding the sword, though. Shouldn't he? Each practice sword was infused with energy, power that could be funneled into a spell via a charm. If the wielder had the gift, at least. Most did not.

Perhaps Nyalin was one of them.

If he had the gift, shouldn't he feel some surge of power? None came. Poor practice sword. Was it better to be an ornamental thing, never intended for combat? Of course, combat and war were bloody and gruesome and to be avoided at all costs... but what purpose did a blade have in a world without such things?

Did blades hunger for adventure the way humans did? Lust for action? Slowly he drew the steel from the scabbard, eying the shine of the blade. It was too shiny. Too clean. Its perfect balance called to him, sang to him, made him long to take a swing.

No. He needed to stop with the idle musing and focus. There'd be plenty of time alone with his whimsical thoughts while he served the Order of the Raven. He set the sheathed blade across his legs and tried to ignore it.

Cerivil had set up three small tests before him. One was a silver bowl of wood shavings. Another was a dark box full of feathers. And the last was an empty wooden bowl, nothing more.

"And here we are—the charms." Opening the lid of the small chest, Cerivil wiggled his fingers as he bent to peer inside. "Yes... Palm Flash. There's that." He plucked a small white stone that hung on a loop of black thread and set it on the table before him. Nyalin picked it up. A small engraving resembling the sun in the center of a hand was chiseled into the stone. "That's what they were working on this morning. And there's... Ignite, yes. A good selection."

The next charm was a solid, deep red stone streaked through with black that hung on a silver chain. Nyalin took this charm now too and rubbed a stone beneath each thumb. He couldn't quite make out what was carved into the dark color of the Ignite stone, but he could feel it. Touching the charms was necessary to focus and channel many spells. With experience, swordmages simply needed the charm close on their person, but never more than an arm's length away. For him, maybe he ought to clutch the thing until his knuckles were white.

"And last but not least..." Cerivil looked back and forth, then frowned. "No water charms? Truly?"

Lara cleared her throat. "He can use mine. If you want."

"If you wouldn't mind."

Lara slipped her hand within the folds of her crossover and drew out her charms.

Nyalin's eyes widened. There must have been a dozen. Maybe more. "No wonder you don't wear all those on your belt. Your pants would fall down."

Her eyes widened.

"Uhh... I mean, how do you manage them all?"

She shrugged. "You mean without a blade of my own? Technically these are all possible as bladeless spells. The blade's primary purpose is to provide energy, like a little well you can carry on your hip. But if you can find a way to access energy some other way, no reason you can't cast them. One or two first-level blade spells occasionally work for me if I'm well rested and trying very, very hard. I just give it a try, and if it doesn't work, I figure I'll put the charm back. They've all worked, though."

Cerivil gave him a sheepish look. "She's always been very talented. Worthy of a blade for sure, if we had any sword smiths, and..."

She pursed her lips. "And if it were more 'appropriate' for me to have one."

Now Cerivil's look turned apologetic.

Lara threw up her hands. "Well, we don't have any sword smiths anyway, and other clans are unlikely to grant me a blade. And the council would have objected too. Even before my brother died, but definitely now."

There was uncharacteristic anger in her brow, and he couldn't say he blamed her. Many believed that magic interfered with the magic of child bearing. Few had really tested it out, though. His mother had carried a blade and borne a child, and she'd been no less powerful while pregnant with him, but her death hadn't exactly helped matters. Many saw the choice of a blade as a literal choice not to bear children.

And that was not an option for a clan leader's wife. He blew out a breath. The world was so damn unfair. And there wasn't a single thing he could do about it.

He thought of the book on clan traditions he hoped to study later. Now was that really true? Not a single thing he could do about it?

She frowned at her lap, then waved it all off in irritation. "I'm stuck with practice blades and ambient magic. Lucky me. Nothing new." She shrugged again and drew the water charm from her chain and handed it to him. "Don't go losing that. Apparently Water Float charms are at a premium."

"I would never." He placed it carefully on the table.

"And since we're not going anywhere," Cerivil said, "losing it seems exceedingly unlikely. But I guess you never know." He gestured at the tests he'd set up before them on the table. "Here we've got some simple spell mediums. The Ignite charm can catch safely on these wood shavings, if you can manage it. Water Float can be used to move the liquid to this bowl from a pitcher— Oh, I forgot the pitcher." He paused as he bustled into the next room and returned with a large pitcher full of water. "And you can shine light into the box. Usually these spells are the easiest to start. And we're all out of Shape Sand charms." He gave an apologetic shrug.

"I'll be perfectly happy if anything happens at all. It hasn't before, so..."

Lara cleared her throat. "Do you want the measuring amulet, Da?"

"Oh, yes." Cerivil pointed a thumb at his daughter as she headed for the shelves. "She could really do this by herself, but I need something to amuse me."

"And a witness that isn't me," Lara muttered.

Cerivil pursed his lips. "Because you've already seen Nyalin's magic. Now we need to up that group of people to two." He slanted a glance at Nyalin again. "Not even your brother Grel?"

Nyalin shook his head. "We're close, but no. And he's tried. Believe me." Should he point out the eyes-glowing act he'd put on in the hall? Did Faytou count? But then he'd sound crazy—and pointing out Andius and his friends had already ganged up on him once didn't seem like the way to make a good impression.

Lara returned with a round, clear lens encircled in silver and hanging on a silver chain, which she promptly hung around his neck before sitting down again. The thing hung on his chest against the crossover like it was any other piece of glass and metal.

"All right, then." Cerivil propped his hands on his hips and surveyed the table. "Have I forgotten anything else?"

"I don't think so, Da."

"Then let us begin."

Nyalin cleared his throat. "Um, pardon me, Clan Leader, but what are we beginning again?"

"Oh! Yes, of course. Well, the first thing is to see if your magic might still be asleep. About half of mages have dormant magic that needs to be awakened with a gentle prodding."

"Uh, prodding?" He shifted in his seat. That didn't sound... comfortable.

"Yes, it's quite mild. Now this is very unlikely for you because I'm certain any reasonable Obsidian would have tried this, including your brother Grel, so unless they've all been lying to you—"

"Which is entirely possible," Lara muttered.

"Lara! Don't say such things. Anyway, chances are good that this is not the issue. Although it'd be delightfully simple if it was!"

"I'm trying not to get my hopes up," Nyalin said, although what he really wanted was for *Cerivil* not to get his hopes up.

"Right. Good. Okay. Let us begin. I'll start by gradually feeding energy to you and—"

"Da, do you want me to do it?" Lara asked.

"Oh?"

"Well, I know it can take some time, and what else am I going to do? Just watch?"

"Hmm. Let's take turns." Cerivil smiled in Nyalin's direction, no doubt attempting to be reassuring.

What exactly did he need reassuring for? Nyalin shifted in his uncomfortable seat again. Here went nothing.

"I'll start," Cerivil said as he slid into a seat across from Nyalin. "This will take time. How about you go get us some tea?"

Lara stared at him for a beat. She wasn't too happy about that request, was she? Nevertheless, she rose and left. He tried not to stare after her. He couldn't exactly blame her; in Elix's house, there had been servants to do menial chores, although Nyalin wasn't so sure that was preferable. He supposed it was any clan member's duty to do the bidding of the clan leader.

Still, he missed her.

"All right, lean back, close your eyes, whatever you like. We'll be lucky if we see any progress before dinner."

Nyalin leaned back and raised his eyebrows. "And if we don't see any progress?" He could already see Cerivil frowning with concentration, so the clan leader must have started something, but he felt no different yet.

"We'll try for a few days. It's hard, unglamorous work." The man paused, frowning, then looked up and grinned. "But rewarding if you get a new mage out of it."

"And if you don't?"

Cerivil waved him off. "That's not the attitude to have. We're going to figure this out. You'll see! Lara saw something, so there must *be* something. We just have to find it."

Nyalin was a little afraid those words were more the clan leader reassuring himself than Nyalin. But he shrugged and shut his eyes.

Silence settled around them but for the wind stirring a wind chime, ruffling the wood shavings. He started to doze off, then inched up in the chair a bit. Amazing he could fall asleep on such a hard, unyielding piece of furniture.

The door opened and shut. Something soft, possibly wooden sat down on the table not far away. Cerivil murmured something unintelligible.

"Anything?" Lara's whisper.

"Not yet." Cerivil's voice sounded strained.

"Let me try."

"It's only been a few minutes. Have some tea."

Of course, he hadn't really asked them what he should expect, what ought to be happening. Would he suddenly be so filled with magic that he'd bolt upright, shout "By Dala's light!" and set fire to everything in the room?

He hoped not.

Behind his closed eyelids, any noise seemed loud, distinct, the room's silence punctured by giant's footsteps, one by one as loud as gongs. Time seemed to slip and stretch and almost stand still. In spite of the breeze, the heat was enough to coat his entire body with sweat. Or was he exerting some kind of effort he didn't know about?

A few minutes or a few hours later, he was entirely unsure, Cerivil sighed. "Your turn."

Nyalin opened his eyes. "Anything?"

Cerivil waved him off. "A little. Nothing significant yet. Let's see if Lara fares better."

Nyalin glanced at her. She was already looking at him, and their gazes locked for a beat, another. Too long.

"Uh, you can shut your eyes again," muttered Cerivil.

Nyalin complied and leaned back in the chair.

Except this time, he didn't have the endless, boundless stretching of time or the sea of giant sounds. For a moment or two, there was nothing, and then...

Like that morning, the weird shifts and flickers of the world returned, even though his eyes were closed. And gradually—there was the grass, the trees.

Except they were several dozen feet below him.

He looked back from the expanse of air below him to the place where Lara had been, where he'd last met her gaze. And in the exact same spot waited the wild-haired man.

"Welcome back." The man grinned, bending in a little seated bow. He was sitting, but there was no chair.

"You again." That was an entirely inane thing to say, but the insane height and the disoriented nausea weren't helping him think clearly.

"Me again, indeed."

Nyalin cleared his throat. "We can't keep meeting this way."

The man smirked. "Sure we can."

Nyalin shook his head and looked around.

"You want to know where you are."

"I guess." Or if I've gone crazy...

The man spread his arms wide. "This is the plane of spirits. Or one of them. This is the next world, the soft world, the mirror world of the one you just came from, before the next hard world in the sequence."

"You mean the series of worlds and all that—it's real?"

"It is."

If he could believe a talking hallucination. "Am I dead?"

The man grinned, and it was more friendly than creepy, thank the goddesses. "No... and yes."

"It can't be both."

He laughed now, which was a little creepy. "Can't it? Are you sure? What is death, really? If only your question were easy to answer. Listen—we haven't much time, and there's something more important than philosophizing or naming this place."

Nyalin frowned. "And that would be...?"

"You are in danger."

"Of course I am. I've been in danger every day of my life." From Raelt, from Elix and Vanae. From everything.

The young man smirked, his eyes twinkling. "What about from a demon?"

Nyalin froze. "Excuse me?"

"A demon from six worlds lower than yours has crossed onto your plane. The world you just came from."

"And you're trying to say he cares about me?" Nyalin rolled his eyes. "I am never taking *any* bread from that baker again. Or eggs."

Snorting, the spirit said, "What do you think this is, a dream?"

"Or a hallucination? What else could it be?" Nyalin

brushed off his clean crossover again. What a day to discover nervous habits. "Or, I know, I've gone mad."

His companion grinned. "Not a believer in the series of worlds, eh?"

"I always thought it was just a way of guilting people into behaving themselves. I certainly didn't tell the monks that, but you know, if I can't see it with my own eyes—" He broke off as the world abruptly flickered again, sickly green fading and surging.

"That's rich. Really. You're one of the few who can. Look, the demon is..."

The voice faded out. Where the young man had been looking at him, Lara's face reappeared, turned to the side now, brow furrowed and shining with sweat.

Nyalin groped for the greenish world again before he lost it completely. Was it something he could control?

Immediately, the world flickered back to the young man. The resemblance to Lara was uncanny—not just the wildness of their hair and manner, but a similarity around the eyes, the smile, especially when he saw them this way.

"Who are you?" Nyalin said quickly. "How can I find you again? Was that you in the library?" Are you who I think you are? But he couldn't say that—it was too far into madness.

"Learn to come here at will, and you'll find me most of the time. I can only talk to you here. Not from the library."

The world wobbled, and Nyalin closed his grip around this strange place as hard as he could for one last moment. "You didn't answer my question—your name?"

"My name is Myandrin."

With that, his strength ran out, and he was propelled back into the normal world with all the gentleness of a whiplash. He hadn't moved from the chair, but he felt like he'd tumbled head over heels down the stairs. His head spun. Was it always going to be this disorienting?

"Nyalin! Nyalin—it happened! Try something!" Lara was standing up beside the chair now. She looked down at him as his head lolled back. "Hey, are you all right? You look a little green."

Oh, goddesses, no. He was not throwing up right here, right now. In front of her.

"Uh—I think I'm fine." But he leaned forward, elbows on his knees, and put his head in his hands. The amulet swung forward and dangled in the air.

"Just when my father left, *of course*, of all times." She fell back down into the chair.

He mustered the energy to look over at her. "What? What happened?"

"Right when he walked out—you did the thing they said your mother did."

He frowned. Again? Maybe it wasn't a hallucination after all.

"Listen, can you try one of the spells?"

He shrugged. "Sure, I'll try." He wasn't sure why, but he picked up the water charm, circled it once with his thumb, concentrating as he'd read how to do in many magical manuals. He tried to imagine funneling some imaginary force that'd come from Lara into the charm, then on into the bowl. Then he tried again—

He stopped when Lara gasped, dropping his charm into the water that poured over the edge of the table and into his lap.

He backed up automatically, as had she. The forgotten practice blade clattered to the floor, and he hastily picked it back up. The table was glistening like someone had poured fifty pitchers of water into the center and then disappeared. The rugs below were darkening where thin streams hit them, and both his and Lara's crossovers were half soaked. The bowl was filled to the brim.

The pitcher he had been supposed to use as a source was also full to the brim, even more so than when Cerivil had left it.

His eyes widened as strands of Lara's hair slowly rose into the thin, static-charged air.

She grinned at the spectacle and then at him. "You did it! Look, you did it! You took it out of the air!"

He frowned. "The water?"

"This is great! See? I knew you could do it! I mean, it wasn't exactly Water Float, which is odd. Almost more like Rain Storm, but—"

"But isn't that a second-order spell?"

"Third actually, but— Da! Look!"

The door opened and Cerivil strode in, eyes wide. "What have we here?"

Lara rushed to him. "I saw it, just like you described used to happen to Linali."

Her father frowned at her, at Nyalin, then at the floor, looking decidedly less delighted.

"His eyes, they were glowing! What is it, Da? Why aren't you happy? It worked."

Cerivil let out a sigh. "Well, my dear dragonfly, this is... both good and bad. Clearly there was magic done here. Unfortunately, I didn't see it. Or smell it. Did you catch a scent?"

She frowned. "It's there," she insisted. "But so faint... That doesn't make any sense. And mine is also muddying the waters."

"I can only smell a whiff of cedar. But I know you wouldn't

lie about this; it's certainly your efforts at the awakening spell. Also, there's much more water than there should be with Water Float." He picked up the dropped water charm, eyed it almost as if the stone were to blame, then handed it dripping back to Lara. "But even worse, his magic clearly does not need to be awakened. If it was asleep, it's awake now. And yet he still appears the same to me."

"The same how?" she asked weakly.

"Hollow."

Nyalin flinched at the word. But it was how he felt—what he feared. Instead of a tree, he was a log. Hollow. Rotting.

Dead. Myandrin's words came back to mind. Who was this Myandrin anyway? Why was he helping—or *was* he even out to help? What had he meant, yes and no? He knew something Nyalin didn't, that much was certain. But he'd have to ponder that later. Lara and her father were arguing.

"Well, there's the measuring amulet. Check that! That should be proof enough for you."

"You know I need to witness it."

"We can just do it again tomorrow."

"Of course. And yes, the amulet, of course." Cerivil strode over, and Nyalin bent down so the shorter man could reach around his neck.

But Cerivil's reassured features fell as he took the amulet, his mouth falling open. "How... That can't be."

Lara was frowning too.

"What?" Nyalin said slowly. "Does it say something bad?"

Cerivil shook his head. "I can't understand it."

Clearly they knew something he didn't. "What? What is it?" he pushed.

"It doesn't say anything at all," said Lara.

Cerivil looked from the amulet to Nyalin. "It's broken.

Somehow you broke it. It's just an ordinary pendant now. The Measure Magic enchantment is just... gone."

Lara looked pointedly at her feet. "And there's water in its place."

Cerivil ran a hand over his features. "Well. We said we were up for a challenge, didn't we, buttercup?"

She nodded. "We did, Da."

"This has been... interesting. I need to think on this. Plot our next steps. Try to understand what might have happened. And also take a nap." Cerivil grinned. "Let's meet again at this time tomorrow, after class."

Nyalin nodded, realizing now that he was fine standing but walking might be another matter. He hadn't thrown up—yet—but the effects of whatever had happened to him were not yet entirely gone. "Okay," he muttered.

"Nyalin, you look exhausted. You didn't eat lunch, did you?" Lara said. Her voice said she knew more than that was going on but didn't care to admit it to her father. He had to admit he was glad of that. It didn't seem like the best impression to make, to just be weakening yourself to the point of exhaustion all the damn time. She took the practice blade and returned it to its shelf before returning to take his arm, steadying him. "Neither did I. Let's go."

"See you both tomorrow." Cerivil wandered out, staring at the amulet in his hand.

~

Lara gripped Nyalin's arm and ignored the little zing that came along with the feeling of his warm skin through the linen of the crossover. Things were weird enough without worrying about that. She guided him back to the chair.

"I did eat lunch," he muttered. "With Faytou."

"Making friends already?" That was admirable, if a little surprising that anyone had been so welcoming.

"I guess so."

She propped her hands on her hips and surveyed him. He didn't look so good. "Good choice. I approve."

"I'm glad." There was an awkward silence. "Anyway, it wasn't much. I'm famished now."

He didn't look at all steady on his feet. "Nyalin, don't take this the wrong way, but I'm not sure you're ready to make it down the stairs. Let's wait a minute, shall we?"

"Okay," he muttered.

She paced around the room, glaring at the water still dripping off the table. All so strange. It didn't make any sense. He obviously had magic. His scent had even returned—blackberries. Though he probably didn't know what it was, did he? It'd be fun to tell him. When he didn't look like he was about to pass out. That handkerchief had been scenting her room with blackberries since she'd dropped it on her desk, and—

She stopped short. "Wait. A couple things don't make sense." How could he... He couldn't be lying to them, could he?

"Only a couple?"

She narrowed her eyes. "If you don't have any magic, what about that handkerchief you gave me?"

He squinted up at her. "What? What about it?

"Well it was chock-full of magic."

He frowned. "How can that be? Maybe someone else could have done it, but why would they?"

She didn't think he was lying. Could someone have been tracking him with the handkerchief? Protecting him? Cursing his luck? "Do you still have it?"

"Sure. I mean—it's in my room. I wasn't exactly running around getting laundry done as a top priority."

Oh. Right. There was still snot on it. It was amazing this man wasn't head over heels in love with her, with the impression she was making. She smacked a hand to her forehead. "Can we go get it?"

"I gotta admit, I'm... still a little dizzy."

"Oh. Right." She'd seen that but was so focused on the handkerchief question she'd forgotten.

"I think I just need to recover for a minute."

"Here." She went back to the still sopping table and returned with a cup of tea, wiping the dripping water from its base with the corner of her crossover. He watched the gesture intently, but she wasn't sure why.

"Thanks." He had his head propped on his knees again.

"Are you all right?"

"I will be. Just a sec. Or two more."

On a whim, she stole a little magic from the practice blade—not that it minded, that one was always a bored sort—and fed it to him again, as she had during the ritual.

He noticeably eased, leaning back in the chair now and tilting his head against the wall.

Hmm. Very strange. Any mage ought to be able to replenish their stores with their own life force or the ambient magic around them. Drawing from the practice blade could be learned, but most mages didn't need to be taught that and did it automatically when pushed this close to the point of exhaustion. What was broken in him that he couldn't? That he didn't? Best not to say anything about it just now.

He gave his head a little shake and straightened. "There. All better. Where were we going again?"

"Lunch. Well, second lunch. And to get the handkerchief."

"Right. Let's go."

They made it to the dining hall in no time, but as they

walked in, she sensed the way the room focused on him. She got her share of attention as Cerivil's daughter and, technically, a noble, but nothing like this.

She gave him a forced smile. "Uhh... let's get something to go."

A few minutes later they were seated on a bench in the now deserted atrium, yak-stuffed bread pockets in hand. Silence stretched on, only the sound of their munching and the water gurgling filling the air. They had both been starving. The handkerchief sat between them on the bench, mostly forgotten. She'd studied it again, but she wasn't surprised. Despite the energy that still clung to the thing, there was no particular spell present. It was as though the cloth had simply, almost naively been imbued with energy without anything to direct the magic to any real purpose.

Strange indeed. She took another bite.

He was the first to break the silence. "Can I ask you a question?"

She braced herself. "Yes?"

He glanced over her shoulder toward the library window for a moment before he spoke. "How exactly did your brother die?"

A pain stabbed at her chest, and she stopped chewing. "How did you know he used to sit there?"

He frowned. "Where? In the library window?"

She nodded. He'd glanced at the exact spot Myandrin had loved to sit and read.

"I didn't know that."

"Then why are you looking?" she demanded.

"I just—I thought I saw something. It's nothing. Would you mind talking about what happened to him?"

She sighed. "As long as you don't mind if the rainfall starts."

To her surprise, he patted her on her shoulder. "I'd never mind that."

She didn't believe him, but it was reassurance enough. But where was she to start? "You know, he always had the worst luck. There were so many accidents over the years."

Now it was his turn to stop chewing. "Really. Like what?"

She shrugged, thinking back. "He wasn't clumsy, mostly. But if something could go wrong? It usually did, and he'd get hurt. Sometimes minor cuts and bruises, sometimes not so minor. I don't know how many times he nicked himself with his own practice blade. Funny thing is, he always seemed to be trying hard *not* to. His face was always so—frustrated."

Nyalin nodded. "I know the feeling."

"You do?"

"I've had more than my fair share of clumsy accidents myself. I always suspected that was why Elix sent me to work as a scribe rather than something harder. How much trouble could I get into in a library? Paper cuts? I found a way often enough, though."

How odd.

"Maybe there's something in the water."

"Or the ink? You boys with your noses in books."

"Perhaps."

"Anyway..." She braced herself, then pushed the words out in a rush. "He was thrown from a horse. It's happened dozens of times, to tell you the truth. He... He, uh, never let it stop him, although our mother worried when she was alive. She passed when I was ten, of a lung disease we couldn't cure. But Mya... He'd broken bones, ribs—but the healers had always made it work, fixed the damage. And he couldn't be a clan leader and not ride a horse, obviously, or a yak, but you have to ride. You can imagine he didn't want to be famous for being a hermit or a coward. Anyway." She took a deep breath. "You know that bridge across Dront River?"

Those concerned eyes darkened. "Yes."

"For no reason whatsoever, his mount reared there on the side of the bridge." Her voice quavered now, but she pushed forward. "And Mya, he... he didn't just hit the ground like all those other times. He hit the side of the bridge and went over. Into the river. People saw it—but by the time anyone got him out, it was too late."

"How awful."

"It was terrible. Just a freak accident."

"I'm so sorry for your loss." Frowning, he chewed his food intently.

She watched him, letting his steady presence ease the sharpness of her grief. Breathe in, breathe out. Those clever eyes scanned the courtyard, studied his sandwich, and then... glanced over his shoulder at the same spot again.

She snapped her fingers in the air between them. "There! You just did it again! Why?"

"I told you—"

"You can't be thinking you saw something behind you."

He shrugged. "It feels like someone is watching me."

She squinted hard at the tower of windows, but there was no one there. She closed her eyes and felt.

There was something. A wisp. Something faint, and far away, but still there. She couldn't explain it, or she'd alert whoever was watching them to what she knew. She would wait for another time and tell him then.

But *why* would anyone be watching him? Or more accurately, them? They were just two young people sitting in an atrium eating sandwiches. Sure, they were nobles with illustrious parents. But that was about all either of them had going for them.

And still... someone watched.

She put down her sandwich, her chewing having slowed to a halt.

"You okay?"

"I think I just lost my appetite."

"I'm almost done. Think I need a rest."

"Here, you can have this back, since it's not telling me anything new." She handed him the handkerchief.

"Oh goodie."

"Well, I'll keep it if you're going to act like that." She snatched it back and tucked it in her pocket again. "I'll walk up with you, and you can take a nap. Or go to bed. I know my days as a young mage included a lot of early bedtimes."

He grinned. "Sounds like an exciting adventure."

"It's not. But it's worth it."

"Maybe you just like naps. You do bring them up a lot."

"How can I argue with that?"

~

The days continued in an easy pattern, morning class and afternoon tests, and two weeks passed before he could blink. The Feast of Souls came and went, which in the Bone Clan included a large roast boar and late night beer, or at least that's what Faytou foisted on him.

The classes continued to teach him little that he hadn't already learned from books, and he continued *doing* very little every time he tried. It might have been frustrating had the company been worse, but between Faytou and Lara, he didn't mind that much.

After one particularly tiring day, he ended up in his room for an early nap and was awake again before the sun had gone down. They'd all been tired and getting a little discouraged on his latest failed magic test—this one had worked when Lara fed him magic, but not Cerivil, and offered no physical proof of his own magic yet again—so Cerivil had insisted they needed a break. The clan leader was probably right, but that didn't keep Nyalin from wondering if the man would suggest an indefinite break sometime soon.

He still hadn't figured out when the clan kitchens stopped serving food, if ever, so he jogged down as soon as he'd shaken the sleep out of his eyes. He scanned the kitchens for the baker with the gray beard and bright blue eyes, as he had every day since that first day. Maybe it was paranoia, but all the hallucinations had started the day the baker had pushed that weird bread on him. He'd had a few more episodes since, but nothing like that first day. Although he also hadn't been caught by Andius's cronies since that first day either.

But even more strangely, he hadn't seen the baker again. He wasn't exactly sure what he was going to say if he ever did track the man down, but he had to *find* the man to begin with.

Once again, the bearded baker and his fallen bread weren't there. Nyalin ate his meal and then stood outside the kitchens for a quarter of an hour, watching the cooks and bakers move. It'd become a habit of late. But again, no sign of the man. Sure, the guy could have simply gotten a job in a different kitchen or part of the clan.

But Nyalin couldn't shake the feeling that something strange was going on.

Sighing, he gave up his vigil and grabbed an extra bag of mutton bites to snack on. All this lack of success at magic seemed to make him extra hungry. Hopefully these bites came without a massive side of next-world hallucinations.

Most nights, he was passing out from exhaustion right

about now. Maybe he could take advantage of his early nap to finally make it over to the Obsidian district and say hello to Grel. He strode toward the exit beyond the kitchens. If Grel wasn't available, maybe he'd say hello to Dalas... or see if the Obsidian library had any books he could "borrow." His research on several topics had stalled so far, including the strange jolts of energy from Lara's touch, his hallucinations, and the glowing eyes everyone kept mentioning to him. At least he'd found plenty about what was involved in each phase of the Bone Clan's Feasts of Contest and how to win.

Out of purely academic curiosity, of course.

Nyalin did a few laps around the kitchen, impressed by the sheer amount of food being prepared even now. From the look of it, a lot of clan members would eat their dinner late. Long days. On his last lap, he caught a glimpse of silvered hair from behind a tree, along the side wall.

It was him. The baker with his beard and bright eyes. Their eyes locked for a moment. Then the baker turned and ran.

Nyalin darted forward. "Hey! Hey, stop!"

The baker did not stop.

Fortunately for Nyalin, though, the only way out was through the front, unwalled portion of the estate. He ran at a diagonal, aiming to cut the baker off as the man ran along the wall. Nyalin followed close and leapt over a low bench and a few flower beds, trying not to damage anything. A flowerpot went spinning to the side, but he refused to look back. One ambitious jump almost sent him tumbling into a small decorative pond, but he got lucky. He usually did in these situations, and he tried not to let that make him nervous.

He had nearly reached the baker, but the man had also nearly reached the end of the walled estate. He'd be out of the grounds and much harder to catch in a heartbeat.

Nyalin jumped, diving headfirst toward the man. They tumbled together to the ground.

But that was far from the end of it. The baker put up a much better fight than Nyalin expected for an older fellow, throwing Nyalin off his back and rolling away. The man staggered to his feet, but so did Nyalin, who lunged at him and tackled him against the last few feet of wall.

"Who are you?" Nyalin spat, dodging as the man tried to grip him for a push or a throw. "And what did you put in that bread?" He shoved an elbow at the man's throat instead, and the baker stilled.

Oddly, there wasn't exactly fear or alarm in the man's eyes, just a slight twitch of his eyebrows. It was hardly conclusive evidence, but Nyalin's gut instinct said the man was actually surprised.

"Didn't put anything in the bread other than not enough flour. I think." Panting, the man frowned at him. "I don't know. If I knew what made it fall, I wouldn't have done it, don't you think?"

"Why did you run away from me?"

"I typically run from people who chase me."

Nyalin frowned. Had he caused all this mess? "No. You were already getting out of here before I saw you. C'mon. You put something *else* in there. Or was it the eggs?"

The baker shook his head but stared at Nyalin intently. "Why do you think so?"

"Because—" he started. But did he want this man, this potential enemy, knowing his secrets? Nyalin shook his head. "Why were you running then? And who *are* you?"

Lips pursing as he frowned, the man scrutinized Nyalin for one long second more. Then, face set in hard decision, he straightened a little. "Release me and I'll explain."

Nyalin hesitated. But what other option did he really have? He wasn't going to brutalize the answers out of the man. This already felt uncomfortably close to Raelt's territory. But he needed to know how he'd been drugged, and why, and by whom. He dropped his hands to his sides.

The baker brushed himself off in an eerily familiar gesture, and Nyalin wondered if that was what he looked like when he did it. Glancing around them and seeing no one, the baker met Nyalin's eyes and then clapped once.

Nyalin's mouth fell open. The sounds of the birds in Cerivil's trees dampened, then faded to silence. The people walking by on the street were moving, but he could no longer hear the calls, the footsteps, the animals.

A silence spell. The baker was a *mage*?

When he glanced back from the road, the baker and his thick white beard were gone. Someone else stood in his place.

The emperor was straightening his tunic. He looked up and grinned.

Bowing wouldn't be low enough. Nyalin threw himself down and pressed his head to the earth. "Emperor Pavan!" Holy Twins, by Seluvae's dark and Dala's light, he was going to be thrown in a dungeon. Did the emperor have a dungeon? No, the sea. No, to the Mushin, to be eaten alive—

"It's all right, Nyalin. Rise. You don't need to bow to me."

"I most certainly do," he said, unmoving.

"I surprised you. And your mother served this nation dutifully and deserved a station as high as any noble." The emperor's voice was a strange mix of warm and stern that Nyalin didn't understand.

"I think bowing is still in order for tackling you and throwing you against this wall."

Pavan chuckled softly. "Consider it forgiven. I am glad

you are looking out for your life and your sanity, even if they were never in danger from me. Please, Nyalin. Rise. We don't have much time."

Frowning, he climbed to his feet. "Pardon my question, Emperor, but—why are you posing as a baker in the Bone Clan's kitchens?"

Pavan smiled. "Why, to keep an eye on you, of course."

"On me. Surely you're joking."

"I am quite serious."

"But *why*?"

"Because your—"

"Don't give me that 'your mother was so special to me' crap. It was twenty years ago."

"Heard that a few times?" Pavan's smile only broadened, laughter lighting his eyes in a way Nyalin had never seen. "If you already know the reason, I won't repeat it."

"I don't believe that's your reason."

"Well, as emperor, I believe I'm allowed to direct the conversation. So... why do you think there was something in your bread?"

Nyalin's frown deepened. "Did you actually make that?"

"Did you think the professional bakers made such failures?" Pavan grinned.

He snorted in response. "No, but—"

"Why did you think I poisoned your bread?"

He bit the inside of his cheek. He definitely wouldn't have told a shifty baker, but his emperor? "I've been... kind of... I don't know. Seeing things?"

"What kind of things?" Pavan leaned forward, his eyes narrowing like a hawk diving at its prey.

He coughed. "People."

Pavan frowned, then glanced at the quiet people in the

street, who were ignoring them, then back to Nyalin. "Care to be more specific?"

"Fine. *Dead* people," Nyalin amended. "At least, I think. No, it can't be real. I must be hallucinating."

Pavan was shaking his head.

"How can you be so sure?"

The emperor's face had sobered now. "Because your mother saw them too."

Well. He hadn't expected *that*. "She did?"

"She did."

"No one ever told me that."

"She didn't tell most people that."

"She saw them... how, exactly?"

"In a trance, usually. Sometimes in her sleep. Sometimes... just any old time. Those weren't common days, though."

Nyalin's eyes widened. "How has no one mentioned this to me before?"

Pavan grinned. "I told you she was special to me. Wait, actually, no I didn't, because you wouldn't let me."

He'd heard that line enough times that it had started to lose meaning, and now suddenly he'd found someone for whom it was really true. There was a light, a distance in Pavan's blue eyes as he spoke of his mother, an expression Nyalin didn't think could be faked. At the very least, that smile and those warm eyes were brimming with affection. He shouldn't be surprised, but he was.

Pavan ducked his head now. "Clearly we need to talk more." Straightening, the emperor patted him on the shoulder and glanced at the street again. "But this is hardly the place. Why don't you and I meet? Tomorrow morning? We can take a walk in the park by the river, away from prying eyes."

"As if I don't have enough problems fitting in with these

people without taking special walks alone with the emperor." He kicked at the dirt and dust on the ground, and when he glanced back up, there was the bearded baker again.

"It won't be with the emperor. Just a new friend from the Bone Clan."

"That's... You're quite good at that."

"I know. Transformation is my best spell."

It was also one of the hardest to master. Some argued that the only thing harder was transforming into something from the plant and animal spheres, humans being slightly more familiar. But Nyalin was not so sure. There were plenty of difficult third-level spells, and most swordmages only grasped one in their lifetimes. His mother had mastered at least three, which was part of what had made her exceptional. Nyalin shut his mouth, which had been hanging open of its own accord. "I—I have class in the morning. Working with Cerivil and Lara in the afternoon."

"At lunchtime then."

"All right. Noon."

Emperor Pavan grinned. "Meet me at the Aoelin Shrine. See you then. Now—if I try to leave, are you going to tackle me again? Good show, by the way."

Numbly, Nyalin shook his head.

"All right then. Until tomorrow." And then he clapped again, and the world flooded with sudden sound. Before Nyalin had recovered from the wave of sensation flooding him, Pavan was turning the corner of the wall and was gone.

Chapter 7

Wild

Lara woke again before morning. The manor and the city were quiet. The black sky outside hung close and warm, like the inside of a cloak.

Yes. Today. Today she would do it. She'd waited long enough.

She rose and dressed in the plainest crossover she had, a faded walnut brown one that matched the dark cloak she tied around her shoulders. She tied the market bag to her belt, as she had the fateful day she'd stolen the thing.

She had gathered a few supplies the day before, and she shouldered them now and slipped out into the hallway. The manor was still quiet under the dark blanket of night.

She would miss the morning's class. But if she rode hard, maybe she could be back by the afternoon for Nyalin's daily lesson. It all depended on how far out she planned to go. Other than that, she shouldn't really be missed.

She would find somewhere desolate to dig her hole. And then no one would know what she'd done.

The sun was beginning to bring a blush to the sky as her horse's hooves pounded down the packed-earth streets. The merchant stalls were still empty, although a few stirred inside, preparing to open for the day.

The city slept. Except for her.

She took the direct route, the bridge across the Elzindor to the Yarow Gate, and headed for the desert.

The blade rested against her hip, tied high and secure so as not to bounce or attract attention. To her surprise, it—and the Bone Dragon—said nothing.

~

The next day's class for Nyalin was far more boring, in part because the students were studying a sand-shaping spell and in part because Lara didn't show up for it. He doubted she needed practice at the simple spell, so he couldn't blame her, but something about her unannounced absence bothered him.

Cerivil discretely gave him a Shape Sand charm—a sandstone one, ironically enough, gritty and cold under his fingers—and so he made his attempts to practice. He imagined the ambient magic gathering at his core, floating into the charm clenched in his fist, and blowing out like a gust of wind to swirl at the dust.

No sand moved across the boards before him. No deluge opened out of the sky.

Between attempts, he wondered where Lara might be. Certainly she must have other responsibilities, other things to do than to tend to him. He was lucky he'd gotten so much of her attention, especially since she's also been attending his afternoon sessions.

He yawned and stretched and leaned back on his fists behind him. Without her he felt... bored.

He missed her, in fact.

Before he could ponder that thought much further, Faytou strode up and plopped down beside him. "How goes it?"

Great. Another heart he had to break. “It doesn’t.” Nyalin shrugged.

“Check this out.” Grinning, Faytou proceeded to hold one hand in the air, palm facing the ground. With the other, he spun his finger like he was winding thread around it. In the space between his hands, sand gathered, even the poor neglected sand scattered in front of Nyalin, and in a matter of seconds it had formed a tiny dragon, its particles shifting and tiny but undeniably there.

“Wow.” He leaned forward to get a better look. “You’ll have to teach me this one. Some day.”

“Glowy-eye trick first.”

“I still have to figure out that trick.” Or any trick, for that matter.

“Still working on waking it up?” the boy asked, cocking his head. The dragon spun and twisted but remained, even as Faytou ignored the spell. He was talented, that was for sure.

“Something like that. It’s sort of… Let’s just say sometimes it wants to play and sometimes it doesn’t and we’re not sure what’s causing what.”

“Ah,” said Faytou, as if that were perfectly normal.

Nyalin didn’t really want to go further into it. Or risk folks like Andius, who was clearly watching out of the corner of his eye, overhearing too many of his weaknesses. “So, will you fight in the Contests this year?”

The boy shrugged. “Doesn’t seem to be much point, does there?”

“I have no idea.”

“Well, you see, my brother has been second to… well, second place for eight years in a row now. Since he started competing.” Faytou’s face fell a bit before he forced a perky grin back on it. Curious. The boy didn’t want to name the deceased heir? Everyone was having a hard time forgetting Lara's brother—they talked about him all the time—yet Nyalin had never caught the young man's actual name. "I don't know if there's much point to it now."

"Why not?"

"Well, I certainly won't win, and there's a good chance I'll get beaten as purple as a grape, so... not sure the risk is worth the reward."

"Beaten purple, eh? How exactly does that happen?"

And that was how Nyalin found himself deep in a discussion about the intricacies of the Contests: the tests in each sphere of magic, the obstacle course, the fights. It was a relief, both because he'd begun wondering and because it was far more interesting than yet another failed Shape Sand attempt.

If they hadn't had an audience, he'd have taken notes.

Lara was panting by the time she'd won a hole the size of her head in the rocky terrain. Clearly there was a reason no one was farming here: soil quality. While that meant no farmer would plow up the precious blade, it didn't make her work any easier.

How deep was it necessary to bury a secret? One foot? Two? Did the size of the secret matter? Did you measure it in physical size, or in its ability to destroy your life?

The Bone Dragon hadn't uttered so much as a growl the whole morning. Dala's light, it was strange. Strange enough she felt almost called to address the dragon herself. But what would she say? She didn't care to apologize.

Was... was Yeska pouting? Was it possible for a dragon to pout?

Perhaps she had now withdrawn her power, as she had

for clan leaders before her. No—she wasn't a clan leader. Just an interim carrier, a guide. A mistake. But Yeska must know of her plans to bury the blade here. And the dragon certainly couldn't approve.

Why didn't she object?

Lara's panting had eased and now she just listened as she surveyed the slopes around her. The silence was deafening. Oh, the wind blew, and children were playing—and shrieking—far in the village below. But there were no words, no laughter.

A rock clattered down the hillside. She'd chosen a stand of trees and brush as her final resting place for the clanblade, and the brush blocked her view of the rock—or whatever had caused it to go rolling down.

Whatever or whoever.

She jumped back just in time as a man leapt into the air she'd so recently occupied. He tumbled to the ground and rolled, crying out as his back slammed into the tree behind the hole she'd dug.

But he wasn't alone. She scampered back, brandishing the shovel, as two more men loomed around the other side of the brush. Their eyes narrowed, suspicious. Appraising.

"What're you doin' up here, woman?" said one, while the other helped up the leaping fool.

"I could ask the same of you," she said back.

"Those boots don't belong out here. What do you think?" he said to his companion, who nodded.

Hell. She could dress down all she wanted, but her boots were too fine, too clean, and probably too flimsy to belong out here. She didn't exactly keep beaten boots around for this purpose.

"These're not your lands."

She pressed her lips together in a thin line to hold in the retort that *all* the lands were hers, that all the lands belonged to the family of the clan leader.

Especially when the clan leader is you.

Oh, now you decide to speak up? Lara struggled not to groan aloud.

And fail to point that out? I couldn't resist.

"Just digging for roots," she said, aiming for demure. Nonthreatening. It wasn't her strong suit.

If you want to be nonthreatening, you should put down the shovel.

Do you think so?

No, I think you should draw me and have at them.

I didn't come out here to attack simple farmers.

What about bandits?

Lara's brow furrowed as she realized the men hadn't answered. They were exchanging glances. Planning something. Lara knew this was a terrible spot to dig for roots, but she could think of no other excuse. But the men weren't pointing that out. She eyed their clothes... Leather, mostly. One had a good button at the wrist.

They're not farmers? she asked Yeska.

No. They are not.

"Leave me be," she said, tightening her grip on the shovel and redrawing their gaze. "I haven't got anything worth taking." Except a sacred and powerful magical sword. Other than that.

They all narrowed their eyes. "What's in that market bag at your belt then?" The last one pointed. They glanced at each other again, and the first one took a step forward.

She hardened her gaze, slowed her breath. She had few charms useful for this sort of thing, and although she had plenty of martial practice, it'd still be three to one. She'd rather scare them away with magic. If she could.

She straightened from her fighting stance even as one ventured a few steps closer. She moved the shovel to one hand and held up a palm.

Light flashed out, white and hot, a brilliant blur. The men staggered back, gasping. She held the light for a moment longer, brightened it a little further, then let it drop.

Cursing now, the men exchanged looks again.

"A mage," one whispered.

"I bet she's a bladed woman," another snapped.

"I'm not—" she started.

Is that technically true? Yeska put in. *You are a woman. You have a blade.*

You are not helping.

They glowered at her now.

"Let's take that magic from her," the third whispered. And they charged.

Well, that had worked well. Instead of frightening them off, she'd incensed them. Excellent.

She dropped her grip lower on the shovel and spun, swinging it in a wide circle around her as the first neared. The broad metal base slammed flat into his side, hard. As this man had been the overzealous tree leaper, his back was already in bad shape, making the second blow to the torso more devastating. He lost his balance along with a variety of curses, and this time his tumble sent him rolling down the hill.

The other two, though, seized the opening to lurch for both of her arms. She caught one of them on the upswing with her weapon, hacking at the knee and then scraping it up his side. She was inches from slamming it into his armpit when the third man clamped down hard on her other shoulder and startled her into losing her grip. The shovel twisted and slipped.

She staggered and fell, the third man's heavy frame falling on top of her. One of his hands still gripped her shoulder, the other groped at her neck. She drove a punch into his gut. His eyes bulged, but his grip didn't falter.

She grappled for leverage, bucking and twisting, but whether because of bad luck or the man's skill, she got no traction. Seconds later, the second bandit had recovered enough to pile on.

Her mind raced for some magical solution. Palm Flash was just for show. Perhaps she could blind them again briefly, but she'd need more than that to truly get away, and without a blade to power herself, she couldn't invoke any of the more powerful spells. Float Water would do nothing but drench them. She'd never been great with Ignite—she was liable to set herself on fire right along with them, and it was a small area anyway.

Although perhaps setting them both on fire would be preferable to whatever *they* had planned.

She continued sorting through her mental list of spells as she kicked, scratched. One hand closed over her mouth, and she bit. Hard. The second man cried out and backed off just a moment.

Small Animals—no, it was too new, she wasn't good at it, and it'd take too much time. Throw Sound might distract them, but who knew if it'd be loud enough for them to hear it? Shape Sand—yes. Yes!

She squeezed her eyes shut as she cast it, flinging nearby dust and dirt into their eyes. One cursed. The other spat it back at her, making her gag.

Perhaps Cast Shadow would frighten them? Darkness looming from above. Yes, but first, more sand.

She gave two or three good throws, her own eyes still squeezed shut, and they backed off a little and were cursing at her like she *had* set them on fire, when a large shadow loomed overhead. It was dark enough she could see it through her eyelids. But… she hadn't cast the spell yet. She hadn't—

A familiar peal of deep, slow laughter rolled around in her mind like rocks in a tumbler.

She scampered back on her butt, brushed as much dust and other nonsense as she could from her face, and squinted up.

A huge gust of wind blew more of the dust away, along with several chunks of hair. The gusts came regular as wing beats, throwing both wind and fear in their midst. Regular as wing beats because they *were* wing beats.

Both she and the men goggled at the creature that slowed and landed with a powerful thud next to the stand of trees.

She was the height of three or four men. Maybe more. Plates and spines stood out in all directions, but especially in a bony ridge along her back. Purple-gray eyes under bony ridges scowled at them all, a low growl emanating from her throat.

"Yeska!" Lara breathed.

The men had no such greeting, nor did they need any further display of power from the Bone Dragon. They rushed so quickly to escape they ran into each other and tumbled end over end down the rocky terrain. She was too stunned to enjoy watching them grunting as rocks hit them in the ass. Mostly.

Not enough of a punishment, if you ask me. Yeska looked blandly down the hill and then swung in Lara's direction. The dragon's head alone was easily the height of Lara's torso, and the spikes on her cheeks flayed out just as wide.

"Thank you," Lara hurried to say.

Yeska's head reared back, as if she were surprised. *Do you still wish to be rid of me?*

Lara hesitated. "No... But you don't wish to be rid of *me*, now?"

No.

Shaking a little still, Lara managed to stagger to her feet. "All right then. What do we do now?"

Either you finish burying the dagger, or you come with me.

"Where?"

You'll see.

"What about my horse?"

I'll carry him.

Her eyes widened. "And give him a heart attack?"

Tie him off here then, and we'll come back. But I can't promise those bandits won't come back and steal him.

"Or worse," Lara muttered. "Fine. Give me a second." She dashed back to where she'd left her things, pulled the cloak back over her shoulders, ignored the stupid shovel she never wanted to see again, and picked up her pack. If she had a blade, she'd have learned spells to talk to the horse. Or at least calm it. But it wasn't to be. Instead, she straightened. "Okay. What now?"

Pardon my eavesdropping but... you do *have a blade.*

Lara blinked. "Oh. I suppose you're right."

As usual.

"You're not too humble, that's for sure. What do you want me to do?"

Humility is for humans, Yeska said. *Climb on.*

~

After class, Nyalin brushed himself off and took a rather scenic route through the city to the park, then wound through several manicured flowered areas until he reached the open grassy area by the broad, dark water. Just a few hundred feet upriver, the Aoelin Shrine waited.

He walked along the paths lined with bloodred and dark purple flowers that were nearly as tall as he was, their petals as large as his head. The flower-lined paths carried him nearly the whole way to the shrine, their scent surprising and sweet.

He almost missed the roundhouse kick while admiring the stupid things.

Almost. He ducked and spun in the same motion, straightening to find the emperor behind him, knees bent, poised to fight. What, did he have a sign on his back asking people to attack him? If so, Raelt had put it there.

"I thought you said walk."

"I did? I must have misspoken. I meant fight."

Pavan launched a flurry of punches, and Nyalin blocked and dodged as best he could. More than once he danced back a few feet, scattering a cloud of dust along the path.

"Not bad. But you don't take the offensive—"

"That's because you're, well, you know, and—"

Pavan's eyes twinkled. "It's not just because of that. And I'm not talking about just this fight."

To prove he would take the lesson to heart, and maybe because he was a little obstinate, Nyalin launched his own roundhouse kick at Pavan's head.

Pavan ducked with a squat and a grin.

"I tackled you just yesterday, didn't I?"

Pavan's assault resumed. "You did."

"And chased you down," Nyalin added, throwing in a half-hearted punch to the sternum.

When his fingers made contact, Pavan froze and stared down at the fist as if horrified, shocked, and offended, straightening.

"I'm sorry, I—"

Pavan smirked. "Got you there."

Nyalin straightened too, dropping his fists to his sides. "You're enjoying this."

Pavan shrugged. "Maybe a little. It's not often people find out about one of my disguises."

He raised an eyebrow. "How many do you have?"

The emperor's already broad grin widened. "A few. But we did not come here to talk about me. We came here to talk about dead people."

"My hallucinations."

"I was thinking of your mother. But yes, we should talk about what you've been seeing too." The emperor glanced around them. The shrine was thoroughly empty, but he gestured toward the gently flowing river. "Come, walk with me."

"Of course." If it hadn't been an order from his sovereign, he'd have done it anyway. Rabid wolves couldn't drag him away. He had so many questions, and too many answers were locked behind iron, barred doors.

They set an easy pace. The river burbled beside them, calm and quiet, and birds flitted overhead.

"I grew up alone, you know," Pavan began. "So did your mother. We had that in common. I was in the orphanage in Tiro. There were people providing a roof overhead, sort of, but little food. We slept on the floor. Some of the older children took to raising up young ones, or we'd probably all have just starved. I helped in my turn as I grew. It taught me how much people truly depend on each other, and how to go from being alone to building something more. But Linali didn't have any of that. She was truly alone."

Nyalin caught his breath at the sound of her name. People never said it. They always said, "your mother." Or if they did use her name, they uttered it with unearthly reverence, like they'd praise Dala. Not with the warmth for someone truly remembered. And clearly the emperor remembered her—and fondly. But who didn't? Nyalin stifled a flash of guilt at the thought.

"What do you mean, alone?" he said instead, as Pavan seemed to be waiting before moving on.

"She was wild. Living with animals. Simple language. Clothing she made herself."

"How could a child possibly survive?"

"The animals helped. And so did the spirits."

"Animals? And did you say spirits?"

"Yes. The animals—she perfected a spell that let her speak with a variety of gentler creatures, or sometimes she just broadcast her need to them instinctively, but yes. She was never sure if it had also been that way when she was a baby or if there had been a time where she had a mother. She always assumed others had come before, but we never knew what happened to them. And yes, there were spirits. Ghosts. Whatever you like to call them. The dead."

"So that's who I'm seeing. I'm not going insane?"

"They are very real."

"The whole series of planes story. It's real?"

"As real as you and me."

"By Seluvae." Nyalin stared across the water and the gardens to the black rooftops of the city beyond.

"What she had was an extremely unique ability. Beyond all the magic you've heard about, it was this ability that made her so strange, so memorable. So powerful."

He frowned. "What was it?"

"She could cross the veil between planes. She could remain alive and exist on both sides, at least mentally. Sometimes physically."

"Both sides? I thought the whole series meant there were

many worlds. Is it possible to go beyond just one world, one afterlife?"

"She was never sure, never had time to try. But I think so. I think she could have made it to others, but our next world was the easiest. I don't see why it couldn't work. But she had enough on her hands dealing with one extra world on top of this one."

Nyalin ran a hand through his hair. "That's amazing."

"Yes. It was. And it is."

"Wait—you're saying that's what I'm doing?"

"Describe it for me."

Nyalin recapped the flickering, the nausea, the greenish earth. The floating. It *had* felt like being in two places at once, he had to admit that. And what had Myandrin said? Both yes and no. Both alive and dead.

Pavan nodded. "It seems the same to me."

"Who can help me?" Nyalin asked quickly.

"No one."

"Well, how did she learn to control it?"

"I'm not sure she *did* control it, honestly. She wanted to, but it didn't always happen at the best time." For a moment, he could see some distant scene replaying in the emperor's eyes, and he wanted desperately for the man to recount it all, detail by detail. But then—Pavan would have already if he truly wanted to. He mustn't wish to if he wasn't already sharing it. "She had no teachers, except the spirits themselves."

Nyalin glanced down at his boots. Well then. He was so concerned about teaching, and his brilliant mother had taught everything to herself.

"She didn't have any choice. She was *alone*, remember?"

"I've been alone," Nyalin muttered. "What about you? How did you learn?"

"I don't know how to contact the world of the dead. But ultimately I ran away from the orphanage and met a mage on the road who taught me a few things. And how to reach the city. Learned much of the rest here, during the war. And from Linali."

"She taught you even though she taught herself?"

"How do you think I got so good at the animal sphere?" He smiled broadly. "Speaking of teaching, how is your learning going?"

"Nowhere yet, but it's only been a couple weeks. It's unpredictable."

"I hope you don't mind I accepted Cerivil's proposition without your input."

Nyalin shrugged. "Beggars can't be choosers."

"But it was what you wanted?"

"Oh, yes." Nyalin nodded. "I mean, I approached him. I thought his loyalty to my mother might help."

"Indeed. He was always a good friend to her."

"Were they..." Nyalin started, suddenly wondering if an answer might be at his fingertips after all. "Did they..."

"Were they in love?" The words rolled off Pavan's tongue as though they tasted bitter, tinged with longing. "No. He was always too wise for her, ultimately. And I believe he was already in love with his future wife."

"Too wise?"

"Her manner of growing up... Let's just say it encouraged risk taking. Boldness. Fearlessness. And a little oddness, I guess you could say? Eccentricity."

"Cerivil is taking a risk on me," Nyalin mused.

"No, he's not." Pavan shook his head. "If he gets what he wants, his clan will rise in power. It already has, just with you joining them."

"I know."

"That's politics. But if he doesn't get what he wants?"

Nyalin shrugged. "He doesn't lose anything but time."

"Exactly. And that is something he has enough of. And he doesn't lose the initial boost. He won't need to save face if he plays his cards right."

"Should I tell him about the... the spirits? Did she mention her ability to him?"

"Doubtful," Pavan said. "But only he would know for sure."

"But she shared it with you."

"Yes. Well, I witnessed it incapacitate her at some... inopportune times. I suppose she felt obligated to explain."

"Such as?" He *had* to get more specifics out of this man. No one ever talked specifics.

The emperor grinned. "Perhaps I'll tell you more on our next walk."

Nyalin raised an eyebrow. "Next?"

"Have I bored you dreadfully?"

"No, no, not at all. I just don't want to waste your time, and—"

"And there are other things about Linali you may need to know. It's time I shared them. Let's meet again in a fortnight. Same place and time."

"All right." Was he about to be dismissed? If he had any questions, he needed to ask them now.

"Was Cerivil the only reason you picked the Bone Clan to approach?" Pavan said, surprising him.

"I—uh." Lying to his emperor seemed like a bad idea. But the truth...

Pavan stopped and gripped both of Nyalin's shoulders warmly. "If it's a woman, I say it's worth taking chances."

His eyes widened. "No—uh—well, maybe—"

"Love is worth going after, Nyalin."

He managed to regain the ability to speak. "That's an odd thing for a bachelor ruler to say."

Pavan's smile widened, but then softened with a sadness that stabbed Nyalin's heart. "Is it?"

"I think so."

"Perhaps I know the value of love better than anyone."

~

Unira tapped a fingernail on the glass a few times. It clinked lightly. Wind whistled and moaned through her family's private catacombs beneath the estate. Well, Giran's family's catacombs, or they had been at one time. She'd long ago burned what was left of the bodies and turned the ashes into the compost heap. Or maybe the dogs had the bones, who knew. What did it matter? The soul went on, once the body was vacated.

She had bodies with souls still in them, living bodies, and storing them was no simple feat. What was she supposed to do, build a bigger closet? Add them to the wine cellar? Oh, no. She needed somewhere special to store *these* bodies. Somewhere where she could tap their power.

And where her father wouldn't know that she had them.

She tapped gently at the glass again and studied the black-haired woman in the chamber.

"Can't you at least go gray?" she murmured. "Just a little?"

But she never did. The woman was frozen in time.

Unira pursed her lips. Her own hair had been peppered with gray for a few years now. In truth, she liked it. It made her feel distinguished and wise. And she was.

But it didn't help that this was just one more way that Linali was perfect. Too perfect.

"I'm going to kill him, you know. I'm going to kill your son."

She shouldn't talk to the woman. Shouldn't taunt her. She had no indication that her long-time rival could even hear her. She had snared many mages into similar traps, but she'd almost never released them, certainly not while they were still alive, so she didn't exactly understand how the spell worked or if Linali was conscious in there. But it was so hard to resist taunting her.

"I know I've said that before. But he finds new ways to put himself in the way. I'm going to the city myself this time. I'm sick of the failures. I'll stab the dagger and drink the blood myself if I must. Your blood would make a potent ingredient in the cauldron, don't you think?"

She stepped closer to the head of the chamber. Bent down as if to speak right in her ear. As she whispered, her breath fogged the glass. "I'm going to end this, and I'm going to enjoy it. Now I have *real* help. And there's not a thing you can do about it."

Straightening, she stalked out, headed to the surface.

Chapter 8

Vindictive

Nothing worked. Nyalin and Cerivil spent three long hours in the breezy meeting rooms, taking all sorts of toys and equipment off the shelves, fooling with them, putting them back.

None of it made a difference. Nothing burst into flame or was doused with water or any such thing. Even with a practice blade, even with Cerivil's help.

He readied himself for one more try. He imagined the magic coming from his core, then added in all the magic around them. Every last ambient drop. Then he could see it move, like a ball of white light, from him through the charm to the wood shavings, sparks flying, and...

And nothing.

Cerivil made a valiant effort to remain encouraging, but Nyalin could see through it. Their puzzlement grew by the hour, and their frustration by the day.

"Why would it work when Lara is here, but not when she isn't?" Nyalin muttered, mostly to himself.

Never mind the bit of aching worry, the concern that she was not yet here. Wasn't coming, it seemed. Had found something better to do? With someone who wasn't so much of a failure?

She had been nothing but obsessively positive while he'd been around, at least verbally. Perhaps now he knew her true feelings.

"Let's break now," Cerivil said, finally admitting defeat. He sank into a sturdy chair and picked up a nearby whittling knife and stick, tinkering away as he spoke. "You've tried well. Labored valiantly. Hard work."

"But no results," he said, acknowledging the obvious.

Cerivil shrugged. "I don't understand it. Lara's presence shouldn't influence anything. And I know she wouldn't just lie about it. Would she?" Cerivil stopped and gazed at the ceiling thoughtfully, as if he'd decided maybe she would. His fingers continued to work.

"No, of course not. Why would she do that? Seems cruel to get my hopes up, and for what?"

"Cruel is definitely not her style, especially for no real gain. But on the other hand..."

"She can't be lying," he insisted. "Maybe it was a coincidence. Something different about that day or how rested I was or something." Today had been harder than most, although he didn't truly think that figured in. "Where is Lara, by the way?"

"I'm not sure," Cerivil said, frowning. "But she's... she's been taking Myandrin's death hard."

Nyalin froze at the name. He could see them now, almost overlaid as they had been the day before, the wild light hair, the similar eyes. It *was* her brother in the afterworld.

He had to tell her. But how? How in a way that she would actually believe him and not think he was crazy? That was a tall order. He needed some kind of evidence, some kind of proof that the afterworld was real, not just a claim he was making. Could he bring something back? Or take her there? Let her see her beloved brother from time to time?

He had *so* much research to do.

Cerivil was still talking, so Nyalin struggled to catch up.

"She's been coming and going as she pleases, and sometimes staying in bed all day. And all night. Wandering the gardens."

"She's lost not just a brother, but also a purpose," Nyalin murmured. "A future."

Cerivil winced. "It's too true. But I do hope she can still have a happy future, even if it isn't the one she wanted or planned. And who knows, in a year or ten, or when children are grown, perhaps she can come back to those dreams."

"Sounds optimistic," Nyalin replied.

"What other option do we have?"

Nyalin shrugged in reply. "Thank you for teaching me today and working with me like this. I can't begin to repay you."

"It will all work out in the end," Cerivil assured him. "We'll figure this out."

"When you see Lara for me, give her my regards, will you?" He sincerely hoped it wasn't sadness that had kept her away. It left him feeling like a self-centered jerk for thinking she'd decided he just wasn't worth her time. It was easy to forget the pain of others when his own problems clouded his mind.

He left Cerivil reading a book on his lounge and headed to find some food. One disadvantage of lunchtime walks with the emperor was that they appeared to include no actual lunch. He'd have to bring something to eat on the walk next time.

On a whim, he asked a woman carrying piles of linens where Lara's room was. It was close, so he stopped and knocked once on the pale wood door. My, she made him bold. But his boldness was wasted, as there was no answer.

Either she was too sad to even get up, or she wasn't there. Whichever it was, he had a bad feeling about it.

~

The horse was unhappy about the ordeal, but not as unhappy as Lara would have expected.

Yeska carried them out over the low mountains and across the steppe. While the height made her heart pound, she couldn't deny the view was stunning. They spiraled down to a stand of trees nestled between two craggy cliffs. The rough rock jutted out from a low mountain—brown, austere, and still quite beautiful. Yeska landed on a rocky outcropping. The entrance to a small cave yawned into the mountain. Water rushed somewhere close by, and cold, humid wind blew past her.

Yeska tucked her wings against her side—and close around Lara—before scooting through the cave entrance. A much larger inner cavern opened up inside. It was here that she dipped her wing and indicated Lara should slide down.

"Is this your home?" she breathed.

Yes. Come. This way.

Lara followed the dragon deeper into the cave. The stone was chipping and flaking, and at times her feet slid against the wet, slick stone. She finally discovered the source of the water when they followed a smaller, narrower tunnel to a new cavern filled with a small, pleasant pool.

And at the other end of the cavern roared a waterfall.

The roof of the cavern was more than four stories high, much larger than Yeska herself, and the air was misty and warm. Sunlight trickled in from somewhere far above the falls. Ferns and other foliage peeked out from behind rocks in the cavern, but rocks dominated. Lara simply marveled at it for a while.

It is a very unlikely spot, isn't it?

"It's beautiful. Amazing, truly."

Sit and rest. I must rest also. I am not used to carrying horses.

You didn't seem to have a problem picking him up. The horse was recovering its sanity, at least, near the entrance to the cave.

I'm used to picking up sheep and other animals of similar size. But then I am also used to eating them.

Lara snickered. *That would be hard to explain to the stable master.*

Don't worry. Horses are not my preference. Too much other utility.

Ah. Of course.

Lara did her best to make herself comfortable, trying out a dozen different rock and wall combinations till she found the least painful one. Her butt was still pretty unhappy with the arrangement.

It was strange to spend time near the dragon like this. It was... almost peaceful. Yeska's breath was loud enough to be heard over the waterfall's roar, and her spines rose and sank with each inhale. She'd shut her eyes for a moment too. If the Bone Dragon was that exhausted from the flight, that was a little alarming. It hadn't *seemed* that long of a flight. Hopefully the dragon was all right. She'd never forgive herself if she'd overworked a sick dragon. Especially one who had been as kind and patient with her as Yeska had been, and one who had saved her from bandits.

One eyelid cracked open, the purple-gray iris peeking out.

Lara cleared her throat. She owed Yeska an apology, and a rest stop was as good a time as any, wasn't it? "Listen, I never thought simply touching the blade would bind me to you. Why doesn't everyone just steal it once it's been relinquished?"

Because that's not how it works.

Lara frowned. "How does it work then?"

A small touch is required, but my preference and acceptance are what truly matters.

"You mean... you picked me?"

I preferred you. I prefer you. You gave me the chance to change my future. My destiny.

"And I thought I was the only one taking my fate into my own hands."

This is why we are a good match. A good team. We don't give up. We fight. We will fight. Together. She blew out two puffs of steam from her nose.

Lara blinked. "I'm sorry I doubted you. And regretted taking it. And tried to bury your soul in a hole in the middle of nowhere."

The bones rattled in something like a shrug. *Some growing pains are to be expected. Not all crowns are easy to don. Not all blades are easy to brandish.*

She looked at the blade in her lap. But that was just it. This blade *was* easy to brandish. It fit her.

That is somewhat the illusion of the imprinting spell, to be honest with you. All clan leaders feel this way.

"Do they all feel like they have something in common with their dragons?"

No. They often don't.

"Ah." She ran her hand along the hilt, thinking. "So... why pick me? If you have shut yourself off from the clan anyway, what's another fool clan leader?"

I do not want *to be shut off from the clan. Cerivil had his moments in which I supported him. Myandrin would have been a great clan leader.*

"I know. Thank you for using his name."

You're welcome. But you will be better.

"I won't be at all. They'll never let me."

The dragon let out a low growl but did not disagree. *I have been thinking on the matter.*

"What did you conclude?"

Nothing yet. I am still thinking.

"No solution is obvious to me."

I agree. It should be that I show my support of you, and they bend to my will. But I fear the withdrawal of my power has diminished my influence with them.

"I'm sorry."

It is not your fault. We have all made our choices.

"My father has often wished I were a boy."

The dragon blew out another pair of twin puffs again, but this time they smacked vaguely of disgust. *The pressures of fools.*

"What?"

To be a woman is good. You should be what you were born to be, what your soul is. Do not change for them, only change for yourself. They are the ones who are wrong.

"But the world is the way it is. We can't change that."

True. But you will give life. You have a privilege they do not understand. I think they envy.

Lara highly doubted that was the case but said nothing. Most men were probably glad not to deal with the pain, the fear, the risk of childbirth, not to mention all that came after. But she hadn't been close to many women who'd borne babies, let alone been privy to their private envies and successes. She only knew that for her, now, a husband meant Andius, and that was a terrifying thought.

"Do you have any children? Dragonlings? Whelps? What are they called?" she asked instead of all that.

I am not yet old enough.

"But—" She searched her mind for the clan's history. "You must be at least three hundred years old."

Yes. I am similar to... a teenager? My time is coming close. But not yet.

"Wow. I... I see."

I have not answered your question. As to why I picked you.

"Oh. Well, tell me, if you care to. I would be curious to know."

You are something different. We need something different. To fight what is coming.

She frowned. "What is coming?"

I can't see it clearly yet. But it is dark. And it has recently intensified. Entered the realm. We will be prepared. That is why I wanted to bring you here. Because we must settle our differences so we can prepare.

"Prepare how?"

You have been dodging this knowledge, but you have a blade now. Perhaps you notice it in your lap.

She took a deep breath. "Yes, I suppose you're right. But no one knows. Bladed women are known. And infamous." She wouldn't have minded being infamous, but they would never let her keep it.

You would have become one of them, the bladed women, given the chance?

"Well. Yes."

Well, I gave you the chance.

She snorted. There was no arguing with that.

You must gain access to higher spells.

"You mean the charms."

That is important, yes. But you must practice them too.

Lara nodded. It was a good idea. And what she would have wanted anyway. "I'm not sure what charms I will be able to find. And I'll probably have to steal them and hide them, because how can I explain that?"

By brandishing my greatness in their face! Yeska reared back a little, spreading her wings before settling to the ground again with a shaking head.

"Ah, not just yet... I'm not ready to die."

Yeska sighed. *Maybe you will only be exiled.*

"But then how will I get any charms?"

You're right. Best to stock up before *you do any brandishing.*

"I agree. Are there certain spells you think we will need?"

Healing and wards are always handy. Otherwise, choose what comes naturally to you.

"It may depend on what I can find," she said, thinking of the missing Water Float charms and the general shortage of charms from the water sphere.

Acquire any skill you can. The battle is coming, and it will be dire.

She was about to press for more details, but the dragon curled her head around toward her tail and shut her eyes. *I must rest a bit. Wait here awhile, and then I'll take you back.*

"Did the flight take a lot out of you?"

That, and it is my nap time.

Lara snorted. Not having much choice in the matter, she leaned back against the cave wall to wait.

Nyalin slumped onto his bed, then lay down on it and closed his eyes. The hours of failed magic had left his head aching, and the lunchtime sparring session with Emperor Pavan still made his joints groan. He was exhausted, and it was barely dinnertime. Maybe Lara was right about sleeping all the time, but he couldn't go to sleep yet. And he hadn't *done* any magic. What was he so tired for?

He ought to find Grel and explain everything that had happened. But perhaps if he only relaxed for a moment, he would have the strength to cross the city and find Grel...

Some time later, he awoke to the purr of a familiar voice. "Well, well, what do we have here?"

He sat up, rubbing his eyes and glancing around. Black robes and long black hair stood at the foot of his bed, tilted at the ceiling and walls around them like their lovely owner was trapped inside a fish bowl.

"Su!" He smiled, tentative. He'd known how his brothers would take the news. Sutamae, well... she could go either way. She always went whichever way she chose, no matter the cost or consequence it seemed.

"Did you drink too much last night?" she said. "You seem to have fallen asleep in the Bone mansion."

He grinned now. "You know me. Such a drinker." Maybe of tea.

"In your drunken haze you seem to have rolled yourself in dust too. Then passed out in someone else's bed. It's a good thing I found you." She smirked at him. "Well, then. Are you fully awake? Stand up and let me look at you."

Complying, he rose and dusted off the nonexistent dust. "Better?"

"Hardly." Her eyes twinkled. "Actually, the colors *are* fitting on you. You'll make a good member of the Bone Clan."

Such direct praise wasn't her usual style. He raised his eyebrows. "What brought you? Come to gawk and make entertaining remarks?"

"I do excel at both. But no, I have much bigger plans for the evening."

Uh-oh. Big plans did not sound like they included Nyalin

staying to recover in bed, tracking down Grel, or researching in the library. "Like what?"

"You know me. Any defeat of my father is a celebration for me. So I mean to celebrate. Amid your new clanmates, if it's all the same to you." A ghost of a smile crossed her lips.

"Why are you always looking for trouble?" he said, but the words had an affectionate bent. He had no idea what made Su hate her father so much, but it was certainly true that she did. Deeply, with an almost vindictive malice. He couldn't exactly blame her. One of the things they shared was their simmering resentment of the great Obsidian clan leader. And that was putting it mildly.

Of course, there was much more than that. They'd grown up together. He'd never been as close to Sutamae as he had been to Grel, and as the only daughter of a very important man, Su had been forced into separate activities from the ones appropriate for an indentured servant like himself. But they were close in age, Su only two years older compared to Grel's four. He remembered building sand castles with her. Playing merchant. She'd sung when the lot of them had played their "music" for Dalas, Uli, and even occasionally Elix. He hadn't always been so hard, or stubborn, or stupid.

She lifted her shoulders a fraction. "Oh, you know me. I just can't help myself where mischief is concerned."

"Care to go to dinner then, sister?" He smiled and held out an arm.

"I would be delighted, brother." She grinned now and took it.

His grin couldn't fade, with an address like that. They headed out. "Have you spoken with Grel? I haven't had the chance to come find him since I moved into the Bone mansion."

"He sends his regards, hopes to stop by soon. But you know Grel. Always busy being too good for his own good."

"You speak the truth."

"Finally someone who'll admit that." She grinned at him. "But I actually heard your news from Raelt."

"Of course you did. I'm sure he was his usual kind and magnanimous self?"

"Yes. Which is to say, not very." Her eyes glittered as if they were cut out of the evening sky. They strolled out a side entrance and down the dark streets. Torches and lamps hung at corners in the Bone District, but nothing compared to the amount of evening illumination Obsidians were used to.

Su continued to gaze around, like some amused tourist visiting a faraway land she had never imagined. He didn't think the often-disheveled wood or stone buildings were particularly interesting, but perhaps just seeing so many crossovers that were not black was a novelty. She had experience at court, though, unlike him, so really it shouldn't have been that unusual. Maybe she was just being willfully rude; he wouldn't put it past her.

"So are they teaching you?" She turned and met his eyes.

He hoped she didn't see his surprise at the question. She cared whether he was being taught? "They are trying. Which is more than Elix was willing to do."

"I'm glad to hear it."

Residences melted into shops and restaurants, and they drifted past a grand-looking facade—maybe a theater? Delicate white flowers grew in the pots outside, and lanterns lit wooden tables with mossy green lace tablecloths where people were dining. Green was a rare color of fabric indeed, primary to no clan and therefore special, produced in low quantities. And lace on top of that? Now they were just showing off. A place successful enough to have all that finery also had to have excellent food.

"What about here?" he suggested. Eating together was going to attract awkward stares no matter where they went. Might as well go somewhere nice. He untied his coin purse and checked. Huh. He could have sworn he'd only had three coppers left after leaving the Obsidian mansion, but in here were five coppers and a silver. Odd that he'd miscounted so wildly. "I think I have enough coin for a beer."

"Oh, no, I'm covering tonight." Sutamae raised her gaze to take in the very grand building and its sandstone façade, with great swaths of dark green silk draped in its doorways and on the eaves. "And not *just* to make my father mad, although it's a bonus. We must celebrate, I told you. This place will do."

A short, cheerful woman led them inside and left them with menus at an elegant table.

"It's even got a candle," said Sutamae, still surveying the place like she'd never been in a restaurant before.

"Are you sure you don't mind paying?"

"I take any chance to spend Elix's coin in a way he'd object to. This is one of the more harmless ones."

He cleared his throat, shifted in his seat. Some of Su's nocturnal exploits were less than wholesome, but he didn't really know the details. And he didn't want to. She had a right to her own choices, her own life.

She picked up the small menu and squinted at it. "Besides. You might as well be a beggar, if my estimates of your finances are correct. Are they?"

He cleared his throat. "You're not wrong."

"Then let me throw my gold in your plate." She grinned. "Besides, these prices are minuscule."

"You won't catch me objecting."

The two of them peered at the menus for a long while. His leg bounced nervously under the table, in spite of his efforts to steady it. A serving woman came by, and Su ordered red wine and steak. Nyalin raised his eyebrows, set down his menu, and ordered the same. Why not?

"I think I need to be on the end of your rebellions against Elix more often."

She smiled, and even now mischief lit her eyes. "You'd probably be safer than my usual quarries."

"If it will please you and anger Elix, you can buy me steak whenever you like."

"Duly noted."

"You know, if you don't mind me asking... what did Elix ever do to earn your wrath?"

Her smile dropped off, and she looked away, at each table near them, at the table cloth, at her plate, before finally meeting his eyes again. "Do I really need a reason? His treatment of you isn't enough?"

He shook his head. "You hated him before all this happened. Although I appreciate the support. What did he do?"

She sighed, staring back down at her hands again. "It's more like what he *didn't* do. He wouldn't teach you. But he wouldn't even have me tested."

He winced. He hadn't known she'd wanted to be, or that she hadn't been. He'd always assumed it wasn't an interest or that the test hadn't panned out. "Why? Why not have you tested?"

"Who knows what's driving his vindictive little mind? I hope to best him at that, at least."

"At being vindictive?" He snorted at her nod. "I don't understand him. Why shut us both down? There's no harm in a test."

“Oh, there’s *plenty* of harm in it.” She ran a hand over her hair, pushing her long, thick locks back over her shoulder. “A positive test means magic. Magic means a sword. A sword means my marriage prospects plummet. And they already don’t know what to do with me. Can you imagine me with a blade?” She laughed, but it wasn’t an amused sound. It was bitter.

“Actually, I can.”

She sobered, dropping her eyes to her lap again. “So can I,” she murmured. “And that’s just it, isn’t it?”

His smile fell, and on impulse, he reached out and squeezed her hand.

She shook herself, forcing a smile. She squeezed his hand back before letting go. “That’s not the *only* reason I like to torture him. But it’s a big one.”

They paused for a moment as a girl who couldn’t have been older than twelve dropped off their wine.

“But enough about me,” Su said breezily. “And definitely enough about Elix. I propose a moratorium on discussion of the man for the rest of the night.”

“Heartily agreed.”

She raised her glass. “To new beginnings?”

“To new beginnings.” Their glasses clinked, the bloodred wine swaying inside.

“May they be more fruitful for you than the last.”

“It’s only uphill from here.”

Smiling, they both drank as the crowd hushed. A small stage took up the far side of the room. A young woman was preparing to play an instrument he couldn’t quite see; it was blocked by the heads of the crowd. If this was a theater, their seats were terrible, but he supposed that shouldn’t be surprising considering that they barely belonged here anyway.

"Dinner and a show," Su cooed. "You're a good date, Nyalin."

It was idiotic, but he blushed. "If anyone is, it's you, since you're the one paying."

She chuckled. "So tell me, are you making any friends? Or do they all hate the Obsidian and his arrogant ways?"

He relayed to her the highlights: working with Lara, eating with Faytou, and the whole Andius gang and his nonsense. He left out everything else, or he'd be talking till the sun rose. "It could have gone better, but it could have gone worse."

"It's good you've had some guidance from Cerivil's daughter. And you're in their house. That does put my mind a bit at ease."

"Worried about me?"

"Maybe a little. Our clans don't exactly have a bloodless history."

"True. You've known Lara some, at court, right? What do you know about her? Raelt made some... comments."

Sutamae rolled her eyes. "He's always criticizing anyone he can think to criticize. The woman gets real exercise, does real work, and then has the gall to show up to a royal function without spending eighty hours primping herself." She pretended to scoff. "As if she—or anyone—needs to care what Raelt thinks of her."

"Can't disagree with that."

"He's not a charmer."

"That I know. But what of Lara?"

"Oh, right. Sorry. Well, let's see. I'd call her the only girl with a story more tragic than mine."

"What do you mean?"

"I'm exaggerating. There are many tragic stories beyond ours. But I never tasted freedom, like she did. Nor will I likely have the weight of the clan on my shoulders, like she will. She was almost there, almost her own woman... only to have it stolen away. Poor Lara."

"I heard as much."

Su shrugged. "Such is the torture of life."

"Know anything else about her?"

"Hmm. A skilled horsewoman, I believe. Good sword-mage. *Her* father cared to have her tested, but she can't get a blade now. Tell me, Nyalin. Are your interests recreational or purely professional?" She arched one finely sculpted brow.

"Uhhh. Professional of course."

"How disappointing."

He hesitated, but he couldn't really admit something to her that he'd hardly admitted in his own head. "She's just helping me a lot. I'd like not to let her down. Or needlessly insult her. Did you know they still hold the Feast of Contests? I'm just focusing on that as a goal. To compete once, even if it's at the lowest level."

"I've heard they hold the Contests, but I've never made the time to see them. Apparently this will be the year. Competing can be quite grueling, I believe. Optimistic, when you came in with no magic at all."

"Well, actually. Lara can see it."

She frowned. "See what?"

"My magic."

"Really? Tell me more."

He further summarized the attempts they'd made, the water spell, the initial time when she'd felt it and jumped.

"Huh. How strange."

"I know. Any idea how that could happen?"

She tapped a finger against her lips. "Well, there are tales. But you swore your interests were purely professional so...

"What does it matter?"

"Oh, my, well it matters all the *world*—"

"Spit it out, Sutamae."

She laughed again. He wasn't sure he'd seen her laugh so much in ages. "I have read a few magic books in my day. Mostly myths and ancient rumors and tales. I'm not sure how much of it is true, so you'll have to double-check. But I've read stories of soul connections."

He frowned. "What?"

"Honestly, it strikes me as implausible because it's such a romantic notion. But the idea is that for any given soul, there are a number of souls out there that have traveled with it through the series of planes, across the worlds and across time. Souls that are fated, compatible. Destined, you might even say."

"Did you say... through the worlds?"

"Yes, well, that's how the stories go. Mind you, there aren't just a pair. There's a handful, perhaps five or six, for any given soul."

"But what does that have to do with magic?"

"In addition to using blades and the ambient world for power, these souls can feed off each other." She sighed a little. "I told you it was romantic."

"Uh... 'feeding off' someone sounds a little creepy, but I see where you're going with this."

Su looked away from the musician and straight into his eyes now. "So, is this Lara your soul mate?"

He raised his eyebrows, leaning back in his chair. "No! Of course not." He swallowed, forced himself to take a drink. "I mean, I don't know."

"You don't like her."

"No! It's not that, it's just—"

"So you *do* like her."

"Sutamae!"

She grinned.

"She's betrothed," he blurted out suddenly, without entirely intending to.

"Ahh. To whom?"

"To whomever wins the Contests."

Her face burst to light with laughter. "Oh, I see! The single thing you're focusing all your energy on."

He winced and let his face fall into his hands. When he spoke, the words were muffled. "You're terrible."

"I try." She sounded delighted.

They sat in silence for a while. Nyalin didn't move.

"Nothing can come of it," he said without moving his hands. It was admitting more than he wanted to, but what was the point of holding back now? "I won't win. I'm optimistic, but I'm not that optimistic."

"You never know, Nyalin. You might surprise yourself."

The streets were dark when Nyalin and Su left the restaurant. Torches danced on two street corners, but the city was mostly empty. Only the sounds of muffled conversation and music reached them.

"Let me walk you back," he said. "I could go find Grel after I see you to the house."

She shook her head. "I'm not going back yet."

He winced but tried to hide it.

She only smiled in return. "Besides, Grel's at a feast with Jylan. He wanted to come along with me instead, trust me, but she was having none of it."

"I bet." Jylan wasn't betrothed to Grel, but everyone

wondered if it was coming soon. Her family was the most powerful in the Obsidian Clan next to Grel's own; her mother ran a vast silk business that had amassed quite a fortune.

"He won't be back until late. Although I shall likely be later."

There was mischief in her smile, but he couldn't return the sentiment. "Tell him I'll come calling. Tomorrow or the next. Or maybe next week. As soon as I have time."

"Of course." She gave him a nod. "Good luck, Nyalin." She hesitated for a moment, then surprised him with an embrace.

He returned the hug, patting her back, and she turned away with one final wave.

He wove through the streets, not taking the most direct route back. With his long nap, he wasn't tired, and there were so many parts of this city he had never seen. He'd kept to the Obsidian District most of his life, and it wasn't like he'd ventured out of his home that much anyway. The city had been built with the six separate districts to encourage peace and cooperation between the clans, without asking anything so crazy as to have them actually live mixed together. They were even buried separately; his mother and Lara's brother were only buried together because of their status, in the emperor's royal graveyard specifically set aside for the nobility.

It had never occurred to him to visit the Bone District, whether because of its general poverty or its distance; it was on the other side of the city. People generally stuck to their own districts, and that helped keep the peace too. He followed the road to the river, then doubled back, gradually making his way closer to the Bone Clan manor. Several of the clans maintained large houses or meeting halls nearer the city center, although Elix's home was deep within the Obsidian District. Why, he had no idea.

The streets were quiet and empty, but the houses and

establishments hummed with muffled life: laughter, the cries of children, the coughs and wheezes of the sick and elderly, the occasional worse sound. Lively music drifted from one tavern, shouts of brawling from another. The smell of beer and bread and the less appealing results of tavern visits drifted past him, memorializing the adventures of people strolling or stumbling or racing down this street.

The city was alive and vibrant, a beating, writhing heart. One he stood just to the side of, watched and even admired but never felt fully a part of.

A strange mixture of loneliness and longing had settled over him by the time he reached the bridge. Perhaps it was the heavy introspection that kept him from noticing them at first, or perhaps they were just skilled assassins, but as he set foot on the bridge's first few cobblestones, he finally saw them.

Both before and behind—at least two dark shadows turning after him from the street he'd just left, three more blocking the way about fifty paces ahead. One of those ones had a limp.

As if in unison, they all began to move, slowly closing in his direction. He quickened his pace, glanced to the side. The river was wide here, which was good, but it was at least a ten-foot drop, maybe more. Not an easy one, and the wider river meant it could be flowing fast and deep at this point.

He would only get a choice or two in this encounter, and he was about to run out of time to make them. Did he rush forward, engage the three head-on, give himself a chance to blow past some of them, or at least avoid being surrounded? Or did he go straight for the river and jump?

He'd fought a lot of fights in his day, both in martial training and in life, but he hadn't jumped over many bridges. The fall *looked* survivable... but it probably wasn't something he should take a chance on.

He centered himself and headed for the pack of three ahead of him at a run.

They didn't shy away or hurry, but they did circle in tighter. The shadows behind him picked up speed.

He stopped just short of meeting them, silent, tense. Waiting. He would meet them head-on, but he would never strike first. Their crossovers were black, although that didn't guarantee they were Obsidians. Or they could be impersonating Obsidians, especially if this was personal and not just a random pack of thieves. Thieves weren't a bad bet, since their faces and heads were also wrapped in black. Only their eyes were showing.

The leader stopped before him and met Nyalin's gaze. A sword hung from his belt. "Oh, look," said a deep masculine voice. Was it familiar, or did he just hope it was? "A runt's wandered away from its pack."

"Dog went looking for a bone," muttered one of them.

"I'd say he found some," said another.

Nyalin said nothing, simply studied them, but their shadowy forms in the darkness didn't reveal much. Nyalin wasn't a bad fighter, though five to one were not good odds. But not many men could use a sword without revealing much about themselves.

"You think you can leave the Obsidian Clan?" murmured the leader.

"You can't," snapped his mouthy sidekick.

"You trying to embarrass us all, becoming a Bone?" said the third.

The two behind remained silent.

Nyalin took a deep, steadying breath and waited, keyed in to every sense.

The leader took a step forward. "Rumor has it you've been lying about our clan. Saying our clan leader is inept. Because he can't see your supposed magical greatness." Voice dripping with derision, the leader caught Nyalin off guard with a sudden step forward and push to the chest.

Nyalin caught his balance but glared up at the man, eyes flashing. Yes. Those eyes were familiar and so was that push.

Raelt.

Raelt caught the recognition in his gaze, Nyalin could see it in the slight narrowing of the eyes.

"Come to kill me, after all these years?" he murmured.

Raelt said nothing. Instead, he sank into a fighting stance, hands hardening into fists.

"We've come to avenge our clan leader," said the second man, oblivious to the tension twisting between the two of them.

"We've come to stop the spread of your lies," added the third.

"It's the rumors that are lies," Nyalin said, voice calm as still water. "I've said no such thing. But that doesn't matter, does it?"

Slowly, Raelt shook his head.

"Did she lead you here?" Nyalin said. He relented and crouched, preparing to fight. All the others tensed now too, even the two behind him. Nyalin swallowed.

"Who?"

"You know who."

But by the slight twitch of Raelt's eyes and tilt of his head, he did not know who. Either he was an excellent actor, or Sutamae had had no part in this.

"No one has led you to this but yourself," said Raelt coolly. "Now. Fight."

"Make me." Nyalin took a deep breath and shifted his

weight forward onto his toes. Raelt braced.

Seconds passed, as tense as cord twisted into a rope.

Finally, Raelt took the bait, aiming for his jaw. Nyalin leapt back, lashing out with a kick and hitting one of the two quiet shadows behind him in the stomach. The man staggered back, hit the wooden handrail of the bridge, and shrieked as he crashed into the water.

The other men froze, eyes wide—long enough for Nyalin to swing round and land another roundhouse kick to the solar plexus of the second man behind him. The blow wasn't powerful enough to send him into the water, or even to the edge of the bridge, but it did send the man tumbling sideways onto his ass.

That was the extent of his streak, though, because an elbow came down on his cheekbone and ear, sending him crumbling toward the pavement. He fell to his knees, then tried to twist away. The kick that should have met his chest whistled past his ear.

A foot crushed down on his fingers, grinding them into the cobblestones. Something hard struck his kidney. He groaned as he forced his twist into a roll, pushing farther away from his assailants and in the direction of the space he'd created. He tried to roll fast, then stagger to his feet, but he wasn't quite fast enough. Hands caught his collar, dragged him up, thrust him forward.

Someone caught him—Raelt. Hot breath puffed against Nyalin's face, and Raelt's eyes were wild.

"You could never kill me before," Nyalin whispered. So what the hell was he doing provoking Raelt to do so now? "What makes you think you can now, just because you brought some friends?"

Raelt's eyes narrowed. "That's not why I'm going to kill

you. It has nothing to do with that."

"Because you're wearing a *practice* sword on your hip?"

Fury ignited in Raelt's gaze as he teetered on the edge of control. So it was true. Raelt didn't have a sword any more than Grel did; he'd simply taken one he wasn't bonded to from the practice rooms.

Nyalin clucked his tongue, for once egging Raelt on. But he didn't want to live in fear of his so-called brother anymore. It was time to call his bluff. "I've taken sounder beatings in my first days as a Bone. You never even use your magic."

"You want magic? I'll give you magic, you little—"

The wave of energy hit Nyalin before Raelt even finished his words, along with the choking, awful smell of pepper. He didn't know what level of spell sent him flying so hard, but Raelt couldn't have achieved it without the borrowed blade. It also couldn't have been an entirely controlled attack, because he collided with the remaining man behind him, who'd only just recovered from the kick to his stomach.

The two of them went sprawling into the street. Footsteps pounded through the night toward them. Then something loud crashed far behind him, near the houses, but he had no idea what. Then another loud rumble, on the other side of the bridge this time.

Nyalin scrambled off the man and onto his hands and knees, wincing at his injured fingers, the ache in his back. Nausea swept him as he tried to steady himself over the cobblestones. They were cool, rough under his palms. Real. Solid.

The cobblestones flickered, swept to the side, then steadied. But then they flickered again.

Oh, no. Oh, *no*.

Raelt's two remaining henchmen reached him at about the same time. The two men each took a side—and launched a kick to his ribs in sync.

He collapsed onto his side, groaning from the pain, his head lolling back. Where was Raelt?

His foster brother's thin form was walking toward him—slow, calm. Controlled. He raised an arm and a palm.

A scream erupted from Nyalin's throat without his consent as the magic washed over him. The energy hot in his veins slashed like a thousand needles over the tender skin of his soul.

Now Raelt stood over him, the blade raised. He wasn't actually going to *use* the practice sword to try to kill him, was he? People never fought with practice swords. Most weren't even sharp. Magical swords were for *magic*, not bloodshed.

But Raelt was gripping the hilt with both hands.

He plunged. The blade dug into Nyalin's stomach, and the power in it radiated through him, covered him like a thick, dark sludge that made it hard to move.

Damn. He should never, ever, *ever* have taunted Raelt about magic—

He was going to die.

But before he could really expound on this regret, his senses dragged him down, the world spun, his head spun, and he screamed.

The sudden scent of fresh grass filled his nose.

He opened eyes that had been squeezed tight. Moonlight. He was bathed in moonlight. He was indeed lying on his back, but he was in a field, not the street. Tall grass waved on all sides of him.

Breathe in, breathe out. He'd crossed over. He was in the afterworld now. What did that mean? Was he dead or still alive? What did he need to do?

He couldn't see or hear his attackers this time. For all he

knew, Raelt was carving up his guts by the minute.

Nyalin sat up and scanned the place. No Myandrin, not much of anything really. Perhaps a few low shadows flickered in the grasses a long way off, but that was all.

When Andius had attacked, the torture had kept on coming, even when he'd crossed over, even though he hadn't felt it. So he had to do something. But what?

He had to figure out how to keep fighting from this side of existence.

He staggered to his feet, dizziness assaulting him and turning the stagger into a jog forward a few feet. Then a few more. Yes, if he could at least run away from them, maybe that could help minimize the damage. When he'd stood in the first fight, he'd stood in real life, as if he'd been invulnerable, according to Faytou.

Perhaps the same applied to staggering. And maybe that would startle them into stopping, especially if he'd just been stabbed.

He stumbled a few feet more, but—no. If he was bleeding, walking around wasn't wise. He really needed to be *there* to get out of this fight. To get to help. Something. He needed to be in his body if he wanted to stay alive.

And to do that, he needed to be able to control this ability of his. If that was even possible. The emperor didn't seem to think it was.

Couldn't hurt to try.

He heaved in a breath, centered himself, and reached for his body, his world—his home.

As before, the pain came flooding in, condensed together with dizzying nausea. The green and the grass faded to the dark navy blues of the nighttime street. His scream was twice as loud this time, raw and animalistic, and richer with agony until he faltered suddenly.

Because the world was back. His body was back. But the bridge... The bridge was gone.

And nothing was underneath him.

To his side, the shouts of men went up, but as pain and nausea swept him, so did a sudden wind.

He fell.

Water enveloped him, ice-cold and hard, smacking into his back with a force to rival the cobblestones. He hadn't had time to even breathe, and the impact forced more air out of him. Immediately he heaved in a lungful of water.

He flailed. No pain was enough to keep him from clawing toward the surface, and to his relief a foot hit the bottom of the river and bounced, sending him skyward.

He broke the surface once, coughing up water and gasping for breath, before another wave of magic hit him.

He fell again, into the world, into the afterworld. But mostly into unconsciousness. The world went neither green nor blue, but black.

Chapter 9

Curses and Locks

Pyaris was just adding another log to the fire when a knock sounded at the door, harsh and loud. She jumped. And dropped the log on her foot.

Stifling curses on the log, her foot, the door, and whoever was knocking, she reached for the power gathered in her cauldron, but only a few souls had yet gathered. If she used up what they offered her, she'd have nothing left to defend herself if this visitor meant her ill. As a necromancer, she had no sword to draw energy from, although her father had certainly tried to get her one. The smiths wouldn't be reasoned with. She could have turned away from magic. But instead, she'd chosen to charm the souls of the dead. It hadn't been an easy choice, and it hadn't earned her any respect from the neighbors—or anyone at all—but turning her back on magic hadn't been an option.

Occasionally, it had also earned her a living after her father's death. Let this be a job and not some fool come to spit in her face. The meager congregation at the cauldron wouldn't be enough if it was someone foul, so she'd have to tap the totem plant she kept by the door for just such emergencies.

The little fern withered as she sucked some of its life

away. She'd have to ask Lara to burnish its energy the next time she saw the girl, or she'd sadly be getting another plant soon.

Then, delicate plant energy in hand, she probed at the person beyond the door.

One energy glowed powerful and bright, reeking of urgency and worry. The other—

The other.

Whatever it was, the creature was dying. But was it even human? It was profoundly strange, different from her. Almost like... almost like... No, it couldn't be.

But when she opened the door, an older man stood, a younger man in his arms. Both were dripping wet, soaked to the bone. Father and son, she guessed. There was a small resemblance between them around the eyes, and in the shade of their skin.

"What?" she demanded, putting up her usual rude shell. She had no intention of letting anyone get too close. Or close at all. She had had enough betrayal for one lifetime.

"A healer. We need a healer." The man was older, with wavy hair and a beard of salt and pepper. He was dressed in something shapeless and black, more a robe than a crossover. A fan of green feathers protruded from one chest pocket. He started forward.

She didn't move, barring him entry with her stance. "I'm no healer."

"You're close enough."

She frowned harder at him as he started forward again. "Do you even know what I am?"

"Of course," he said breezily, edging to the side of her.

This time she relented as the boy's face grew paler. Guilt for delaying his treatment pricked at her a little, so she shut the door behind them.

"You are a sorceress of the dead." The man was laying the boy on her cot in the corner now.

She raised her eyebrows at his use of the more preferred, more respectful term—and his use of her own bed. So much for a dry and warm night's sleep. "And are you...?"

"No," he said, shaking his head. He straightened and gestured at the boy. "Please. It matters not what I am, only that we help him."

"Why are you here?"

"Because there is not just a wound, but a curse."

Raising her eyebrows, she rushed from the door to the bed, angry at herself for not checking. What if the curse transferred over to her home, her luck, if the boy died? There were incantations that worked that way. She should have checked harder, but she'd been so thrown off by his... otherness.

She knelt beside the cot and floated her hands above the abdomen's injury. And sure enough, it was there. A curse.

"Can you lift it?" the man murmured.

"Perhaps. Because the cauldron is already going. Go and add this vial to it, will you?" She took a vial of wolf's blood from the shelf and held it up to the man. Time to see how much he cared about this boy's life. Or if he was squeamish.

He was either not afraid of blood, or he cared very much, for he strode to the fire and added the vial's contents without question.

"Stir it," she commanded. "Slowly."

He complied, much to her great surprise.

She turned back to the boy and closed her eyes. It was still a bit risky to let her guard down... but if he'd wanted to kill her, there were much simpler ways of doing it and they didn't involve following her directives.

She dug into the curse like kneading into dough. There was something here, all right. She was no healer and could do nothing for the cuts or bleeding, but someone had already tried to heal it. The wound had an odd shape, something like a stab wound but soft at the edges. The original wound had likely exited the back, but that much had been healed already.

The curse had prevented full healing, though. That was why he was here. He needed her help.

Technically all magic wielders *could* work the same spells if they wished. She suppressed an urge to taunt him about his lack. Whether power was drawn from cauldron or blade, whether a charm was used as a crutch or if the caster did the hard work of spinning the energy themselves—magic was magic.

But in practice, the spells employed by sword mages and necromancers were very different. Necromancers sneered at silly charms—imagine needing an aid to prop up your mental abilities. And many mages curled a lip at the sight of a cauldron, believing that drawing power from swords was cleaner, more ethical.

Necromancers knew better. Necromancers knew the truth. About the swords, and about other things.

Mages were aware of curse spells but didn't deign to learn to fight them. They deemed the dark magics beneath them—immoral, dirty, corrupt. And yet, when a curse took hold, did they ignore the magic then? Oh, no. Then they knocked on her door, as he did now, and mingled with the darkness. It wasn't the spells themselves or the sources of magic that were right or wrong, good or evil. What really mattered was intent—how they were used. Any necromancer worth their salt knew that.

Any sorceress of the dead, too.

She felt a little sting of foolish pride at the words, and at the idea that he needed her. By Seluvae, this was not the time for feeling superior or inwardly gloating. It was time to wrestle with the curse—and hope she didn't lose.

It was far from a sure bet. This one was powerful and clung around the abdomen like cords cutting in, restricting the body's attempts to heal, seeping rot.

She opened her eyes and glanced at her shelves. She needed something stronger in the pot, something better to ensure the curse didn't overtake her. Silver was what they should use, but it was one of her most expensive tools. She'd hoarded it for an emergency, for herself.

The man appeared by the shelf, picking up the small vial her eyes had been locked on.

She swallowed. He would demand she use it. He could *make* her use it, if he so chose. A boy's life was certainly worth it.

"Is this what you need?" he asked. "In the pot?" His voice was surprisingly controlled.

"Yes," she murmured. She squeezed her eyes shut and turned back to face the curse.

"What's wrong? Why do you hesitate? Is it dangerous?"

"No. It lures better spirits, stabilizes the concoction. It's just expensive. Cost me three years of labor to put that away, and I have no job to speak of now. But it'll do me no good if the curse takes me over and we all end up dead. Besides, a life is worth three years." She said the last bit at least as much for herself as for him.

"I'll repay you for it if you'll allow me to add it for you." His footsteps moved from beside her back to the hearth.

Yeah, right. So he said now. But she should just get over the cost. Safe and poor was better than dead. Or cursed. "Go on. Add it."

The silver sliding into the concoction hit her with a burst of fiery energy, spirits dancing to a new and different tune. A good one. Farmers and merchants and bankers came to play and lend their aid. She wasted no time.

In her mind's eye, the silver flames engulfed her hands, and she tore away the bonds of the curse, unwound the tightly spun spell, ripped it if she had to. She flung their sticky tendrils into the clean, consecrated fire beneath the cauldron. Spirits spit and dashed dust on the filthy remains.

The young man groaned, but that was a good sign.

She probed the wound further, rooting out bits of rot sown by the curse. She couldn't heal him, but his body would heal itself, with time, now that the curse was gone. Strangely, there was a glimmer of something else curse-like, something hard and unyielding but hidden and inert. But she lost track even as she reached for it and couldn't find it again. As the flames diminished and flickered out, she sat back on her heels and opened her eyes.

The man was still standing by the hearth, poised to do her bidding.

She blew out a breath, feeling woozy, her forehead slick with sweat. "It is done. Check for yourself. He will be all right."

The man approached the bed and stood beside her even as his fingers poked around in his chest pocket, brushing the green feathers across his knuckles. His concerned frown slowly eased. "Brilliant work. You are very talented." He withdrew a small pouch, opened it, and handed her a neat stack of five gold coins.

She stared at them in her palm. If these were real and not some illusion, this was enough for five years' work. Maybe more. Without requiring her to find someone willing to actually hire her for a job. It repaid the silver and then some.

"You are too generous, I—"

He cut her off with a slash of his hand. "For that sum, you

have done your work. Will you do one more task for me as part of that payment?"

"Of course." She nodded, although belatedly she realized she should have found out what the task *was* first. She was being sloppy tonight. But the man seemed so trustworthy, it was hard to summon up her defenses, her suspicion.

"Contact Lara naCerivil moMyra. She'll know what to do with him." He was moving toward the door.

"I can do that. Lara is a friend."

"I know."

"You know? How? But—you're not taking him?"

"No."

"Who are you? Where are you going?"

"It doesn't matter."

"He'll want to know who saved his life."

For a moment, the man paused in her open doorway and looked sad. "I know. He'd like to know a lot of things. But it's better this way."

Then he shut the door. She groped tentatively past it, at the street beyond, but he was already gone.

And he'd left her with this... this... very strange young man on her bed.

She sighed. She had better call one of the children next door to send a message to Lara.

They were lounging by a fire Lara had built when Yeska's ears suddenly perked. The dragon jerked awake.

"What is it?"

Your friend. He is in danger. We must go.

The words "your friend" had dripped with sarcasm, as if he were anything but. "Who? Do you mean Nyalin?" Perhaps she revealed too much by asking after him first.

Of course Nyalin.

There was no time to argue labels, though. Yeska had already reared up and begun to stretch her wings. Lara grabbed her bags, tossed them on her shoulder, and then took a running leap atop Yeska's back. They were in the air before half a minute had passed.

"What kind of trouble?" she shouted into the wind.

You know you can talk to me without speaking aloud.

"I know, but it feels strange." She swallowed. *Fine, I will try. Tell me what happened to him.*

I'm not sure. I only know that something did.

How can you tell?

He has an unusual soul. I have a few such souls I like to watch. His light is wavering.

Lara bit her lip. *I don't like the sound of that.*

Well, I don't like the look of it.

The dragon's wing beats were powerful, and she and Yeska covered the distance back much more quickly than she would've expected. In no time at all, the city had moved from the horizon to a dark patch speckled with light and fire directly beneath them. She craned her neck to look down at it, despite the wave of vertigo that came along with the move. The city from above was beautiful.

Can you fly here without being seen? Is being seen a worry? Maybe you want to be seen?

They see me from time to time. Some are excited, thinking it a lucky omen. Others... well. You'd be surprised how much people will ignore just so they don't have to inconvenience themselves. She laughed darkly. *I land where I choose. It hasn't been a problem, but it does draw attention.*

Were dragons known for being honest? Or were they

wont to leave things out? Even as the clan leader's daughter, she had never seen the Bone Dragon, so sightings among the average folk must be rarer than Yeska believed.

The dragon settled on the rooftop of the manor, and Lara slid down the dragon's side. The roof up here had a small, flat terrace with stairs that led down. The space was suspiciously appropriate in size for a dragon. She brushed away her curious questions but made a note to ask Yeska more about the past of her clan. Later. When Nyalin was safe. She turned toward the stairs. Although a few shouts went up from the gardens below, it wasn't as many as she'd feared.

Where is he?

I'm not sure exactly. I'm not bonded with him the way I am with you. Yet.

Don't start.

Give me a moment. There was a pause. *I believe a messenger has been sent. They're already looking for you.*

Lara cursed. *They know I was gone?*

It appears so.

Terrible timing.

I am sorry it took so long.

Oh, it's not your fault. It's just my bad luck. I hope hanging around you is a good omen, because I'm sorely in need of one.

Yeska nuzzled her shoulder affectionately, and Lara patted a hand on the dragon's snout. Huh. Yeska was comforting her. And it was kind of working.

We forgot your horse. I will make another trip. It was worth it; the boy is in danger. You must go. Now. The light flickers further.

Thank you, Yeska. She squeezed a hug against the bony plates of Yeska's head before racing down the stairs.

She found people when she reached the lobby. And this—well, this was worse than she'd hoped.

Andius stood, organizing the guards and ordering them into three groups. As she came down the stairs, he rounded on her. "Where have you been?"

"Lara!" Da exclaimed. "We were so worried."

She pressed her lips together. She didn't think Andius was particularly worried, just excited for a chance to kidney-punch her while she was down.

She forced an intentionally fake smile. "Oh, just wandering the city. I needed a day to myself. "

"Wandering." Andius huffed.

His frown told her he wasn't buying one bit of it, but Da rushed to her with a hug, patting her back almost gently for once. "You should have let someone know. We were looking for you. I was terrified."

"What's wrong? Pirates put a ransom on my head?" She grinned and played dumb.

"There isn't, of course—" Cerivil started.

"I didn't think there was anything wrong with a little walk," she said. "You're not usually looking for me at this time of day."

Andius jumped in, his voice dripping with disapproval. "Are you *usually* out for a walk at this time of day?"

"I don't think it's any of your business if I am." Of course, she rarely took walks at all, never at night. Walks were for sunshine. But any comment that pissed him off was worth uttering.

Da cleared his throat. "We were looking for you because we received a message from Pyaris. She said you are needed urgently."

"Pyaris?" Her surprised exclamation was almost in time with Andius's own.

"Yes," Da said. "I was surprised too."

"You can't go." Andius cut at the air with his hand. "It will have to wait till morning."

Lara's glare was accompanied by a sharp look from Cerivil.

"You can't tell me what to do," she shot back. "I'm going."

Andius looked to Cerivil. "It is not appropriate for her to be out at night like this."

"This is obviously not a normal situation." Cerivil's expression hardened further. "She has a friend who needs help."

Two, most likely. But she definitely wasn't letting Andius know Nyalin might be in a weakened state. And how was Nyalin connected to Pyaris, anyway?

Andius was not backing down. He took a step forward, chest puffing, tilting his head back. "Nor is it appropriate for her to be associated with necromancers."

To her surprise, Da mirrored the gesture, stepping to meet Andius halfway. His own shoulders lifted, his back straightened, his chin rose, till he looked twice as haughty even with half the stature.

There was a moment of pure tension. And then, after a second or two, Andius relented and stepped back.

Cerivil nodded sharply, and when he spoke, it was loud, for the guards to hear. "Pyaris is a respected clanswoman and a longtime friend to our family. If she says she is in need of urgent aid, we will not desert her. We would never abandon our own or our allies. Isn't that so, Andius?"

The young man gave a curt, bitter nod, but Da was already turning to her.

"Go. Take a horse. Send the child back on a pony," he said indicating the messenger Pyaris had sent. "And send for us if you need anything."

"I will, Da. Thank you."

She jogged out as fast as she dared, the messenger girl

following on her heels, before one of them could change their minds.

Her feet carried her to the stables in a blur, her mind racing. What could have happened? What could be wrong? Pyaris did not live close by; why was Nyalin in that area of the city anyway? And Pyaris was so private, reclusive even. The chances that he had simply met her out and about were slim to none. But the message had come from her, and there was no way to find out why but to go there.

She saddled her horse as the stable hand prepared the pony. She'd barely led the horse out of the stall when Andius rounded in front of the startled animal. She clutched the reins as it skittered back. She patted its neck, but it didn't trust her. Her usual mount was back in Yeska's cavern.

Andius stopped dead ahead of her, eyes aflame with fury. He was panting. Had he run the whole way here?

He started forward, the back of his hand raised, and she skittered back herself this time, dragging the alarmed horse with her.

"You have no right—" she started.

His head cocked in the direction of two guards and a stable hand approaching, and he dropped his arm. He glared in their direction, then back at her.

"I *will* tell you what to do," he whispered. "And you'll do it. Mark my words."

"I'd rather die."

The words came out before she could really think them through. Was that the truth? They had the definite feel of it.

He scoffed, a puff of laughter in her direction. "You wish," he growled. "I won't be so merciful."

Their gazes locked for one moment longer. She had to end this. If Yeska was right, Nyalin needed her. She swallowed.

"Get out of my way," she whispered.

His lip curled, and he looked like he would start forward again, but the loud guffaws of a guard stilled him. Others were still close. They shooed the wary girl on the pony out into the street.

"Wouldn't want to disillusion your audience," she sneered. "Or should we put on a show?"

"They are more loyal to me than they've ever been to you or your father. So gloat all you like. You are mine either way."

He turned and was gone, robe swirling.

She was shaking as she mounted the horse, cursing his name, and she just clung there a long moment. The messenger was gone. The guards and stable hand had retired to sharing their jokes on stools near the stable's gate. She needed to hurry.

But she couldn't stop shaking,

Finally, she touched her hand to the pouch at her side. To the clanblade. To Yeska.

To her friend.

Andius was wrong. She would never be his, one way or another. She'd seen to that. She might be dead, but she wouldn't be his.

Sighing, she clutched the reins, dug in her heels, and brought the horse to a canter and then a gallop.

What mattered right now was that she was alive, and Nyalin needed her.

Lara knocked on the old, warped door. Worn as it was it looked heavy enough to stop a crowd. Footsteps shuffled, a crossbar lifted with a scraping, and a familiar face appeared, rimmed in gold firelight with warm brown eyes shining. "Pyaris!"

"Lara!" Her friend threw her arms around her neck and hugged her close, Pyaris's cloud of springy ebony coils brushing her face. She smelled of incense, and Lara let herself sink into the hug. She needed this more than she cared to admit. "It's been too long."

She drew a little away, although she didn't let go of her friend's arms just yet. "I know. I haven't been doing much since... well, since, you know."

"I know." Pyaris patted her arm.

"You look well," Lara said. And she did. When had her childhood friend grown into a woman? It hadn't been so long ago they'd hidden in tree branches together, evading boys and tutors equally. Now enviable curves were hidden beneath that wine-colored dress and dark sable skin.

"Thanks." Pyaris gave her one last squeeze, then released her. "Come on in."

As Pyaris stepped aside, Lara's eyes caught on the still, pale figure on her cot in the corner.

"Nyalin!" The word was a cry of her own pain. Before she knew it, she'd fallen to her knees at his side and grabbed his hand. Energy snapped between them, stinging her fingertips, but fainter than she'd ever felt it. Something wet and sticky slid against her skin.

She gritted her teeth. Blood. "Who did this to him?"

"We don't know. I tried to patch it some," Pyaris explained. "But I don't have the right supplies. The injury is bad, but it's not that bad. He's just lost a lot of blood. If you take him back to a proper clan healer, he should be all right."

The first damn charms she was going to look for were the healing charms. There was no reason why she couldn't learn to do this. What a waste of time—she could have been spending the last six months mastering these spells if she'd bothered. And some healing spells would probably come in handy when they executed or exiled her for stealing the clanblade. She wanted to be the one to heal him, damn it.

"Who wants your friend dead?" drawled a third voice.

It was only then that Lara took in the rest of Pyaris's abode—and Kedwin, the second necromancer who lounged at the table watching them. Not much else had changed; the home was still the same dark but cozy cave, its walls lined with dried things, oddities, artifacts, and of course vials of blood from every creature imaginable. Except maybe Kedwin. Hopefully his blood wasn't in stock. All were ingredients to draw spirits and harness their power the way a swordmage harnessed a sword.

"Oh hello. Nice to see you again." She didn't really mean it this time.

"Nice to see you too, Lara." He grinned and tipped a wide-brimmed hat at her with a slight seated bow. "Someone got it out for your friend?"

"I have no idea," she said, although the back of her mind was picturing Andius blocking the way in the stables. "How did he get here? And what're you doing here, Kedwin?"

"I could sense the energy coming off him for blocks. Had to track him down here and see what the fuss was all about. If I hadn't known better, I'd have thought someone summoned a—"

"That's not possible," Pyaris cut him off.

"I think it is."

"He's just a boy. Don't start rumors."

"He is hardly just a boy! But suit yourself." Kedwin

shrugged.

"A what? What were you going to say?" Lara stood, letting go of Nyalin's hand for a moment.

Kedwin opened his mouth, but a scowling Pyaris spoke first. "In some ways, his astral presence appears like that of a demon or a spirit. Something not of this world but belonging to the next plane."

"A demon?" Lara stared at them, blinking. "I have no idea what that means."

Kedwin shrugged. "Is that why someone wants to kill him?"

"Why do you say that?"

Pyaris folded her arms. "Well, it was just one wound, but it was very deep. Also, it was cursed. Someone meant for this to stick."

"Cursed?"

"Yes. I lifted it."

"By Dala's light." She bit her lip. "So, a necromancer?"

"No." Pyaris cut at the air. "Anyone could do this with the right blade."

"Blade was crafted by a necromancer, though," Kedwin said.

Lara stood. "I understand. I had better send for help. Send for a stretcher. Can you call your messenger friend back?"

"I'll leave you ladies to your freak." Kedwin rose to bow and smirk at them. "He seems mostly harmless. For now."

"Kedwin, by the goddesses' gray—" Pyaris started, but he was already at the door. He waved goodbye and was gone, the two of them staring after him.

"Asshole," Lara muttered. "I don't know why you

hang around him."

"I don't exactly have the pick of men in the city, given my chosen profession," Pyaris muttered. "Besides, I didn't invite him. He showed up knocking when he sensed—what is your friend's name?"

"Not the freak?"

Pyaris winced. "There's definitely something unusual about him, but you know I'd never call anyone that."

Lara felt herself blushing. "Sorry. I know. I know better, I was just—"

"Angry. Deservedly so."

"His name is Nyalin."

"Kedwin showed up when he sensed Nyalin's presence. Now—shall I call back the girl?"

"Yes, please."

Soon the little messenger and the pony were on their way back to request men and a stretcher. More time lost. Lara did her best with what little bandages Pyaris had, cleaning the wound some and staunching the bleeding.

"So how do you know this young man?" Pyaris asked.

"You first."

"No, you first. I asked first."

"Your tale is more interesting." Lara grinned. "But I'll relent. He came to Da for help with his magic—"

Nyalin moaned softly, cutting off her explanation. Which was good. The sound meant he was alive.

"What do you mean, demon? Spirit?" Lara barely permitted herself to whisper it, but she needed to know.

Pyaris frowned, regret in her eyes. "I wish I could explain. The more you delve into communing with spirits, the more you start to understand them, to recognize different types, different personalities. Most spirits are weak, wisps and memories of their past lives, collections of thoughts and regrets and desires. Some aren't, though."

"They aren't what?"

"They aren't weak. They're strong, more like people, but different. It's just a different feeling. They're almost... more substantial than they should be. As if their presence is more comfortable in the spirit world than in this one."

Her eyes were wide as she struggled to make sense of Pyaris's words. "And... his is like that?"

"Somewhat. Not entirely. I've never seen anything like it before, to be honest. It feels human in some ways and in other ways... not. The way Kedwin saw it, he's got a crack in his soul."

She winced. "A crack?"

"It didn't look like a crack to me, but I can't get a handle on it. It was almost like... a lock? A cage buried in the soul somewhere? Something is wrong with him. Is that why he moved to join our clan?"

She shook her head. "His clan said he had no magic. Won't teach him."

Pyaris snorted. "That's ridiculous."

"I know. You can see it too? I can but no one else can seem to. Maybe you can testify to Da or give him some tips."

"Yeah, I'm sure they'll believe us. The necromancer and the wanderer."

She snorted. "No one's called me that in ages."

"But I still see you wandering in that heart." Pyaris winked. "But come on. That boy is oozing magic right now. That's actually what's weird. Can't you feel it?"

She could in fact feel it, and it had obviously drawn Kedwin, so they weren't alone. "At first I thought you had some artifact. Or something special in the cauldron."

"I wish. We did put in some silver, but that's for stability, not power." Her friend waved a hand.

"These demons and spirits—do they have more magic? Less?"

Pyaris's eyes met hers and narrowed. "More. Much, much more. Why do you think Kedwin showed up? The right astral spirit can be bargained with, employed, even bound. It can change everything for a necromancer to snare the right spirit. Or partner with one. Instead of enticing wisps to my cauldron every night, I could have a permanent partner, maybe even a friend I could trust. Which would you pick?"

Lara frowned down at Nyalin, disturbed at the image of necromancers circling like vultures, looking to exploit the power of this boy who couldn't find a way to wield it himself. "I'd definitely pick a friend," she murmured.

Pyaris stepped closer and propped her hands on her hips as she, too, surveyed Nyalin on her bed. "My, my. He makes powerful magic, and he's tasty looking too. Can I keep him?"

"No." She was startled by the coldness in her own voice but couldn't bring herself to correct it.

Pyaris grinned.

"What?"

"I see. I see what's going on here. I suspected, but I wasn't sure."

"What?"

"You can't hide from your oldest friend."

"No! I mean—ugh. You don't see anything."

"I see perfectly well. You like him, clearly. How can I blame you?"

"I don't. Or... even if I did. Liking him—or not—doesn't matter."

"Sorry." Pyaris studied her face. "Sometimes we want

most what we cannot have."

Her eyes flared. "No." The indignant tone to her voice all but guaranteed she meant the opposite.

"Ah. Obviously. No want there at all. Do you want everyone else to look but not touch?" Eyes twinkling, her friend looked back at Nyalin.

"Maybe," she admitted grudgingly.

"He's certainly special," Pyaris murmured.

"I know..." She shook her head, trying to throw off Pyaris's spell. Oh, not a real one, but Pyaris had it in her nature to draw the truth out of Lara. And to bring out her romantic, whimsical side. "Usually he has the opposite problem; he doesn't usually emanate energy like this. He doesn't seem to have any until I feed him a bit." She paused. She'd never thought of it so clearly before, but that was the simplest way to put it. It was almost like he could use the magic she gave him, but he didn't have any working magic to start with. The ability, but no well. But how was that possible? "Is there such a thing as an affinity for necromancy? The magic of the dead?"

"No. That's not how it works. All sources are equal in the eyes of magic. It's humans that restrict them. Judge them. Which, now that you mention it..."

Lara raised an eyebrow.

"This attack got me thinking. If you are really going to be his 'friend,' then maybe you should learn how to break these curses too."

Her mouth dropped open. "But... I..."

Pyaris scowled. "Are you truly his friend or not?"

Lara hung her head. "You're right. I just..."

"You don't need a cauldron. Here." She picked a thin volume bound in black leather off the shelves of ingredients. "Breaking a curse is a useful skill for any kind of mage. If the man who'd brought him to me had known how, maybe he'd be healed already."

"Wait—a man found him?" she said as she accepted the book and tucked it into a fold in her crossover.

"He showed up on my doorstep, asked for you, helped me add to the cauldron even. Surprisingly respectful. But he left without giving me his name. Oh, and look at this—he gave me five gold."

"So much?"

"I know."

Lara frowned. How many people carry that much gold around on them? "Strange."

"Indeed. Maybe one of the attackers had some regrets?"

Lara shrugged. "It doesn't matter. We can't know. But if you see the man again, try to get his name."

"Obviously. I won't have much luck, but I would have tried either way. Listen—"

A knock sounded at the door. Lara cracked it open and peered outside. Four guards whose faces she recognized peered back in. She opened the door. "Over there," she directed them. "We need to take him back to our healers."

"Lara, one more thing before you go." Pyaris edged into a corner away from the men and waved her close.

"What?" She followed Pyaris, keeping her voice soft.

"I don't know what's different about him, if it's a crack, a lock, or whatever, but... You should really be careful. I'm not exaggerating when I say he doesn't feel entirely human."

"I don't know what to do with that. He seems pretty human to me." She gestured at his form, all lean muscle and quiet, thoughtful strength being lifted from the bed onto the stretcher on the floor.

"I don't know what to do with it either. But I had to share

it. I'd regret it if I didn't. And I just want to say... you know his magic is strange. Unusual. I... Well, if it *was* a lock I sensed, please consider why it might have been put there in the first place. Maybe some locks aren't supposed to be broken. Maybe the lock is holding something in."

"Like what?" She raised her eyebrows. "Pyaris, I—"

"I know it sounds crazy. Just be careful, okay?"

"I will." She glanced over at the guards, who were almost finished. "Sorry about your bed."

Pyaris snorted. "Time to practice a little Water Float, don't you think?"

Lara grinned. "I hope it's enough."

"But not so much that I can't smell delicious boy for the next few hours."

"Pyaris!"

"What?"

"Nothing. Never mind."

And with that, the men had Nyalin loaded on the stretcher. She followed them to the door.

"Lara," Pyaris said, sobering. "Don't forget what I said."

"I won't! Goodbye, my friend." Lara waved and headed out again into the night.

Two days after the failed attack, Unira had made her preparations to travel the day's ride from the silk farms and her estate into the Salt City. No horse was comfortable holding Zama, though, so they took a carriage down into the basin and across the plain.

In the end, she was glad she'd taken the carriage anyway. He was too handsome, too strange. People might suspect something. Or talk. Or look at him sideways.

They arrived at the Obsidian mansion around nightfall and forced their way in. Of course, Vanae had her objections, and Unira kept her own house in the city, but they weren't going to stay long.

"Raelt." Unira sank into an orange armchair by the window and steepled her fingers. "Bring him."

Vanae froze. "Why?"

Unira's gaze only hardened.

"No, Unira—please—I beg you—"

Zama's expression was hard. "Produce him, or I shall. I don't think you will prefer my methods."

Nodding, Vanae trudged up the stairs.

Barely a few moments later, the young man came down. Slowly, pausing at the bottom of the steps, eye cold and wary, left hand shaking. Afraid.

He should be.

"We gave you an extraordinary dagger," Unira started. "Did we not?"

"You did," he murmured.

"And the exact location. And a team of men to help you. And what did you accomplish?"

He swallowed. "Nothing. I apologize, clanswoman."

Her rage flared for a moment. How could any gnat of a child be so hard to kill? She waited until she'd calmed to speak again. "What happened?"

"He vanished."

"Vanished?" said Zama, more dubious than ever.

"He somehow leapt from right in front of me on the bridge, into the air, then fell in the water. But he never came out. I also didn't hear him go in. We searched the bottom, and for several miles up and downstream we kept watch. There was *no* way we missed him."

Oh, she doubted very much that that was true, but she did believe he'd disappeared. Something strange was up with that boy, and it was more than his mother's strange blood. Although Linali had pulled her share of vanishing acts, if Unira let herself be honest about it.

If she didn't know better, she'd think he had someone watching out for him. Actively thwarting her efforts. Keeping him alive.

A damned thorn in her side.

She faked a yawn. "What do you think, my friend?" She didn't use his name around others, especially around one like Raelt. It wasn't a simple necromantic spell, but knowing a demon's name was key to taking control of them, and she didn't need a battle over *that* right now. "Should we kill him or just make him suffer a little?"

Raelt's eyes widened, but to his credit, he didn't move.

Zama looked at Raelt, those silver eyes boring like needles. "Just kill him."

"No!" Vanae rushed down the stairs. Meanwhile, Raelt had gone white and very still. "You promised—" Vanae cut herself short, as Raelt had never been privy to details of their plans against Grel. Mostly because Unira knew they wouldn't work out for Raelt the way Vanae thought they would. "By Seluvae, please—"

Zama burst into laughter. "It doesn't take much to get her goat, does it?"

Unira smiled. "No, indeed." She waved at them like the annoyances they were. "Do with them what you will. I suppose he can live. This time."

Zama chuckled again, cracked his knuckles, and approached.

"Have your fun, and then take a portal back to our estate.

He certainly can't stay here."

"Wait—what does that mean? Why can't he stay here?" Vanae was frantic.

"Her too." Unira ignored her and gazed out the window. Thank the goddesses for the Silent Sphere spell. And for the whole damn sound sphere while she was at it, one of the few conventional schools of spells that she made use of.

It was just so handy for quieting the screams, she couldn't resist.

Chapter 10

Empty

Nyalin opened his eyes to the light of dawn filtering down between broad green leaves. Plants wound up walls made of stacked sticks and across slats of a narrow trellis high above him. The sound of water trickling through the walls tickled his ears. The air was rich and wet and humid. He blinked. Where was he?

The only familiar feeling was a ball of warmth near his calf. He lifted his head and sure enough, Smoke was snuggled beside him on an unfamiliar cot. As he scanned the strange place, he spotted Lara reclined in a woven chair to his right with what looked like a sketchbook in her lap. She frowned at it and pursed her lips. He could imagine kissing those lips, smacking one on her as she frowned and surprising her into giggling. Her eyes would go suddenly bright, and—

Whoa. Like it or not, there was not going to be *any* kissing. She was effectively promised to someone else. He needed to focus on casting even one basic spell. Or simply not dying. Winning her hand was a fool's daydream.

Still. It *was* the middle of the day, and it was past time he admitted he had a thing for her, so perhaps fool was a fitting label.

He permitted himself to watch her a few moments longer, sans dreams. She was so rarely unguarded like this, relaxed, that the seconds ticking by seemed precious. She frowned at some part of the sketch, biting her lip, which only made him want to bite it for her.

He took another deep, ragged breath. He was ridiculous.

The air was humid, crisp, and scented with cedar. Was that the wood around them? Seemingly annoyed at the drawing, Lara threw down her chalk, wiped off her hands, and picked up a small black book that had been resting open beside her.

After another moment's indulgence, he decided to sit up and surprise her. A shot of pain coupled with her startled look helped him remember that that was a terrible idea. He groaned involuntarily as he let himself fall back down. He was staring at the ivy overhead in pain when her form leaned over him.

A smile twisted her lips. "I leave you alone for one class..."

"I think it was an entire day," he replied.

With a delicate feline yawn, Smoke chose that moment to rise, stretch, and leap onto his chest, peering into his face. "How did you get in here?" he murmured, running a hand down her back.

Lara shrugged. "She just wandered in. Who am I to argue with determination?"

"Clearly even an hour alone is too much. You'll just have to not leave my side." What was he doing?

"I should think that would get awkward sometimes."

"Awkward in a good way or a bad way?" Some things were awkward because they were new. New things could be good.

She cocked her head to one side, eyes laughing. "A bit of both?" But she looked down to his stomach, sobering. "How are you feeling?"

"Not dead." At least not at the current moment.

"Well, that's always good. Low bar, though."

"I know. But you weren't there for the attack."

"What happened?"

It hurt, but he managed to prop himself up on his elbows. "You should have seen it. The entire Mushin army showed up at the Troker Gate. I fended them all off. Would have been fine except for this one scratch."

She snorted. "It's a good thing we have you to defend us from the hordes."

He grinned, but then the memory of what had really happened sobered him up quickly. "It was my brother Raelt. And cronies."

"Really? I wish I could say I'm surprised."

"*I* am surprised. A little. He's never been this direct. He can be cruel, vindictive, annoying, but it was always harassment, not real harm. Why now? Why try to actually kill me after all this time?"

"Thank the Twins he didn't."

"He wanted to. He was just getting started before..." His voice trailed off, not knowing how to explain. "Before."

"Before what?"

He frowned. It was all a bit blurry, but when he thought back to the attack, it seemed as though his movement in the afterworld had moved him here in this world too. But how could he explain all that? Where did he start, when even the afterworld's existence was hardly certain to someone who hadn't seen it? "Uh. It's all fuzzy. Maybe it will come back to me in a few minutes." He sighed, and his stomach grumbled.

"Of course. You need to rest." She pushed his shoulder back down onto the cot. "Can I get you some food? Tea? Something stronger to ease the pain?" Her hand still rested on his shoulder as she studied his face.

"Some simple food would be good. Please. If you wouldn't mind."

"All right, hold on. I'll be right back." She rushed off without any of the hesitation she'd shown the time she fetched her father tea.

While he waited, he breathed in the rich smell of water and cedar, ran his fingers over Smoke's back as she curled up on his chest, and felt all the tension ooze out of him.

Lara returned with broth and tea and helped him to a sitting position against a cushion to drink it. To his relief, he didn't have to lean against the millions of piled sticks.

As he sipped, she sat on the corner of his bed and looked around, taking a deep breath.

"How long was I out?"

"Two days and two nights."

"It's relaxing in here." It must have been, for him to sleep so long and so soundly.

"Yes, that's the idea." She smiled. "It's the Soothe spells."

"Ah. I thought it just smelled really good. Is that cedar-wood?"

She grinned. "No. The cedar's my magic."

"Oh!" He'd caught the scent so often now. He should have realized.

"Which reminds me, no one's told you *your* scent yet, have they?"

He raised his eyebrows. "You caught it? I mean, no one's been able to sense it, so they certainly haven't."

"It's blackberries," she said with a prim, self-satisfied nod. "Quite refreshing."

"Blackberries." He blew out a breath. "I'll be damned."

"You seem to have noticed it yourself a few times without

realizing it was your magic."

He frowned. "I suppose I did."

"That's a lucky scent, I'm sure of it. It could be a lot worse."

"It's not cedar."

"I am blessed by Dala."

"But Grel's is chocolate."

"Ooh," Lara cooed, looking hungry.

"It might sound good, but it is not a cool scent for a twelve-year-old boy to have."

"What's Raelt's? Maybe I can tease him the next time we're together."

"Pepper."

"That figures. But not nearly as unpleasant as I'd hoped."

"I know. It suits. Too well."

He'd finished sipping and handed her the bowl, then eased back down. He was already feeling lightheaded from the effort.

"Our best healer was by just a few hours ago. She had to recharge, but she'll be back later. It'll be a few more days before you're well, though."

"Oh. Good." That was lucky. He hadn't expected the clan's best healer. Or any healer at all. "I thought I was dead for sure." Or... more dead. All the way dead? Permanently dead. He probably shouldn't explain that just now.

She put an end to his morbid thoughts as she eased onto the cot by his feet—ignoring, he noted, the perfectly functional lounge not five feet away. She scooted back and folded her legs, her thigh resting along his calf, the thick blanket a barrier between them. "I'm glad you are not. Would you have had regrets?"

"Not learning magic, of course."

She nodded. "An obvious one."

He pressed his lips together, thinking. "Not having a family some day would be disappointing."

She nodded, said nothing.

"Not figuring out who my father was. I'd really hate not to have finished *that* quest."

She tilted her head. "Are you searching hard to find out?"

"I exhausted every avenue I could years ago, but I'm always looking for new ones. But the thought didn't flash before my eyes as he stabbed me, if that's what you're thinking."

"What did?" she murmured.

You.

He said nothing for a long moment, searching for a believable lie while also wanting never to lie to her in the first place. "I... it doesn't matter."

"Sorry. Too personal."

He shrugged. It wasn't really; most things he would have told her. If it had been another woman, he'd have told her.

But it hadn't been. It had been her.

He needed something to distract from the awkward chasm opening between them, so he searched for something else to cut open and bleed. "I just... It would have been nice to reach some level of accomplishment, you know? Be someone standing on my own two feet. Someone who was more than my mother's son. I don't think I ever will be, though."

"Don't say that. We'll solve this puzzle. We've only just begun trying."

"It's not that. It's just her reputation. It's larger than life. I never will be more than her son. Even if I had all the magic she had and more."

Her eyes were deep with concern when he looked up to meet her gaze. "Maybe it *would* be better if you didn't have any magic then. Maybe it's better if we don't find anything."

"What?" He frowned.

"Not that that's possible, because I know you have it. But if you didn't, then you could just get on with being yourself. Making your own life on your own terms. What's so wrong with being ordinary?"

He tilted his head to one side. "I don't know... I don't think my mother would have wanted to give up all the good she could do for the world just to have a son that was... ordinary."

Now it was her turn to cock her head. "Are you sure? Having the weight of the world on your shoulders can't be fun. Maybe she would be glad to give you a life more ordinary than hers. More peaceful. No demands from clan or emperor to pull you this way and that." She looked away for a moment.

That was a... very good point. "You are a unique woman, you know that?"

She let out a sharp laugh. "Yes, yes. Far from ordinary. But I'm hardly a woman, barely a girl. They all say I'm too dusty and too high up in the trees."

He snorted. "It doesn't look that way to me."

Their gazes locked for a long moment, then she tore hers way, staring up again at the ivy and branches above. "Tell me. If you could leave the Salt City, where would you go? Anywhere in the empire. No, the world. Knowing you, you've read the geography of many places."

"I have, but— Leave? What do you mean, leave?"

"You know what I mean. What if you left, took off? Just picked up and went. You could remake yourself. Don't tell them Nyalin moLinali. Just Nyalin. Or something new."

He tilted his head the other way now. "I never even thought. I have no idea. I'd have to do some research, figure out how far I could get with five coppers to my name." And one silver that shouldn't have been there. Where had it come from?

She snorted. "You're too practical. You're supposed to assume you could go wherever you wanted!"

"Where would you go?" he said instead.

Her eyes got dreamy. "The Hiven Mountains. It's beautiful there. Crystal-blue lakes, green slopes."

"No city. Few people. Fewer books." He pretended to shudder. "What would you do? Fish all day?"

She giggled. "I don't know. Take a walk? Swim? I didn't get that far. I've never been fishing."

"I've never been out of the city."

"Really?"

"Have you?"

"Oh, yes. I—" She hesitated. "I had hoped to lead caravans. Explore."

"Really? All alone?"

She laughed. "Oh no. Caravans are heavily guarded, and I'd have my magic. The clan's territory includes several untamed regions. The desert is in the way, you see. Blocks our view of the beyond. But if I could just see past that... Well, there might be resources there. Something more than sand. Something to make us not the poorest clan anymore. And even if there aren't resources, there might be new cities, new people more friendly to trade with than the Mushin.

He rubbed his chin. "So it's work for the clan."

"Of course. I never considered anything else."

"You could still do that as a clan leader's wife."

She winced. "I could. But not as Andius's wife. He's made that abundantly clear."

"Ah. I see."

"Anyway. It was a nice dream. You should think about the Hiven Mountains. Getting away from all this. If I could escape, I—" She stopped. "Well, I hear they are beautiful."

"I hadn't intended to ever leave, but you might be onto something. Oh—how did I get back here, by the way?"

"Pyaris is a friend. She called me. I had some guards bring you back, since I couldn't carry you myself. We shared a tutor when we were young."

"Who's Pyaris? A tutor of what?"

"She's the necromancer who helped to heal you. Our tutor taught us herbs and gardening, if you can imagine." She smiled. "Her father was very wealthy, for our clan, once upon a time, but he died young. He tried, but he couldn't get her a sword either."

"The sword smiths are corrupt little toads. Even my brother can't get one."

Her eyes widened. "You're surely joking."

"*Not* Raelt," he was quick to add. "You'll never catch me referring to him as a brother. But Grel's been denied at least ten times now. Maybe more. I think he may have stopped telling me. Or asking them."

"That can't be."

"I'm sure he'll get it eventually... But could you not repeat that? He probably doesn't want people to know."

"Of course. I guess Pyaris shouldn't be too bitter either then."

"But I don't understand. How did I get there? Why did she call you?"

"The man who showed up at her door told her to."

"The man—who?" He bolted upright, then gasped at the pain. Bad idea.

She jumped forward to brace the wound and support his shoulder. "I don't think that's advisable—will you lie back down? By Dala."

He relented but grunted through clenched teeth. "What

man? The last thing I remember is..." How little could he explain? "Is falling in the river."

Her eyes flickered with something—worry? concern?—and she seemed to know he was omitting something. "I don't know who the man was. Neither did she. He refused to share his name. We both knew you would want to know, and we wanted to know ourselves, but it didn't matter. He paid her five fat gold coins, though, so he must be wealthy. Unless he stole them from you? Pyaris wondered if perhaps he was an attacker who'd changed his mind."

Nyalin shook his head numbly, still clutching both hands over the wound. "Why... No, I've barely got five coppers, let alone five golds."

"Duly noted. I didn't realize the 'five coppers' was literal."

"It is. But, who would do such a thing?"

"I wondered that myself. She also said the wound was cursed. She removed the curse first. Which was lucky, or someone might have missed it, and you might have wasted away while we all wondered why the healing wasn't working."

"So... the man knew the wound was cursed, how to find her, and he paid her handsomely."

"Yes."

"Bizarre."

"I agree. Especially when he then fled the scene and refused any credit for his heroism."

"Hmm." Nyalin stroked Smoke again, trying to think. "If the blade was cursed, does that mean a necromancer was involved?"

"Not necessarily. Pyaris stressed the blade could have been made by a necromancer for someone else. Did you see one, though?"

He shook his head. "But it's not like they wear EVIL

NECROMANCER tattooed on their foreheads."

"Yes, most people prefer forehead tattoos strictly for fashion purposes."

He laughed as her eyes twinkled. It eased some worry from her face, and that eased something in his chest. Su's words about fated something or other came back to him, the memory a bit blurry now. He'd have to look it up. But something about the theory, the fairy tale felt right. He had felt connected to her from the moment he saw her in that graveyard. Without her, he was... less than he was with her at his side.

"All my attempts at magic fail when you aren't there," he muttered. He meant it simply to share the information, but it came out like an accusation.

She winced, and he regretted the word choice. "Sorry. I had... something I had to do. It wasn't fun, if it's any consolation."

"No, no. You don't owe me anything."

She opened her mouth as if to disagree, frowned, and then looked away.

"I just meant to apprise you of what had happened. I didn't mean you should have been there."

"I had hoped to be. I was... delayed."

He frowned. Her caginess on the topic was highly unusual. Her typical mode was burbling openness. What had she been up to? Not that he wasn't hiding something himself.

She seemed to sense his intensifying stare and looked up with the fear of a hunted rabbit in her eyes. She opened her mouth to speak, but a knock sounded at the door. She looked to him, and he nodded. "Come in."

The door opened to reveal Grel's familiar, worried face. "You're awake!"

Lara smiled. He had the distinct sense she felt she'd dodged something difficult. "He stopped several times while you've been out."

"You had us worried sick."

"Us?" But Nyalin saw suddenly what he meant as Elix's scowling form lumbered through the doorway. At a much slower rate. "Oh." He highly doubted more than Grel or perhaps Sutamae had been involved in any worrying.

"What happened? Who—" Grel started.

"It was Raelt," he said quickly, forcing himself to spit out the words. He couldn't meet Elix's eye. His foster father had never chosen sides between them, but the man hadn't defended Nyalin from Raelt's harassment either.

Grel cursed his brother for a good five seconds.

"Well, that explains why he vanished." Even Elix's scowl had deepened, though. He let out a slow, seemingly disappointed sigh.

"You believe me?" Nyalin struggled not to look incredulous. "I mean—it surprised even me."

"I might have struggled a few days ago, but Father's right. He was just up and gone, the same morning we got word from Clan Leader Cerivil that something had happened. Good thing your new friends have the right friends, I guess?" Grel glanced at Lara who smiled but ducked her had. Necromancers weren't usually considered the 'right' friends.

"I better check that that healer is coming," she muttered, sheepish.

"No." Elix held up a hand to stop her.

She stopped short at the bold command.

"We will only be a moment. He must rest."

"And we saw the healer preparing on the way here," Grel said. "I'm sure it'll only be a few minutes. Is there anything I—uh, we—can do?"

Nyalin frowned from Grel to Elix to Lara then back again.

He wouldn't have imagined two out of three of these folks would care a few months ago. How things could change. He shook his head. "No, I'm in good hands here."

Now Grel's eyes flicked to Elix, his expression darkening. "We have to find Raelt."

"Better ask your Bone friends for some luck, then."

Grel scowled harder. "Don't you care? Raelt could have killed him."

"He didn't." Elix sniffed haughtily, the meaning of the gesture totally lost on Nyalin.

"But he could have. This is attempted *murder*. Arguably of a ward of *two* clan leaders."

Elix pursed his lips. "I don't dispute that. Look. Hunt. But you won't find him."

"Why not?"

"They're two steps ahead already. Maybe more, by now." Elix's eyes rested on Nyalin and flickered with some emotion Nyalin couldn't read. "Strength to you, son. And for once, I mean it." He bowed.

Nyalin nodded to return the gesture as best he could.

Grel was still fuming as Elix turned to walk away, black robes swaying behind him. But the heir to the Obsidian blade hadn't come up with anything by the time Elix had vanished. He gritted his teeth and looked at Nyalin. "He might be right. But I won't stop looking. Raelt won't live in this city and get away with this under my watch."

With one last embrace, Grel followed his father and was gone.

He raised his eyebrows as he looked to Lara, but she was nervously gathering her things. She'd remembered all that while that she was trying to dodge something? He didn't even remember what they'd been talking about. "I'll get you some more of that tea—"

"Lara, wait—"

But before he got the words out, she was already out the door after them.

He tilted his head again and frowned. What a curious creature she was. Not that he was one to criticize. They made a curious pair. Ah, but that was the stuff of daydreams, very foolish ones. Or Su's romantic tales.

But at the moment he had all day. And not even a book. What else was he to do? Live in Elix's world of reality and the probability that enemies could nearly get away with murder if they planned well enough?

He sighed, shut his eyes, and breathed deep the smell of cedar. And dreamed.

—

It was three more days before Nyalin was back on his feet again. By then, he was dying to be up and about and actually doing something. So once the healer finally cleared him, he headed to class practically at a jog. For breakfast, maybe some fruit this time. Sure, the bearded baker had been Emperor Pavan, and the bread hadn't truly given him mad hallucinations, but it just seemed safer to try something else.

He walked around corners a little more warily, and jumped at odd sounds a little more quickly, but the hard work of the Bone Clan had made it like his attack had never happened.

There was barely a scar. Physically.

But his already jangled nerves ratcheted up a level higher when Lara again was absent from class. To add to the fun, Faytou started off the day sitting at Nyalin's side, and Andius leveled them plenty of glares communicating his disapproval.

The lesson for the day was in the water sphere. All of magic could be divided up among one of thirteen known spheres—or schools—of magic, and each sphere had a few spells all mages could learn. The base spells could be mastered by any swordmage—except for Nyalin, apparently.

The youngest students were working on just such a spell: levitating the water, as he'd been supposed to do in his first test. Andius was scowling at a cauldron before him and practicing a second-level spell that boiled the water down to nothing. A requisite practice sword sat across his lap, powering the feat. Two other students had steaming bowls as well. A shame they didn't throw in some potatoes and carrots and make a stew. Faytou and many of the students were practicing the first-level Water Bubble spell, though.

Beyond the base spells, the first-level spells required a blade most of the time, and they nearly all involved bubbles—Fire, Acid, Dirt, Shadow. Nothing like a Dirt Bubble popped over your head to ruin your day. That was where the practice swords came in, for those who hadn't yet been granted one by the greedy, ever-stingy sword smiths.

Nyalin scratched his head as he surveyed the students. Not a one of them seemed to have anything other than a community practice sword. None wore sword belts or scabbards at the hip. In the Obsidian Clan, every swordmage would eventually receive a sword, as soon as they could afford one and the sword smiths granted them one.

Theoretically. But in practice it had mostly held true until now.

Here, though, Nyalin wasn't sure if *any* of them expected to get one. Or were they all practicing under the illusion that the Contests were still potentially winnable by anyone? If that was the only chance many of them had, his new clan was weak indeed. A shame, but if they had no smiths of their own, it seemed likely that was the case.

Faytou shadowed him again for lunch. Nyalin stuck close to the large, busy hallways and convinced Faytou to eat in the kitchens, amid the throngs.

"How do you stand it?" said Faytou, sliding onto the bench across from Nyalin with a bowl of stew.

"Stares are uncomfortable, but they're better than cursed blades to the gut."

Faytou blew out a breath. "Wow, it was cursed? Someone's got it out for you. Bad."

Nyalin winced. "It looks that way, doesn't it."

"Could it have been a thief or something?"

"Like I've got anything to steal."

"It's true you don't make a good target." Faytou swirled a finger at the room around them. "We're the poorest clan. And most of the money we do have is pooled into shared communal resources like this. This hypothetical thief would have to be serious with his weapons, but not with his targets. Literally any other clan would be more lucrative. Plus you're young. They'd know you probably don't have much wealth to your name yet." Faytou arched an eyebrow now, wondering. "I mean, unless you do."

Nyalin snorted. "Do five coppers count as wealth?"

"No. Not even in the Bone Clan."

"Then I am a typical young man of your clan."

"Our clan."

"Right. Our clan."

Faytou grinned. "Okay, well—there you go. But why else would someone want to kill you?"

He shrugged. He had no idea why Raelt had suddenly decided to kill him. None of it made any sense.

The discussion around Myandrin nagged at his mind. And of all the "accidents." Myandrin's attack, too, had happened on a bridge. Had it really been an accident, or had he simply not lived to point the finger?

Because he couldn't teleport by crossing into another dimension?

What kind of a spell could cause a horse to rear enough to kick off its rider? How hard was it to get a cursed blade?

The silence had dragged on, though, and he was no closer to explaining all that to Faytou. He needed some other topic.

"What about you, Faytou? Your family have a little money?"

It was Faytou's turn to snort. "Heh, yeah, right. Not even a little. Why do you think my brother is so determined? This is a huge chance to remake his fortunes."

"What about your fortunes?"

Faytou shrugged. "I have no idea what if anything he'll share, and I'm not sure I want him to. People mistake his bluster for strength, but I see it for what it is."

Nyalin frowned. "What is it?"

"Greed."

"You've thought a lot about this."

The boy shrugged again as he took a bite of his pita. "Nah. I've just had years to observe. He's always had a chip on his shoulder. I guess it isn't easy to always come in second place. Not just in the Contests, but all throughout our classes. Lara's brother outshone everyone, every time, without trying very hard. I guess he figures now it's his turn. Or maybe he doesn't care, and he just wants to win."

"Do you think his greed is intense enough to use a cursed blade on someone?" Nyalin murmured quietly. Even if it had been Raelt, something didn't add up. His foster brother had had ample opportunity to kill him before last night. Who had pushed Raelt to act?

His companion's eyebrows rose. "Uh... possibly." He chewed on the idea for a moment. "Except... no. He'd stab you for sure, but curses aren't really his style. My brother's got enough of a sadistic streak I think he'd prefer to stab you himself."

"I agree." If curses had been Andius's preference, then he could have employed one in his very first attack. But he hadn't. Although that had been an impromptu ambush, so perhaps that accounted for the difference.

He couldn't ask Faytou if hiring an assassin would be Andius's style. But, if their family was truly poor, what could Andius have to offer Raelt? That didn't add up.

But then what had pushed Raelt to action?

Were curses Elix's style? That didn't add up either. Elix had had even more opportunity to kill him than Raelt had. It was Elix who might be the most embarrassed by Nyalin's change of clan, though.

The gong rang in the distant tower. Their food was long gone anyway. He said farewell to Faytou and headed again to Cerivil's office, the pit of his stomach sinking.

~

Lara scanned the pages as her father and Nyalin pulled equipment she didn't recognize off the shelves. "I can't believe we've made it through so many of these." She shook her head. Another long, frustrating week had swept by with no answers. It'd been four weeks since he'd joined them and they'd started this search for his magic, but it felt like much longer.

Da nodded. "We have been quite productive."

"If you can call failure productive." Nyalin's grin was more good-natured than hers would have been.

She swallowed. “But there’s only three more tests left in here.”

“I know.” Da’s expression grew grave.

She let the page drop from her fingertips. “What then?”

“I’m not sure,” he admitted. “Let’s hope it doesn’t come to that, shall we?”

“I’m sorry this is so much trouble.” Nyalin sank into a seat across from her at the table.

“It’s quite all right.” Da stopped beside her, set down a stack of long twigs she had no idea had even been stored in this room, and leaned over the book. “Like striking flint for a fire, sometimes it just takes time to get the hang of it.”

Nyalin did not look consoled at all by that sentiment.

“We knew what we were getting into,” she added. His expression softened.

Cerivil rubbed his hands together. “Yes. Yes, we did. Let the trouble begin!”

“Let’s see...” Lara squinted at the page. “This one uses Summon Small Animals? Is that right? Unusual.”

“Yes. We’re into odd territory now. Way beyond your run-of-the-mill sparks and flashes.”

She scanned further down the page. “This works by using a salt circle for a focus instead of a charm. The salt works like a giant temporary charm. Huh, who knew you could do that? You pour the salt in the shape of a... squirrel?” She bent closer to make out a smudged word. “Oh, no, that’s just the example. You can choose anything you want, if you can draw it reasonably well.”

Nyalin snorted. “Well, that boils down to... nothing. Just because I’m a scribe doesn’t mean I draw well.”

“No doodles in your margins?” She smiled.

“Elix prized speed over creativity.”

"A shame."

"It's not the only thing he was wrong about." His eyes twinkled.

Da cleared his throat. "Why don't you help him draw the animal, Lara?"

She held up her hands. "I don't want to help too much and get accused of anything."

Da rolled his eyes. "It's all part of standard practice. There's variations on the next page, see?"

They spread a large, clean blanket of rich grassy green on an open portico and got to work.

She frowned at the book as she knelt. This seemed almost harder than using a charm, but perhaps if the difficulty lay in directing the energy from the sword into the charm, then replacing the charm with something else, something simpler and larger, might work. They were nearly out of options anyway, so it wasn't like they had anything to lose.

"What shall we call? Anything that's small and will respond to the spell. Do you like squirrels?"

Nyalin snorted. "Not particularly."

"Cats, like your little black friend?"

"Hmm, seems dangerous. Like they might not leave."

"She seems pretty determined to stick to you. Good point. What then?"

He thought for a moment. "Ravens?"

"Ooh, stubborn, smart creatures—I like a challenge."

"That explains a lot."

She smiled but didn't acknowledge the comment, peering at the diagram. "Let's see. Here's the salt."

"That's one thing we've got enough of," laughed Da. He set down a large silver pitcher with a long, thin spout she would have expected to hold tea, but it didn't, at least not today.

She placed the book on the floorboards between them and raised the pitcher, holding it out to Nyalin. "All right. You pour, I'll direct."

"Got it."

Quiet settled over them as the focus gradually took shape, her hand over his on the pitcher's handle. They made a reasonable representation of a raven, especially since she had no reference. At least it looked birdlike; hopefully that'd be enough. She'd cast this spell before, but she'd used a charm and only when it had been required in class. The spell—and the entire sphere of animal magic—wasn't one of her favorites. She never knew what she was supposed to do with the small animal once it showed up, since she hadn't mastered the spell necessary to talk to it. What was the point? To stare at them?

Still, she was glad for this test and its carefully crafted focus. It was peaceful today, a breeze blowing and a warm autumn sun casting a gentle warmth. A good day to coax something shy or stubborn out into the light.

The back of his hand was cool and smooth under hers, and his forefinger and thumb still bore ink stains. Was he still writing away in that room every night? She imagined him penning notes or romantic sonnets to some Obsidian girl he'd left behind, writing long after the sun had fallen behind the mountains and the sea.

She sighed at herself. What was it about him that brought out these strange, fanciful thoughts?

Birds sang nearby in the trees, as if cheering them on, and the salt pouring from the metal was a quiet susurration as the focus formed. Da putzed around behind them for a while, gradually moving farther down the long room to one bookcase, then another, tidying or inspecting or what, she wasn't sure.

She glanced over at Nyalin. To her surprise, he was already looking at her. The deep brown-black of his eyes gave her a jolt. He quickly looked back at his work.

After a minute or two, she risked another glance and then let her gaze linger. After a moment he met hers again. Their hands stopped, neither of them watching what they were doing enough to keep moving. Fortunately, he lifted the pitcher so it didn't leave a mountain in the spot where they'd halted.

Cerivil fumbled a book, the loud clatter of leather and paper hitting the ground breaking the moment.

She forced herself to finish the drawing even as she felt the weight of Nyalin's gaze. What was she doing? What was she hoping to accomplish with long, deep stares anyway? There was nothing to be gained.

"All right," she breathed as soon as the shape was complete, more breathless than she would have liked. "Let me read the rest of the procedure to you. This is the heart of the spell." She picked up the book, glanced around for Da in case he wanted to read, but he was at the farthest corner buried headfirst in a chest, tossing what looked to be colorful scarves out left and right. Seemed busy. So it should be fine if they just proceeded...

She cleared her throat. "Let's see... Center your mind. Bring into your focus a creature. Describe it to yourself." She improvised the next part. "Black. Winged. Elegant. Wise."

"Too wise," he murmured. "Stubborn. Smart."

"Too smart," she echoed. "Let your mind flow into the grains of salt, taking each one into your power. Feel the expanse of the world slim down to only this focus. Tighten, spin your source energy in this image, into the way and the spirit of the raven. Call the creature you have chosen with the depths of your being. Whisper the promise of reward from your center out, focusing on harmony, on grace. Other offerings can corrupt the spell. See the creature in your mind's eye, one of many, joining you in its natural home, even if that is not where you are right now. And call again. Reach. Repeat as necessary."

His eyes were closed, sweat breaking out on his forehead, face contorted in concentration—and frustration.

She scanned the buildings, the roofs, the treetops.

Nothing came. Not a blackbird. Or even a fly to mock them.

After a while, he sighed. "Let me see that, so I can see if I'm forgetting anything."

"Sure." She handed him the book, then glanced over her shoulder.

Da was watching. His eyebrows lifted quizzically. She shook her head, but he strode over anyway.

Nyalin sighed and sat down as Cerivil approached. "Another dud, sorry. Or no, it's me that's the dud."

She bit her lip. "Don't say that. C'mon, we'll figure it."

"If you say so."

"Let me observe and check if anything is off," Da said. "Try one more time."

He did so. There was no evidence he was doing anything other than frowning at the sky. The silenced seemed to stretch on and on, and what was a few minutes seemed like ages. She'd resorted to nervous fidgeting, cleaning the dirt out from under her fingernails, when finally Cerivil sighed.

"Enough. You can't say we haven't tried."

Nyalin's sigh settled across her shoulders with the weight of a tree trunk.

"Perhaps we could try another animal—" she started, but the sheer exhaustion in both their eyes brought her up short.

"There's a book on the last two tests. Let me go get it. But this has been enough for the day, I think. I'll be right back."

Da's footsteps seemed to echo as he headed for the door. Nyalin hung his head and didn't look at her. The air around them was tense as a bowstring, pulled tight. And as much as his slumped shoulders told her to leave well enough alone, something nagged at her.

The narrow space between them yawned like a cliff on the steppes. Her fingertips traced the back of her hand, remembering the foreign feel of his skin instead of hers. She hadn't touched him since they'd completed the focus, not since he'd started casting the spell. She had an idea of what might work, not that she wanted it to. Not that it solved anything. It only raised more questions. But what if it did?

"Can I try something?"

He frowned. "With the spell?"

"Yes. Can you try one more time? Just once."

His gaze was pained, and he didn't say yes. But he didn't say no either.

"For me. Please." She glanced over her shoulder again, but Da hadn't returned.

"All right, fine," he grumbled. Nyalin closed his eyes, and his brow crinkled.

She reached out, closed her palm over his hand, and sent a gentle pulse of energy.

The sudden chorus of avian shrieking was almost instantaneous. She jumped, snatching her hand from his. Nyalin's eyes snapped open too.

"Where is that coming from?" It seemed to be peppering them from all sides.

"I don't know," Nyalin murmured just as a raven alighted on the tip of the manor rooftop.

She gasped. A second appeared. Then a third.

Ravens proceeded to arrive in droves. They covered the tree branches and every reasonable place to land on the top and edge of a nearby roof. Newcomers were settling for the ground or flitting around, hoping to startle some other bird into giving up their spot. A handful of bold birds went straight for the portico and stopped before their green, salt-covered focus. And waited.

"What-what happened?" Nyalin leaned forward, clutching her forearm.

"I gave you a bit of my magic, ambient magic pulled from the world like a more powerful swordmage pulls magic from their blade."

He frowned. "Is... is this what you did the last time? With the water?"

"I think it might be."

"So you cast the spell?"

"No. Take a sniff."

He obeyed. "Blackberries. Huh."

"And I never get *this* kind of response when I try to call them."

One raven hopped forward.

"Why do I need your help? And, uh, what do we do now?" Nyalin blinked at the bird, as if fighting the urge to back away from it.

"Thank them," Lara said, "and send them on their way. Or we could ask them to do something but don't ask me what."

He met her eyes. "Do we want your father to see this or not? I can't decide if this is a success or a failure."

"Maybe it's a little of both? But my gut says send them off before he gets back."

"How do I do it?"

“Shut your eyes and give them your message through the focus. Just like when you called them. I’ll give you a burst, see if it confirms our theory.”

He was nodding even as he shut his eyes. She couldn’t help but admire him for a moment. Either Linali or whoever she’d chosen as a mate—or both—must have been very handsome. It was hard not to just sit and admire him.

And forget what she was doing. She sent a quick pulse before he got tired of waiting and realized she was ogling him. Or Da returned.

The cries from the ravens were more peaceful now, and they meandered away with none of the urgency with which they’d arrived. She hoped that was because Nyalin had thanked them thoroughly, but she wasn’t about to ask for details.

They were still leaving the rooftops when Cerivil returned, a book in hand. And she had both a powerful desire to tell him, and the strong feeling that she should not. Odd. She had *never* not confided in Da... But this was not normal. This was not right. Some part of her was certain that if she told him what they’d just discovered, he’d decide Nyalin was permanently broken, not just a very tough case.

If only she could just hide this bond between them, make her father forget it, secret it away as something only she and Nyalin knew about. Something Andius couldn’t take away from her, a lifeline to sanity in the madness of marriage. But no, she’d never let herself become his wife. That marriage wasn’t going to happen. She’d find another way. She had to.

A dangerous flicker of an idea stirred, tinged with desperation. What if... If no one knew about the strange connection between her and Nyalin, if no one understood it, could they *fake* being normal? What if he—with her help—

No. That’d be wrong. And he’d never go along with it.

Even so, the pieces of a plan started to slide together. What was the alternative?

The scowl on Da's face wasn't much more pleasant than the war going on inside her.

"What is it?" Nyalin asked.

"Oh, I just hate these tests, that's all. That's why they're last on the list."

"Why?" Nyalin asked.

"You'll have to decide if you really want to try these, son. Because these are nicknamed the 'pain tests' for good reason—they attempt to use pain to draw out magic. Pain, injury, threat of certain death. We only consider using them when all other tests have failed."

Nyalin frowned down at the floor.

"These final two tests are not to be undertaken lightly." Da laid a book on the table beside Nyalin. "This is what I was looking for: a manual specific to the pair. They are complex, uncomfortable, arduous, and take a lot of time to boot. I think you should start by taking this and reading it over in detail."

"That, I'm sure I can do." Nyalin drew the book to him and flipped through a few pages.

Da straightened and cleared his throat. "For my money, I'll admit I would rather not try them. For all their cruelty, there's still no guarantee they will work."

"Really?"

"Yes. We've gone through sixty-eight other tests. What are the chances that one of these two awful things is the effective one? Seems a much greater risk of pain and effort and still no reward. Also, with the time they take, we will need to wait till after the Contests, since preparations for the feasts have already started."

Nyalin's expression was grave. "Of course."

Preparations had already started... and the transfer of power to Andius had already begun, were his unspoken words in her mind. She winced. "Are we giving up? It's seems like we are giving up—"

"No! No, no, no." Da waved his hands in the air. "I simply think more research would be a better strategy. Clearly something unusual is going on. We should exhaust every tome we can get our hands on for clues. Exhaust the knowledge of other clans. Figure out a new angle of attack. Theories and new tests. There must be a logical explanation for your awareness of his magic but his inability to reach it."

"That sounds a lot like giving up to me, Da."

"What do you have against research, my little fruit pie?"

For once, his affection sent a thrill of irritation through her that she didn't understand. "We need to *do* and try, not sit and ponder. I thought Nyalin wanted *out* of the library, out into the world of living and breathing magic."

"Hey, I never said I wanted out of a library," Nyalin cut in. "I love libraries."

"Hmm." Da tapped a finger to his beard. "Well, now that you mention it. Maybe there is one other way."

She smiled, pleased with herself. "What?"

"I could ask the dragon."

The blood in her veins ran cold and slowed to a frozen stop.

"You said the Obsidian dragon wouldn't say?" Da seemed oblivious to her internal panic as he turned to Nyalin.

"Correct. Just kind of... passed me over. Refused to acknowledge me. Almost like she couldn't see me."

"How odd. But even if our dragon wouldn't care to comment, it couldn't hurt to ask. I can't summon her after... after everything. But I'd really rather Nyalin not have to torture himself to find his magic."

"Kind of you," said Nyalin.

Da smiled, but his eyes were absent, thinking. "I relinquished the clanblade, but perhaps the dragon would deign to speak to me one more time, to answer me just this once." He looked thoughtful, wistful even.

Males. They never appreciate you until you are gone, Yeska cut in.

Don't be so smug. I'm in trouble here. Lara fought to keep her breathing normal, her stance even. Sweat was starting to bead on her forehead. Goddesses, keep them from noticing it.

Wait. All this quiet—that would give her away. Act normal. Act normal. What would she usually do? "Well then, we should try! What are we waiting for?"

Very subtle. Yeska snorted.

Exuberance clearly means innocence.

Clearly.

"You're right. Let's go." Da rose and waved for them to follow. "I'll ask and see what she says." He led them out of the office and down the stairwell.

Save everyone time and tell them I agree with you, the kid's got talent. The sensation of Yeska pacing in her den rippled through Lara. The dragon twitched, tense and worried even if her words were flippant.

That'd go over well.

The truth rarely does.

Lara faltered and missed a step as she forgot to pay attention, focusing instead on Yeska's anxious pacing. *You're not helping here.*

Sorry.

Da waved at the two guards stationed outside the armory, all smiles, and the three of them went inside.

The case was the same as it ever was, still in its usual spot.

Still closed. But when Da's fingers lifted the case, he froze.

They all saw it. The polished wood of the case, the sea of black velvet lining.

But no blade. No Dagger of Bone.

Cerivil just stood and stared for a long moment. She felt the weight of Nyalin's gaze on her, but she didn't dare return it, nor could she keep still. She bounced and stared and dug at her fingernails some more.

Finally, she couldn't help herself and broke the silence. "Da—what's wrong? Where is it?"

Da stared, blinking a moment longer before his voice croaked out. "It's missing."

"Did you loan it to someone?" What a weak attempt.

"No. How can it be missing? How..."

"Guards!" Lara barked, taking a chance. Maybe if she acted outraged, indignant, surprised, they wouldn't suspect that she was their true quarry. "Guards!"

Two hapless men stumbled in from outside, surprised. Cerivil stabbed a finger at the empty case, and they froze. Neither spoke. They, too, were now statues.

Lara tried hard not to crawl under the carpet and die.

She forced the lashing torrent of worry inside her into her voice instead. "Search the premises!" she demanded. "The clanblade is missing."

Her sharp words roused Da. "Yes, they can't have gone far. Muster the rest of the guard. Search every room, but speak of this theft to no one else. It's of dire importance that no one knows our sacred blade was stolen—and from our own armory no less. Go."

The men were already tripping over themselves in their effort to obey.

Chapter 11

THIEF

EVERY NOOK AND CRANNY OF THE BONE MANSION was searched. Bedrooms, kitchens, store rooms, meeting rooms, stable stalls. Even the chicken coop. The surrounding gardens came next, guards lifting benches and overturning stones.

Nyalin had never seen so many guards so focused on one purpose. At first, he considered offering to help, but with him so new to the clan, getting involved at all could be fraught with danger. So he simply backed out of the way. Plus he'd never even seen the thing. He wouldn't know what to look for.

Cerivil roused from his initial stupor and kept the orders coming, heading off after the guards in the direction of the cellars last Nyalin had seen him.

This left Nyalin and Lara standing in the hallway, open-mouthed and very confused.

"This is crazy," he muttered. When she didn't respond, he squinted at her. She was practically bouncing with energy. Anger? The scent of the hunt? "Can you believe this?"

She glanced at him as if remembering he was there and shook her head. "No, frankly."

"How could something guarded like this just disappear?"

She bit her lip, looked about to say something, then shut her mouth again. After a moment, she started again. "We just can't catch a break, can we?"

He chuckled. "Nope. Even impossibly powerful and well-protected magical objects flee from solving *my* mystery."

"And those pain tests are the only option left? I don't think anyone's tried them for as long as I can remember. What if they're not even real?"

"Maybe people don't like to talk about being truly desperate."

"Maybe this is all not fair."

"Well, no, it's not." He shrugged. "But what else can we do?"

"There's plenty more." Her arms folded across her chest. Anger vibrated from her now. No, bitterness.

"I'm honestly trying not to think too hard about it. More research might turn up something." Of course, by then, it'd hardly matter. It'd be too late to fight for her. Not that he had a chance anyway.

She slanted a gaze at him, eyes narrowing. "Do you *really* want to figure this out or not?"

He scowled. "Of course I do, damn it. But beggars can't be choosers. Cerivil is my best chance, so if I have to wait... I'll wait. Or lash myself if I have to. But yes, if it matters to you, I think both options are abysmal. Don't repeat that to your father."

She studied him closely. "He's not your best chance," she said slowly.

"What do you mean?"

"He's not your best chance. I am."

He blinked. "What?"

She squared her shoulders with his and looked him dead

in the eye. "You could run off. Like we talked about. Make a different life for yourself. I've got two gold I can give you. Maybe three. It can get you at least to Tiro."

Tiro, where the emperor had been born. Funny that she should pick the same place. He kept his eyes locked with hers, as hard and certain as he could make them. "I'm not running off to Tiro. Not yet anyway."

"Good. Then meet me in my room at the evening gong instead."

He opened his mouth—what did she even intend to do?—but her eyes were so steely he abandoned the idea. A little voice said that meeting the clan leader's daughter at night alone in her room might not be the wisest decision. But that glint in her eyes—he couldn't fight it.

"All right. But until then, I'll be reading this." He waved the horrible little volume.

"Lucky you. Don't go running any dangerous tests without me."

"I wouldn't dream of it."

Her smile now was tentative, and she bounced up on her toes and back to her heels before turning to go. "See you?"

"See you."

~

When Nyalin was completely out of sight and the echoes of his footsteps had faded up the stairwell, Lara changed directions, turning around and heading back to the practice room.

No one would question her presence here among the equipment at this time of day. It was the perfect opportunity, so she wouldn't pass it by. Even if she was shaking.

She'd have to work fast. The guards could decide to search her room at any time, although she wasn't sure her being there would help or hurt matters. She could think of nowhere better to hide the blade than amid her silks, so it wasn't like she could move it, and she definitely wasn't going to carry it around right now. Much as Yeska might prefer that.

The practice room they'd left was predictably empty, the salt focus still on the floor.

She grabbed an empty crate from the shelf and went shopping, filling it with a little used, slightly rusted practice sword, two more boxes of salt since that had seemed to work well, a blank amulet designed to accept wards, and a few colorful scarves, mostly to hide the other items.

Then she eased the box onto the table and listened for anyone else in the rooms, anyone approaching.

Silence met her. So she strode to the shelves and found the charm chest. Its rough-hewn wood was bound by gold, and she lifted the lid to reveal the pale-satin-lined interior, the colorful stones bright against the backdrop.

Normally a swordmage would choose their sphere of specialization carefully. They'd figure in a number of things, including natural talent, interest, and temperament, as well as utility to the clan.

She, however, would be choosing based on what she could pilfer from this box.

She chewed on her lip as she surveyed what was in stock. No higher-level light charms, or fire or water. Those were popular classics and had been mostly cleaned out. Da should really be commissioning some more. What was the holdup? She could only find one charm in the energy sphere, and it was too high for her. Sound was plentiful but also so very useless.

A few more were present in abundance: acid, shadow, caution, and control. Harder, darker. Less showy, but still useful. People sometimes stayed away from them, as they had more overlap with the spells necromancers preferred, but that attitude had always seemed a little silly to her. Thinking of Pyaris's comments about locks, she pocketed all the levels of charms for control, which would allow her to master magical locks of every kind with enough practice. Then she stared at the other spells. So dark. While she wasn't afraid at all of being mistaken for a necromancer, they were very far from her warm, sunny personality.

Shrugging, she filled her pocket with shadow charms of each level. And what the hell, why not caution and sound too. Who knew? Depending on what was going on in her room, she might not get another chance.

They are not here yet, Yeska offered. *But they're getting close.*

Still, there had been one more set she'd hoped to find. Even a small broken one might do. She felt around the edges of the top and then lifted out the tray. If she could have managed it, she'd have crossed her fingers for good luck as she looked beneath.

Yes! Thank the goddesses.

A full set of healing charms shimmered, carved from pearly white moonstone. Perfection. She jammed them in her pocket with the others. She'd thread them all onto a thong later. After the attack and all this talk of pain tests, mastering the healing spells was her highest priority. Plus, if she ended up exiled in the wilderness, they might come in handy.

Time to quit while she was ahead. She'd taken enough that their absence might be noticed, so it'd be worth getting out of the practice room without being seen.

And now to go find out if her other theft had been, er, noticed in the box in her room.

Not just yet, Yeska added. *But they* are *busy little bees.*

She shut and replaced the chest, propped the crate on her

hip, and stepped out into the hallway.

Her heart was in her throat as she trudged up the stairs. Turning onto her floor, she hesitated as a guard entered her room, calling out something unintelligible to another inside.

By Dala's greatest light. They were just opening the door, heading into *her* room. She had assumed they would, but what were the chances that they'd be doing it just as she was approaching?

What if they'd found it already?

She hesitated a moment longer, but standing around looking nervous would be sure to draw unwanted attention.

Plastering a fake but pleasant smile on her face, she strolled as casually as she could manage up to the room—her room—and offered the nearest guard a bright hello.

"Oh—by the great dragon! Forgive us, Lara, but we have to check everywhere." Mep, the guard, gave her a toothy grin.

She waved him off. "Of course. Don't mind me." She flashed a practiced, unworried smile, donned her best confident swagger, and lifted the crate to place it on her desk—

And at that point, she stopped short.

The other guard had out the box of silks and was rubbing the corner of one of her dressing gowns between two fingers.

She couldn't help herself. Acting innocent be damned, she stopped and stared.

His fingers had to be a hair's breadth from the blade. He must have grazed it already, surely.

"Hejim!" Mep snapped. "What are you doing, you perverted louse? Get out of there! I'm sure there's no damned clanblade in her undergarments."

Hejim scuttled back, then returned to push the box back under the bed. He cleared his throat, trying his best to act as if nothing untoward had happened. "Nothing here, Mep, I think that's just about it." Pretending that his cheeks weren't beet red, Hejim bowed and fled.

She stared at the empty doorway.

When she'd finally accepted that they were really gone, she locked her door, flopped back on her bed, and stared at the ceiling.

Goddesses above, what a close call.

Yes. Yeska's voice was more jovial than she would have expected. *I... may have inspired him with some creative imagery.*

She winced. *Not of me, I hope.*

He has a wife, in fact, but she's never afforded undergarments like those.

When they exile or execute me, can you have Andius let the woman inherit my things?

When did you become so negative?

She knew the moment, but Lara shook her head and didn't answer. She just stretched out a little further, slid her hand into her pocket to finger her newly acquired charms, and sighed.

When had she become such a thief?

Her heart hurt for it. She had never kept things from her father. She'd been closer to her mother, when the woman was alive. But Lara had been young then, and her mother had been dead for a long time now. Long enough for Lara to forget much. But now that it was just the two of them, after mourning Myandrin together too... Well, she'd never felt closer to Da. Secrets should have been unthinkable.

But everything had changed. She had secrets now, big ones, and they were multiplying.

~

Nyalin spent the intervening hours in the library. Not only was it a comfort to be away from the rushing anxious guards, cocooned in the serenity of the books, but he also had something he wished to find. And it had nothing to do with the pain tests, the book of which lay abandoned and ignored on a nearby pine table.

No, he traced leather spine after leather spine looking for something else: the fairy tales Sutamae had mentioned, or something like them.

The afternoon drifted away, not serving up anything, until he was almost faint with hunger. And then the library relented a little and revealed one slim volume. *Ronigot and Dewinter, and the Magic of Fate.*

He carried the book to the kitchens and skimmed the tale as he downed a yak kebab and tried to pretend his other clan members weren't staring at him. If he was going to be an ordinary member of the Bone Clan, a member of the larger rank and file that lived their whole lives without even any magic, they were going to have to get used to him being around.

Or he was going to have to get used to them staring.

The book was disappointing in that it didn't explain much more than Su already had. Ronigot and Dewinter had been powerful mages in the early years of the wars with the Mushin. They'd met in the market, and they'd felt drawn together inexplicably, even only as friends. Check. Their touches had sent zings through them, sparks flying so to speak. Double check. And together they'd been able to achieve things they couldn't alone. Although some details were vague, they'd mastered a much larger than average number of spells and, on their own, successfully defended a Glass Clan village from three thousand Mushin troops.

Interesting.

Unfortunately for these two, they'd also been members of families who hated each other. The lovers had defied their families and attempted to sail south only to be lost in a storm at sea. Supposedly only the narrator had lived to tell the tale.

He dropped the book on the table with disgust. By the Twins, he hated stories with unhappy endings.

Yak bits consumed, he eyed the sky and decided the gong would ring soon. It was time to seek Lara out. But first, he stashed his very depressing pile of books in his room.

It was probably a bad sign that he felt compelled to make sure no one saw him knocking on Lara's door. But given his experiences with Andius, and with half the clan on edge looking for the clanblade and the other half wondering what the hell was going on, extra caution wasn't a bad idea.

She opened the door, her usual halo of gold hair falling around her shoulders, braids like enchanted snakes bound into peaceful slumber. Same glint of steel in her eye. He might be a bit of a failure, or maybe more than a bit, but he felt a kick of pride that she was bothering to help him.

She stood aside and let him in, closing the door behind him. The same black book from the days when he'd been healing lay open on her bed.

"What's this about, Lara?"

She propped her hands on her hips, apparently winding herself up to say something. "Listen, I don't know why you've been fated to deal with all this nonsense. Why you've had such bad luck. Why Elix and the Obsidians would lie or why my father can't see what I can. But... well..." She faltered.

"You said it yourself," he muttered. "It's just fate." He considered volunteering that fate might be more concrete and less nebulous than it sounded, but what would she say to that? To fairy tales, theories, and conjecture? Probably the last thing she needed was for him to get all moon-eyed over her. Did the black book have anything to do with this? Maybe she'd been reading something too.

"I'll just come out and say it. Nyalin, I..." She took a deep breath and straightened. "I have a proposition for you."

He raised an eyebrow. "Yes?"

"I think you should sign up for the Contests... and I should feed you power like we've been doing. But all the time, for every spell."

He frowned. "Do you think they would go for that?"

"No. Definitely not."

"I guess we could ask."

She winced. "I was... sort of thinking we wouldn't."

Both eyebrows got in on the action now. "You mean... you want to cheat?"

"Yes." Her nod was vigorous. "Specifically, I want you to cheat with my help. What do you think?"

He just stared. "Wow. That never occurred to me."

She shrugged. "That's because you're a better person than me."

"No. Just less desperate."

"Well, it wouldn't be my preference either. But I have to do something."

He paused, rubbing his chin. "What would happen if we got caught? You might be safe, but they might kill me."

She shook her head. "They'd kill us both, I'd guess. Exile. Imprisonment, perhaps. Nothing good."

"That's... big."

"Don't think I don't know that. But I'm not going to lie to you about the weight of this decision." They sat in silence for a long moment.

A knock split the air, making him jump.

"Lara!" Andius's voice rang out as his fist pounded on the door. "Lara. Open up."

Her eyes darted from the door to him and back, fear tensing her body.

"I know it was you, Lara! Open up."

He didn't need to think. He pointed at the closet. She nodded, and he slipped inside, shutting the curtain.

She opened the door.

Nyalin watched through the sliver between one sheet of heavy brown velvet and the other. Andius crowded her, pushing her back into the room. He slapped the door behind him, harder than he needed to, and it slammed shut.

"You have it, don't you?" Andius whispered.

"I don't know what you're talking about." She took a step back.

"The sacred clanblade. *My* sword. The Dagger of Bone. You took it."

She shook her head.

"*You're* the one. It had to have been someone inside the house, to get by the guards. It had to be someone who knew how to use it and who had a reason to deny me the blade. Everyone loves me. Why would they do such a thing? Everyone but *you*."

"You're insane, I don't have anything."

He leaned closer still, but she didn't give up her ground now. "When you're my wife, they'll be penalties for lying."

"I'm not lying."

"It doesn't matter. I'm having them make another blade."

"What? You can't make another blade."

"Does that upset you?" He smirked. "They can, and they will."

"You don't have a dragon scale."

"Yes, I do."

"Who is the liar now? The dragon won't give you one. She

won't give *anyone* one."

Even more angry that she wasn't buying his claim, he threw up his hands, then leaned in again. "I don't *need* a dragon scale, woman. It will be a fake one. Because the dragon isn't *real* and doesn't matter."

Nyalin caught his breath. Thankfully the sound was masked by Lara's sharp inhale as well. "What are you *talking* about?"

Andius only sneered in response.

Inside Nyalin's mind, there was a low, angry growl.

What the hell? There was no reason for him to cross over now, and he'd never seen anything that could growl in the afterworld. Was he actually going mad this time?

"You don't deserve to lead this clan." Her voice was acid.

He straightened, chest expanding. "I'm the most powerful. Of course I do."

"You're not more powerful than me."

"You're a pathetic woman. Of course I am. Draw your sword, and let's see. Oh, wait, you don't have one."

"Neither do you. And you don't honor the dragon."

"And *you* don't honor your betters."

"You're not my better. I don't answer to you."

"You will."

"I won't. Ever."

"That too can be arranged, if you insist. But I'd rather not."

"Are you threatening me?"

"What? Of course not. What an imagination." His voice was smug. Andius grabbed her by the hair and pulled her closer, and Nyalin clenched his teeth to stifle a second gasp.

"Let me go," she spat, her hands clawing at his wrists. Lines of blood welled against his skin, but he didn't let go. "Get out of my room."

Nyalin edged closer, trying to see better, his blood boiling.

At what point would he no longer hide? If he hurt her—

"I don't care if you stole it," Andius whispered. He smiled at her then, a smile that could freeze a hot spring. "Because you'll be mine either way."

"Get—out," she grunted, digging her nails in even harder.

He released her, sending her staggering. The door slammed shut behind him.

Nyalin shoved the curtain aside, grabbed her shoulders, steadied her. For a moment she just leaned against him as they listened for any chance Andius might return. His footsteps faded into silence.

"You're shaking like a leaf." He pulled her toward the nightstand. "Here. Have some water." He held up a glass.

Still shaking, she ignored the glass and bent over the wash basin, splashing some water on her face and gulping some down. Slowly he set the glass by her bedside. A mirror hung over the wash table, and now she stared at it, panting.

Then, hand as fast as an adder, she seized scissors from beside the basin and lopped off a lock of hair. Then another, and another.

"Lara—whoa—stop!" He grabbed for her hand, but he didn't want to get stabbed. Or worse, stab her. "Wait—what are you—" She'd shorn off several more handfuls before he'd disarmed her. Golden locks scattered across the wood of the nightstand and floor.

She turned wild eyes on him. "I'll *never* be his, Nyalin. Never. Do you understand?"

"Let's not be hasty."

"You saw what he did. What he is."

"I did—and I don't want you to let him win. You can leave. Run away. There's so much of the world you still want to see, remember?"

An edge of the madness in her eyes lifted. "Run away?"

"Yes. Look—I'll go along with your plan. We can try to win this thing together. But in exchange, you've got to promise me you'll work on a backup plan. Pack supplies. Some transportation."

She sniffed. "Are you sure you want to deal with all of this? With me?"

He squeezed her shoulder. "I've never been more sure. I always regretted not having magic, because it meant my mother's sacrifice was meaningless. I've been searching for something big enough to make it matter. Somehow—this is my chance. I can help you even without magic, or maybe even *because* I don't have it."

"But you do—"

He held up a hand to quiet her. "You deserve to be the clan leader just as much as your brother did. You can use me to achieve it. I never thought being a puppet would be meaningful, but I'll take it."

"You'll still cast the spells."

"Whatever. Just promise me—"

"I promise." She glanced at her reflection. "Although I may have to trim off more to look presentable."

He winced, ran a hand over the remaining locks. "They're beautiful, so that's a shame, but they'll grow back."

She leaned toward the mirror as if searching for something in her appearance. After a long moment, her eyes flicked to meet his in the reflection. "You think they're beautiful? Not wild? Not uncouth?"

"No, not at all. I think of them like... your crown of gold." Hell, had he just admitted that out loud? That was a ridiculous thing to say, especially given the situation.

"You think of them?" She straightened and turned

toward him.

"Maybe. So what if I do?"

She stepped forward once, then again, and surprised him by pressing her mouth against his. No part of them touched but their lips, but that same feeling ran through him, of fire and energy igniting like a star in the sky. It was achingly sweet and still timid, fragile like the first snowflake against the warm ground. It was exactly what he wanted.

And also entirely wrong.

He lifted a hand to brush her cheek, trying to memorize this feeling. Then after a long moment, and then one more to savor the sensation he'd certainly never feel again after what he was about to say, he gently gripped her shoulders and eased her away.

"Don't, Lara," he whispered. "A kiss isn't a thank-you. Or a payment." And he didn't want to labor under the illusion that her gratitude was anything deeper or grander than it was. His imagination would run wild.

"It wasn't—" she started.

"Let's promise to be honest with each other. As allies at war, we'll have to be. Always." His hands squeezed her shoulders tighter.

Her brow was furrowed as her eyes searched his face. He had no idea if she found what she was looking for, but eventually she murmured, "Always. Of course. I promise."

"All right, then." He let go of her shoulders, took a slight step back, and pretended nothing had happened and that her hair wasn't two radically different lengths.

It was time to start figuring out how to cheat.

"Now tell me. Just exactly how do you think we're going to do this? Are you going to use a practice blade to power all this? We're going to need more than first-level spells."

She raised one shoulder. "Not exactly."

"I'll have to learn higher spells. We have a lot of work to do, and not much time to do it in."

"Agreed." She dove in—showing him a crate of goods and a dozen new charms. She explained her theories, what she thought would work, what they needed to do.

He nodded along. It wasn't a bad plan. It wasn't a great one—but there was no time for perfection.

Still. As they continued to plan, a bad feeling brewed in his stomach. The ending of this story of theirs... It might not be a happy one. But while there were many easier paths, this was the only one that had a chance at something meaningful, and it was the only one he wanted to take. He was hopelessly devoted to her, and he had been since that first day in the graveyard.

There was no going back, and there never had been.

Chapter 12

BRAVE

IT WAS A LONG TWO WEEKS, WITH MORE than a few sleepless nights. But they'd had a lot of spells to spin, and a lot of practice at modulating her magic so that he had enough for the appropriate spells. There were whole spheres of magic they didn't have the charms for—or any practice at—but he hoped to the Twins it would be enough.

They rotated between their rooms and the library late at night or early in the morning. Somehow Smoke always found them, as if she had no interest in returning to her Obsidian home. She'd curl in his lap, or Lara's, or do figure eights between their legs if they were on their feet, practicing the combat spells of the shadow sphere as well as one could, given the lack of time and resources and their all-around secrecy.

But they made something like progress.

On the day he usually visited his mother, he made the trek to the stadium grounds just after dawn. Of course, he'd visited her grave first. He needed all the support or luck he could get. But then he'd headed off to do something a little ridiculous.

Throw his name in for the Contests.

Built by the emperor and used by all the clans, the

stadiums were a series of tall, round buildings open to the sky. They facilitated clan competitions as well as empire-wide festivals and more.

But today, he lined up outside the smaller one, with about four dozen other young men in similar bone-pale garb. And he waited.

At the front, it wasn't Cerivil taking names, nor any clan member he'd ever met before. An elderly woman with sharp blue eyes and a beige hood raised her eyebrows at him.

"I'd like to sign up for the Contests."

She frowned at him and said nothing for a long moment.

He cleared his throat uneasily. "Is there a problem?"

Silence. Except for the whispers that started to swirl behind him.

"Do I need to pay something, or...?" he asked, even though he knew he didn't.

The woman's eyes narrowed like an eagle zeroing in on prey. "I thought you were the one with no magic."

He shrugged. "Rumors are wild. It's true that I'm not very good, though."

She reared back a little. "Not much like your mother, eh?"

The words stung, but he brushed the feeling aside. "I'd just like to get a little experience. Now that I'm in the Bone Clan, I'm getting better every day."

She eyed him for a moment longer, then finally relented. "Fine. Nyalin moLinali—write it down," she said to a hooded assistant who never looked up. "Be here the day after next. The midday gong exactly. And bring anything you plan to use to compete. Questions?"

"No, ma'am."

"Next."

And just like that, the deed was done.

Walking away, he shook his head. What the hell was he doing? Trying to steal the leadership of this clan he'd only been in for not even a month?

No. Of course not. He'd never cared for leadership or power. He was just trying to save someone very worthy from a torturous, tragic end. Someone who'd become a great friend, who was loyal and smart and kind. Though friend wasn't quite the right word for it.

Did the end justify the means, though? Was it the act or the consequences that mattered?

Maybe it was a little of both. If the rule requiring her to marry was unjust, was defying that law by cheating the right thing to do? Or was it just a convenient excuse?

He had no answers to questions like these. And it didn't change the fact that, for Lara, he was going to do this.

Later that night, as he was getting into his bed, Smoke already curled on the linens and the dresser pushed over to block the doorway, he noticed one of the books had fallen off his shelf.

Odd.

He bent to pick it up. It was the book Grel had left for him in his room. *Unusual Magical Phenomena.*

As if interested, the cat sniffed at it as he sat down with it on the bed and began to read.

~

As the days passed, Lara's sense of the dragon grew. It seemed to grow by the hour, in fact, until just under every waking moment was another one, a parallel existence. Yeska bathing in her glorious mountain waterfall, diving and spinning through the air, snacking on fish.

Even now, as Lara lay in bed trying to sleep, another part

of her mind was gliding over the waving grasslands, lit only by the moon, a dark velvet-blue sky stretching above. The scent of woodsmoke and mutton caught her nose on the wind, and she veered to the east. Perhaps there would be a roast going near the village... either forgotten or unattended.

In bed, Lara's stomach growled even though she'd eaten *plenty* for dinner. She rolled from her back to her stomach, grumbling. Then she punched her pillow, pulled her covers up in a bunch near her chin, and, in spite of all the images and the worry, fell asleep.

The great gray-purple eye blinked. The dream had enveloped her, and now for the first time, she could look around, away from the great eye. They were at the waterfall. The dragon lounged in the water, ripples from the falls lapping against her bony plates. Lara sat on a sandy beach that she did not remember being quite so large, or maybe it hadn't existed at all. She wrapped her arms around her knees and hugged them close.

Tell me how to help you, daughter. The dragon gave a little flutter of its wings in the water, shaking them dry. The gesture was surprisingly doglike.

She only hesitated for a moment. "Did you hear what I suggested to my friend? To Nyalin?"

Your friend... The one you insisted is not your mate.

Uh. Yeah, that one.

You kissed him.

Her face flushed. *I know! I don't know what I was thinking.*

You were thinking he should be your mate in things other than magic.

Lara slapped a hand over her face. Her punishment for the theft of the clanblade was going to be Yeska's permanent over-the-shoulder commentary. *Can we just focus on what I asked him? He wasn't interested.*

Only if you admit I was right.

She rolled her eyes. *About what?*

You have wanted him as a mate all along.

Damn it, Yeska! She let out a frustrated moan. *Okay, fine. Fine. You were right all along. He's handsome and smart. And even better, he's actually nice to me. Imagine that. Now can we talk about my plans?*

Yes. Yeska's voice purred, she was so pleased with herself. *It is a bold and daring deception. I love it.*

Lara couldn't help but wince. "I hate to lie. Can you think of any other way? Anything?"

It is not only lying, I believe. It is outright cheating.

You're not helping.

The dragon chuffed through its nose. *I admire that you will do what it takes to change our fates. I do not mean to judge you. I wish you to win. And succeed. You have found a way you might be able to lead without risk of death—through him.*

She blew out a breath. She'd been worried the dragon might hate the idea, and then what would Lara do? *But can you think of any way cheating could be avoided?*

And still fight for the clan? You could always simply leave and abandon them.

"No, no. I still want to fight."

Then fight. I know of no other way. This one is strange enough.

Lara hung her head for a moment. Yes. She hadn't seen it before, because to see it required questionable morals, something she was rapidly acquiring. "So this young man, the one you flew me back to save—"

Yes, I like that one for you. Exotic, but good stock.

She frowned. "I have no idea what that means."

Well matched in more than just magic.

"That's not what I meant!"

It's what I meant. Yes, perhaps aunt is the correct term for me. Do aunts not concern themselves with encouraging the marriage and mating of their families?

Shaking her head, she rubbed her forehead. "He doesn't want me. He made that clear enough."

Does that matter? If I were your age, I would fly to Resravakot and insist that—

"I am not sure I want to know this."

Fine. What do *you want to know then?*

"He's been told he has no magic. But I can see it, and sometimes if he's using my energy, he can cast spells anyway. Why would that be? And how can I help him?"

A lock—a magical one, the Dragon offered.

"Truly?" Pyaris had mentioned something like that. Damn, she should have consulted Yeska earlier.

I know, I'm very useful. Magical locks are possible at the highest levels of 'control magic,' I believe you call it. A soul lock is a simple spell if you know it, although not as simple as locks on boxes. It requires training and a great deal of energy. The mage must specialize to reach it, of course, as with all the highest-level spells.

"What does it do?"

It cuts the target off from their source.

The blades? Their source. Of course. But when she fed him magic, he wasn't so cut off.

There are many sources of magic. The blades are one source, but there are others too. A soul lock cuts the target off from ambient magic as well as their internal source, their own life force. From everything. Blades may be usable, temporarily, or magic if it is loaned. Or they can borrow from the dead.

She frowned. "You talk like those are all equal."

The dragon sent a ruffle through her plates that sent

water flying, almost like a shrug. *Because they are.*

"I wouldn't take advantage of the dead."

No, you're quite content to exploit the power of the living.

"What do you mean?"

You're happy to take advantage of my power, aren't you? And I'm happy to let you. But blades are not so different from the blood magic or whatever you call this thing that you're doing.

"What are you saying?"

Where do you think the blades get their power from?

She faltered. "I-I don't know."

What makes you so right to use my soul, and them so wrong to use the souls of the dead? Is the blood of frogs so beneath mine?

"Of course not. I-I didn't realize. I didn't mean it like that."

Of course you did. But now you know better and can take care to not let your friend know of these thoughts.

"I will correct them. And I want to know more about what you mean about the blades. But first—Pyaris could see the lock or thought she could. Why would she, as a necromancer, be able to see it, but my father and I can't?"

A good question.

"Could it be because a necromancer put it there?"

Possibly, but nonnecromantic mages cast lock spells just as often. There is no reason to prefer one over the other.

"Damn. Thought I was onto something. How can I know for sure if a soul lock is responsible?"

Well, if he has a soul lock, he's been cut off from his source. Many sources, it seems, not just the ambient. It should be all sources, including you. But somehow you are exempt.

"There's never an end to the strangeness with him."

Indeed. It could be my power coming through. Or... there is another option.

"What is it?"

You are mates.

She winced. "I told you—"

No, you do not understand. Extraordinarily well-matched pairs exist among all magic-wielding species. And across them. Are we not linked? This sort of bonding is not necessarily romantic or sexual. You humans are so obsessed with reproduction. Just because you attempt it more often than every three hundred years. I don't see what the fuss is all about.

Her eyes widened. She had no response to that.

This is more like paired in magic. And think—your two fates become more entwined each day, yet a month ago you did not know each other. Mates of this sort are born attuned to each other. Drawn to each other like magnets, and just as natural.

"Can't we use some other word?"

No.

She sighed. "Is there any way to test this theory of yours?"

Not really.

"Then I guess it doesn't tell us much either, except maybe a reason why I can see and help him when no one else can. But I'm not exactly telling my father or Andius or the council *that*."

I agree it would not go over well.

"Listen, this lock. If he is locked, is there any way to verify that? Or break it?"

I am not sure.

"And Pyaris was concerned. She said—what if something was being locked in? Or out? What if someone put it there for a reason? Why would someone do that?"

I have no idea. But I can ask around.

"Ask around? Who?"

The other dragons.

She hesitated.

I will not name names.

"We don't have many leads, so I suppose you ought to try."

I will, Clan Leader.

She winced again.

Do not suffer at your title. You and the boy will win the day, and all will be right.

She shrugged. "I wish I could be that sure. We might win. Or we might both be executed."

The dragon rose up suddenly, her wings spreading with the dreadful clacking and knocking of bone against bone, droplets spraying wildly into the air and rivulets streaming down into the pool. *They are my clan. You are my clan leader. Do not doubt my power or yours.*

"I'm sorry, I didn't mean that. I'm just afraid."

The dragon sank back into the water. *I know. And I'm just angry.*

"I know." She did, of course, think they had a good chance to win, or she wouldn't have suggested it. But she had nonetheless filled a pack heavy with supplies, as Nyalin had asked, and stashed it in her closet.

As I was saying. He is your clan now, and potentially a mighty warrior. Strengthening all warriors in defense of the clan is only prudent.

"Andius wouldn't see it that way, I bet."

I am not talking to Andius. I am talking to you. *Forget him.*

She swallowed.

I will think on this matter of the new child of my clan and his strange magic.

"He said the Obsidian Dragon waved him aside."

Curious. She is powerful. She ought not to miss a soul lock. I will look at him myself and then ask her. Most strange.

"What if Elix put the lock there? Then the dragon

wouldn't go against him, would she?"

You're right, she wouldn't. She may even have helped. But why would they do such a thing?

"I don't know. Why does Elix do anything?"

Enough now. You must rest. If you need other aid from me, you have only to ask.

How about figuring out what to do when her theft was discovered? But she didn't ask that. Instead she said only, "Understood. And thank you."

Help was not something she could afford to turn down.

~

Smoke was purring hard and shedding a fair amount of black hair on Nyalin's lap that morning as he finished off a chapter in *Unusual Magical Phenomena* and waited for Lara to arrive. The air was still a little cold, but Smoke's warmth helped. Her big blue eyes blinked up at him, slow and steady. He'd always noticed those eyes. Black cats never seemed to have blue ones, usually copper or yellow or green-gold. But Smoke was unique in more ways than one.

She nudged the book with her snout, rubbing her face along the edge, and he took her hint and resumed reading.

Before he'd gone a page or two further, something occurred to him. Very occasionally, for dense books such as this, authors would mention a list of the key topics in the back, as a sort of key for finding things. Maybe he could look for soul mates or something. The irony of looking for a soul mate in the back of an obscure magical tome did not escape him. But there was no index or key or any kind of additional help. The last chapter just ended with a note that perhaps future volumes might be written as more unusual phenomena were observed.

Disappointed, he paged through the book again, studying the cover, the title page, things he'd skipped when he'd first started diving into the book. The title page caught his eye. *Written by D. C. Ronigot and Ona Dewinter.*

Eyebrows raised, he dropped the book on the bed and stared. Well, damn. What did that mean? If they'd died on some ship somewhere, when had this book been written?

A knock sounded at the door. Smoke hopped up and headed expectantly to greet their favorite tutor. He swung it open without much ceremony—Lara should have been here a few minutes ago—and stopped short.

Four girls huddled together outside the door. About his age, maybe a little older. They were... giggling.

"Is that a cat?" one whispered.

"By Dala's light, he has a cat!" A second cupped her hand toward the ear of another, but hardly lowered her voice.

"Um..." Nyalin cleared his throat. "Excuse me? Who are you?"

That sent a ruffle of smiling murmurs through them. They all looked at each other, as if trying to decide who should speak, except one who kept her eyes fixed on him. This apparently elected her the de facto leader as all the others began elbowing her. She frowned, elbowed them back, and bowed slightly.

The others followed suit, and so he returned the gesture in kind.

"The hero is also polite." Her words were delicate and quiet, her head bowed.

"Hero? Uh, I'm no hero." Goddesses, what fresh insanity was this?

"We heard Linali's son had signed up for our clan Contests and that he's fighting tomorrow."

"Well, that is a true statement. That hardly makes me a hero."

"He's humble too!" the hand cupper said again in a loud whisper.

"Did you... want something? I'm a little busy." He gestured at the book, which was really a weak excuse as it hadn't told him a damn thing yet, but anything to get out of this awkward situation.

"Just to let you know you'll have our support," the leader said, actually batting her eyelashes now. "We'll be cheering for you."

"Oh, uh..." He stared dumbly for a second before marshaling enough wits to exit the conversation without embarrassing himself. "Thanks." He started to shut the door.

"Wait! We made you this." The fourth one, who heretofore had not whispered or batted any eyelashes but had simply stared, shuffled forward and slid a scroll onto the open book in his hands.

"Uh... thanks again." And before it could go any further, he quickly shut the door.

Pressing his ear against the door, he listened to make sure they were gone before he examined the scroll. The paper looked like ordinary stock, four sheets rolled up, the holy glyphs for good luck carefully painted by skillful brushes. It seemed harmless enough, but he frowned at them on the desk.

Another knock sounded. This time he cracked the door open only slightly and peeked out.

It wasn't Lara this time either, but when he saw who it was, he threw the door wide anyway.

"Grel!"

His brother greeted him with a huge hug and a slap on the back that did not rival Cerivil's but was hearty nonetheless.

"Nyalin! Look at you! I'm sorry it's taken me so long to stop by."

"I'm sorry I haven't made it back to the Obsidian house too."

"Well, you've clearly been busy. Starting any ice storms yet?"

A nervous laugh escaped him. "Not exactly." He hadn't thought of their cheating plan when it came to Grel—should he tell his brother the whole truth? Part of it? None of it? What would Lara prefer? He had no idea, and it didn't seem fair to choose without consulting her.

But Grel was his brother. The only person he trusted in nearly all the world.

"Su said you were doing well." Grel grinned.

"Yes, improved. Magic still hasn't come easily, but things are improving. We're finding a few... workarounds. I'm actually due for a lesson in a few minutes."

"That's great. I won't stay long." Grel ran a hand through his overlong dark hair and sank down to a seat on Nyalin's bed beside where Smoke had curled up. "What's this I hear about Contests? You're fighting tomorrow?"

"I've signed up."

"Wow. Exciting. I'll be there to watch, by the way. I had to get over here to talk to you before the big day. So you think you have a chance?"

He shrugged. "No idea. Not really. I figured it'd be good experience either way."

"I'm sure you'll learn a lot. But no one knows the book-learning part better than you."

"And that is worth what exactly? Nothing."

Grel shook his head. "Don't be silly. It's worth a lot. Su was right, you look well in brown."

Nyalin held out his arms and twisted back and forth, showing off the crossover. "What can I say? I look good in everything."

Grel snorted as there was another knock.

By Seluvae, let it please be Lara this time.

And thank the goddesses it was. She smiled wide and looked about to launch into something when she caught sight of his brother on the bed and stopped short.

Grel's eyebrows flew up, and he rose to his feet. "Lara! Well met. Strength to you and your father." He bowed deeply.

She bowed in return. "Thank you. Luck to you, as well."

"You look different. Your hair—"

"Is more manageable now," she said, more of the joy draining from her face.

"Both ways suit you," Grel said graciously.

"You're too kind."

"No such thing," Grel shot back. "I make an effort of trying to find out, but I haven't found a limit just yet."

That was enough to charm a small smile out of her. "Were you two busy with something? I can return later—"

"No, no," his brother said quickly. "Don't let me keep you from your lesson."

"Well, I just... found something in my research I wanted to share." She looked at Nyalin hesitantly.

He shrugged. "I have no secrets from my brother," he said slowly. "I'd trust him with my life. But of course, you're the one who knows what you're going to say."

Grel raised his eyes, but Lara seemed appeased and launched forward.

"Have you ever heard of magical locks?"

"Of course," said Nyalin. "One of the spheres of magic is basically all locks. Big things, small things. Isn't that one of the basic spells?"

"Yes, and we should tackle that one tomorrow. I have the charm for it." She said the words casually but of course there was more to that meaning than Grel would know. "But I discovered that at the highest levels, the locks can be applied to things *other* than physical things."

"Like what?"

"Like souls. Like *magic.*"

Nyalin blinked. "What does that mean?"

Grel was rubbing his chin. "Huh. I've never met anyone who could cast it. But it's supposedly possible."

"I never have either, of course. And why would you? But it might account for some of our difficulty."

"Is there anyone we could ask more about it?" Nyalin asked. "Where did you hear about it?"

She faltered for a minute, a strange look crossing her face. Ah, yes. It was easy to forget and feel close to her, but they both had their secrets still, didn't they? But what could she be hiding related to this?

Grel spoke first. "My father specialized in fire, so he's no help. Not that he would have helped anyway. There are several scholar monks with the Holy Sect of the Wolf who might know something, but the monastery is a day's ride out of the city. At least. Maybe Varial of the Silver Clan... Or Attatu of Pearl has studied some magical curiosities. And of course, Emperor Pavan knows more high-level spells than anyone I know. Hey, I heard you talked to him to get this all arranged. How did that come about, anyway?"

Lara's cheeks flushed a little. "My father's doing, actually."

Grel smiled. "A cleverer man than others, I think."

"Maybe." She shifted her weight.

"I can ask the emperor," said Nyalin. "He's been taking an interest, telling me tales about my mother."

"Now *that's* a meeting I'd like to attend. But sadly I must go to a different one now. The feuds over market stall allocation never cease." Grel rolled his eyes.

"Thank you for coming by." Nyalin bowed. "I'll have to return the favor soon."

"No need. Stopping by is a nice way to escape the nonsense. At least for a little while." His brother rose and ran a hand through his hair again, shoving it out of his eyes.

"Oh, thank you for that book by the way," Nyalin added. "It's been... very interesting."

"What book?"

"The one you left on my desk right before I left. I figured it was a gift. *Unusual Magical Phenomena*."

Grel blinked. "I didn't bring you any book. Not recently, anyway."

Nyalin frowned. "What? Where did it come from then?"

"No idea." He shrugged. "See you later. And good luck in those Contests!"

As Grel shut the door on his way out, Lara turned to him. "He heard about the Contests already?"

Nyalin nodded. "I wasn't sure how much to tell him. I never hid anything from him, but, well, this is different. I kept it vague. Wanted to talk to you first."

She smiled. "I appreciate that."

"So now that he's gone, can you tell me where you heard about this? And if we have any chance of breaking a lock of that kind?"

She frowned hard. "I... I can't really. I promised I wouldn't."

What was the big deal? "So someone told you. You didn't just read it in a book. How do we know we can trust them?"

Her expression darkened further. "I just... it's complicated. We can trust each other, I swear it."

He sighed and tried to repress the sudden wave of hurt, but it didn't work. "You said you'd be honest with me. I'm being honest with you." Although he had a few of his own secrets too. Damn, he was a hypocrite.

"I *am* being honest with you," she insisted.

He swallowed. "Okay. Okay, fine. I thought we were beyond keeping secrets from each other, but let's move on. How do we break it?"

She stepped closer to him, her eyes searching his face. "No, you're right. We are beyond that."

Some weight in his chest lifted. He forced himself to wait. She'd tell him when she was ready.

"The best way is to just show you. C'mon." She started for the door, then slowed at the desk as she saw the half-unrolled scrolls. "What's this?"

He groaned. "Four girls with batting eyelashes showed up this morning and handed me these."

Lara raised an eyebrow. "News travels fast, apparently."

"Can you tell if they are harmless?"

She frowned. "Do you have reason to worry?"

"I always worry."

"Well, I don't notice anything, but we can ask Pyaris to check for curses too. Okay, c'mon." She gathered them up. On the way out into the hall, she flagged down a servant and asked them to send the scrolls with a brief message to Pyaris.

He followed her to her room. After so many trips back and forth between their rooms the last two weeks, he'd stopped trying to avoid being seen. Was that a good thing or a bad thing?

Lara closed the door behind them. "Okay, I, uh, have something to show you. But you can't tell anyone."

"Do you need me to sign in blood?"

"I considered it, but I figure we are already risking each other's lives. What's one more thing? But... but it's a big thing."

"How big?"

"Very."

"Hmm. Well, in for a copper, in for a gold." He knelt beside her. "You can trust me, Lara. I won't share this, even with Grel. Unless you tell me to, of course."

She nodded, but she was sweating now, her nerves more apparent after his words, not less.

He reached out and laid a hand over hers.

She stared at him for a long moment and brushed the side of his hand with her thumb. Then she pulled her hand away as she leaned forward. "All right. Brace yourself."

She drew a box out from under the bed. Inside it, shining satin and smooth silk swam in various shades of milk and honey, and for a moment his mind sketched just how exactly these garments might look like in grand detail.

But her fingers just pushed the garments out of the way, and he pulled his thoughts back down to earth. A glimmer of something metallic caught his eye. Then something pale. Almost... bone colored.

His breath stopped as it came into view.

"It was you," he whispered.

She nodded, her face a mixture of calm resignation and numb fear. The dagger lay between them, loud in the silence.

"Why?"

"If I have it, they can't give it to Andius, right?"

"You didn't anticipate he might try to fake a new one."

"He may still fail that." An edge of hope rang in her voice.

"Or we may succeed. And then what?"

"I don't know. I didn't want to bring you in on this, because it would incriminate you too. But I figured you had a right to know where the magic I was funneling to you is coming from."

He raised his eyebrows. "Goddesses... we have that much

power on our side?"

Her features relaxed somewhat. "Yes. So you're not going to turn me in to my father?"

He snorted. "So Andius can have the blade and be clan leader too? Not likely. Did you really think I would?"

"I didn't think so. But you never know, one can always be wrong. Anyway, I mentioned it today... because it was the Bone Dragon who told me about magical locks."

He stared at her. "Really? You can talk to it?"

"*Her*, and yes. She won't stop talking half the time."

A low growl sounded in his head once again.

"Hush," Lara said to the air. "I'm just kidding."

"Did she have any advice on the lock? If it's truly real?"

I can offer no advice.

Nyalin's eyes widened.

"Is she talking to you too now?"

"Uh-huh."

We would need to know more about how the lock was created in order to break it. But I have inspected you, child of Linali, and there is definitely a lock preventing you from reaching most magical sources.

"Wow." He caught Lara's eye and grabbed her hand again. "That's wonderful. Finally something solid, a clue I can work on."

"You don't think I'm awful for taking the dagger?"

"I think they're awful for putting you in this position, and that's it. And it sure helps me that you're talking to her now. I'm sure Andius wouldn't ask the great dragon questions on my behalf."

The dragon snorted a sulfurous puff into his mind. *And if he asked, I wouldn't answer anyway.*

Lara rolled her eyes.

"Besides," Nyalin continued. "It's not like you have a lot

of options. Your brother would have had options, right?"

He almost missed the glimmer of a tear in her eye as she smiled. She squeezed his hand and let it go. Then she covered the dagger and pushed it back under the bed.

He eyed her for a moment longer. "You know, I knew you were brave. But I had no idea."

Her cheeks flushed, bright round twin spots. "No, I'm not."

"Yes, you are."

"What are you going to do about the lock now?"

"I'm going to talk to the emperor."

Chapter 13
Sort of Dead

Dawn had barely tinged the sky with light when Nyalin set out into the city. The Contests would start at noon, as soon as the sun hit its zenith and the gong rang. He needed to track down the emperor before then.

Of course, that was easier said than done. The emperor had written to delay their usual lunch meeting, and Nyalin had been so caught up in preparing for the Contests that he hadn't thought anything of it.

He did make a stop at the graveyard first, though. He was never sure why, but perhaps this time it was for luck. Maybe he'd been in the Bone Clan too long, focusing on luck at a time like this.

He cleared away wilting flowers from the cool stone, knelt in the small prayer square, bowed his head, and sat for a long moment.

"I'm trying," he whispered. "But I'm not sure about any of this."

Of course, no answer came.

The emperor's palace wasn't somewhere he'd visited often. He'd come there to receive his gems as a young

Obsidian—the same ones he'd traded to Cerivil for his Bone Clan ones. Maybe there had been a festival or two? It couldn't have been more times than fingers on his hand.

Still, he pretended complete comfort with the idea and marched inside the large, beautiful arches. The walls were covered with blue and white tiles, and the fountain in the center featured six dragons spouting water in various artful directions.

He stopped and looked around. Was he too early? There was no one here.

As if materializing out of thin air, a woman in glorious azure appeared, the fabric draping around her instead of crossed and belted in the usual style. Her skin was olive too but darker than his, and a birthmark was dotted under one eye.

He spoke up quickly, before she could. "Pardon me, but I need to speak with the emperor."

She bowed her head briefly in acknowledgment, and when she spoke, her voice was sweet and excessively polite. "Petitioners' hours begin at the afternoon's gong, young one. We must—"

"Please. I can't wait. I must see him. It's urgent."

"What details can I carry to his advisors to explain the urgency?"

She seemed earnest, but he froze. He didn't even want to explain the true urgency to *Pavan*. Oh, I'm planning to cheat like hell to win one of the clan's Contests in a few hours, but you know it'd be really great if I could not do that, so just on the off chance you know how I could compete legitimately, could you tell me? Thanks.

Yeah. That'd be just great.

"It is difficult to explain," he said more politely. "And sensitive. Could you perhaps tell him Nyalin moLinali humbly requests—no, begs—his presence for no more than ten minutes?"

His request must have seemed reasonable enough, because she measured him for a long moment before nodding again, deep and graceful as a swan, and then glided away.

He tried sitting on the edge of the fountain, but his leg tapped so incessantly it annoyed even him. He was going to sprain something. Instead, he took to pacing back and forth, and then around the thing, and then when that had him dizzy, he reversed directions.

"Nyalin! Well met. Honor and great luck to you, these days."

He whirled. By the dark dragon, his humble request had worked. Emperor Pavan strode in his direction. He was in full court regalia today, something Nyalin hadn't seen on their walks. The emperor's crossover was impossibly fine, bold red and bordered in thin, intricate patterns of azure and gold, and his striking sword Shadow Wing hung on his hip. Nyalin bowed deeply. "Emperor. Luck to you, as well." The greeting still felt strange and a little weak on his lips. Wishing people strength was a tough greeting to follow. "Thank you for seeing me. I only ask for a few minutes."

The man grinned, sweeping his long, curling hair back over his shoulder. His robes were a lapis blue today but woven with gold and green and belted in black. His sword hung at his hip as always. "I was just about to eat breakfast. Why don't you join me?"

"If it's not too much of an imposition, Emperor."

"Not at all. Come."

He led Nyalin through a smaller archway to the left side, down a hallway, and into a bright, yellow-painted room with blue tiled floors—and a huge table set with a lavish breakfast for two.

"Were you expecting someone?" Nyalin asked, uneasily

sliding into the second chair.

"No. But my staff are quick and skilled." He smiled broadly again, gentle eyes twinkling. "Eggs? Bread? This one's properly baked this time, and I promise I didn't make it."

Nyalin couldn't help but smile back, and it drained some of his nerves. In a blink, Pavan had his plate piled high with food, and Nyalin began to eat automatically. No one had tried to take care of him like this since he'd last seen Dalas, and the sudden pang of homesickness made him glad his mouth was full.

After sampling the vast array of meats and eggs and teas and even a little wine, Pavan leaned back in his high-backed chair. "So how are you faring, Nyalin moLinali? How do Cerivil and Lara fare at unearthing your magic?"

Nyalin cleared his throat and gulped one more drink of tea to buy time. "Well, to be frank, Emperor, we've been struggling. But I think I may finally have found a clue as to why."

"Oh?" Pavan raised one eyebrow.

"I think someone may have placed a lock on my magic. I have no idea who or how or why. But it's a theory."

"Whoever gave you that idea?" Pavan asked, head cocked to one side.

"Someone shared the idea with Lara in her research, who shared the idea with me," he demurred. "Do you know anything about spells like that? Grel pointed out that you know more higher-levels spells than anyone."

Pavan smiled as he took a sip of tea. "Linali knew a few more."

"True. But she's no longer with us."

"I hear you keep her grave well tended."

"You hear a lot of things, it seems."

"It's my job as an emperor." He took another sip of tea,

and Nyalin refused to fill the silence, waiting for his answer. "Yes, I've heard of magical locks used from time to time. Mostly in very dangerous scenarios."

"Dangerous?"

"Yes, like locking in a dangerous animal, things like that."

"But this would be a lock on my soul. Or at least my magic."

Pavan's eyes widened. "Really. Fascinating. I suppose it's theoretically possible."

"If I have one, I need to break it. Do you know anyone who could help?"

Pavan hesitated. "Now, now. Let's not be hasty. What if you don't want to break it?"

He shrugged. "How can I know? There's no way to know, without trying. What else can I do, just go become a scribe?" It had seemed so reasonable once. Before he really knew. "I can't just forget about all of it and live an ordinary life. Not now."

"Is ordinary so bad?" Pavan's lips twisted.

"That's an easy thing for an emperor to say."

"I've wished for ordinary more than a few times in my life."

He heaved a deep breath. "Well... I haven't. I have to find a way. Have to. I'm determined."

The emperor sighed deeply. "Is there any way I could talk you out of it?"

Nyalin frowned. "Why would you want to do that?"

All the mirth had faded from the emperor's face. He gazed out the window of the room into the gardens, which were just starting to glow with the fresh morning sunlight hitting the dew. But in Pavan's features, there was no sign of appreciation for that beauty. Instead, he suddenly looked old, and tired, and somber, like he saw someone or something long ago or far away.

"Emperor?" Nyalin said softly. "Are you all right?"

"You can call me Pavan, you know."

Nyalin frowned harder. "Is something wrong?"

He sighed again, then straightened, looking for all the world as if he were about to deliver a thunderous verbal blow. "All right. It is beyond time. You asked, how can you know what will happen? I will tell you. I know what will happen. And you do not want to know. And most of all, you do not want to break that lock."

Nyalin stared, blinking, for a long minute before questions took over. "What do you mean? Tell me then if you know. What will happen?"

"I can't."

"Why not?"

"It's... hard to explain."

"How do you know what will happen, anyway?"

The emperor's lips pursed as he leaned forward, as if he were pondering what to say. Or possibly simply waiting to see if Nyalin would figure it out so he didn't have to.

"How do you know so much about this?" Nyalin murmured, numb to his core.

Pavan's expression slipped further into a scowl. Nyalin stared back, blinking and not wanting it to be true.

Finally, Pavan grunted, shook his head, and leaned back again in the chair. "I know because I'm one of the ones who put it there."

His breath caught. The air went still, crackling with static. Every piece of the world as he knew it shifted and tilted, the foundations of his life shuddering under him.

"What?" he whispered. "*You* put it there?"

"It wasn't just me, but yes."

"Why would you do that?" His voice was barely audible.

"To protect you."

The faintest hint of anger curdled in his gut at those words, waking him from his shocked stupor. All this time, he'd thought himself a failure. All this time, he'd mourned the waste of his mother's talent... and none of it was true?

"Who else?" Nyalin demanded.

"I can't say."

"Who else, damn it? Was it Elix?"

"He helped."

"That son of a bitch. Were there others?"

Pavan winced. "Your mother too."

"What?" He reared up out of the chair, sending it toppling behind him. Pavan stood in turn. "What the—why? How could you? What does that even mean? You should have told me."

"You're probably right. But we were afraid."

"Of what? The emperor, the empire's most powerful clan leader, and its most powerful mage—what by the goddesses were you afraid of?" He was shouting now.

"Of you!" Pavan thundered back.

That slowed the burn of Nyalin's anger for a moment.

Pavan gritted his teeth, swallowed, then spoke. "You don't understand, Nyalin. You were so fragile, and so powerful, and... And she was *dying*." The word came out broken, cracked. Pavan heaved in a heavy breath and let it back out again before continuing. "Who would have protected you, a baby on the other side? She wasn't going to be there to guide you. We were under siege. She had enemies you don't know of, still has them, and they are more powerful than you think. And there was so much blood, so much, and—and—I—"

Nyalin took a sudden step back, his blood running cold. A revelation was forming in his gut, the realization of something he wasn't sure he wanted to know. "You were there," he whispered, stabbing a finger at Pavan. "You were there when she died."

"Sort of. Yes." The man looked like he stood before an execution squad.

"What do you mean sort of?" Nyalin demanded.

"It's complicated."

"Did she *sort of* die? Like I'm *sort of* alive?" He paused, and questions exploded in his mind as Pavan seemed to grope for an answer. Anything other than a simple *She's dead* made the whole world flip further on end. "I'm so sick of hearing it's complicated, it's not so simple, it's hard to explain, everything's different for you, Nyalin. It's usually not so hard, Nyalin."

"I am trying to explain."

"You were there. When I was born."

"Yes."

"Why?" he said slowly, drawing out the word. His voice was heavy with his thoughts, his fears. His sudden certainty.

For an eternity, Pavan said nothing. But Nyalin didn't really need to hear anything. He already knew.

"It was *you*, wasn't it?" he breathed. "You. And you left me with Elix? To rot? To think I was all alone? To *be* all alone?"

"Nyalin, I—"

"I thought my father was dead. Or he didn't know. Or he had some good *reason* for leaving me. Not that he was too busy running his empire to be bothered. To hell with you." He turned and stormed down the hallway, toward the fountain.

He had to get out of here. He needed time to think. To collect his thoughts. Especially before he'd say something he'd regret. The Contests, sweet goddesses, how would he put this out of his mind to compete? What would Lara think? Could he even tell her? The woman in azure hovered near a pillar, frowning as she watched him go.

"Nyalin!"

He didn't stop. He turned out of the palace courtyard and headed down the street.

"Nyalin! Wait."

The voice that echoed down the city street wasn't Emperor Pavan's. Nyalin turned and froze, tripping and just barely keeping himself from wiping out on the cobblestones.

"Dalas?" His voice cracked, like a boy's. Like a child's. Fraught with tears but fighting them hard.

"Nyalin." The emperor's face had transformed, except the expression was just as mournful as before. Maybe more so. "You were never alone."

"Why? I—" Nyalin had drifted back without meaning to, and now he stopped.

"I tried to be there. I tried to help when I could, without drawing suspicion. I left you books, coin. Locked the door when you forgot to. And a lot of other things."

What did this even mean? "I wanted to know the answers. The secrets. I wanted to know who my father was. But now I'm not so sure."

Pavan-Dalas said nothing but crossed the distance between them, stopping barely a foot away.

"Was it you that day?" Nyalin whispered. "Who found me and took me to Pyaris?"

"The necromancer? Yes. I knew Raelt was up to something."

"Smoke? Is that you too?"

"No... Not exactly."

"Not exactly? By Seluvae! Who is—"

"I can explain, all that and more," said Pavan-Dalas. And seeing him up close, it *was* Dalas, Nyalin was sure of it. Not an impersonation. How had he not made the connection before? "But you are competing today in the Contests, aren't you? This will take... a lot of time. Probably more than you have.

And not all is easy to hear."

"I'm not even sure I want to hear it at this point."

Dalas blew out a long breath. "I knew when I agreed to all this that you might hate me for it someday. But you must believe me, I was trying to do what was best for you."

Nyalin gritted his teeth and said nothing.

"Go to the Contests, fight your heart out, and then come back and I will tell you all."

"Fine. But if you want to help me fight—and win—and if you're *really* my father, do one thing for me."

"What is it?" said Dalas, and Nyalin could hear the desire in the man's voice, the hope it was a wish he could fulfill.

"Break the lock," Nyalin whispered. "If you truly put it there, let me stand on my own two feet in this test."

His expression crumbled. "I can't."

"I just want to fight like a normal mage," he shouted. "Is that so much to ask?"

"You can't! That's not what would happen. It's not what you think."

"You've given me *nothing* my whole life, and you can't even give me this?"

The man's face creased with frustration as he searched for words. "No, Nyalin, no—I— I will try to explain. What happens to you when you have access to magic? Lara shares with you, does she not?"

"I can fight," he growled, ignoring the warnings going off in his mind that the emperor might catch on to their scheme if he understood so much. They hadn't counted on that. And anyone else who had helped create the lock, for that matter. "I can fight like a normal mage. Cast any spell. Like I should always have been able to."

"Every time?"

His jaw clenched. "Most of the time."

"And what happens the other times?"

"I... cross over."

"And how does that go for the fight?"

"Well, I can't feel myself getting beaten, so that's a plus. But I can't see to fight back either."

Dalas was nodding. "Your mother grew up constantly in and out of two worlds. Learning two sets of rules about everything. Constant nausea, constant incapacitation. Suddenly ending up somewhere she hadn't started. She was lucky. She had several spirits that looked after her, her father in particular, and he taught her to seek the animals' help in this realm. She had more help in that world than this one. But two worlds for a child? A toddler? It's enough to drive anyone insane. She is lucky she made it out with her mind intact. Mostly intact."

"Why?" he demanded. "Why do we have this ability?"

"Because her father was a spirit," Dalas breathed. "A ghost. Some would say, a demon."

"A *demon*?"

"Whatever you want to call a creature that can move between the worlds. Just like you can move between them."

Nyalin was shaking his head. "You're saying she was... part demon? Are you saying *I* am—"

"She was half spirit," said Dalas, refusing to go the demon route. "And you are a quarter. But what I've told you, it's only the very edge of the blade. Her struggle didn't end there. If Lara had more to give you, if she had a blade, if you had your own magic... you could be very, very dangerous, and in grave danger yourself."

But she *did* have a blade. And he was going to find out what they could do with it whether Dalas liked it or not.

A minor gong rang out in the tower, the hour passing. Both

their heads shot up, like dogs on the hunt. It was almost time.

"I will go to the Contests," Nyalin spat out. He backed away, needing to move but not wanting to turn away just yet. "But then we'll talk. We're not done here."

"I know." Dalas nodded. "Please. Whatever you do. Don't break that lock."

"No promises," Nyalin said.

Dalas wrung his hands around his wrists but seemed to accept Nyalin's words. He took one more hopeful step forward, but Nyalin danced back. "Go on. I will explain all when you return. And good luck, my son."

Nyalin's steps faltered, but he could think of no answer. In spite of all the anger, and all the questions, something surged and eased in his chest at the emperor's words.

He gave Dalas one sharp nod, turned, and ran.

Considering she'd spent most of her mornings with Nyalin for the last few weeks, Lara found herself unsure of exactly what to do while he was off with the emperor. They'd practiced every spell and charm they could. They'd perfected the flow of energy, talked through strategies if she was drawn away for a time—like giving him a bit of a well to work with, or for either of them to delay and excuse themselves so they could return.

There was nothing left. If they hadn't tried it by now, one morning wasn't going to change anything.

While she was tempted to go sit in the stadium and wait, that would hardly be comfortable. And people might misinterpret her enthusiasm.

Instead, she took to the gardens again. But the cold morning air chilled the stone benches, the trees were wet with morning dew, and the air bit through her cloak and crossover and into her bones. And so she hit the streets for a walk.

Anything to burn off this nervous, reckless energy.

And so she wasn't sure exactly what part of the district she was in when a bag closed over her head.

She jabbed an elbow backward, and from the sound of it she made contact, but there was more than one attacker. How many limbs were there, pulling her back and down? She stomped as hard as she could, aiming for toes and insteps, and lashed out when she got an arm free. She threw bubbles of shadow and water left and right, but being unable to aim, what good would they do? If any? There were way, way too many. She went down, and rope tightened around her wrists, hands crushing her fingers to keep her from breaking their hold.

Yeska!

My daughter! I am coming!

Her ankles, too, were bound, and her body was hoisted up over someone's shoulder, and try as she might, her kicks accomplished nothing but making her feel sick. And throwing up while a bag was tied over her head didn't seem like the greatest idea.

She gritted her teeth, pricked her ears, and listened. She would figure out who they were and where they were taking her, and then she'd make them pay.

Chapter 14

UNDERGROUND

THE JOG AWAY FROM THE EMPEROR WAS A hazy mess. Nyalin ran and ran, and he wasn't even sure in which direction or how far, but somehow he ended up in the Bone District again. The day was still early, and he'd run off half his energy—or maybe all of it.

But his head was still whirling with questions.

He stopped to catch his breath for a moment next to some large clan storehouses. He planted his hands on his knees and panted.

His father was the emperor.

He wasn't just Linali's son. He was the emperor's son. What the hell did that mean?

He didn't want it to mean *anything*. But he wondered now if, like Lara, the title would come with some obligations, even if he hadn't known it until an hour before.

And Pavan... was Dalas. And Dalas had always been there, always cared for him. More than a random servant should have, he realized now. It had never seemed odd because it had always been that way. He'd always felt Dalas's love for him, and the man had been like a father to him. Nyalin had even seen it in Pavan today, in the way the man had heaped food on his plate.

What could possibly make an emperor give up his only son for someone else to raise?

That was the real question.

He started off on a slower walk, headed back toward the Bone manor and eventually the stadiums. He still had a little time. He had what he needed on him, aside from a practice blade, which he could also get at the Contests, he'd heard. One that looked less rusty might be a good thing...

By the goddesses. He hoped this wasn't going to be horrifically embarrassing. What if somehow their plan didn't work? And even worse, what if it did? Emperor Pavan would know of their deception. Elix would know too. Who else had helped them? Surely not Cerivil, but other clan leaders? They would all know he and Lara had cheated.

The plan had been imperfect, but he'd never counted on this.

He had to find Lara and tell her. He needed to get back to the Bone manor, catch her before she left for the stadium. He leapt into a run again.

Even in his disturbed haze, he sensed the lunge of the first man from the alley. He spun, whirled, and dove into a roll. But there was another to greet him at the end, launching a punch at the cobblestones and his head.

Nyalin rolled back the other way. Not now. Not again.

Three more ran up and jumped toward him, but he never even saw them arrive. A slam of energy hit him hard, then another, then a third, and the world didn't even get to shiver this time. He was thrust into the afterworld, any grip on his original one lost like sand through his hands.

He was lying in a sea of waving grass. He was alone. And

he had no idea what they were doing to his body, or if he would live.

~

When the bag flew up over her face, Lara spat blindly at whoever was doing the lifting. And she wasn't wrong.

Andius glared at her, slowly wiping his cheek clean.

"You," she whispered, shaking the hair out of her eyes. "I should have known."

"Tell me where the clanblade is." Andius straightened.

She surveyed the room around them. Over a dozen men crowded behind Andius. It was dark, cave-like, underground maybe, but there weren't many identifying details. Most concerning, another form slumped nearby on the floor.

"Tell me," he commanded again, kicking at her foot to draw her attention. Between them he dangled her charms—the ones they'd discovered and taken as they searched her for the dagger. "Where is it? And you can have your charms back."

"I don't have it. I told you. How would I of all people know that?"

Andius sighed and tossed the charms recklessly over his shoulder like a stray handful of salt. "Guess you won't be getting these, then. You never were easy." He looked coldly to the man to his right, and that man pulled a bag off the head of the other form.

Nyalin. It shouldn't have been surprising, but she caught her breath. Blood dripped from his nose, the corner of his mouth. She wasn't sure if it was encouraging or terrifying, but there was a faint shine of white at the edges of his eyelids. Was it something like his mother's power? They'd triggered it a few times in their practices, but it had been something he'd worked hard to avoid, not going into many details. What was triggering it now?

Andius drew a small knife from inside his crossover, crouched, and held it to Nyalin's neck, where his heartbeat pulsed under his skin.

"Tell me, or I'll kill him."

Lara stared, eyes wild, darting back and forth from Nyalin to Andius and back again. In all her attempts to escape this man, she'd never expected something like this. This was certainly a worst-case scenario. And Nyalin being in danger was entirely her fault.

"I told you..." she started, her voice faltering.

"Lara?" Nyalin's eyes had opened, and he raised his head slightly. Andius rewarded this with a swift palm strike to the temple, bouncing his head off the packed dirt beneath them.

"Stop!" Her breath was ragged, her voice a shrill scream. "Fine. Fine, damn it. I'll tell you. But you have to let us go."

"You're in no position to negotiate, Lara." Andius gave her one of his small, slick smiles. "I'm keeping you both here until after the Contests are over. I don't know what you were planning, but you're not going to get to try it. I'm going to win, with the clanblade or without it, and then I'll come back and claim you."

"You still won't be clan leader."

"I didn't mean as clan leader. I simply mean as my property. You would have made a decent wife for a clan leader. Not a great one, but you have the looks for it and the people like you well enough. But as it is, you've caused me far too much trouble. I think you're much better off to me... out of the way, so to speak."

"You wouldn't."

"Kill you? I haven't decided yet. Maybe I could sell you to the Mushin or simply send you to a tower in the steppes.

Or better yet, a root cellar. Chaining you in a cell for a few years should do wonders to tame that wild streak of yours. But killing you *would* be fun." He shook his head. "Decisions, decisions. Always so difficult. But first, you'll decide. Does Nyalin live, or does he die? Last chance, little *dragonfly*. Tell me where the clanblade is."

Her eyes locked with Nyalin's. He shook his head subtly, but she had no idea if that meant don't tell him or don't let me die. Not that it mattered. She couldn't possibly. But if Andius got his hands on the clanblade...

I'm coming, daughter! But you are buried... I can't find you. I am near, but you are so far down.

It's okay, Yeska. I'll work my way out of this.

She swallowed and straightened. "Fine. I took it. And I'd take it again."

"I *knew* it. Tell me where it is. Now," he said, fingers tightening on the knife.

Somewhere far, hard to reach, but not so far it seemed implausible she might have smuggled it there... "I dropped it in the bottom of the well in the Glass District main square. Now at least let him go."

He gaped at her. "You threw a sacred clanblade into a *well*? In *another* clan's district?"

She jutted out her chin. "I had to do something once they started looking. C'mon, Andius. Keep me, but let him go." This wasn't helping her arguing position, but she didn't have much of one at this point.

Andius laughed in her face. "Oh, no. I don't think so. Then he'd come to the Contests and enact whatever you two have planned. I think instead I'll lock you both in here for a long, long time, while I think on what to do with you. Maybe the rats will eat you first. Or maybe you'll eat each other." He smiled as if he were talking of choosing a place to have tea. "Wouldn't that be fun. Lock them up."

The men hauled her across the ground and down two shallow stairs, their rough grips causing all manner of injuries as her hip, backside, and wrist bounced against the floor. They sent her tumbling onto her side, her shoulder pulling hard. Nyalin fell too, disturbingly without reaction or exclamation of pain, and a heavy iron door slammed shut.

The lock clicked. The place was pitch-black except for the light cast by a single torch outside the cell door. What would happen when it burned low?

She struggled to her knees and crawled to the bars, trying to catch a glimpse of if they left her charms behind. But it was all a blur of black robe, cloak, and shadow. The men's voices laughed and rumbled, but eventually they drifted away, and it was silent. Could she reach the charms? She tried, but she couldn't get a sense of their different energies. They were just a little too far, if they remained at all.

The dagger was distant but still present in her mind, so she worked her basic healing spell, the magic slow to come and slow to work. But better than nothing at all. Her shoulder eased. The ache arching from her wrist toward her elbow faded. She couldn't resist chafing against the rope bindings, but they weren't coming off that way.

Through it all, Nyalin didn't move. Sweet goddesses, if he'd died, here in some cellar because he agreed to help her— The glowing light had faded from his eyes. Examining him closer, it didn't look like they'd even bothered to bind him. How hard had they beaten him? She chewed on her lip and risked nudging him with her foot.

"Nyalin?" she whispered.

His eyes flickered open. "I..." He stopped and groaned.

"Thank the Twins, you're alive," she whispered.

He nodded weakly. "Barely." Something tugged at the corners of his mouth.

"Are you laughing? What could possibly be funny right now?"

"Long story."

"Well, time is one thing we got. Listen, I'm going to try to heal you a little. What I can—they took my charms. But it'd be nice if you could get well enough to untie me."

"Wake me up in five minutes, and I'll try then." He half rolled, half collapsed onto his back and shut his eyes, and she began her work.

"Is it getting better?" Lara's voice cut through his haze. Nyalin opened his eyes and squinted at her. The golden halo was tighter around her crown now, but the dim light made it no less striking. What had she asked him? Oh, yes, the healing. He focused on his body for a moment.

"Better," he said. "I'll see if... I can move... in a minute."

She snorted, even if it wasn't really that funny. "You know, you did that thing with your eyes again. The glowy thing. That your mother did."

"I know."

"How do you know if you can't see it?"

"It's... complicated," he said, and then started to laugh. Oh, the irony.

"Are... are you sure you're all right?"

"Let's just say it's been a tough morning."

"I know. Me too. But you look like you had it worse."

"The Contests are probably starting now."

"Screw the Contests," she said. "I'll be glad to get out of

here alive."

He had not given up hope for either of those things just yet, but he didn't say anything. He cleared his throat instead. "When you see that light in my eyes, when the ability is triggered, I see some pretty strange things too." That was a weak explanation. But actually coming out and saying it... she was going to think he was crazy. Probably wonder if he'd been hit a little too hard on the head.

Which maybe he had, but it wasn't causing *that* problem.

"Try sitting up now," she suggested gently.

He did, although his head swam at first. He was far from healed, but he was also still planning to show up to those Contests, so there wasn't time to lose. He gingerly got on all fours and crawled to untie her, trying to hide the grunts and gasps that came with each new pain.

She heaved a deep, satisfied sigh as her wrists came free. She rubbed where the rope had been. Getting to her feet, she paced around the outside of their small cell, dug at the floor with one foot.

"Dirt," she said dryly. "What is this, a wine cellar? Or just a hole in the ground?"

There was no other window or door, only the heavy iron one, and her investigation of it revealed little in the way of weaknesses.

"Any magical locks?" Nyalin asked. "You know we love those."

"No, unfortunately. Only metal ones."

"Damn."

"What did the emperor have to say, anyway?"

"It was a very eventful morning."

"Which means?"

He hesitated. He didn't want to hide *anything* from her

at this point. It was just a matter of breaking it all to her in the right way, at the right time. This didn't seem like the right time for anything, really. But he had no choice.

"Well, there was a lot. But the lock is real. And he admitted to putting it there, with the help of Elix and my mother."

She gaped at him. "But *why*? And why didn't they tell you?"

"That, I don't know. But he urged me not to break it."

She frowned. "Pyaris said the same thing. Or something along those lines."

"Really? Maybe she can tell us more. I couldn't get him to answer half my questions. He promised to tell me more after the Contests."

"And now this." She threw out her hands, then slapped them to her sides. "Now we'll never know, cause we're going to rot in here."

"No, no." He groaned as he forced himself to stand up too. "We'll figure a way out of here."

In fact, he had a theory. He'd lost consciousness during this latest attack, so his soul seemed to have followed his body and returned to it on its own. But he *had* used the afterworld to move—to teleport—away from Raelt. Could he use it to teleport out of this cell? Could he bring Lara with him? What happened if he went too far and teleported them into the solid dirt beyond?

He swallowed. Nothing worth having was ever easy... He eyed the distance to the door, the length of the hallway beyond. Was space the same across worlds? *Exactly* the same?

"Let me try something," he said. "Give me some power. A lot, if you can manage. Let's trigger my mother's power again. I think I may be able to use it to get us out of here."

"Really?" She tilted her head and came closer. He could already feel the magic flowing in.

The vertigo hit—awful, since his head was spinning just fine on its own if he moved—and the world flickered gently. He reached for it this time, embraced the transition like diving into deep water.

The green world was dark around him and nondescript. Was he underground? Did that matter in the afterlife?

He stood. It didn't ache to do so; that was a nice side effect. He took exactly seven steps in the direction he'd faced himself. Then he opened his eyes and reached for Lara, for the other world once again.

Dark brown enveloped him, easier this time. He faced a blank dirt wall.

"You're out!" Lara shouted from behind him, clutching the bars and grinning. "How did you do that? Your eyes went all white, and then it was just like—*boom*. A flash. And you're out there now."

"A gift from my mother, I guess." He shrugged. That was as good an explanation as any.

"Look for a key."

He limped around and searched through the rubble, but his strained efforts produced nothing. No key. Just a few supplies, discarded bags and rope, a lantern. "There's not much out here. No keys. No charms."

"Damn." She pounded a fist against the cell door once. "Okay, well, go and get help and come back for me. No, go beat Andius at the Contests, *then* come back for me—"

"Let me try one other idea. Just a little more power, please."

She nodded, and the energy surged on in. He reached more directly this time, waited less, and crossed over easily. Seven steps more, and he slipped back.

Well, this could get interesting.

He stepped toward her. "You had your secrets. I guess I

have a few too." She frowned up at him, but there was trust in her eyes. "Can you hold on to me?"

She hesitated. "Sure. If you want me to."

Her words were casual, but as he slipped his arms around her, her returning grip was like a vise. He took a deep breath, her scent fortifying him, and then he reached for the next world again, imagining the green covering them, easing into them both.

He opened his eyes, not realizing he'd closed them, and there she was, lit by pale, sickly green but eyes as bright as ever.

She stared around them, her expression wild. "What is this?"

"It's the next world. The next in the sequence. Our mirror world."

"Where there are ghosts?" she whispered.

"Yes. But not many. I didn't see any nearby."

"You see them?" Her eyebrows flew higher.

"From time to time when I'm here. This is what I see when my power is triggered. I cross over to this other world. But it matches up to our world somewhat. Follow me this way." He eased her the seven steps forward.

"Ready to go back?"

She nodded numbly, mouth hanging open, and he reached for their original world. It was harder this time, took more effort, but he squeezed her tighter and focused as hard as he could. He opened his eyes as he felt the vertigo fade and her grip on him loosen. He was loath to release her, but he understood his magic so poorly, he didn't want to risk anything experimental with her in his arms.

Laughter burbled out of her. "We're out! You did it! We're out!"

He grinned. "We better get to the Contests."

But she sobered quickly. "No—you get there. I've got to get the clanblade before Andius realizes I... well, you know." She gave him a knowing look and glanced up the hallway. She'd clammed up because some of Andius's cronies might still be nearby. "And they took all my charms."

"Mine too. I can get by with the basic spells in the first round. It'd be better not to, but..."

"No, it will be quick to get more. I have a backup set of charms in my pack in my room. You said to have a backup plan, remember? I'll meet you there."

"Good. Let's go." Climbing the stairs bruised and bleeding wasn't easy, but nothing could have stopped him.

Chapter 15

Birthright

"You're late."

Of course, it was the eagle-eyed old woman who caught him just outside the stadium. He nearly collapsed at her feet from panting.

"I came—as soon as—I could."

"Oh, did our timing inconvenience you?"

"No, I—was unfortunately—indisposed—but I'm—here now."

She pursed her lips, looked him up and down once, but apparently he was suitably miserable-looking. "Are you all right? What happened?"

He waved at the air. "It's a—long story."

"Fine, fine. We haven't completed round one. The spheres test. Get in the line, and you shan't be too late."

He nodded and raced toward a young man in a bone-colored crossover, the last in a short line.

In the center of the wide stadium, thirteen copper bowls shone in the midday sun on elegant pale wood pedestals, one for each sphere of magic. He struggled to catch his breath without the others noticing as he peered around to watch.

A contestant strode forward, bowed to the crowd, then reached one arm out to the bowl at his left. His hand twisted, rotating palm up, and flame plumed up from the bowl.

The crowd gave a smattering of polite applause. It was a basic fire sphere spell, Ignite, and it would earn him one point. Any basic spell earned one point, while any higher-level spell earned double its level. Thus a third-level spell could accrue six points. Together they'd only practiced one of those, and he wasn't sure he was going to try it. If only he knew how many points Andius had earned and what he was dealing with.

The current contestant skipped the next bowl to the disappointed sighs of the onlookers. Nyalin shook his head. With thirteen overall spheres of magic, there were going to be some spheres the young swordmages had not yet mastered. Too bad skipping any sphere resulted in a penalty.

Nyalin scratched his chin. He was back with all the young and inexperienced mages at the end of the line, wasn't he? Or perhaps the experienced swordmages hadn't even shown up, because they were all content to let Andius win.

Would it kill them to post the contestants or scores on the wall somewhere?

As he watched, the current mage managed to Palm Flash some white light and cast two Water and Earth Bubbles, which would get him nice first-level bonuses. Finally, he blossomed one flower and summoned a butterfly before he bowed his goodbyes.

His magic had earned him seven points total. Sadly, the young man earned just as many penalty points, as seven bowls remained quiet and empty. The crowd gave a muted reaction to this showing, and Contest officials ran up from the sides to douse flames, remove buds, and lay fresh soil and other spell substrates.

The other contestants waiting in line smiled and waved at the most recent one as he walked past, the scent of rosemary following him. His spirits seemed high. The boy hadn't had any problems or embarrassments. He just hadn't come here to win. Perhaps it was practice. Or tradition.

Nyalin couldn't settle for that.

He fidgeted in his empty pocket where he'd taken to rolling his cold charms, Lara's stolen gifts that would be his only chance of a decent showing here. They should get him through the round. If Lara made it back and showed up with another set. And if Cerivil didn't ask what the hell Nyalin was doing with them.

He stayed low behind the young man in front of him, who fortunately was a tall, beefy youth, and scanned the crowd for Andius while he waited.

There—across the stadium, sitting near Cerivil. Andius's face was flushed, forehead shiny with sweat. Had that snake tried to find the clanblade in the well, or had he sent his cronies to do it for him? Either way, he must have hurried to get all the way back here and compete already.

"Nyalin." The voice behind him froze him to his very core. A voice from his childhood, and not a good one. "I've been looking all over for you."

Slowly Nyalin turned to face Elix.

"What are you doing here?" Nyalin's voice was quiet, but inside panic danced through his veins. Elix knew about the lock. Had the emperor talked to Elix in such a short period of time? Past his foster father, a panting horse milled in imperial livery. Had Elix been at the palace even at the same time Nyalin had?

He braced himself for Elix's words while his brain searched for a loophole. Elix would want to stop him. To tell everyone it was impossible that this weak boy cast any spells at all, let alone these. How could he cut the argument down? His mind raced but he came up with nothing. If Elix knew the truth, then he knew the truth.

It was going to be over before it began.

Elix's voice was gruff. "I would have liked to do this some other time, under different circumstances. I've imagined this moment time and time again over the years. A time to explain things. But we're out of time. For now, this will have to do."

"What are you talking about?"

The Obsidian Clan leader had drawn nearly every contestant and hooded Contest official that could see him, although they were still out of sight of most people inside the stadium. Surprise grew as Elix dropped to a knee and held up a scabbard spread flat across both palms. Nyalin hadn't noticed he'd been holding anything, he'd been so afraid it was all over.

"What is this?" he said, even as he reached to take it.

"Your mother's sword." Rising, Elix produced a sword belt as well and handed it to Nyalin.

"My—my what?"

"The sword of Linali. Your birthright."

"By Seluvae..." he muttered. Old habits died hard.

Then, to Nyalin's surprise, the huge man clutched him in a hug, the sword an awkward bar between their stomachs.

"It won't do you much good," Elix murmured in his ear.

Nyalin winced; that was the usual attitude he expected from his foster father, not this... weird generosity.

But Elix wasn't done. "It doesn't have the energy it once did. We don't know why. But it will give you the excuse you need."

Nyalin's mouth hung open as Elix released him. Only then did Elix's eyes seem to scan his face and notice the blood.

"What happened to you?"

"Long story."

"Was one of my sons involved?" His already hard face hardened further.

"Not this time."

Elix's eyes closed for just a moment, barely longer than a blink, but the wave of power hit Nyalin like flames licking across his skin. He jumped—but the sudden absence of pain stilled him quickly. Elix had healed him. Elix. What insanity was this?

He was so stunned he almost forgot to bow as his former clan leader bowed to him. "Fight well, child. Seluvae's blessings upon you."

"Thank you, Clan Leader." He bowed deeper even as he felt the other men in line bristle. He was only using the proper title—what else was he supposed to call the man?

Then, just like that, Elix turned and left without another word.

Nyalin stared down at the sword.

It radiated nothing, not even the little a practice sword did. Just wood and metal in his hands, although the scabbard was a beautiful, shining red lacquer. He untied the scabbard and drew the blade an inch. The shining metal was etched with leaves.

What the hell had just happened?

Lara is here, a deep voice growled in his head. *She's sending a messenger, hang on.*

Thanks. I will. He hesitated. Did he need to say something more to properly thank a great dragon? Would she even hear him? *This will take some getting used to.*

Yes, it tends to. And no, I'm thoroughly thanked, and no need for titles.

He wasn't going to have much chance to call her anything if this day didn't start improving. He glanced at the shortening line ahead of him, wiped the sweat off his brow, and watched the next contestant stride out. Then he set to putting the belt on and getting the sword properly hung at his hip.

Elix had had it all this time and never mentioned it. What did he mean by imagining a time to explain things? What did he have to explain? The lock?

He scowled. If they were hiding all this, what else were they hiding?

The excuse you need. The sword could be the excuse for why he could now suddenly do magic when two weeks ago he'd been as magical as a doorframe. Was that the intent? Pavan *knew* Nyalin was cheating today, because he knew about the lock. And that meant that Elix knew too.

And that meant they weren't stopping him.

What was going on? They both had a lot of explaining to do.

Just as another contestant left him and the line shortened further, a little dusty girl scampered up with a fabric bag. She held it up wordlessly, and he took it, bowing.

She waited.

Eying her uncomfortably, like a raven he'd summoned and didn't know what to do with, he opened the drawstring. Indeed, inside were the goddess-given charms. Thank the Twins. He pocketed the charms, reassured by their cool weight.

The sun was beating down. The little girl was still there.

He groped inside the bag, a smile forming. If he had to partner with someone to cheat, he'd chosen just the right person. She'd foreseen this. He drew the silver from the bag and gave it to the girl.

Her eyes narrowed and went from him to the bag and back again.

Sighing, he handed over the empty bag too.

She fled.

His nerves should have been rubbed raw by the time his turn came after all that. But he was far too focused on remembering his spells and distracted by the sword and his damn father. He rubbed the charms, turned them over again and again, and tried to focus on memory rather than worry.

That was true, at least, until he stepped out onto the sand.

As he entered the arena, the bored crowd roused, and acid rushed his veins. Whispers—and some louder comments—flew.

"Who is this one?"

"Don't you know? It's Linali's son."

"Look at that sword!"

"Oh, this should be good."

"No, no, I heard he flunked out as an Obsidian."

"Why's he here then? And why'd he come crawling down to us?"

Because he was clearly a glutton for punishment, it seemed. He lifted his chin, brushed off his robes, and strove to ignore the murmurs by bowing deeply to Cerivil and the officials.

Cerivil's eyes flicked to the sword and widened. The excuse you need indeed—yes. Nyalin caught sight of Grel too, in a row just behind Cerivil, gaze intent. Sutamae clutched Grel's arm and waved, a wicked twist of a smile on her face, although her eyebrows raised at the sword too. Damn—Grel might think Nyalin had earned this somehow. No, he doubted the damn sword smiths would have spent a moment to deny him. He'd have to find Grel afterward and explain.

And there was Andius, next to Cerivil, eyes wide and nostrils flared, looking ready to storm onto the sand and kill him. But Andius didn't move.

Nyalin didn't move either. The mood of the stadium quieted, knotting with anticipation. Then he simply reached out with his mind, finding the first bowl, the pedestal dedicated to all magic of the fire sphere. Sparks dashed off the rim of the copper bowl and into the dirt before the dry wood in the bowl burst into flames.

One point down. Many more to go.

The crowd's applause was more than polite this time.

He could work his way around like several contestants had, but he didn't want to. It was time to take some risks.

He focused on the bowl designated for sound, small symbols set inside as a potential medium. The highest-level spelled he'd attempted was Silent Space. And okay, maybe the emperor had inspired him a little. His admiration felt a little naïve and almost silly now, but Pavan was good at it, and the spell was impressive. Lara hadn't been sure the higher level spell was strictly necessary, so they hadn't settled on how far to go. Given the physical beating he'd taken, he should probably be playing it safe.

But he only had one shot at winning this thing.

He concentrated, drawing the energy together in his core, then gathering it at the charm. Then he flattened his palms against each other and clapped. It was more a social indicator than practical, as he still needed to twist the energy through the charm and—

The wave of silence exploded from his center out, magic moving through him fast. Maybe too fast. Maybe he'd run out and—

No. There she was—new energy flowed in, and just as fast. Thank the goddesses for her. The amount that flew through him startled him. It *had* to be bolstered by the dragon.

You're welcome.

The scent of blackberries was like a punch in the nose, it was so strong. And the clan members in the highest seats had risen to their feet, shouting and waving hands. But he couldn't hear them.

And neither could most of the stadium.

He stared. The space he'd carved out was ten times larger than what he'd planned. And many people *inside* the silent space were stunned into a different kind of silence. He glanced down at the sword on his hip.

Nah, that was all me. Yeska again.

Well. Thanks.

You're welcome. This is fun!

Nyalin released the spell, and the murmurs only grew into cheering and shouts. But he had eleven copper bowls left, and no more tricks up his sleeve.

Lara hid in a far corner of the stadium and prayed to both goddesses that she was reading Nyalin right from this distance—and that her father wouldn't spot her. Andius was sitting beside him, and if Da saw her, Andius would follow his gaze. And who knew what the snake might do if he realized she'd arrived?

Especially since the clanblade was tucked in her bag at her hip. If he demanded she be searched, it would all be over.

She'd wrapped a scarf over her hair and mouth, and thank the Twins it was cold enough to wear a cloak. With the hood up. If anything, she probably looked too covered and a little suspicious this way, but people weren't going to easily recognize her.

The shadow bubble Nyalin blew off his palm was as dark

as the night. It drifted lazily, floating down to a satisfying pop in the appropriate bowl. Shadow sphere—they had mastered it well. Another two points.

He also managed to demonstrate the base Water Float and Bloom spells, solid single points. The lock he made for the sphere of control magic was a thing of sheer beauty.

The boy had so much talent it made her ache.

She pondered what he'd said about the emperor as they worked, but feeding him energy was natural. Easy, even. So Pavan had admitted there was a lock and that he'd known about it all along. Did that mean he'd known her and Da's efforts to help Nyalin would fail? Had the emperor *intentionally* wasted their time? Or had he hoped they would break it?

Or had she conveniently given him the illusion of attempting to help Nyalin without ever actually doing so? Maybe a man who controlled an empire didn't need young upstart rebels with fine pedigrees like Nyalin challenging him. That hardly seemed like Pavan, but it was hard to know what to think anymore.

Nyalin cast a second-level ward from the sphere of caution, and she beamed like a proud parent behind her scarf. They'd practiced that one long and hard. Thank goodness it'd paid off.

He nailed a first-level healing spell too, stitching shut a mock wound that awaited just such a treatment to quite a bit of applause. She had to glance at Da at that one, but his face was turned so she couldn't see his reaction. Or Andius's.

In the end, every sphere had been addressed, each bowl touched by some bit of Nyalin's—and hers and Yeska's—magic. The place pretty much reeked of blackberries.

She sighed in relief. No penalties. That was huge. They'd done all they could.

The crowd's applause was much more vigorous than it had been for the last few contestants, and it swelled when Cerivil stood. He held out his arms wide, embracing them, and gradually they quieted.

"The first round of our Contest is complete. And what a magnificent showing we've seen. First and foremost, a sword-mage warrior of our clan should have a mastery of magic. That mastery should be both broad—and deep. And this is why we begin with these basic demonstrations.

"But there is more to a clan leader than the mechanical casting of spells. Is there not?" An agreeing murmur answered him. "A clan leader must be brave. Bold. Able to defend his clan, his family, himself. Able to smite enemies of the clan should the need arise." He pounded one fist into an open palm, and the crowd roared its approval. He waited till it settled. "We will test that ability to fight—both with the aid of magic and without it. But first, the scores."

The crowd stamped and shouted to spit it out already.

Cerivil cleared his throat. "In the lead, with twenty-eight points of skill demonstrated, is honored clansman Andius naLevin moShra."

A bit of a cheer went up. Andius stood beside Cerivil and waved, spinning to gaze adoringly at his crowd. Her heart flipped when he almost looked right at her. She ducked closer to the stairwell that led out of the stadium and into the street.

"In second place is Faytou naLevin moShra with twenty-six points."

Faytou waved at the crowd from the jumble of young men that stood in the stadium's entryway arch. That was where most contenders who weren't as arrogant as Andius remained. She scanned the group, searching for Nyalin.

"And in third, we have Miros naZalay moNiiseu, with

twenty-three points."

Lara caught her breath. If her accounting was right, Nyalin had twenty-two. He was just behind the leaders. If only she could spot him, see if his expression told her the same thing.

"A great showing for the clan. We shall now begin the second phase of our great clan's tournament. And after that, the feast will begin in the main hall." Cerivil paused as the crowd's excited murmurs swelled and subsided. "The second phase is of course the obstacle course. We have a last minute change, however." The murmurs swelled again as many frowned, especially as Cerivil's face grew especially grim. "One of our contenders has provided some proof of last-minute attempts to cheat at the course. So we have changed the venue to keep the contest fair and the playing field level."

Lara swallowed. Damn. Separation was something they'd considered, practiced for, but it was basically their worst-case scenario. Well, that and being found out. Damn all that time wasted learning the original course—it had been built and waiting in the stadiums next door. Everyone had had the chance to practice that one. Whatever the new one would be... Could it actually be the opposite? Maybe Andius had bribed them to change it to a course only he had gotten to practice?

"Observers may wait at the beginning of the course in the Garden of Dala's Fountain, or near the end of the course at Yakanuk's on the square. Now, contestants please follow me. To the catacombs."

Her eyes picked just that moment to find Nyalin's in the swarm of contestants, and their gazes locked. His expression was somber, and she bit her lip, although he certainly couldn't see it. He nodded slightly.

She nodded back. But a split second later, a chill went through her, a sense of being watched not just by Nyalin.

Andius. Andius had spotted her. And was climbing the stairs.

She ran for the street like her life depended on it. It probably did.

―

He tried not to worry at the way Lara had fled like a hunted doe. She was probably just getting a head start to the course, hoping to meet him there.

But his gut said something else was wrong.

There was nothing he could do to figure that out, though. All the contestants were funneled en masse out of the stadium. They were on the opposite side of where Lara would have reached the street. Officials marched them down the street, left, then another quick right, and he lost hope. There was no way she could have followed fast enough to know where they were.

I know where you are, said Yeska.

That's comforting.

I can tell her, but she's a bit busy at the moment.

Is she okay?

Yes. Just fine, worry not. I can give you magic too, you know. But if I come too close, they might see me.

Is that bad?

I am never sure.

They reached the mouth of the catacombs and stopped.

"You will enter in three groups." The eagle-eyed woman was back, officiating this time. "Listen for your name to be called for your group. The time delay will be subtracted from your final time." Behind her a table was covered with an impressive array of hourglasses and a myriad of labels.

As the names were read off, someone angled out of the crowd in front of him and grinned.

"Faytou!" Nyalin exclaimed. "Great score you had in the first round."

"Thanks, you didn't do so bad yourself. Blew everybody away."

Nyalin shook his head. "Not as good as you. I'm just doing what I can."

"One sec." Faytou held up a finger and paused as his name was called. Nyalin's hadn't been yet; they finished the first group and headed into group two. "Too bad we won't be in the same heat, huh? We could have worked together or something." His eyes twinkled. He said it lightly, but he definitely meant it.

Nyalin shrugged. "We may still see each other on the inside. Think you have a shot of winning this thing?"

Some of Faytou's mirth faded. "I might have a chance at this course, but not in the third round. I'm half his size, and I always preferred books to blades. That's where Andius can beat me, no matter what he does in these other rounds."

"You never know. You might surprise yourself." He would much rather Faytou end up with Lara than Andius. He'd hate it, certainly, but it'd be easier if Lara wouldn't suffer. If Faytou was kind. If they were happy... Hmm, maybe he was kidding himself.

He'd had no idea Faytou was so powerful, although his friend was always excelling in the morning classes. He really shouldn't have been surprised.

They waited together, listening to the names. Nyalin was in the third group. Lara had to be far away now. He shook his head. This wouldn't be good. If it were sheer physical prowess to get them through the catacombs, Nyalin might have a chance, but Cerivil and his books had said this test was specifically about using magic.

He cleared his throat, searching for something to talk about to keep his mind off his rattled nerves. "Nervous about the new course?"

Faytou smirked a little. "Nah, not too worried."

He narrowed his eyes. "What?"

"Nothing."

"Why are you laughing like that?"

Faytou grinned and leaned in closer to whisper. "Because my brother bribed the workers building the original course. Had secret passages built in just for him."

His eyes widened. "*You* asked for the course change?"

Faytou's eyes crinkled as he grinned. "I asked for a fair race."

They quieted to listen to an older man explain the proper path through the catacombs to the exit. "Only those who remember this well will get through quickly enough. Also beware. We have set traps to test what you're made of in every sphere. Flames must be doused, earth shifted, darkness lit. And others. Good luck. Those in the first group, come to the front and prepare."

More than half the young men surged forward, which of course didn't make any sense. Were they cheating or just stupid? Some ended up hanging back though at the last second, and the first group clustered up as they disappeared at a run down the stairs into the darkness, all battling for a position in the narrow tunnel.

When his group came, Nyalin didn't bother. In the second group, one man had gone down in the surging crowd and taken quite a few hard hits before anyone let him stand again. The last thing he wanted was a head injury right now. So he hung back.

And besides. He couldn't make it if he needed magic that only Lara had to get past obstacles. Could the dragon really give him any? The sword hanging on his hip felt useless and quiet.

Unless—

Could he teleport?

At his first chance, he tucked himself into a corner, gathered as much energy as he could—with Yeska's support—and pulled himself into the afterlife. This time he slipped in like a calm bath in an easy, cool pond.

This part of their mirror world was the same, although doused in shades of green. The structure of the catacombs was there in its entirety. Fascinating. Was it because they were homes for the dead? Nyalin raced backward, out of the tunnels, up the stairs. When he reached the flat grassland that seemed to cover most of this afterworld, he raced along, the grass whipping at his legs all too real. Let the other entrance to the catacombs be there too—

It was. He had to nudge aside some overgrown grass and pry open a heavy wooden doorway, but it was there all right. And on the steps sat Lara's brother.

"Where have you been?" Nyalin said slowly, praying to both goddesses his real body wasn't somewhere saying just this same thing in front of a Contest official.

Myandrin grinned. "I could say the same of you."

"Hanging out with your sister."

His face softened. "Tell her I said hello, will you?"

"As soon as I can find a way to bring all this up."

The spirit grinned. "The demon is here, you know."

Nyalin glanced sharply to his right.

"Not here, in this world. In yours. He's with a necromancer that's bound him. They've been watching you compete."

"Well. That's great news."

"Watch out in the third phase. They're helping Andius."

"Of course they are."

Myandrin smiled. "You really like her, don't you?"

Nyalin frowned. "Uh... why would you say that?"

"Aren't you competing to marry her as we speak?"

How many had missed that obvious implication? "You're insightful, for a ghost."

"Treat her right. Or I'll haunt you." Myandrin winked.

"Can you do that?"

"Aren't I already? I'm sure I can figure something out while you're in my world at least."

"You're not going to need to."

"That's what I want to hear. Now—you better get going. Turn in a record time."

"Yeah, for a cheater."

"This is magic too. Seems legitimate to me."

Nyalin shrugged, starting down the steps past Myandrin. Then he turned back. "Wait—any tips for me? Weaknesses Andius has? I won't have magic to help me in the third round."

"Well, he will, so you might want to keep up that cheating streak. Because he is. I don't know what the demon's planning, but they want him to win. But yeah—I fought him for eight years, I know a thing or two." He paused, thinking. "He has only one rhythm. He changes up the exact moves, but he always favors that certain timing. Learn it, and you can predict his attacks. Predictable. And a little overconfident too."

Nyalin's lips thinned. "Imagine that."

"I know. Luck to you." Myandrin waved.

He bowed. "Luck to you as well." And for the first time, the greeting of the Bone Clan felt natural, at home on his lips.

He descended into the darkness. Three flights down, he crept back into the tombs and found an isolated spot.

He jumped back into the real world, icy reality splashing over him like the great river waterfalls. His breath caught as he realized that just in front of him were the backs of a woman's knees. A woman dressed in the azure swinging robes of the emperor.

Struggling to keep his breath calm, he scanned the space. Did he have enough energy for a Throw Sound? What if it sent him crossing back over, for who knew how long? If he could just distract her...

A cracked piece of wall plaster lay on the floor by his foot. Of course—there was always the mundane way. He picked up a shard and tossed it as far as he could past her feet and into the far doorway. He held his breath.

She tilted her head but didn't move.

He groped around, found a smaller one, threw.

Finally, she shuffled over, and while she stood in the doorway, he lunged back into the last tunnel, hoping to both goddesses he wouldn't get caught.

Pressing himself against the quiet stone, he listened and calmed his panting breath. There were no other competitors nearby. The woman shuffled back to her original spot.

Here went nothing.

He turned and jogged forward, as if coming out of the course.

"Excellent! Our first contender!" She grinned. A dozen other officials and members of the Bone Clan rushed in at her call.

Whispers flew.

"So fast."

"Powerful magic indeed—"

"Truly gifted."

"Nyalin moLinali takes first place!" It was the eagle-eyed woman, and to his surprise, she was smiling. "The first contender receives fifty points and a seat at the head of the table for the feast. But don't drink too much. You've got to be ready for the final phase tomorrow. Total score for Nyalin moLinali: seventy-two points. This will be very close!"

Whispers followed him as he escaped the mouth of the catacombs. Andius had to be there, down in the catacombs, still going, if Nyalin had come in first.

That meant he had better get out of here—and fast—unless he wanted to face Andius.

Yeska's voice growled in his mind. *Lara says to meet her at the horse statue. She knows where you can hide.*

He knew the one, and he set off for it at a jog. The crowd loved his enthusiasm and cheered even louder as he raced away.

Hide. Right. Neither of them would be safe in their own rooms, especially with Andius looking for the dagger. And her. And probably him too. They were supposed to be still buried in that root cellar.

As he loped along, the streets were quiet, and his body hummed with well-spent effort. The evening wind ruffled his hair, and he let himself savor that for right now—just for now—he was in the lead.

Chapter 16

Feast

Lara opened the door at the quiet knock. She'd practically chewed her lip raw with worry. When Nyalin's frame filled the doorway, she threw her arms around him.

Subtle, girl. Really subtle. He doesn't want to kiss you, remember? Allies at war—and that's all.

But he didn't push her away this time, and in fact, he squeezed her closer even as he angled her to the side and pushed the door shut behind them. He smelled of sweat and blackberries—as always—and dust.

"You made it," she murmured against his shoulder. "You survived. I was so worried. Who knew what Andius would do if he found you down there in the catacombs? In that free-for-all. It's chaos."

He frowned. "Well, there's always tomorrow."

She leaned back to scrutinize his face. "You got by him? The traps? The tests?"

His smile was laughing. "You could say that."

"What is it?"

"Remember how we got out of that cell in the root cellar?"

"Yes."

"Tried that again. Bit farther this time."

"Really?" She burst out laughing. "Brilliant!" A throat cleared behind her, and her face flushed. "Oh—sorry. Nyalin, this is Pyaris. One of my dearest childhood friends. This is her home."

Nyalin bowed almost more quickly than Pyaris did, and she felt a little flicker of gratitude for that.

"It's a pleasure to actually meet you this time." Pyaris's grin was white and brilliant against ebony skin.

He smiled back. "Sorry I wasn't much of a house guest the first time. Thank you for lifting the curse."

"You're welcome. Speaking of curses, those scrolls you sent by?"

"Yes?" Lara asked.

"Two of them were just normal paper, but you were right. Two of them had necromantic charms on them."

Nyalin raised his eyebrows as he looked at Lara. "Guess it's good we checked."

Pyaris's glance flicked to his arm, which was still curled around Lara's waist. She wanted to groan as he cleared his throat and released her—but she had no right to demand closeness of him. Or anyone.

Although with all the other rules she'd thrown out the window, why keep to that one?

"And thank you for hiding us," she said. "I didn't know where else to turn."

"I'm sure your father would want to help," Pyaris offered. "But I think neither you or he would like to test the loyalty of your guards right now."

"Agreed."

Pyaris spread her arms wide, long sleeves jangling with small purple bells on the cuffs. "Here—it *is* a feast night. I used one of the golds I earned breaking your curse to buy a few things. Wine, mead, lamb. You know us necromancers are excellent cooks. No spirits included, I promise."

Nyalin snorted, surveying the meal on a small table set for two. "That's not something *I'm* worried about."

Pyaris raised her eyebrows, giving Lara a look that Nyalin missed.

I'll explain later, Lara mouthed.

Pyaris nodded, then strode to the door and reached for her cloak.

"Wait—are you going somewhere?" she asked.

Smiling, her friend nodded. "Just next door. The neighbors are having a feast of their own. And Kedwin will be there."

"You can stay," Lara added quickly. Bleh, Kedwin.

"That's all right. I was planning to go and take food with me anyway."

"When will you be back?"

Pyaris grinned and shrugged. "I may not be. Don't wait up. Oh, and bar the door. I can knock loudly, but you have people looking for you."

And with that she was gone, leaving them alone. Very, very alone.

Despite all the time they'd spent together studying in the Bone manor, this felt strange. Different. At home, someone could and would stop by anytime—servants, Da, even Andius. Now, they were truly alone. No one other than Pyaris knew were they were.

And they absolutely had to stay here till the morning.

She must have stared at the door for quite some time, because Nyalin had finished barring the door and was staring at her before she realized it.

"You all right? You were, uh, hoping she'd stay?"

"Oh, no. It doesn't matter."

"Well, guess you're stuck here with me now." He spread his hands.

"We're safe. For now. That's what matters."

He strode past her toward the table, and she turned to follow him. "Who's Kedwin?"

She waved it off. "No one important."

"Think this was intended for him? Er, the two of them?"

"Probably," she sighed. "I owe her big time."

"I'm sure if she's a good friend she'd trade a fancy dinner for your safety anytime."

"Good point."

He lifted a lid on a large pot that she hoped to the Twins wasn't the usual magical cauldron. But inside was a scrumptious-looking lamb stew stuffed full of carrots, potatoes, and peas. "Looks good." He took a deep breath. "Smells good too. Should we dig in?"

She nodded and scooted into Pyaris's chair.

To her delight, she found a steaming loaf of bread and broke it for them. Had Pyaris bothered with Heat Water spells or was this just that fresh? Either way, it was a divine treat. She poured both wine and mead for each of them while he doled out the stew, and they started eating without speaking. He looked ravenous, probably from the day's exertions, and the first bowl vanished in no time.

The wine in her glass was dangerously low; she might have been drinking at the rate that he'd been eating. She sipped and studied him as he ladled out another helping—this man who had done so much for her without getting anything concrete in return. She wanted to thank him. No, she wanted to kiss him. Last time, that combination had meant utter disaster. She *definitely* wasn't going to mention how deeply grateful she felt right now. But he was out there risking himself, dealing with Andius, for her. Even if he wasn't doing it with romance in mind, it was hard not to feel swoony about it.

She needed some other topic, but the wine only drew her to things that were heavy, emotional—or things she shouldn't talk about.

"You know, that first day when you gave me that handkerchief. I tried to play it off, even to myself, but it really meant a lot to me." Yep. She'd definitely had too much wine. Those words had escaped her before she'd even realized it.

He blinked.

"I was miserable and trying so hard not to be miserable all the time. And it was just the reminder I needed that there was a wider world out there. That everything isn't awful *all* the time."

"Just most of the time."

She laughed. "Maybe."

"You were there mourning your brother? Myandrin?"

"Yes, and asking his forgiveness," she said, smiling. "You have no idea how great it feels to hear you call him by his name. No one ever calls him by his name."

He laughed a little. "I know the feeling. People rarely use my mother's name either. It's always either part of my name or 'you're *her* son!' "

She nodded, taking a drink, but stopped short before she could set her glass down. There was something strange in his eyes. "What? What is it?"

"He, uh..." He stopped, swallowed, continued. "I don't know quite how to put this but I'm not sure if I'll get another chance to try."

Something inexplicable in her chest soared. By the goddesses, what was he going to say?

"He told me to say hello."

She froze, and he met her eyes with a careful gaze. Those eyes were so, so... They were the same too-clever eyes that had pierced her soul that first day. But now there was something more in them. She could have sworn it was affection. The power of his gaze was so intense that she almost missed the fact that he'd just tried to deliver a message to her from someone who was dead. From Myandrin. "What—how—" she managed.

"I told you there are spirits over there. In the green world—the afterworld you saw."

Even having seen the strange green world for herself, she stared at him. That was... delusional. You couldn't talk to the dead in the next world. You couldn't travel there either, though. Nyalin had never seemed delusional, except maybe in his persistent optimism. Still, what could she say to that?

"I've seen him in there. Near the Bone manor. And in the catacombs today. He sits in the library too."

She flinched at that. But that did sound like her brother, and the way she'd caught Nyalin glancing at the library like someone had been there came to mind. Was Myandrin really wandering some other not-so-far away world, strolling quiet halls and reading books? That didn't sound so bad.

She needed to say something. Her staring was getting awkward. "W-was he all right?"

"Of course." He eyed her, not missing her hesitation. "I know it's hard to believe. I'll show you when this is all over, okay? I didn't realize I could take you there, or I'd have done it sooner. I didn't think you'd believe me."

"Of course I believe you," she said automatically. She'd seen the green world after all.

He snorted.

"Okay, it's a little challenging, but I'm working on it over here. Do you know why hasn't he crossed over further?"

"I have no idea, I don't know how it works. Seemed to be looking out for you."

She glanced around uncomfortably.

"Well, not every second of the day, I'm sure."

She forced a smile, still feeling unsure about it all.

"Look, I promise, if we don't get ourselves killed, we'll go see him." His smile vanished. "I almost forgot... While I was down in the catacombs, he also told me there is a demon here. One who is after me. Not sure how he knows that."

"A demon?" She winced and glanced away, thinking of Pyaris's words about Nyalin himself.

He shouldn't have, but he seemed to understand the wince. "I know what you're thinking."

"You do?" She shifted uneasily in her chair.

"You're wondering why I can cross over like that. And talk to dead people. And other people can't."

"Maybe."

"The emperor told me... well, he told me a lot of crazy things I didn't get to tell you. But one of them was that my mother's father was... well, not a demon exactly. A spirit? A ghost? Not a man."

"How—"

"I have no idea. I'm going to go back when the Contests are over and try to find out."

She nodded. "So that makes you... a quarter demon?"

"I prefer to think of it as a quarter dead. But as you like."

Huh. She'd known there had been something odd about him. But she hadn't expected it'd be *this*. It was a little hard to believe. Would have been harder to believe if she hadn't seen the strange green world herself. "Does this have something to do with the lock?"

"I think so. But I'm not sure I understand it. He said they were afraid of me. That that's why they put it there." He couldn't hide the hurt in his voice.

She winced on his behalf.

"Are you afraid of me, Lara? Now that you know?"

Not half as afraid as I am of Andius. But that'd be the wrong answer. While the idea made her a little uneasy, she certainly wouldn't call it fear. "No," she breathed.

"At least somebody's on my side."

"Well, you've been the only one on my side. It's the least I could do."

His face darkened. "You think he might try to kill me tomorrow? He obviously didn't want me there in the first place."

She didn't need him to name who. "It's against the rules. But yeah. Given what he did today, I think he might try."

"Faytou was in second this morning, can you believe that?"

She smiled. "That's great."

"He said he had no hope for the third phase, though. That Andius always beats him."

"He's a lot younger than you."

"But he's probably been battling Andius his whole life."

"True."

"All Andius has to do is be the last one standing. That's the rules, right?"

She nodded. "Last one of the top sixteen." The scores so far determined who went to the final round, but ultimately the third phase was a vicious, free-for-all fight for survival. Figurative survival, as defeated contestants were expected to yield—and victors were expected to grant that request. That meant that all Andius had to do was pummel each one of them into submission. Or they had to pummel him. Teaming up was strictly against the rules, however, as was any use of magic.

"At least he can't get them to gang up on me," he said, as if his thoughts had taken a similar turn.

Her lips twisted. "Theoretically."

"What do you mean—theoretically?"

"He'll probably avoid the appearance of alliances. But if other finalists support him, they can still do things to help him win. Like yield quickly. Or choose more skilled opponents, decreasing the likelihood that Andius is gravely injured or loses by chance. After they defeat their goddess-chosen opponent, of course." The initial phase was always determined by the goddess—or if one were a little more honest about it, a random draw of a number from a basket.

"And if he bribed those who built the original course, how do we know he hasn't bribed the officials monitoring this competition?"

"I wouldn't put anything past him."

He frowned, thoughtfully. "I wonder who Andius and his friends might think the weakest opponents are. They don't know me. My score based on magic should tell them little about my martial abilities. I didn't fight when Andius ambushed me. Maybe they'll think I'm nothing to worry about and leave me for Andius."

"You're still an Obsidian."

He scowled.

"What? In their minds, you are. And even if you're not in every important sense of the word, you still trained with them in sword fighting." She raised an eyebrow at his frown. "Assuming you were trained at all?"

"At Grel's side," he admitted.

"So by the very best, then."

"Fine, I see your point."

"Who will you choose? After the first?"

"Assuming I win the first match?"

"Obviously. You have to have a strategy ready."

"I thought I'd sit back and see who if anyone came to me, size up the fighters as best I can. They all know more about each other than I know about them. But if I must choose, I'll just go for Andius."

"Andius! Why?"

He shrugged. "Ultimately Andius has won for years. So he's beaten all of them before at one time or another. But he hasn't beaten me."

She was quiet for a moment, not sure whether she liked that idea—or hated it. "What a ridiculous way to decide the future of our clan. What does beating each other into submission have to do with being a good clan leader?" Or a good husband. Or just a good person.

"What does being born a boy to the right father have to do with being a good clan leader either?" He shrugged. "Sure, you can be trained from birth, receive the wisdom of previous generations... Does that work out well every time?"

She snorted. "Fair point. But the goddess-chosen pairs? Please. Dala has better things to do than shift around shards in a box. The temples just want their hands in this. People could be matched based on ability, or their current score."

"Sometimes in war and in life, you get lucky. Sometimes you don't. Isn't this the same?"

"I suppose it is. But there's got to be a better way."

He smiled. "When you're clan leader, you can decree a better way."

She bit her lip as her heart gave a little flutter in her chest. Whether it was out of hope or anxiety, she wasn't sure.

"Until then, we fight." He shrugged again. "I suppose it's

this way because a leader must be strong enough not to be killed *too* easily. They may need to overcome long odds. And if he or she can just be toppled by a blink and a flick of a sword, that's not strength or stability for the clan."

"Except that magic isn't easily taken away."

"True."

"The fight should at least include magic."

"If we weren't cheating, that wouldn't help me much."

"True. And there's also the power a leader grows in their people—the power of having men and women around you that support you. People that would defend you. None of that matters here."

"I suppose. Although hasn't Andius won—or bribed—plenty of people to his side? He's a charmer. And if Andius has already arranged for some of them to yield to him, perhaps that's the same thing. Do you really want that mattering?"

She sighed. "Obviously choosing a leader is far from a simple or perfect process."

"Good thing they're clan leader for life!"

She pursed her lips. "Let's talk about something else."

"Sure. This isn't exactly easing my nerves."

"You never said—how did the course go?"

"Teleportation earned me fifty points."

Her eyes widened. "You came in first? Congratulations! Here, drink up." She forced a wine glass into his hand and toasted him. "There's something to celebrate. If you got the highest course score, you've got to be up there in the rankings."

"For better or worse. As if I wasn't enough of a target already."

"Don't think like that. Andius is the real target. Anyone ambitious will want to take him down, not you."

"Both Faytou and Myandrin suggested Andius will be cheating and not to hold back."

"I guess that's only fair, since we are too," she quipped.

"I know, as if we're ones to criticize." He leaned his chair back, balancing it on two legs. The firelight caught in his eyes, in the shine of his dark hair, making something in her clench up for a second.

"Don't die on my behalf." She blinked. Had she really just said that aloud?

One corner of his mouth crooked up in a half smile. "I wasn't exactly planning on it, but your request is duly noted."

"I'm serious, Nyalin. You can't end up dead because of me."

"If I end up dead, it will be because of my own mistakes—and mine alone."

She pressed her lips into a thin line. "We both know that's not true. You entered that Contest to help me. Because of me. I pushed you into it. You gave me hope when I had none. Even now, I—" She stopped short. She didn't want him to know all the different hopes that stirred in her. "It was always going to be this way. No sense in dying over it."

"We're all dying. I'm about halfway to dead already."

"I thought you said it as more like a quarter."

He barked out a laugh but sobered as she slowly set down her wine.

"I already lost Myandrin. My mother. I don't know if I could stand to lose you too. I'd much rather be yoked to Andius and know you're alive in the world rather than live in one where you're dead."

He opened his mouth to say something, stopped short, then frowned. His eyes locked on the table, and she could almost see his wheels turning. He looked like... like he disagreed with her but couldn't quite figure out how to tell her so. What was there to disagree with?

His hard, intense gaze flicked up from the table. "We should get to bed. Got a long day and an early start tomorrow."

She bit her lip. He hadn't promised her he wouldn't do anything rash. Far from it. He'd avoided answering altogether. The realization made her heart thud against her rib cage.

He stood up. "You take the bed; I'll take the floor."

"Not a chance." She stood up now too. "You're competing. Fighting. You can't be all stiff and achy for that."

"You're competing too. If you pass out and don't feed me magic, we're both screwed."

"Magic so you can cast what? They smell blackberries, and you're done for."

"I thought we'd at least cheat enough to heal me." He smiled. "Just a little?"

"I think I'm rubbing off on you in all the wrong ways. But cedar is an unusual smell. If *I* cast the spells, we'll be in even bigger trouble."

He grabbed her by her shoulders and marched her to Pyaris's cot. "Then you can use all your energy to heal my aches and pains in the morning, because you won't need it for anything else. C'mon now."

But when he released her, she spun in his arms, catching his elbows before he could quite let them fall.

"Let's both take the bed." The words escaped her before she could second-guess them, and she winced.

He shook his head and opened his mouth to say something.

Before he could, she dove. This might be her last shot, for all she knew. On tiptoes, she crushed her mouth to his, looping hands around his neck and pulling him in hungrily.

He gasped and was still as a statue for a moment. And

then the tension abruptly eased. He melted into her, his lips giving in to the kiss, teasing her mouth open.

A pounding at the door cut through the silence.

"It's me! I'm back."

They broke apart, breathless and wide-eyed.

"That's Pyaris," she murmured. "Damn."

He bent down and pressed one more hard kiss to her mouth, then strode to the door. It left her swaying, and a little dizzy.

But that last one... he'd kissed her of his own accord. She dragged the back of her hand hastily across her mouth.

"Don't bar that, I'm headed back out again." Pyaris waltzed in, all smiles. She had the glow of a feast, or wine. Or a lover's attention. That was nice—even if the lover was Kedwin. "I just forgot the pie. Did you have any?"

Lara shook her head numbly. "We were just finishing up. Everything was delicious. I can't thank you enough." Thank the goddesses the words came automatically.

Her friend swept a pie into her arms, beamed at them, and headed back toward the door. "We're barely started with the festivities—so I'll see you in the morning. Good night!"

Nyalin replaced the bar on the door with a thud like a mountain crashing down. But he didn't move. He ran his hands through the air and stared at the closed door for she didn't know how long.

The air was tense, and thick, and awkward.

"Lara—" he started, finally turning. But he stopped when he saw her face.

"This isn't just about gratitude," she whispered. "Can't I have gratitude and other feelings too?"

He swallowed.

"You're not just a... convenient coincidence to me. Not

just a less bad fate than Andius. Don't you see that? I could have sworn you felt something too."

"Tomorrow is coming whether we like it or not. What we feel doesn't matter."

"It matters. I'll *make* it matter. There has to be a way."

"That's not true. Things don't always work out, just because you work hard or you want them to. There's not always a way."

She gritted her teeth at the echo of Da's words. "Well, there *is* a way for you to kiss me right now. If you want to."

"You think that's going to make it easier for me to watch Andius win tomorrow? To know I can never do it again?" He took a few steps toward her as he spoke, crossing half the distance, then stopped.

"I don't *want* it to be easy for you. It shouldn't be easy. It should be hard, because none of this is fair."

He was breathing hard. "I..."

"If we can't work a miracle tomorrow, we lose all this. The days practicing. The evenings. All of it."

Some of the agitation seemed to drain out of him at that. "I'm going to miss it."

"Are you giving up? We may lose the war, Nyalin, but we are fighting. We *are fighting*. That matters."

"I know."

"Then don't give up on me yet."

"I would never." He frowned, coming another few steps back to her. "How can you even say that?"

"Because there are only two reasons not to kiss me right now. One is that you don't want to. The other is that you've already given up."

He flinched. His eyes dimmed with hurt.

She stepped closer to him. Barely a pace apart now.

"Kiss me," she whispered. "And sleep beside me until sunrise. In case it's our last chance."

He took a measured breath. That subtle hurt in his eyes melted into wariness, and then... determination.

She crossed the remaining distance between them. His hand found her hip; he bent his head and closed his eyes. And she raised her lips to his for one last taste of freedom.

Chapter 17

The Wind

"And now we see how the goddesses favor you all."

Outside of the stadium, Nyalin shifted from foot to foot among the sixteen final contenders. They clumped around the officials of the final phase. Cerivil stood at their center, his expression stern, with several officials including the old woman at his side. She held a simple basket in her weathered hands, a closed sphere with one hole in the top just large enough for a hand to reach in.

Even Nyalin stilled as she raised her chin, preparing to speak. The wind teased at the bottoms of the tan and brown crossovers of those gathered, the only motion in a long tense moment.

"Who asks their fate of the goddesses—" she started.

Andius stepped forward and thrust his hand in before she'd even gotten the words out. He drew out his shard and shot his hand into the air, holding the shard high.

"Eight."

The old woman held out her hand, but he tossed it on the ground at her feet. Her eagle eyes narrowed as he stalked away. Andius cast a vicious glare at Nyalin too, before striding off.

And what had gotten into his usual charismatic self? The knowledge that there wasn't a real clanblade waiting at the end of this contest? Or the escape of his prisoners? Even if Andius made a fake sword to spite Lara, that wouldn't be the same for his magical potential. A fake blade would be dwarfed by the real clanblades of other clan leaders. If he could even make a fake at all.

But he wasn't going to need to, was he? Because Nyalin was going to win.

He swallowed as the line moved closer to the woman. Another contestant drew a thirteen, then another a seven. Laughter and jeering went up as he and Andius sized each other up with laughing eyes and nods.

The pit of nervousness in Nyalin's stomach deepened. There was too much knowing in those eyes. Even a few officials seemed to be nodding, too. Maybe it was just encouragement. Maybe something more.

Faytou stepped forward and drew. Two.

Nyalin strode up after him. Might as well get this over with. The inside of the basket scraped his fingers with its rough weave, and he accidentally jammed a bone shard into the tip of his thumb before he got a grip on one and pulled it out.

He blinked at the number painted in russet ink onto the large fragment of bone.

"One," he said softly.

He glanced at the old woman, who gently took the shard from him as he turned aside—and drifted toward Faytou.

"Looks like it's you and me, friend." Faytou's smile was weak but not forced as he patted Nyalin on the shoulder. "There's no opponent I'd rather have."

Nyalin snorted. “That’s kind of you to say. It’s probably because you know you can beat me.”

“I’m trying to be brave. I’ll be going up against an Obsidian, you know, unlike those fools.”

Nyalin scowled but cut it off at the glitter of amusement in Faytou’s eyes. “You’re just trying to make me mad, so I’ll get hasty.”

“What other chance do I have to beat an Obsidian-trained swordsman?” Faytou gave him a wink. Hmm, perhaps he was saying that loudly not just to tease Nyalin, but so the other contestants would hear. Whether that was a good or bad strategy, he wasn’t sure.

“I don’t want to fight you at all,” he admitted. “Certainly not first.”

Faytou shrugged. “We’re goddess-chosen to fight. Sometimes you get lucky, sometimes you don’t.”

“Which one is this?”

“I’m not sure.”

The early morning sun wasn’t doing much to fend off the cold, so Unira pulled her cloak a little tighter around her.

Zama, apparently unaffected by anything so mundane, grinned and took a bite of his doughy bread puff. “I had no idea when you called me here I’d be going to sporting events. This is even more fun than I imagined.”

She shrugged. “Just think what the future might hold.” Like the sight of this ridiculous building in ruins.

Drums pounded and sticks clacked, stoking the audience and signaling the start was near. The longing for the fight throbbed around her. For these barbarians, it meant choosing a leader, but to her, the sound was the heartbeat of drums of war. Not so long ago, such energy seethed through every clan, toward each other and toward the Mushin. The energy was so powerful it felt palpable in the air.

The public stadium echoed with hundreds of excited Bone Clan voices, too, but she and Zama sat surrounded by the paid guards of her household. Any minute now, they'd begin.

And the death of Linali's spawn would be soon to follow. By the hands of her puppets. Or her own, if necessary.

Her sources had searched all last evening, but none of them had been able to track the bastard down, much to her annoyance. Not annoyance—rage.

"Your life is so unpredictable." Zama popped the last bit of dough in his mouth, a mocking twist to his lips. Did he actually have a stomach to digest any of that or was there just a portal to some other world where chewed bits of dough were popping out and landing on someone's head? Perhaps a mess for servants in some other realm.

His attention, however, intensified, so she turned her gaze to the sand in the center of the stadium just as the drums came to a halt.

Silence fell. Clan Leader Cerivil stood front and center, and the top sixteen contenders were entering the stadium behind him, walking in pairs.

A speech about the ideal qualities of a clan leader. Yada, yada, kindness, generosity, peacekeeping, blah, blah, blah, wisdom, honor, whatever. Everyone knew this Contest would end in blood. It was the last and final Contest for good reason.

Because all the wise words in the empire wouldn't change the fact that everything always came down to blood. Who could draw more of it, when, and if they wanted to. In combat, in birth, in death.

Even Cerivil admitted it: "The phase will end when the

last contestant remains standing."

The crowd liked this bit of theatrics and sent up a feisty cheer.

"Contestants driven to the point of exhaustion shall yield and be removed from battle," Cerivil continued. "Magic is strictly forbidden. Officials will be monitoring for any scents as well as using their Ward spells to be sure none is used. Lastly, all fighters must fight their current opponent until one of them yields before moving on to the next. Initial matchups are goddess-chosen, but after these matches are decided, anyone is free to choose who they will, until we have our winner."

How cute, they had rules and pathetic attempts to make things fair. Nothing in life was fair.

She scanned for Linali's whelp. And yes, there he was. He'd been matched with the third-place contender, a young man of barely thirteen. She frowned at such an easy match. Of course he'd get off easy, riding on *her* reputation.

Goddess-chosen, what a bunch of dragon droppings.

With a crash of the gong, the fighting began. She scanned the other competitors— who would be a challenge and who would fall quickly? Just because they could earn points with magic didn't mean they knew a sword's hilt from its point.

"Oh, this should be fun," Zama murmured. "Look—they must be friends. They don't want to hurt each other."

She refocused on the boy. Ah, yes. The two were tentative with each other, slow. The younger man took a chance at a kick as their swords crossed, and they passed each other.

The kick landed with a dozen times more force than he'd applied, and Zama cackled. It connected with the back of Nyalin's knee and sent him toppling forward with a grunt.

"Oh, good one. Keep it up, my friend." She took a bite of

her own snack, a fluffy strawberry confection.

"Would have been better if I'd gotten it a little sooner. The side of the knee is so much more devastating. But I'm still learning the boy's timing."

The young man hung back even more now, but he had to fight. His next swing got lucky and hit his opponent's sword squarely when it would usually have missed.

Nyalin easily deflected it but clutched at his arm.

"What did you do?"

"Only gave that strike the force of a boulder smashing, that's all."

"Ahh."

This repeated several more times, with high lunges and dives followed by crushing blows. And then suddenly—the blows seemed to stop.

Zama frowned.

"What's wrong?" she hissed, fighting a shout. "Why did you stop? Break his arms!"

"I didn't stop. Someone is pushing back. Someone other than him."

"You mean someone is defending him?" she growled. She scanned the stadium, before stopping, realizing that was far too obvious. Perhaps her instincts weren't so paranoid after all.

Zama began to vary his attacks, and Unira watched in horror as only some of them got through.

Linali's spawn still took a beating, but he kept his moves measured, controlled, his passion low. Confusion creased both fighters' features.

Hah. Let them wonder.

Zama, always one to push a boundary, steered the young man's next opportunistic kick off-center a bit—straight into

Nyalin's kidney.

Unira could barely contain her giggles. "The neck! Go for the neck! And stick to the blade. You'll never kill him this way."

A few people nearby sent her frowning glances. She rolled her eyes. As if they could prove anything. The demon's magic had no scent unless he wished it to, and it wasn't Unira doing a bit of it. They'd have to assume she was cheering for the little underdog.

Zama ignored the onlookers and shrugged. "The young one is cautious, even more so now. We must bide our time for the right opponent."

Unira nodded her agreement. But then her eyes caught on a few of the details of the boy's sword. The engraved inlay. The glistening red scabbard.

How by Seluvae's dark hand did that boy have Linali's sword? Where had he hidden it all these years?

She stood straight up. Something about the motion or perhaps her intensity drew the boy's gaze, and for a moment their eyes locked. He scowled at her.

She forced herself to sit and gritted her teeth. Today she would destroy that pup once and for all. And she even knew what to get as a memento.

Nyalin wasn't sure what it was about the woman who stood so abruptly in the stands that caught his eye. But for a moment, the fight froze in time, and he'd only seen her.

It'd been barely a moment, strange and cold, and then she sank back into her seat. Even now, though, he could still feel her dark eyes scowling at him.

The crash of Faytou's sword against his broke his gaze.

He staggered back. But there was a darkness there almost blocking out his vision—in the corner of the stadium and the corner of his mind. He couldn't blot it out. He glanced back again.

She had black hair that cut off sharply at her chin. Her gown was clearly the finest black silk, adorned in a filigree of silver. An Obsidian? Not someone he recognized, which seemed a little odd, as anyone of import had usually visited Elix's house enough for Nyalin to catch a glance.

And there was someone beside her... His gaze darted to the stands again. Silver eyes caught Nyalin's and bored in like a thunderstorm rolling at him, a wave tumbling him over, dragging him down into the sea—

The next crash of the sword came even harder, and much faster, and Nyalin realized why. From Faytou's eyes, he was realizing it too.

"What is going on?" Faytou whispered. "Who... Why?"

Nyalin shook his head minutely before he lunged, then retreated. "I think we know why."

Nyalin furiously parried a series of blows, dancing back. Panting, he twisted and swung wide now. The slice went horribly astray, almost as if knocked aside in midair.

Faytou spun too and pushed him back with a marvelous lunge. By the Twins. If only Lara weren't at stake, he might even wish for Faytou to win. The kid was very good. At best, they were equals, and Faytou was five years his junior.

Some of those feelings were chased away by the next unnaturally heavy blow that left only aching joints behind. He clutched at his shoulder with a growl. He wouldn't last, if this kept up at this rate. Meanwhile, Faytou's face had gone pale with horror—and a little rage.

"Goddess-chosen," he was murmuring, mostly to himself.

"How dare they. And how..."

His arm flooded with warmth.

That's my doing, murmured Yeska. *No scent to dragon magic, you know. Although sometimes I like to add in a little cinnamon, just for fun.*

A little busy here, Yeska.

Someone is cheating. Or should I say some thing? *Whoever or whatever, they have no scent.*

Faytou returned with an unusually timid thrust, and after knocking it aside, Nyalin risked a glance at Andius. He looked just in time to see that Andius had defeated his man. The man, who hadn't bowed out as quickly as Nyalin had worried he would, was sprawled unconscious in the sand.

So much for yielding. At least he didn't see any blood.

Andius rounded on the next nearest pair of men and pointed his sword, fire raging in his eyes.

Even though they were barely engaged, one cast his sword aside and ran for the archway. Andius turned to point his sword at the second, the apparent winner of that matchup, who fell to both knees and dropped his sword before him.

"I yield. May the goddesses guide Clan Leader Andius."

The crowd's voices rose in surprise, whipped back and forth with both shock and admiration. Was that move legal? Did they care?

Slowly, Andius spun and looked Nyalin directly in the eye. He raised his sword—a challenge.

But someone cut him to the chase. Cold steel suddenly pressed to his throat. Dark dragon, he'd paid for his distraction. He froze.

Faytou met his eyes as he moved closer, not moving the sword. Was there truly an option here? Faytou could kill him easily if that was truly his aim. He should just yield, as those other men had. Let brothers battle it out.

And yet... the memory of Lara's head on his shoulder the night before stilled his lips. If there was a way out of this, he had to find it. If he tried to stagger back, could he get out of it fast enough to keep fighting? His friend wouldn't slit his throat, would he?

But he wasn't sure enough of that to actually try it.

Over Faytou's shoulder, Andius started toward them.

Faytou felt it too, glancing back just once. His eyes were cold, narrowed. More determined than Nyalin could remember seeing them.

"You've been a good friend to me, Nyalin moLinali," Faytou said softly. "And I do believe the goddesses chose us to fight for a reason."

"What reason?" he whispered.

Faytou glanced back again. "I've fought my brother. He's my brother. He's beaten me before many times."

"You may have gotten better."

Behind him, Andius reached them and stopped short. Panting. Waiting.

"It doesn't matter." Faytou shook his head. "You should be the clan leader, not me. And not him."

The cold was suddenly gone, and Faytou sunk out of view.

Nyalin staggered back to see his friend before him. On one knee, his sword offered up across his palms.

"I yield," Faytou shouted. "And I pledge my support to Nyalin moLinali."

The crowd erupted, murmurs and shouts crashing against them like the sea.

Nyalin didn't have much time to absorb it though. Faytou barely got out of the way as Andius crashed past him.

And the fight was joined again. Andius didn't have the

finesse that Faytou did, but what he lacked in style he made up for in strength.

But what had Myandrin told him? Andius was predictable.

Yes, now that he watched, it was the same five or seven strokes each time. And the cheating was the same, but it too was regular.

The fifth blow this time was the strange one. Four strikes in a row of similar force were easily parried and then—*wham*. It was like a tree had fallen on his sword.

He staggered back, collapsing to the ground, every bone in his arm aching. His shoulder and elbow screamed in pain. Andius stood panting, frowning at his sword in his hand. Didn't he know who was tampering on his behalf?

Or were they only cheating *against* Nyalin, not in favor of Andius?

Nyalin dragged himself to his feet. The next sequence began, and this time Nyalin waited... waited... and then just as the fifth, stronger blow began, he ducked, swinging his leg out wide.

Andius's feet went out from beneath him, and he went down with a cry. From the ground, he writhed for a moment, swearing and slashing in Nyalin's direction as he rolled away.

Nyalin hurried after him. Andius started to scramble to his feet but only made it to his knees. Unfortunately, he was perfectly capable of parrying from there.

Nyalin struck down with all the force he could muster, willing the sword to fall from the man's hands, willing him to yield.

Instead, his next blow hit like he'd struck an iron anvil. Both his arms shook, streaking with fresh pain, and then something outright knocked him back.

A few cries went up from the crowd, suddenly suspicious.

Yes, you could hide using energy spells to push a sword harder down, but knocking a man around was much more obvious.

Whoever was helping Andius, they were protecting him too. And they might not even care if anyone knew.

This was going to be a long battle.

~

Both men were dripping with sweat—and a few drops of blood—as the sun rose higher in the sky. The first round of matches settled, and new opponents squared off. Unira's man went straight for Linali's boy, just as he'd been told.

But it was dragging on. And on. And on. They hadn't counted on *both* sides cheating. And who could even be helping him? It didn't matter. Since they paid off the officials to ignore the signs of cheating, there'd be no hope they'd figure it out anyway.

Several of the second round of matches settled, with the losers yielding and limping from the field. A few eyed Andius, waiting to see the outcome.

It wasn't nearly as close as Unira would have liked. She folded her hands in her lap as an idea began to form. She'd never be able to cast the spell here, in front of all these people, with the precision she'd need to keep it hidden and without a scent. But maybe Zama could. His abilities seemed greater than hers—although she was still figuring out how exactly—but at times, at a basic level, they weren't so different.

"I know how to end this," Unira whispered, a delicious smile on her lips.

Zama raised an eyebrow.

She bent closer and cupped a hand to whisper in his ear. "If the boy can't speak, the boy can't yield. Even if he wants to. Give him a taste of death that's waiting for him a little early."

Chuckling, Zama rubbed his palms together. "My dear, it would be my pleasure."

~

The fight dragged on and on, every brutal cheating blow followed by dragon magic and Nyalin's increasingly desperate attempts to turn the tide. Every muscle in his body ached, so it was hard to notice exactly when it started. But at some point, a tightness started to form in his jaw.

The tightness morphed into an ache, even though he hadn't been struck there. Yet. And though Yeska toiled away healing his other wounds, this one seemed to get no attention. It just got worse and worse.

Was it getting harder to breathe?

He had to end this.

Fortunately, they were both exhausted, in spite of any help that might have been bolstering them. He dare not glance around to see how many men were left standing, but the ring itself was quieter than before. They had more space around them.

He had always been fast. And better with his hands. Strength with a blade, splitting a practice dummy in two with both hands on the hilt—those had never been his style. All this nonsense was making him play directly into his weaknesses. He needed to try something new.

On the next attack, he didn't focus on parrying. He let himself focus, slow down, and as Andius went through his motions—one, two, three, four, thrust hard—Nyalin kept his calm. The thrust was wild, Andius having lost much of his usual control to fatigue, and Nyalin slipped just slightly to one side and lunged forward as well.

He was open, and he had to be fast—but fortunately the

move was just different enough to startle Andius, leaving a breath of an opening. Nyalin grabbed Andius's wrist with his left and yanked him forward, his blade resting awkwardly against the length of Andius's arm. Then Nyalin brought up his knee and drove it into his opponent's stomach.

Andius doubled forward, groaning, and almost lost his grip on his sword. Almost.

But it didn't matter because Nyalin followed up quickly. He slid his mother's sword the last few inches to rest the cold steel against Andius's throat.

They both froze.

Nyalin was panting hard now, and his whole jaw ached so much he could barely part his lips to take in air. But it didn't matter. It was close. It was almost over.

"Yield," he whispered. Although the words were more of an unintelligible grunt than anything else.

Andius's eyes narrowed as he growled low in the back of his throat. "I'll never yield to you."

He jerked, trying to jostle free, but Nyalin still held his wrist too. He pressed the blade harder against the skin.

Last chance, he wanted to whisper, but it ached too much. Was he really going to have to kill Andius to end this? And if Andius really did refuse to yield—what would that mean? Was it still possible to win? Would he have broken the rules if he spilled Andius's blood into the sand?

The hesitation was just too long. The force that was helping Andius chose that moment to act, slamming him in the stomach. Sucker punched—and he couldn't even see his attacker. A flicker of the green world threatened to overwhelm, but he shoved it away. He couldn't do that here—there would be too many questions. And crossing over was technically magic. And whoever was helping Andius wasn't usually attacking with energy, so he might not have enough power to cross over anyway.

He hadn't recovered from the gut punch before it was followed up with another blow—this time to the jaw. The agony made yellow blotches flash before his eyes, and his lip split, sending blood spraying. He collapsed back into the sand, sprawling.

The air thudded out of his lungs and wouldn't return.

Gasping, heaving for breath, he struggled and desperately twisted to get to his stomach, to his hands and knees. Anything was better than this.

The crowd was jeering, nearly roaring. They hadn't missed that. Whoever was helping Andius was not hiding it anymore. Officials had stepped forward, but there was no magic from Andius for them to detect. One held up a Ward spell whose shape glittered in the sunlight but didn't change or give warning.

Andius's laugh as he staggered forward was cruel, brutal. As he neared Nyalin, he kicked at the sand. A spray hit Nyalin straight into his face.

He struggled to breathe, to clear the sand even as Andius's foot met his ribs. He swore at the pain—or he tried to.

No sound came out. In fact, his entire jaw, lips, teeth—none of it would move.

And suddenly he understood.

Yeska—something's wrong. Very, very wrong. It's like my jaw is... frozen. He rolled hastily away. By the Twins, let him not collide with another fight. He might not get away from Andius this way, but he had to try. If the bastard got a knife to his Nyalin's throat right now, everyone would say, well, the boy should have yielded. What a loss.

It is the darkness. It grows bold, growled Yeska.

I don't know what that means.

I'll tell Lara. It means you've been cursed. By a necromancer—or worse.

~

Lara was chewing viciously on a nail when Yeska's voice bit into her thoughts. She jumped, almost knocking back the hood.

That darkness that I told you is coming?

Lara's eyes widened. She pulled the hood tighter around her face. She'd barely been aware of anything other than the match playing out before her. *Yes?*

It is here. Here in the stadium.

Lara glanced around. As if that would help. Not like there'd be a heavy storm cloud floating in the stands. A quarter of the crowd was ominous-looking and black-clad just because they were Obsidians. *What's going on?*

It has cursed his vocal cords. Or maybe his mouth. He can't speak. It's spreading.

Sweet goddesses—we've got to do *something.*

Yes. I am trying, but this is complex. And still being cast.

Her heart leapt out of her chest at those words, and it leapt harder as he went down. Think—think! Pyaris's book had talked all about curses, but she'd never tried any of it. She hadn't had the occasion to even see a curse, let alone break one. She groped blindly, hunting the dark energy.

Andius swung. Nyalin rolled right.

The blow crashed into the stadium's sandy floor, cracking it like a dish shattering.

The next swing came. Nyalin rolled to dodge left. He couldn't get a moment to get to his feet. Lara couldn't get a moment to get a handle on the curse. He kept moving, and even when he was still, she hardly knew what she was looking for.

The third blow smashed an even larger crater into the sand and concrete floor. Nyalin was clutching his sword arm to him like it was useless, barely hanging onto the weapon as he rolled.

Yeska poured energy into the wound, but it wouldn't be enough. Andius had too much of an advantage now, there wasn't enough time to find the curse, let alone break it. She should have brought Pyaris. She should have guessed this might happen.

Nyalin brought his sword up just enough to block as Andius fell over him, pressing their locked swords across his neck, twisting, turning, trying to get traction.

"Yield!" cried someone in the stands, horrified.

"Yield!" another cry, and another.

The blades slid with a horrific sound—brutal and abrupt. She stopped breathing.

"Yield! Yield! Yield!" The stands were chanting, unending.

But he couldn't, could he. His chin was raised high, avoiding the blade, but it didn't move.

Damn her lack of energy spells. She glanced around hopelessly. What could she do? She couldn't push back the blade. Most other magic that could torment Andius would be obvious and clearly visible.

She raced from her position high in the stadium down the nearby stairs, not out of the place now but toward the center, toward the teeming front row of seats.

Andius pressed the blade harder.

She couldn't even hear Nyalin grunt, and maybe he couldn't, but the strain was apparent on his face. She caught a glimpse of a pocket of black, seething energy, but lost it right away.

She stopped at the railing, colliding with it almost

absently. By Dala's light, she had to do *something*. This was all because of her.

All her fault.

Should I throw Andius off him?

You can't. Then they'll know. Or they'll think Nyalin did it and that he cheated.

Well, he did.

But not like that. And all of this will all be for naught.

It is all for naught anyway, because you are already their clan leader.

This isn't the time, Yeska. We have to help him.

I'm holding back the blade as delicately as I can. Curses aren't my specialty, and whoever keeps casting it is strong. They're not letting it slide. Aside from smashing Andius into the city wall, what would you suggest?

She bit her lip, having no answer to that. The image was gratifying, though. She'd told him not to get himself killed, damn it!

She caught hold of the curse. It was nothing familiar—a hideous dark mass of energy. Odorless and black. Reeling at the sensation, she clutched at her chest as Nyalin's blade slipped. Andius's reached an inch closer, touching the skin.

Yeska!

Sorry! I was looking at the curse too.

Fixing that doesn't help—I don't want him to yield. If he does, Andius wins.

I'm sorry, my daughter. But Andius has won, it seems. We simply must save the boy's life. He doesn't deserve to die here.

No, he doesn't.

And then the blood pounding in her ears, the screaming crowd, the seething dark, the grunts and groans—all of it fell away. She would never belong to Andius. And it was true, there as no way out of this that wouldn't make their cheating obvious. Both sides hadn't played fair, but one side was winning. But she would never belong to Andius. Ever. She already belonged to someone else.

She knew what she had to do.

She threw back the hood and leapt over the rail. Cries of shock and shouts went up as her boots landed in the dirt.

There was really no going back now. There never had been. She dug into her bag as she ran, gripped the bone handle.

Yeska. Are you close?

Yes.

I will need you.

I know. I am coming. I am ready.

Good.

So are you.

She leapt over the remains of a broken sword stand, dodged a crater in the sand, and sprinted for them.

She stopped just behind the man she was supposed to marry. The one she'd sworn she never would.

"Andius." Her voice was cold. The crowd hushed, straining to hear her words. "Put down the sword."

Several officials had staggered a few steps forward, but they stopped, torn between duty and curiosity as to what this mad girl was doing on the field.

Andius froze, glancing back once over his shoulder. He let out a crazed bark of incredulous laughter. "Have you lost your mind? Get out of here, before you get dust on your pretty crossover."

Gasps went up left and right, the crowd quieting further to listen.

"I said, step back." Her eyes on Andius were harder than granite, but her hair blew around her face like flames licking at the sky. "Step back and leave him be."

"Why should I listen to you, woman? I'm the clan leader here, and everyone knows it. Except maybe this Obsidian dog. And I'm about to show him for certain."

"No, you aren't."

"Yes. I. Am." He jerked, pressing harder. Nyalin frowned. It might have been a wince if his mouth could move. Was that a trickle of red under Andius's blade?

There was no more time for negotiation.

She drew her hand from her pocket. Sunlight caught on the shining blade, as nearly an entire stadium caught its breath.

"Our clanblade is mine. That makes *me* the clan leader." Her voice wasn't loud, but it seemed to echo in the stunned silence.

Silence except for Yeska's triumphant chortle in her mind.

That's right. She had it. Let them know. Let them *all* know the truth, damn it. She had it. She *deserved* it. The dragon that had withdrawn its power from their clan talked to her, chose her, served her. Not him.

She pressed the cold tip of the Dagger of Bone against the base of his skull.

"Are you a loyal member of your clan? I've given you my orders. Drop. Your. Sword."

Whispers flew through the crowd, even as it struggled to be silent.

Andius froze, eyes flicking back and widening when he realized what she held. "*You* were the one who stole it," he shouted, playacting as if he'd just figured it out. "Never. I'll never submit to a charlatan."

He's not going to give up, Yeska growled.

Pour on the energy. Tell Nyalin. Tell him it's time to cross over and get out of there. Really far out of here.

For a moment, there was only silence and the crowd's confusion at her lack of response. And then—thank the Twins—a glimmer by his eyes.

By the time they glowed white hot, the crowd roared. But that was quiet compared to the tumult a few moments later when he vanished completely.

Instantly, he reappeared a dozen paces away on his stomach. He quickly scrambled to his feet. A red line of blood streaked across the skin of his neck. She poured healing spells at him with as much energy as she dared.

Andius staggered forward, rounding on them both. "You—you—"

"I believe the term you're looking for is clan leader," she whispered, quiet enough so that few in the crowds could hear. People had leapt to their feet and were quieting others to hear their words.

"You'll *never* be clan leader." He spat at her feet, fire raging in his eyes.

"Who is it again that holds the clanblade?"

"Not you."

She cocked her head as she glanced to the dagger in her hand then back to him. "It appears that I am."

"Not for long." He lunged at her.

She easily danced back and away, out of reach. "It wasn't my idea to keep it, but I will admit I'm growing fond of it."

Louder gasps and murmurs went up all around the stadium, then dulled again.

Da's eyes were on her, but she couldn't risk a moment to look, to read his expression. Andius might try to take the dagger the moment her attention wavered.

It would not waver. Not until they were safe.

The beat of leathery wings sounded somewhere close.

She'd promised him she'd have a backup plan.

"How dare you defy our tradition, the council, this very Contest! How dare you wield the sacred blade, *woman*." He looked around him as he spoke, raised his arms, beckoning the crowd to support him.

The rising shouts and murmurs said it was working.

"You're not worthy of the dagger or the clan," she hissed back. He continued to lunge closer, then back away. She circled toward Nyalin, not taking her eyes off Andius. "You don't even believe the dragon is real. Well, she is. You've lied and cheated and bought your way to favor. You tried to kill Nyalin and me only *yesterday*, all in hopes of finding this blade. I hid it from you to save myself, sure. But I also did it for *all* of us. You don't deserve to lead the clan. You don't deserve to even be one of us."

"Lies. All lies! Try to throw your shame on me, but who should they believe? You? The thief? The liar? The one who has broken our ways? Who took the blade without even taking part in the Contests—"

"No one would let me!"

A familiar growl vibrated the air and filled her ears, and she didn't think it was just in her mind this time.

Fear gripped the crowd, silencing it again.

Andius continued, oblivious. "None of this is an excuse to steal the clanblade. It belongs to *me*." He reached for it, and she sliced at his palm, stopping him even though she missed. He scowled at her.

The noise around her rose at that, emboldened. She risked a glance, and indeed, the crowd had pressed forward, some officials only a few paces away. Frightened faces mixed with enraged ones, dashed with confusion and alarm. Sympathy too.

Something hard hit her hand.

Her fingers lost their grip, but she lunged forward, trying to throw her body between the dagger and whatever had knocked it from her grasp.

Her body collided with Andius.

The two of them went down in the sand, scrambling after the blade, shoving, and kicking.

Then Nyalin was on him, pulling Andius away from her.

Andius lashed out, aiming for Nyalin's head and throat, and then kicked at her. His foot caught her in the jaw and sent a wave of stars through her eyes and gasps through the crowd.

Her head knocked back, and she hit the sand. Stars covered her vision, and the world spun, but she kept groping in the dirt—it had to be here, it couldn't be far, he couldn't have gotten it that easily—

Her fingers brushed rough bone and curled.

Even in her dazed state, she gripped it hard and rolled away from him. She staggered to her feet with little grace, swaying.

Now she was just as dirty and dust-covered as they always said. But she'd never felt so much like she belonged. Her lip was bleeding, but she was fighting for herself, her dragon—her people, even. They deserved better than this greedy, selfish idiot.

Nyalin had held his attention briefly, but Andius realized she'd recovered. He whirled on her and roared. Eyes flashing, he charged her, and she was hardly sure what he even planned to do. She put both hands on the bone handle, planted her feet, and braced herself.

But there was no need.

A bellow answered Andius's roar. A much, much louder bellow thundering out from behind her, keening something ancient and inhuman, dripping with magic. Hot wind and dust blew past her like opening a door during a sandstorm.

The shouts fell away. Only whispers flitted here and there as the arena went silent. Andius, too, froze, staring about thirty feet into the air behind her head.

Nyalin's eyes were wide. His hands dropped from his defensive position as he stepped back.

Lara knew what they saw.

Daughter. I am here. Let not this unworthy one trouble you.

What do I do, Yeska? She glanced around her, searching for some solution. Did her voice sound as panicked and small as it felt? Her head spun. *I've made a real mess of things.*

No. This mess was already here. You were born into it.

I still have to deal with it. And I can't find a way to clean it up.

There are not always easy ways to solve hard problems. This mess was not made in a day and won't be fixed in one. You know what you must do.

She could take a moment now, stare around her. Nearly everyone had fallen silent, eyes wide, children pointing, people clutching each other. She backed slowly toward Yeska. Some seemed to think she didn't know the dragon was behind her and waved and pointed in warning.

She caught Da's eyes. He didn't look angry, at least not yet. Now he only looked... stunned.

You wanted my help, said Yeska. *Now take it.*

If I do, there will be no going back.

There never was. Climb my back. Bring your mate.

She swallowed. *He's not my—*

I saw that kiss. Those kisses.

She winced. *Can't a clan leader get a little privacy?*

If she asks a dragon nicely.

Lara swallowed, uncertain. Where would they go? How would they live?

We shall figure it out. Bring your... friend, and let us be gone from these fools.

This is your clan, great Bone Dragon.

If that is the case, they will learn to respect me and my choice. And you as their leader. Now come. I found some berries I'd like to show you.

She stood frozen a second longer. But what else was there to do? Yeska was right.

She met Da's gaze. Some of the shock had faded, and now his eyes held only curiosity as to what she would do. The lack of anger or judgment or betrayal eased her last hesitation.

She nodded slightly. He nodded back.

She caught Nyalin's eye. "C'mon." She nudged with her head toward the dragon, all the while keeping the blade trained on Andius.

"What?" Andius whispered. "What do you think you're doing?"

As Nyalin reached her side, they both turned and ran.

Her massive, craggy scales bristled, but the dragon took a knee and extended her wing, lowering her back for them to scramble up the bony plates like a ladder.

Climbing up was a blur. The murmurs rose up again, alongside Andius's scream of rage.

"You can't do this! You can't—goddesses curse you!"

"Bring that back!" shouted someone from the stands.

"Thief!"

"But the dragon is—"

"Get her! Stop her!"

But even as the people rushed onto the sand of the arena, Yeska took a great leap into the air. Her mighty wings flapped once, the powerful gust staggering those who had rushed forward, and with a second mighty blast she was well above the arena. A few more, and she was in the sky.

Lara clung to the bone spike in front of her, her body wedged between one spiny bit of the back ridge and the next. Nyalin clung to the one behind her—and to her. One hand rested lightly on her hip.

She returned the clanblade to her pouch. She was going to need an actual scabbard or something. Too bad she hadn't thought to steal all the accoutrements to wear it in public.

Yes. Yes! This is how you should think.

About stealing?

Yeska only laughed, both in her mind and in a low rumbling growl that vibrated her body beneath them.

"Are you all right?" she called back to Nyalin, turning.

He was clutching the ridge spike before him as he gave a weak shake of his head. His face looked pale—a little blue.

Goddesses above. That damn spell still had a hold—how had she forgotten?

She poked and prodded at the awful blackness. *Yeska. Any ideas?*

It's a necromantic curse. Very similar to a spell. Touch of Death is similar to a healing spell, and this curse is similar to Touch of Death but more targeted. Masterful.

How nice for us. Done by the darkness you mentioned?

Yes.

What does Touch of Death do?

Makes the living appear dead temporarily, freezing them in time. It is like a curse but not exactly one. Usually the spell is applied to the whole body.

Lara tightened her grip as most of her mind focused on the curse. That might be just enough to piece together how the thing worked. Could she untwist, unfocus the thing like a spell in reverse?

She tried. It twitched and twisted but went back to the same.

Gritting her teeth, she groped for the charms in Nyalin's pocket. Now between the two of them they only had one set—maybe. But there were second level healing spells. Could it be that simple, when combined with what she'd learned from Pyaris's book? Curse breaking demanded absolute concentration, or one could acquire the spell—the primary difference between spells and curses. Curses had a mind of their own and didn't like to die.

Of course, a dragon's back midflight wasn't the best place for this, but she didn't have much choice in the matter. They were barely out of the city. If Yeska stopped, it put them at risk that pursuers would follow. And she had no idea how long it would take her to break the curse.

She had to do it and do it now. If she caught the curse from him, so be it. It would be fairer for her to die than him since she'd started all this. She tightened her arms into a bear hug around the spike and hoped that would be enough as she reached out and began.

The Dagger's energy flowed through the charm, spinning into raw life-giving power. She funneled it at the curse as she would a wound, forgetting her body, the wind around her, everything but the energy flowing through the world at her command.

Nyalin heaving in a deep breath was the sweetest sound she'd ever heard. But it was accompanied by a sickening falling sensation.

"Oh, thank the—Lara!"

Her fingers groped at the spine. But it was too far already. She only caught air. She was sliding now, and the wind was disorienting. She groped again, at another spine, at anything—

Yeska banked to the side. The dragon's body shoved her

up into the air, and suddenly hands caught her groping ones, hauling her up. She found the spine once again and clung to it like a drenched cat returned to dry land. Nyalin patted her hard on her shoulder, busy heaving in breaths himself probably.

No taking a nap now. Yeska almost seemed to be smiling as she glanced back over her shoulder at them as she flew. *Look at you, little curse breaker.*

One learns something new every day, it seems.

You will do great things, daughter.

Thank you. I hope you're right.

She eased up enough to take a deep breath, glance back at the city, and caught Nyalin's smile over her shoulder as his face leaned against the dragon spine.

That chased the rest of the tension away, and she grinned into the wind. They were high up now, but she didn't dare look down. Clouds floated past them and grew denser ahead. Sun beat down on her skin, but not enough, as the chilled air raised goosebumps down her arms.

"Where are we going?" he coughed.

To my home. By the way he jumped, Yeska must have spoken into both their minds.

She turned back to him. "I didn't know what else to do. They were going to kill you!"

"I'm glad you broke the rules."

"None of their rules made sense. None of them."

"Obviously. Who's the one riding away on a dragon?" He laughed. "I think it'll be a long time before I tire of watching you get angry. Such lovely rage, it's refreshing."

"What if I'm angry at you?"

"Well, I hope you're not. I'll be wrong, most likely. But you'll still be lovely."

She whipped back around, her cheeks hot. The dragon's

words flashed through her mind again. Mate. Well-matched souls. That day so long ago at the graveyard. "We have some things to figure out, don't we?"

She was tiring of yelling, and she wasn't sure he'd heard that bit over the rush of the wind. But a moment later he shouted, "What's new?"

She chuckled, her tension draining away. Her laughter and her stress were carried off by the icy wind, lost, forgotten, and inconsequential for now.

She rode away from everything she'd ever known, ever loved. Beneath the joy lurked fear. But one thing was certain: she was trapped no longer.

Afterword

Thanks for reading Dagger of Bone. I hope you had as much fun reading it as much as I did writing it. If you have a moment, consider leaving a review. Reviews help others like you discover books they may love for themselves. I love hearing from readers and appreciate your honest feedback!

For new release notifications and extra free bonuses, sign up for my monthly newsletter at **www.rkthorne.com/getupdates**. You'll get news and goodies like free stories, extra scenes, maps, and character interviews.

The next book in the Clanblades series is already in flight... stay tuned.

Acknowledgements

Special thanks to Hilary Meuer and Steve Martinez for blessing this book with their beta reading. Or at least for tolerating my typos. And much gratitude to Terrance Mayes for the wonderful map and the brainstorming and fun that went into that part of the worldbuilding!

Share what you thought

If you are on Instagram, join me there by tagging this book with **#rkthorne** and **#clanblades**! I'm posting pictures of books, notebooks, games, and random flowers at **www.instagram.com/rk_thorne**.

Also by R. K. Thorne

The Enslaved Chronicles

Mage Slave

Mage Strike

Star Mage

Legends of the Clanblades

Dagger of Bone

Blade of the Moon (Forthcoming)

The Audacity Saga

The Empress Capsule

Capital Games

Child of Wrath

Songbird Rising

Oath of Duty (Forthcoming)

Check **www.rkthorne.com/books**
for the most up-to-date listing.

About the Author

R. K. Thorne is an independent fantasy and science fiction author fueled by notebooks, role-playing games, coffee, and imperial stouts.

She has read speculative fiction since before she was probably much too young to be doing so and encourages you to do the same.

She lives in the green hills of Pennsylvania with her family and two gray cats that may or may not pull her chariot in their spare time.

For more information:

Web | rkthorne.com
Facebook | facebook.com/ThorneBooks
Instagram | instagram.com/rk_thorne
Pinterest | pinterest.com/rk_thorne
Twitter | @rk_thorne

Made in the USA
Middletown, DE
07 October 2023